PROJECT DUPLICITY

SERENA J. BISHOP

Project Duplicity

The Kari Chronicles
Book 2

Serena J. Bishop

Also by Serena J. Bishop

The Kari Chronicles

Book 1 - Project O.R.C.A.

The Dreams Trilogy

Dreams

Miracles

Heroes

Other Novels

Beards

Leveled

To Dad
*Thank you for being such a loving, funny, and artistic man. I've
learned a tremendous amount from you. I love you.*

Chapter One

Anchorage, Alaska, United States

The VIP boat motored away from the Hinewai in an aquatic crawl. "Don't worry," Mitchell said to Kari from the stern. "It happened so fast it didn't hurt at all. No pain, promise."

Kari's brow furrowed as the boat increased its distance. "What are you talking about? What didn't hurt?" Kari shouted, hoping to be heard over the smaller boat's double engines.

"Death!" Santos answered with his hands cupped around his mouth. "Try not to get murdered like us! To stay safe, you need to ..."

She strained to hear the advice but couldn't. "What did you say?" Kari ran the extra few steps to the railing, as if that would make his words audible. "How do I stay safe?"

He didn't answer. Or at least he hadn't provided one Kari could hear. And she wasn't going to hear it any time soon with the boat now a speck in the distance.

Confused and annoyed, Kari turned away from the ocean and started toward the deck stairs. Her foot landed on the first metal step with a bang. Another gunshot pierced the sea air, and she whipped her head back to the area where the boat had disappeared. Kari raised her hand to her forehead to shield her brown eyes from the blinding sun and saw nothing but the horizon. However, her nose detected an odor that wasn't salt water or diesel from the boat. It was sulfur. Had someone lit a match?

Kari lowered her hand but paused mid-motion as something odd caught her attention. A patch of fine black hairs on her forearm were gone. Singed away. Kari examined her smooth, light bronze skin, mesmerized by the sudden change. Then, her skin began to bubble and thin as fluid beneath it started to collect and grow. Another blister appeared. Then another.

In a matter of seconds, her entire arm was hairless and covered in hundreds of growing and pulsating blisters. But they didn't hurt. Kari studied one of the sores on her index finger's knuckle with fascination as the liquid beneath started what looked like a rolling boil.

Every blister exploded at once.

Kari dropped to her knees on the metal grated deck and screamed. Mitchell had lied. This was excruciating. The physical pain transitioned from sharp to dull and then to nothingness. The absence of physical agony allowed her to think. No pain meant nerve death. Through her tears, she stared at the new pink and white mottled colors of her right arm as the blister process started on the other. "No," she whimpered.

"I'm afraid so." Madeleine came down the stairs in an icy blue suit while holding a small black remote. "Do you want this to stop?"

"Yes!"

"Then tell me, have you learned your lessons about discretion and obedience yet?"

"Yes!"

———

"Chickpea!"

Kari's eyes shot open to see the silhouette of Mom A against the blackout curtains. She scanned her surroundings and realized she was in the rental home for family vacation. Once her mother released her non-burned arms, she pushed herself up to a seated position and slowed her breathing. "I was having a nightmare."

"I'll say." Mom A sat on the edge of the bed. "You were screaming or trying to scream or something. I shook you out of it."

"Thanks for that." Thanks to summertime Alaska, there was plenty of light bleeding through the curtains for her to notice the concerned wrinkles in Mom A's forehead. "I'm sorry if I scared you. And woke you."

"I don't think you could really help it."

Kari rubbed the sleep from her eyes. "I'm still sorry that I woke you. What time is it, anyway?"

"About two in the morning, and you didn't wake me. Dad walking around on loose wooden boards and flushing the toilet did that. I was trying to go back to sleep when I heard you. Do you want to talk about it?"

Since it was after midnight, it was officially the last day of vacation. Did she want to ruin fond memories by telling her mother that she had nightmares every single night for a week, most likely due to family campfires? No, but talking about her dreams might help ease her subconscious a little.

"I was burning alive, probably a lot like how Mitchell and Santos died in the boat explosion." Kari's telepathy was inactivated thanks to her new device, but she could still tell what her mother was thinking. The soft, kind eyes directed toward her told an epic tale.

"Oh, chickpea." Mom A put her arms around her.

Kari's head instinctually nestled in the crook of her mother's neck. "I'll be okay. I promise I'll set up a teletherapy session tomorrow—well, today—with Dr. Will."

Mom A wore a sad grin and nodded. "I'm glad, but . . . maybe don't go back to the ship."

Kari would have loved nothing more than to put the *Hinewai*, Madeleine, and Henry behind her, but she couldn't. Not while her mothers were still threatened if Kari didn't do everything Madeleine and Henry wanted. "I promise I'll be fine. I'm taking steps toward good mental health."

"Okay. I'm going to trust you to know what's best for you." Mom A hugged her again. "I love you so much, chickpea." As if Kari hadn't quite received the message, she kissed her cheek before letting go and heading to the door. Where she walked into Mom L. "I'm sorry if we woke you, Leela."

"Hot flashes did that. But I heard you two talking and wanted to double-check that everything was okay. Is it?"

Mom A looked back at Kari. "What do you think? Is it?"

Kari managed a tired smile. "Yeah, I'm good. Thanks for checking in."

"Of course." Mom L came over to the bed and kissed the crown of her head. "Try to get some more sleep, chickpea."

On cue, her cousin's snoring came through the thin paneled wall like a fog horn.

Kari chuckled. "Yeah, I'll get on that. Goodnight part two, Moms." Once they left, Kari laid back once again, closed her eyes, and fell into her four-seven-eight breathing until sleep took her once more.

Chapter Two

"What do you mean Dr. Will's on sabbatical?" Kari shouted into her phone so loud her voice no doubt carried through the open window and into the forest.

"I'm sorry he didn't tell you in person." The office receptionist sounded genuinely apologetic. "Maybe the email notification went to your spam? But the good news is that I can see Dr. Ola Egbe is accepting patients and has availability this week. Would she work?"

Kari was going to have to make it work, since solid sleep was something she wanted back in her life. "Yeah, that's fine, but because of my work it'll have to be Thursday or Friday." Her shift schedule as a VIP assistant consisted of a twelve-hour shift four days straight with three days off. The alternating am and pm shift was a grind, but the entire week off every four weeks was a nice bonus for the hassle.

There was a few seconds of keyboard clacking on the other end of the line. "Dr. Egbe can see you Thursday at noon in cabin 115."

A shiver passed through Kari, both because the cool, spruce-scented summer breeze tickled her neck and the location of the appointment. "Whoa! What do you mean cabin? I've been doing telehealth visits and would like to continue doing that."

"Those have been eliminated from Dr. Egbe's office."

"Why?" Kari realized she had yelled but wasn't going to apologize for it. This was dumb and a total deal breaker. "I can't do in-person."

"Okay, then you should know that the next available telehealth appointment will be three weeks from now with Dr. Simon."

"Fine, I'll take that one." She had enough coping strategies to get through twenty-one days. Yes, there would be more nightmares, but she had her breathing techniques and a few friends she could talk to. That was basically the same thing as therapy.

After her appointment was set, Kari finished packing and went into the living room where her grandparents, Ata Niq and Noko Ani, were back at the puzzle table. There were no signs of the others. "Where's everyone else?"

"Your moms went upstairs to gather their stuff," Ata Niq said.

"River and Wade are outside taking pictures of bear tracks and its scat," Noko Ani said. "They're trying to figure out what species it is."

"I think a more direct approach would be if Wade stayed outside tonight with breakfast scraps in his pockets and a camera." This would be an excellent use of her cousin's time and resources. "In case the battery dies, you all can watch from the windows as a redundancy measure." Kari may not have worked in a lab anymore, but her mind still operated like a scientist.

"That's enough," Mom A reprimanded as she used careful footwork to descend the stairs with a gigantic suitcase.

Mom L followed with a smaller and cushier duffle bag. "She's just showing us her dedication to research. Isn't that right?"

"Absolutely." Kari pointed to their luggage. "Let's get that rental car loaded. I have to make the noon tender or I'll be stuck at the dock for five hours."

Her extended family met them outside for the formal good-byes. Uncle River warmed up his back with a few bends and twists before he picked her up in a spinning hug. Ata Niq kissed her cheek and made her promise to take pictures of all the extravagant planes and cars she might see. Noko Ani wrapped her in a gentle hug, kissed her forehead, and asked her to try to accept her paranormal gifts. Kari knew she would say that because she always did. Then, she looked at Wade's not-bear-mauled face. "Bye."

He waved and promptly walked back to the cabin.

"I love you," Kari called out to the remaining family, blowing kisses or waving as she got into the backseat of the rental car and shut the door. "I wish Logan could have come instead." He was the much more mature and non-cockwaffle cousin.

Mom A turned to face her from the front seat. "I really thought Wade showed some maturity this time."

"No, he didn't," Mom L said. "Hopefully, despite his presence, you still enjoyed this vacation before you sail off on your swanky boat."

Kari gave her mother a slight smile. The *Hinewai* did have every luxury one could imagine: high-end suites with waterfall hot tubs, day trips with the helicopter, big game sport fishing with marine scientists as the guide, and desserts with gold flakes. She and the other VIP assistants coordinated all of it so the rich and famous had every whim catered to. Except they couldn't use the exterior rock climbing wall while intoxicated.

There had been an incident before Kari's time.

The sights Kari had seen, the conversations she had overhead—normal or telepathic—were fascinating at times, but every observation had come at a cost. The remote that controlled her telepathy was in the hands of that frosty, murderous bitch-queen, Madeleine, and all of the information gathered went to expanding Henry Wibawa's megalomaniacal quest for global dominance and acceptance into a secretive organization. Kari was eager to expose Henry and Madeleine's dirty secrets with a little help from ENN journalist, Adam Cho.

"Don't worry, Moms, this vacation represented luxury in a different way. We can't grow trees that high on the ship or play with the sled dog puppies." Their fluffiness and sweet breath may have been the highlight of Kari's year.

"That made me miss Sage," Mom A said from the passenger's seat.

"I'm sure he got all the belly rubs while we were gone," Mom L said as she entered the dock's address into the GPS. "Well, dogs and trees aside, I know it meant a lot to Niq and Ani that you came. Going from seeing them twice a year to over an entire year was a pretty long lapse for them."

"And she's not saying that to make you feel guilty," Mom A quickly added. "That's just what happens when you get older and move out on your own. It becomes difficult trying to schedule everything."

"That's right." Mom L jerked the car to avoid a massive pothole in the road. "The new intern from World University starts soon, right? That ought to free up your schedule some."

"Correct on both accounts."

"Do you have to start work as soon as you get back on

board?" Mom A asked. "If you're like me, you had fun with the family but need a break before returning to the working world."

"You mean, Noko Ani's charades tournament isn't your idea of a relaxing good time?"

Mom A snickered. "I was more a fan of the animal tours and riding bikes along the coastal trail."

Those had been some of Kari's favorite activities, too. Although, she felt a pang of sadness when she saw a bald eagle. Because Madeleine had switched on her neurological implant when she left the ship, she didn't have access to her telepathy, empathic link to Mom L, or her connection to raptors.

"I liked the Indigenous art museum, too," Kari said. "I'll have to tell Neill about that."

Neill was her only friend who was aware of her entire situation and could commiserate with her. Kari still didn't know his entire story, but she knew three critical facts about him. One, he was on the run from the South African Defence Force. Two, he loved art, especially painting. And three, he had a good heart.

Mom L sighed long and loud once she put the car in park. With both hands on the wheel, she looked at the *Hinewai* anchored in the distance. "I guess this is as close as I can get to dropping you off at your doorstep."

From the passenger seat, Mom A turned around with her sunglasses perched on her head. Her eyes weren't glassy, but she did reach for the bottom of her braid, an anxious fidget. "Are you sure you can't stay for a quick bite? The place with the reindeer jerky you liked is only five minutes away."

Kari understood it was hard to say goodbye. She wanted more quality time with her mothers, too, especially now that she didn't have to hear every thought that ran through their heads. They were both kind, smart, and strong women whom she admired and loved. It was because Kari loved them to pieces, she had to leave. If she didn't return to her duties, Madeleine may plot their murders, too. Or Sage's.

Or their chickens.

"I'm sorry, but I should go," Kari said. "There's a storm brewing in the Pacific, and if the weather comes in faster than anticipated . . . You know what happens."

"Yeah," Mom L drawled, "the *Hinewai* leaves regardless if you're on it."

"Come on"—Mom A took Mom L's hand and kissed it—"let's see our chickpea off."

Kari got out of the car and took all of her belongings with her. "I hope you two have an uneventful and peaceful journey back home."

Mom L put her arms around her and squeezed tight, causing the orange-ginger scent of her soap to envelope Kari. "You're the only screaming baby on an airplane I ever tolerated. I love you." She got on her tiptoes to kiss Kari's cheek and then released her from the embrace.

"I love you, too." Kari waved Mom A over next. She was rewarded with a broad smile and excited wiggle.

Mom A kissed her cheeks first before coming in for a hug of the evergreen-scent variety. "I love you so much. Please take more pictures this time around the globe."

"And maybe try to avoid brain surgery," Mom L added. "That was stressful for us."

Kari stifled a laugh. "I promise no more brain surgeries and I will take more pictures." Her emotions lately had come in various degrees of dread, paranoia, and guilt, but she was excited to see new places this time around the globe.

As Kari distanced herself from the hug, she expected to see Mom A's eyes shimmer with unshed tears and Mom L anxiously rocking on her heels, but all eyes were dry and feet were steady. It took a full year, but both were able to watch her leave without having to wrestle with their emotions.

Mom A pointed out to the water. "Looks like your next ride is here."

Kari turned to see the *Hinewai*'s afternoon tender headed toward the dock. She balled her hand into a fist and stuck her thumb up. "Got my biometric boarding pass right here."

The family of three group-hugged again, then she made her way to the passenger loading area. Her progress stopped, like guilt had slapped her face, when she recognized Charlotte, Santos's girlfriend. Kari continued forward and gave her a nod to say a silent hello. Not wanting to linger with awkward eye contact with the pseudo-widow, Kari scanned the area before she settled on finding her moms one last time. They waved from the parking lot, and after she blew them one last kiss good-bye, they drove away to return to their lives of small-town politics and world-saving environmental solutions.

"Was that your family?"

Kari recognized the guy who asked as a six pm cafeteria regular and deduced he was a maintenance worker based on the white and burgundy uniform. "Yep. We're a small but mighty estrogen-packed trio." She pointed to the paper bags in his hand and the various cardboard boxes, some as small as a shoebox and some as large as a kitchen appliance, surrounding him. "Looks like you did some shopping?"

"A bunch of specialty parts we had to order for a VIP suite renovation came in."

That was news to her. "What are they doing?"

"Adding areas to play virtual golf, gold fixtures for the master bathrooms, and Japanese-style toilets with lumbar support pillows."

Kari had no idea they made pillows for that. She knew ship

upgrades happened, but all of that work now didn't make sense. "I would have thought our annual maintenance spot in Papua New Guinea would have been the best time to renovate. Why now?"

"Apparently, we have a super-duper VIP coming at the Vancouver stop, so it couldn't wait. You're a VIP assistant, right?"

"I am, but I didn't hear anything about this." Kari didn't want her first client back from vacation to be a pain-in-the-ass who sat on the toilet so long they needed chiropractic accessories. VIPs were already rude to the service staff; rude and constipated made the worst combination ever. "Are there any rumors about who the VIP is?"

"No clue, but I'm guessing you'll find out soon enough," he said as the tender hand tied the boat to the dock.

Another maintenance crew person hustled off the boat and helped bring the renovation boxes and bags on board first. After several trips, the rest of the passengers, including Kari, had their thumb prints scanned and they took their various spots on the boat. Kari opted to stand at the railing so as the tender pulled away, she could watch downtown Anchorage grow smaller. She wouldn't be able to set foot on land for at least another week, so she took advantage of observing all the buildings, roads, green grass, and mountains.

The snow-capped mountains.

A shiver went through her, so she folded her arms across her chest for added warmth. She should have worn a hooded sweatshirt. It was times like this she missed her long hair. Although, if she ever wanted to reminisce about her long hair, she could always visit it in the ornate wooden box Finn had gotten her for her nineteenth birthday. A twinge of loss pierced her as she reminisced. The gorgeous, sneaky, funny, non-binary redhead who had won over her friendship, and then her heart.

Well, maybe not her heart.

They had only gone on one date, so that was taking her emotions a bit far. But since wallowing in self-pity was not her preferred method of expending energy, Kari took out her phone to text Finn.

> Vacation with the family is over. How are you? Did you know they make lumbar support for toilets?

It wasn't the most romantic text—and it couldn't be since they had agreed to be friends—but it let Finn know she was thinking of them. She pocketed her phone again and prepared for her next and last transfer.

The size of the *Hinewai* still gave her pause every time she came aboard. It was a massive vessel and a true engineering achievement with all of the different environmentally-friendly modifications to the amenities and cabins. The thought of her own cabin made her long for her bed, which was now her one true indulgence in life. When the ship had been in Japan, she had sprung for a new mattress, the highest thread count sheets, the fluffiest yet most supportive pillows, and a new comforter with a pearl-like luster that reminded her of the abalone inlay of her acoustic guitar. But despite the comforts, there were still nightmares.

Kari took the long walk with her luggage up to deck seven. The extra strength and stamina she had as a result of being a miracle child helped her make the trip without the need to catch her breath before she stopped outside her cabin door. The door that had a sticky note on it from Jade.

Welcome back! Let's hit the game room at 4, then get our dinner. I have A LOT to tell you.

That gave Kari time to do a load of laundry, play a few songs, check the outlets and switch covers for listening devices, see if their ship-based entertainment system had updated the movie selection, and, most importantly, do her preliminary research on the various ways she could contact Adam Cho to destroy her bosses. Then, she could hang out with her neighbor.

———

Kari walked down the passageway to her cabin with her canvas sack of clean clothes slung over her shoulder like Santa Claus.

Jade stood outside her door.

"I'm coming!"

Jade put her hand on her hip and wore an expression of pure annoyance. The stern face disappeared as she laughed at her own antics and pushed her glasses back up the bridge of her nose. For a woman who was a little more than twice Kari's age, she hadn't lost her childlike penchant for play. Everything about Jade was fun yet balanced with wisdom. Her job. Her attitude on life. And her bright pink orthotic sneakers.

"Sorry I'm late," Kari said. "I had to run the dryer an extra few minutes."

"Don't worry about it, I think I'm early." Jade followed Kari into her cabin and then planted her butt on the loveseat. "We have a lot to talk about."

"I was only gone a week." Kari dumped her clean sack of laundry on top of her comforter.

"Yeah, but in that week something very surprising happened. But"—Jade held both of her hands up in a stop gesture—"before I get to that, tell me about your vacation."

"It was nice."

"You look tired."

"I didn't really sleep well. Strange bed and I had more than a couple of nightmares." Kari could be honest with Jade about that since she had supported her through the immediate aftermath of the explosion. But Kari wanted to stay positive and instead began to sort her clean laundry by using the different corners of the bed. "I saw a lot of beautiful scenery, ate a variety of game, and didn't kill my cousin."

"Which one?"

"Wade. Logan's the good one, but he couldn't come since he had to wrap up teaching for the school year. The time with my moms was nice. They really, really liked it that you took the time to say hello when we first docked. Having a friend on board I think reassured them that I do have a support system here." Kari picked up a pair of black lace panties and tossed them to the undergarment corner.

"Whoa!" Jade's mouth formed a perfect O as she pointed to the dark splash on the bed. "You wore sexy panties. Did you get over your Finn withdrawal with some Anchorage action?"

Kari raised her brow. "Um, no. I bought those in Japan along with the new bedding."

"I sense a theme."

There was no point denying it to her one and only girlfriend. "I may have been a little depressed and thought buying lingerie would cheer me up, because a character in a book I read did that once. I have to say the tactic did work." Kari went back to sorting her typical, non-sexy clothes: socks, hoodie, cargo pants that were no longer sticky from a leaky ice cream cone.

Jade pursed her lips. "I find this side of you fascinating, just so you know."

"The side of me that buys lingerie for myself?"

Jade nodded.

Kari's shoulders slumped. "Is it weird that I did that?"

"No," Jade said gently. "We have to do nice things for ourselves in life and, face it, given our situation on the ship, it's not like we can draw ourselves a candlelit bubble bath. When I divorced my ex, I did all the sexy shopping. Including the kind that isn't clothes."

Kari tossed a tank top with a grin. She had picked up something of that variety in Japan, too. "Well, it's good to know that I'm not abnormal in that way."

"Heavens, no! You're better off doing all of that than . . ." Jade averted her eyes in the direction of the TV and the three framed pictures featuring the moms, the inCog crew having dinner, and her surprise birthday party a few months back. "Dammit, Neill," Jade muttered.

The tonal shift and mention of Neill raised alarms. Kari threw down the sports bra in her hand and went to sit beside Jade on the loveseat. Given his line of security work with Henry and Madeleine, he encountered direct risks. Like them. Had they killed him because he'd also witnessed the murders and was a loose end? "What happened to Neill?" Kari asked in a panic. "Is he okay?"

"Calm down. He's fine. I maybe"— Jade sighed—"asked him out on a date."

"No way!" Kari did not have that on her year two *Hinewai* bingo card. And that answer was so much better than Neill being dead. "When did you ask? How?"

"I'm going to preface this by saying I was feeling down and my typical pick-me-ups hadn't worked. Now, we already had air hockey time scheduled together and I wanted to cancel but also didn't want to leave Neill hanging, so I went anyway."

"But that wasn't the date, right?"

"Right. But I had such a good time! And it completely turned my mood around. You know, when other people aren't around, Neill really opens up. He revealed so much sensitivity and depth and"—she slapped Kari's leg—"he was funny! I couldn't believe it. Then he rolled up the sleeves of that black button down and I could see those muscular, tattooed forearms. Yum! You put all of those things together, and I asked him out on a date."

Kari winced. She had a feeling she knew where this was headed but didn't want to make the assumption. "And he said … ?"

"The kiss of death. He likes me as a friend and that his life is complicated." Jade shook her head. "That was five days ago and it's making me do dumb shit now. When I saw him in the passageway doing security rounds, I ducked into a random club room where everyone was praying. It was awkward so I just stayed and bowed my head. Now I feel stupid."

"But I don't hang around stupid people." After Jade snickered, Kari continued. "Knowing Neill, he was probably stunned and didn't know how to respond."

"Maybe. I still wish I would have taken my own advice and bought a thong."

Kari hated seeing her friend so down, especially when she knew Neill was such a wonderful man. "I'll see him at work tomorrow. Do you want me to say anything to him?"

"No, but thanks for offering." Jade patted Kari's knee and smiled. "I love that you feel comfortable enough around me now to sit right beside me and not on the other side of the room."

Since Kari couldn't say, 'Uncontrolled telepathy is a bitch,' she said, "You're my unofficial big sister now, so I feel more comfortable."

Now, if only that comfort extended to her job.

Chapter Three

Gulf of Alaska

The shrill ring of her alarm at five am woke Kari from an improved night's rest. She tossed the covers off and commenced her workday routine. She showered, dressed, finished her cup of divine French press coffee, and studied her reflection in the mirror. Her black Oxfords shined. Thanks to vacation, her belt's prong was in the next hole. Her black trousers had a crisp pleat down the center of the straight leg cut. The only disruption to the pants' lines was her multi-tool in one pocket and her work cell phone in the other. She wasn't allowed to carry any personal devices during shift, as that created paranoia among the clientele that photos or recordings could be taken. Her black button-down shirt was buttoned high enough so that none of her cleavage was exposed, but low enough so her firestarter necklace was visible. She still hadn't used it to start a fire, but it connected her to her mothers.

And provided a constant reminder that she needed to comply with Henry and Madeleine's demands of discretion and obedience.

The cafeteria was nearly empty during the earliest breakfast time slot, so it was easy to find a quiet corner to enjoy her smoked salmon omelet with berries and sourdough toast. Due to the variability of her VIP's needs, Kari had learned it was best to preorder the heaviest breakfast option on the brand new *Hinewai* app.

As far as Kari could tell, Charlotte's grief over Santos meant that she had thrown herself into work and completed the app ahead of schedule. In addition to meal scheduling, the app included nautical information about the ship, the port arrival and tender schedules, weather alerts, and club room reservations. There was even a game designed around evacuations and safety. Someone called Seaman4Life had the high score on *Pirate Protocol.*

After breakfast, Kari headed up the stairs for work, as she rarely used the secret elevator system these days, and walked straight into the administrative hive to start her day. The land of cubicles was still dim and quiet at six am, but she knew someone who would be at work. And Kari dreaded seeing her bony face—both in texture and color—once more.

She knocked on Madeleine's closed door.

"You may enter," Madeleine said in her cultivated Australian accent.

Kari rolled her eyes and walked into the office of the Chief Acquisition of Talent Officer and VIP Coordinator. Only Kari, Henry, Neill, and another security guard, Josef, knew that through Madeleine's office bathroom there was a second clandestine office where she performed the illegal activities of Wibawa Enterprises.

"Good morning, ma'am." Kari hated the required greeting when, 'Fuck you, and why haven't you died yet?' would have rolled off the tongue so much better.

"Welcome back," Madeleine said as she lifted her teacup of

Earl Grey to her lips. Icy blue eyes peered at Kari over the fine china. "Was your vacation restorative?"

Kari closed the door behind her. "It was. The family was glad I could participate in the fun. Also, reindeer is delicious."

"You didn't find it too gamey? That was my experience."

"No. Maybe our reindeer had slightly different diets."

"Mine, no doubt, had some of Santa's cookies before the slaughter." Madeleine tipped her head back with a cackle.

Kari refused to join in, even though she liked the joke. Madeleine was evil—her scarlet suit added to her devil vibes—but sometimes she was funny about it.

Madeleine scoffed. "It seems you left your sense of humor on shore."

"If it's alright with you, I'd like to focus on work."

"Suit yourself," she said with a shrug. "You don't have a VIP until Vancouver, because you'll be training our new intern, Belle."

Surprises around every corner. "How can I train someone when I just started a month ago? Matthew and Ahmed have been VIP assistants for years."

Madeleine tightened her thin lips, which was the epitome of her annoyed face. "The intern coordinator at World University, Doug, insisted on you based on personality profiles." Kari opened her mouth to speak, but Madeleine cut her off. "I know, it's stupid, but in this case, it wasn't a battle I wished to fight. Too much energy for something so insignificant, and I didn't want HR sending me another email about 'teamwork'."

At least Kari knew her feelings on the matter. "Alright. So, I'm training Belle. With what? It's not like we have a manual."

"Make one." Madeleine sat up straighter, as though a brilliant idea suddenly flew up her tight rear end. "Yes, be honest with her that there's no training manual, so you two are tasked to create one. I'm sure she has to turn in reports to Doug, so this will help her."

The report made sense, but the logistics did not. "Is she going to shadow me?"

"Only during Vancouver. Hopefully after that she's competent enough to fly solo. Any other questions?"

"When does this start?"

"I told her to come to my office at six-fifteen, so"—Madeleine checked her rose gold watch—"shortly. That means we should get to other matters." Madeleine went into the bathroom behind her, slid open the closet, popped the faux back wall with a press, and walked through to her secret office.

It was an elaborate process.

Kari followed, her eyes were drawn to the small black box with a glass scanner on its top. There was a quiet click after Madeleine placed her right thumb on the glass. "Hold on a second, you said I didn't have a VIP. Why do I have to have telepathy if there are no important minds to read?"

Madeleine proceeded to take a small remote out of the box. "Matthew and Ahmed do have one, and should you happen to be around Ms. Sokolov—and you will—I want to know what's going on in that head of hers." Madeleine pressed the single button on the remote, placed it back into the box, and steered clear of Kari as she left. Madeleine rarely allowed Kari access to her thoughts. The only times were if she wanted to make a point.

Once Madeleine snapped her fingers as the 'safe to return signal', Kari went back to the proper office. "Have a great day, ma'am. I'll come back to collect Belle soon." She shook her head at the saccharin sweet, cotton candy pink office pillow that read *Hope & Kindness* as she left and almost walked straight into a blond wall as she opened the door.

Great first impression. "I'm sorry, I'm a little early," she said with a slight US southern—maybe Tennessee—accent.

Kari was slightly above average height, but she needed to tilt her head up to make eye contact with the young woman who was constructed of long, wavy blond hair pinned back and a lot of leg. She wore the same black uniform as Kari and held two to-go cups. "I take it you're Belle."

"I am." *Has to be Karishma.* "Are you Karishma?"

"Kari's fine. Only Henry calls me by my full name here." Kari faced Madeleine. "Do you need to talk to Belle?"

"Not one bit. Off you two go and shut the door."

"Bye." Belle waved at Madeleine before the door closed. *She's surly.*

At least the newbie caught on quickly to that fact. Kari turned back to Belle and pointed at the cups. "You must get thirsty in the mornings."

Belle let out a bubbly laugh that somehow managed to soften her square jawline. "I brought us drinks. One is a coffee with French vanilla creamer and the other is a decaf herbal something. Whichever one you don't want, I'll have." *Please Jesus, take the coffee.*

Kari didn't need more caffeine, but the gesture was nice. "I'll take the coffee, thanks. What are the odds that you'd pick my favorite creamer?"

"Pretty high since I asked. A blessing and a curse that the *Hinewai* is a pretty small community, so anybody can learn about you."

Kari debated stepping away from her for a little more brain quiet, but she couldn't resist the opportunity to learn more. "Did you ask anything else about me?"

Now thinks I'm a gossip. "Oh no! I didn't mean that. I grew up in a real small town—graduating class of twenty-five—so I respect people's privacy."

"I had a graduating class of one."

What? Her blond brow knit together. "Did you say 'one'?"

"Never mind. How about we take our drinks to the lounge and talk about what it means to be a VIP assistant?" Kari led the way out, but Belle's excited thoughts of learning about the VIPs and Henry kept rushing into her brain. "I hope this doesn't sound rude, but could you give me a step or two. I like a good personal space bubble."

"Oh! I can absolutely do that and thank you for telling me."

Was Belle the politest person on the planet? If so, the next year of working with disrespectful, spoiled clients would be interesting.

Kari placed her coffee down on a high-top table for six and took a seat in the covered portion of the outdoor lounge. As expected, Belle sat across from her, giving a healthy distance between the two.

"I don't think I've ever sat out here before," Belle said. "It's real nice."

Kari admired the dark blue ocean through a crinkle in the plastic wall. "The first time I sat out here was last summer in Manhattan's harbor. A very different view."

At that time, she and Mitchell had engaged in small talk, rather than discuss neuroscience, over coffee. It was nice. Kari supposed that was why she had grown so close to Mitchell and Santos. She had known them as more than scientists. She knew who they were as people outside of work. Since she was Belle's trainer now, she supposed that would be a good ice breaking strategy to use.

"I had a very brief talk with Madeleine this morning, and she told me that between now and Vancouver—basically this week—my job is to lay down the basics of what it means to be a VIP assistant. Then, I can write it up formally as an SOP and you can use the information for one of your reports to Doug or something."

Belle nodded. "That tracks with what he told me."

"Good. So, considering we have some time before we start all of that, I think it makes sense if I get to know you better. I might be able to tailor your training to your strengths that way. What do you think?" Kari sipped her coffee.

"That sounds fine to me, but what about you?"

"What about me?"

"Well . . ." Belle smiled. "Do I get to know about you? You're a bit mysterious."

"Mysterious?" Kari repeated with a chuckle. "I'm sorry, but that's the first I've heard that."

"Really?" Belle's nose scrunched as she grinned. "I have oodles of questions."

Kari was first thrown by the usage of 'oodles' but leaned into her intrigue, despite some fear, about what information was out there about her. "Okay, ask away."

"One person graduated in your high school?"

Okay, Kari would give her that one as being a bit unique. "I was homeschooled because I'm a little . . . We'll say accelerated. Next question."

"You said that Henry calls you by your first name, which—oh my God—I can't believe you get to work with Mr. Wibawa and get to call him Henry. Does anyone else call you Karishma?"

"My moms, but only when they're mad. If that happens, I get the full first and last name treatment, Karishma Okpik-Bakshi."

A flash of a smile crossed Belle's lips, and her sapphire blue eyes opened wider for a fraction of a second. "You have moms, plural? Do you also have dads?"

Given Kari and her family's past with the extremist group God and Country, the cross Belle wore, and her thoughts of Jesus earlier gave Kari the slightest pause before answering. "I have a Mom A and a Mom L. No dads."

"That's great! I mean, it's great to have two parents, regardless of who and how they came into the picture. Do you get along well with them?"

"Very." Kari realized from their brief interaction that not only was Belle an attentive listener, but she asked so many follow-ups she naturally steered the conversation in her direction. "Enough about me. What made you want to be a VIP intern?"

Belle took a sip of tea. "Like I said, I grew up in a small town and went to an itsy-bitsy private high school where I played volleyball. I just loved going to different schools and meeting new people. I had a dream of playing in college, but I hurt my shoulder pretty bad. Surgery and rehab didn't go well, so that eliminated my chances at getting a scholarship. But my grades were good, so I was still able to go to a small school for a bit where I majored in Hospitality Management. Then, one day on campus I saw an ad for World University. The idea that I could finish my degree and travel the world . . . Sign me up!"

"That means you had to transfer schools. Sounds like a pain."

"It was, but I got a good financial aid package to WU, so I transferred here last fall. And this year"—Belle beamed—"I'm a VIP assistant intern on the *Hinewai* and graduate in May! Can you believe it?"

"I mean, you're sitting here across from me in a matching black outfit, so yes, I do believe it."

Belle laughed and finished with a content sigh. "I'm still so excited. Last year we stopped at every five-star hotel or resort we docked at. Barcelona was my favorite. I think I saw you on the tender, actually. Your hair was longer then, like in that viral video where you put that creep in a joint lock."

She had hoped those five minutes of fame where she had almost been trafficked were over. "I'm surprised you recognized me from then to now."

"I have a great memory for details, including faces. Why did you cut your hair?"

It was official, Belle asked more questions than a toddler. "I had brain surgery." Since the curiosity was inevitable, Kari prepared the same show-and-tell lie she told others. She turned her head slightly and, behind her ear, positioned her index and middle finger on either side of her device nub. "I had a procedure to stop my seizures. When I wasn't working, I spent most of my free time in my room healing."

Belle grinned. "Or playing table tennis? I hear you're good."

"Wh . . ." Kari's mouth momentarily froze, preventing her from finishing the question. "Why do you know that?"

"When I found out you were going to be my mentor, I asked around to learn more about you. I went to your JobConnect page, but it hadn't been updated in a while." Belle's hand shot out across the table, as if she were going to touch Kari's hand. "I'm sorry if that invaded your privacy. I was hoping it would be seen as proactive."

"Okay," Kari drawled. "I can see why you'd do that, but I like to keep to myself and don't like to put myself out there. Also, there is nothing about tabletop sports on my JobConnect page."

"Oh! That's not where I found that tidbit out. Chef Boudreaux overheard me talking about the internship at a WU picnic."

"Wait. Jade told you?"

Belle nodded with a smile. "Aside from your favorite creamer, she told me that you're neighbors and play table games together."

Kari's shoulders dropped their tension. No one was dropping personal information about her for some new blackmail plot. But in her moment of relief, she realized Belle had veered her away from the conversation again! "Okay, back to you. You've seen some fabulous hotels, but have you worked with the clientele?"

"No, and that's what I'm really hoping to get out of this internship." Belle bit her lower lip and winced. "I've never really had a job-job before, but I don't want you to think that I don't know how to work hard. I do." Belle took a sip of tea and then appeared as though she was thinking of something else. "Aside from volleyball practice and off-season training, I did volunteer work at the local animal shelter."

"I love dogs." Kari's muscles involuntarily relaxed as she smiled.

"Do you?" Belle asked, tickled. "What's your favorite breed?"

"Um. We can talk dogs later." At least Kari hoped so. That topic was preferable to anything related to their actual job. "The reason why I asked about working with clientele is because that while the VIP assistant position is an easy job, it can be emotionally difficult."

"How do you mean?"

"It's because of the way most of the VIPs treat us. I mean, yes, it is our job to cater to them, but almost all of them are already used to that and they do not hold back when it's not perfect. Even when it is perfect don't expect a 'thank you'. We're not even people to some of them." Kari recalled her first

VIP taking a sip of his Scotch whisky, tossing the full glass overboard, and bad-mouthing the 'help' as if she had distilled the liquor. "If you don't have thick skin, their comments can get to you."

A dark cloud passed over Belle's pleasant features. "You don't need to worry about that with me. My skin is plenty thick."

The sudden switch in tone and gravitas she used gave Kari pause. "I'm sorry if I sounded patronizing, I just didn't want you to be surprised the first time someone was a real cockwaffle to you."

The bubbly laugh returned. "I don't think I've ever heard that word before." Belle chuckled again but softer. "What else should I know?"

"For today, I figured I'd give you a tour of all the VIP things." Kari's phone buzzed in her pocket. She pulled it out and read the text from Madeleine:

> Come to Ms. Sokolov's happy hour at 4pm.
> Let Belle leave early for the day.

Kari slipped the phone back in its place. "Good news for you. Your day ends at four today, so I can tend to a Russian oligarch." Maybe she could even use some of the Russian she had been learning.

"You're sure I can't come? A Russian oligarch sounds exciting!"

"Sorry, but maybe next time." Kari drank the rest of her coffee and then pointed to Belle's cup. "Would you like to finish your tea here or start the tour?"

"Oh, the tour, for sure." Belle didn't have to hop down from the high seat, rather her feet were already on the ground. "I want to thank you for taking the time to get to know me a little bit and sharing more about yourself before we jumped into things. I can tell you're a very patient mentor. No wonder your guitar students like you. And I only know that because I saw your ad pinned to the corkboard outside the prayer club room and someone drew a smiley face on it."

Patient had never been a word used to describe her in the past, but maybe giving lessons had taught her some. "If it's okay with you, I see this more of a partnership than a mentor-mentee thing. Sound good?" Kari held out her hand to shake.

Belle grasped it in a firm shake. *My reports filled to edges.* "Sounds great." She released her hand, walked away, and tossed her to-go cup into the recycling bin. "Where to first, partner?"

"Let's start at the top of the ship and work our way down."

———

During the tour, Belle asked questions at every stop and about every person. How often did VIPs ask to go fishing? Snorkeling? ATVing? Who did the VIP assistant consult when they wanted to do those things? Could Chef Jon make them anything at any time? Who was responsible for turning over the suites? How long had lumbar-support for toilets been around?

Once they reached deck one, Kari braced herself once her feet touched the VIP area. The weather was cooler than that day in the Philippine Sea, but the ocean looked the same. The railing was the same. Her foot placement on the grated deck was the same. She expected to see a fireball and black smoke rise into the sky at any moment.

Something's wrong. "Kari?" Belle placed a gentle hand on her arm.

She quickly turned to Belle and stepped back. "Yeah. So"— she pointed to the dual-motored boat—"this is the VIP boat. We use it like a tender but also for sunset cruises, snorkeling, diving, and some fishing. We rent the marine science lab's boat for the sport-type fish."

Belle gave her a hesitant nod, then approached the boat. She appeared as though she were inspecting the dual motors. "Did they ever find out why the last one exploded?"

A sound Kari didn't know she could make escaped her. It was equal parts whimper and scream. Her heart raced. A cold sweat broke out. She lost control of her breathing.

Belle rushed from the boat and back to her. *Oh, no. Forgot.* "I'm so—"

In a daze, Kari wandered through the tunnel, dividing the two sides of the deck. Belle followed. "No! You stay over there."

"I'm so, so sorry. I forgot you worked with them."

She made it to the tender queue's bench and gripped the edge of her seat. "You know how I take cafeteria coffee, that I give guitar lessons, play table tennis with Jade, and read my JobConnect page, but you can't remember that my friends and colleagues died in a boat explosion a few months ago?" she yelled. "And then you asked about it?"

"I . . . You're right. I'm so, so sorry. That was an awful mistake to make." Belle bit her upper lip and fidgeted with her hand, scraping her thumbnail across her forefinger. "God, I feel like I've done a lot of apologizing today, but I am so sorry. Would it help if we left?"

Removal from the situation—and Belle—was what she needed. Kari took a deep breath to center her emotions to ensure her most mature, calm voice. "Yes, but I need five minutes alone. Can you go back to the lounge area where we started and wait for me?"

"Sure," Belle said softly. "I'll review my notes and see if I have any more questions."

Once Belle disappeared up the stairs, Kari closed her eyes and rubbed her face. She reminded herself that she hadn't caused the explosion, but she had antagonized Madeleine enough to instruct Josef to do it. How was she going to live with that guilt? Get in the VIP replacement boat? Not think of Santos whenever she saw Charlotte? Not think of Mitchell whenever she saw a medical doctor?

Surely she could wait a few weeks for her therapy appointment.

After she collected herself further with her go-to breathing technique, Kari headed back to the lounge. Now that it was late afternoon, the plastic sides were rolled up, allowing the breeze to cool off the flurry of activity.

Belle sat in the same place as before and read the screen on her phone.

Kari weaved through the crowd to reach her.

Doesn't taste decaf.

Yes! New high score!

Am I allergic to bananas?

Shoe always unties itself.

Jon is head chef. Ahmed is most senior VIP assistant. Matthew is jolly. Don't ask Madeleine questions. Stay away from Madeleine. Kari really wants me to avoid her.

At least Belle's notes and thoughts demonstrated she had listened to her during the tour. "Thank you for giving me some space back there," Kari said as she took her seat. "I . . . ah . . . Every time I think I'm better, something unexpected triggers me and I . . . ah . . . lash out. I'm sorry you took the brunt of that."

All traces of cheerful Belle were gone. Her eyes were sad. Lips downturned. *Apologize again?*

"And I accept your apology from earlier," Kari said. "Let's move on. Do you have any final questions about your first day?"

Blond hair that had escaped Belle's hair clip stuck to her faint grin. She brushed the strands away. "Only about a hundred, but they're all swirling around my brain right now like my hair. If it's alright with you, I'd like to sit with my thoughts and ask questions tomorrow morning before we get started." *Think needs a break from me.*

So Belle was an organized thinker who gave her space when she did not ask for it. Kari approved. "I like that plan. Between now and then, I hope you have fun filling out your first report for Doug." Kari gave her a tiny wave and walked away.

"Sorry, one last thing." Belle jogged after her, each strike of her foot covering an impressive distance. "Can I give you my phone number? I know I'm not allowed to attend this thing you're headed to, but I'd appreciate some pictures of the set up so I know what to expect. I understand if you need to censor the faces or"—she dropped her voice to a whisper—"something else censor-worthy." *Hope no nudity.*

"I'm not allowed to send pics to a non-VIP phone. However, I will tell Madeleine you need a work cell phone and a name tag ASAP." Kari pointed to her own, which had her nickname and pronouns. "What would you like yours to read?"

"Annabelle Jenkins has too many syllables to remember, so Belle, she/her is fine."

"Consider it done."

"Thank you so much," Belle said with a broad smile. "I'll see you tomorrow morning."

Since Belle was on her way to report writing, Kari headed to happy hour. She passed the VIP kitchen, which smelled like freshly baked rosemary bread, then took in the deck makeover. While she had been in Alaska, there had been even more changes to the VIP space than her chat with the maintenance guy had suggested. There wasn't anything new, per se, but everything had been upgraded. The simple teak bar had a face covered in an elaborate mosaic of broken tile. Kari didn't know why a ship would want a large, threatening wave as an art piece, but it was well done. The dining area was larger, with electric heaters above and below the table.

The lounge area wasn't nearly as interesting.

Madeleine and Henry sat beside each other while the VIP, Eva Sokolov, sat across from them with her feet kicked up on the low table. The Russian centimillionaire gave off an unexpected friendly, warm energy. She had an airy laugh, a casual posture of her arm draped over her oversized chair, and jeans! Actual denim jeans paired with a knit cardigan. Then, Kari saw something even more shocking. She was drinking beer.

"Hey, Kari," Neill said from behind her. "Welcome back."

She turned to her massive friend and matched the grin he gave her. "Looks like they made some changes last week. What's the occasion?"

Big wig. "The Vancouver VIP is a really big deal. Henry has been adamant that the visit has to be perfect, so everything has been improved."

Since the trio in the lounge chairs continued to chat, now was the chance to pull some personal details out of Neill before her arrival was noticed. "Did you do anything interesting while I was gone?"

Asking about Jade? Just stall. As if in slow motion he spun toward her.

"Just so you know, my little device is activated."

He groaned and shuffled his feet like an annoyed over-sized child.

"If it helps, I promised Jade that I wouldn't ask you about it, so I'm not. But if you wanted to talk about it, I'm here."

He kept his stare on the rich and tipsy. "There's not much to say." *Bad guy.*

Kari waited for more, but there was nothing. "Okay, b—"

"If my life was different, I would have said yes, but I can't live a double life like you can. I can't lie to someone."

She grimaced like an actual cheese grater passed over a nerve. "I choose to think of it as protecting my loved ones."

"I'm sorry, I didn't mean it like that, I know your situation is different than mine." He faced her and sighed. *So ugly. Bad.* "My story is so much uglier. You know that."

"Actually, I don't know that. I only know that you were a military guy and, based on what Madeleine has said, had a 'chain of command issue'. I figured you'd tell me the rest when you were ready." She shrugged. "I didn't want to be pushy."

Deserves to know. But can't.

Like a waking dream, she saw combat boots flailing and limbs grappling on dirty tile floor while, in the corner, a bruised body laid motionless. "Oh, shit."

He took one large and dramatic step away from her.

"Fine. Be that way."

Neill faced forward. "All you need to know is that Jade's too sweet a person to be with me. I'd rather not darken her world."

To Kari's ears it sounded as though it was also a case of self-inflicted punishment. She also heard a cackling and chorus of excited Russian words from the interior stairway.

Kari caught Madeleine's eye, who gave her a slight head tilt to the bar area where Ahmed was stationed. "Speaking of, I gotta go. Duty calls."

For the next two hours, Kari plastered on a fake smile and tended to every want and need of the happy hour. Ahmed kept pouring beer and wine and mixing cocktails. Aside from taking their drink and food orders, they hadn't said anything to Kari. But despite the lack of direct conversation with her, Kari was able to gather plenty of details.

"So," Madeleine said from behind her desk in her secret office, "what did we learn?"

Kari stood with her hands clasped behind her back and delivered her report of family drama, plans for wedding sabotage, and a yoga instructor affair.

"I'll see if the analysts can dig up some downward dog pictures for future blackmail." Madeleine snickered at her joke. "Before you go, how was Belle?"

"Fine enough, I guess. She's excited for this opportunity and is as attentive as she is inquisitive." A little too inquisitive for Kari's liking. She'd have to monitor that for Belle's own safety. "She does need a work cell phone and a name badge. Belle, she/her."

Madeleine nodded. "She'll have them tomorrow. Note: I want her well prepared for our Vancouver guest. Squeeze in time the rest of this week to study him together, as I think that'll give you both an advantage." She placed her thumb on the black box.

"Who's the VIP?"

"Jack Weatherby and his son, JJ."

Kari's eyes nearly bugged out of her head, but not from hearing the click of the box. It was the tycoon's name.

When Kari had been sent to spy on one of Adam Cho's journalism contacts in Brisbane, she had found a notebook. In it, Jack Weatherby had been listed along with Gabriella Fermi and five more of the world's most powerful people. But it wasn't only names. There were also pages categorizing Henry's assets and a crude blueprint showing a large room with columns. Kari had reason to believe it was all a part of a secret organization called In Virtute.

Madeleine pointed the remote at Kari, pressed the button, and placed it back in the black box. "Dismissed."

On Kari's stroll to her cabin, she made more connections. If

Jack Weatherby was coming on board, was Henry officially a member of In Virtute? Regardless if he was or not, Adam Cho would want to know. She didn't think her personal cell phone was tapped, but Henry and Madeleine had the means, and if she was discovered trying to contact Adam the consequences would be dire. She needed a disposable phone or burner, as they were known, and to get away from the *Hinewai* as far as possible.

Chapter Four

Vancouver, British Columbia, Canada

Kari's bike ride was similar to the one she had with her family in Alaska. Clean air. Big trees. Lots of water. Except here, she didn't have to monitor her pace. Kari could push the pedals to the max so that after an hour she had given herself a healthy distance away from the *Hinewai* or from any onlookers. She stopped at a stream that seemed like an abandoned locals-only fishing spot. An empty reel wedged between the rocks and smashed beer can with a discontinued logo provided evidence to that theory.

Before she dismounted, she double-checked to make sure there were no wildlife cameras in view. Since there were none, she dismounted and leaned her cash-purchased, used bike against a tree. Satisfied no one could hear or see her, she called Adam Cho's personal assistant with one of the burner phones she had bought—also in cash—at the convenience store. With each ring and passing second ticking by on her analog watch, her heart pounded harder. On the sixth ring, an automated voicemail message instructed her to leave her name and message.

"Hello," Kari said in a cultivated Australian accent. She had heard it enough times to perfect the tone. "This message is for Adam Cho. My name is—" Shit. She had thought of everything except a fake name. She looked up at the clouds and down to the reel. "My name is Sky Fisher and I have information regarding billionaire targets written on the Brisbane list. I don't seek any type of payment or favor. I'd appreciate an in-person meeting to communicate this to Adam and only Adam. I won't use this phone again, but you can confirm you received this call at eat_the_rich on CryptCodE, the encrypted messaging app. I'll check for a message using a different device."

Kari hung up and checked her watch: The call was under one minute. Good. To complete her safety protocol, she popped the backing off the phone and removed the SIM card, then placed the thin chip on top of a flat rock before pulverizing it with a rounder stone. She kicked the SIM fragments into the stream and made a plan to toss the phone off a bridge. Kari hated polluting, but it was worth peace of mind.

With her primary errand completed, she had plenty of time to donate her bike before she returned to the *Hinewai* for her relaxing day off. She knew Jade had work with the curriculum committee, so she'd eat lunch alone in her cabin. The self-help book about trauma and checking her outlets and switches for surveillance bugs would help pass the time until dinner. Which she would also eat alone, since Jade had a planned call with Diana and Neill was working. By the time evening rolled around, she'd pick up her guitar to play a few songs and watch a movie until it was time for bed.

Everything went to plan, except the going to bed part.

Kari stood in her pajamas at the side of her wonderful comfy bed and stared. She couldn't turn down the covers. Considering her secretive work contacting Adam earlier in the day, she could almost guarantee she would have a nightmare. She sat on the edge and rubbed her face in her hands. Only two more weeks and she could talk to a professional again. She could do this. All she had to do was exhaust her body into sleep and avoid REM. She took off her pajamas, put on some workout clothes, and headed to the gym.

Since the ship worked twenty-four hours, the common areas always had people in them and the gym was no exception. She joined the dozen or so people in the cardio area for a 5K on the treadmill. Afterward, she was sweaty but not tired. Since exhaustion was her goal, she headed to the weight machine circuit next. While she was mid chest press, Neill walked in front of her, his muscles huge and his shorts and tank tiny.

"Where have you been hiding all of those muscles?" he asked.

Kari smiled as she exhaled and put the weights in rest position. "I should ask you the same question about your tattoos. Is that Frida Kahlo?"

Neill shifted his leg so he could see his outer quadricep featuring the famous Mexican painter. The flex of his muscles caused the artist's trademark brow to dance. "I just love her work." He took a seat on the chest fly machine beside her and put his protein drink between his feet. "You're here really late."

"Yeah, I didn't want to sleep."

"Nightmares, huh?" At her nod, he said, "I've been there. What's your therapist said?"

Kari gave him the summary of her doctor's sabbatical, the immediate on-ship option she declined, and the more belated teletherapy option she had booked.

"Dr. Egbe—she prefers Ola—is amazing! She really helped me out when I got on the ship, which funnily enough Madeleine suggested to me. Why don't you want to go to her?"

"Isn't it obvious?" She pointed at the security cameras in every corner. "And those are the ones we know about."

"I think you're fine. You're a genius and can talk your way around certain things—well, people—while still talking about it. I mean, it's not like people don't know about the explosion."

"Maybe, but it still sounds risky."

Neill took a swig from his drink. "Kari, you're in a gym close to midnight because you're afraid to go to bed. That's risky in its own way. I really think Ola could help you."

Kari wanted to argue, but she was equal parts too tired and knowing he was right. "What did she do for you that was so helpful?"

"Aside from having someone to talk to, she did this thing called EMDR. She'd asked me to picture my trauma while I followed her moving finger. I know it sounds weird."

"It doesn't. I actually did some of that when I was a kid." Back then her therapist would ask her to talk about specific elements about the God and Country attack on the farm all while following a light move.

"Did it work for you back then?"

"It did. It's just seeing a therapist in person makes me feel so . . ."

"Vulnerable?"

Kari nodded.

"I get that. My fear was judgement for what had happened." He dropped his head then took a deep inhale, causing his pecs to strain against his barely there tank top. "I was part of the military police. One day I walked in on a commanding officer roughing up a hand-cuffed prisoner. And I'm not talking a slap here. He was practically naked and I could see bruises all over him. When I yelled at him to stop, the colonel kicked him in the mouth. I saw that man's teeth fly out and roll on the tile."

"That's awful! Why would you think a therapist would judge you for wanting to stop that?"

"Because that's not the end of the story." Neill took another drink. "I pulled the colonel off, which resulted in a fist fight and wrestling on the ground, but then he went for his sidearm. I got in a good kick to that bastard's knee, which gave me enough time to shoot him before he could shoot me. I didn't kill him, but that made my situation worse because he lied about what happened."

"But the prisoner could vouch for you?"

"Colonel shot the prisoner in the head as the other guards were coming."

Kari covered her mouth, but that didn't stop the gasp from coming out.

Neill's eyes glazed over. "He did it right in front of me. There were no cameras so it was my word against his regarding who had beaten and killed the prisoner. If I stayed, the trial would have been fixed—ballistic evidence ignored—and I'd spend the rest of my life in the worst military prison imaginable. So, I ran. The *Hinewai* happened to be in Cape Town and I found my way on board. When security found me, I proved my worth by identifying flaws in their system and they gave me a job. At the time, I thought it was a gift, but I quickly realized I had started a different type of prison sentence. But," he said with a sigh, "someday my contract will end and I'll get my freedom back."

Neill had shared a massive secret, his worst trauma, and had exposed so much vulnerability. It took Kari a few moments to choose the best, most precise words to say to him. "That's really fucked up."

His shoulders bounced the slightest amount. "I'm inclined to agree."

"But thank you for trusting me enough to tell me all of that. You didn't have to."

Neill shrugged. "It was time that you knew. Plus, if I can help you or encourage you to get into Ola's office, I'm going to do it." He picked his drink up and stood. "What happened to Mitchell and Santos was the worst kind of crime, but please don't punish yourself for it."

The message was received. "I'll make an appointment to see her after the Weatherby visit."

Neill smiled. "I'm happy to hear it."

Chapter Five

The Weatherby last name had been synonymous with wealth in North America for two centuries. They had their hands in oil drilling, land acquisition—stolen and bought—the railroad, and the trade of the enslaved. With the family fortune also came a reputation for being cold, calculating, and ruthless. It was rumored that Jack had once stabbed his son, JJ's, hand with a corkscrew before a dinner meeting because he'd ordered wine with a screw top. He had three daughters, none of whom spoke to him. Perhaps somewhere within Jack's numerous divorce settlements was the answer as to why, but those legal filings had been locked tighter than his rumored penchant for handcuff play.

Kari had no desire to meet this vile man and his offspring, but she was ready to start her day and entered Madeleine's office.

"Ah, Karishma!" Henry said with a broad smile from one of the visitor seats. Kari couldn't help but notice he wore a tie with his navy suit. He never wore a tie. "Come in and please close the door behind you."

She did as she was asked and remained standing with her hands clasped behind her back. There was no point getting comfortable when they were going to go to Madeleine's other office for remote activation anyway. Except neither Madeleine nor Henry moved. "Aren't we going back there so you can do the clicky thing?"

Madeleine grimaced but tried to cover it with an awkward grin. "Not today, apparently."

"Are you serious?" Kari asked.

"Yes, Karishma, she is," Henry said. "There may be a time when I want you to have that ability, but for now, please attend to your typical VIP duties. However, those duties must be executed without any flaws!" Henry stood, buttoned his jacket, and then adjusted the elaborate knot on his boring diagonally striped tie. "I'll see you later this morning when Jack and JJ arrive." He left the room and shut the door behind him.

Madeleine picked up her teacup. "I think you're as surprised by this change as I am."

"I'm not complaining, but yeah." Kari took a seat in the chair Henry had occupied. "I would think that Henry would be dying to know what Jack's thinking. The fact that he's not is just . . ."

"Weird? Strange? Uncharacteristic? All of the above?"

"Yeah." Kari crossed her legs and racked her brain trying to think of Henry's motivation. "The only way it makes sense is if Henry's worried we'll learn something about him this way."

"And that's my theory as well." Madeleine placed the empty teacup back in its saucer. "I haven't shared this with you because there's been some . . . friction, at times, between us."

"I think that's because I hate you, everything Henry represents, and forced servitude to despicable people."

Madeleine pointed a finger at Kari. "Watch the attitude. And don't forget, you got free brain surgery because of it."

It was heaven not having a constant barrage of other people's thoughts. "Point made. Please continue."

"What I was going to say was that you were right about something you said on that particular day of the boat." Madeleine mimed an explosion with her hands. "Henry has been keeping me in the dark about something major and I don't like it."

"Oh, no. My heart is"—Kari mimed breaking with her hands—"for you."

Madeleine *tsked* and laced her fingers on her desk. "Could I ask you to provide reports about Henry to me?"

"You want me to spy on Henry?" Kari yelled.

"Keep your voice down," Madeleine whispered sternly. "But no, not 'spy'. I don't want you to go through his things or plant bugs. I simply would like to know at the end of the day what he and Jack discussed."

Kari brow knit together. "But you'll know. You're always there when Henry wines and dines the super VIPs."

Madeleine shook her head. "Not this time."

"You're not invited?" Kari shrieked.

"Would you stop yelling." Madeleine kept her razor edge voice down.

"Everything okay in there?" a twangy voice asked from outside the door.

Madeleine rolled her eyes. "Everything is fine. Please, come in Belle."

Belle poked her head into the room first. "Are you sure? I know I'm a little early."

Madeleine waved her in then gestured to the other guest chair with the *Faith, Family, Footy* pillow. "You're certainly excited to get started."

"Yes, ma'am, I am." Belle sat and crossed her long legs. "I woke up at four am and couldn't go back to sleep, so I just got up and did more research on the Weatherbys. I gasped really loud though when I learned about the Sacramento Swindle controversy and woke my roommate. I'll have to make it up to her later. Poor thing stayed up late studying for her exam about continental plate formations."

Kari watched in amusement as Madeleine's forehead made the slightest twitch. Clearly, she didn't know what to make of Belle yet either. And her latest Botox treatment had kicked in.

"Well, continents are large. I'm sure there's a lot of material to cover." Madeleine opened her desk drawer and pulled out two sheets of paper. She gave one to each. "Here's a list of requests that were sent last night for both Weatherbys. Please see that they are attended to, in addition to the usual checklist, by nine. They're due on the helipad at ten." From the open drawer, she pulled out a phone and name tag for Belle. "The phone's pre-programmed."

While Belle rejoiced over getting her first ever work phone, Kari read the list of forty items. Half were ridiculous but within the realm of super wealthy comfort, like spherical ice only, but others were preposterous. "Where are we supposed to find a print copy of a porno magazine? No store that sells that would be open at this hour and I don't even know if they sell actual magazines anymore."

"I can handle that," Belle said, and Kari knew by Madeleine's wide eyes that she was as surprised as she was. "I'll ask around the WU cafeteria during breakfast. I can think of one person specifically who may have something."

"That's rather unexpected, but also good outside-of-the-box thinking," Madeleine said. "I'll see you both at six pm when Matthew relieves you. Dismissed."

Kari followed Belle out of the office but kept reading. "Okay, what do you say we divide and conquer this and meet up at the suites? If you run into any snags, you can text me."

Belle hadn't taken her eyes off the list either. "Does that sound like a good plan to you?"

Belle looked up. "Huh? I'm sorry. Yeah, that sounds good. I was stuck on filtered water flavored with Persian cucumbers, chilled to thirty-four degrees Fahrenheit. I didn't know Persians had their own cucumber."

"The world is chock-full of wonders." Kari walked them to the VIP assistant office. "For the magazine errand, what times are breakfast for the WU students?"

"There's not enough of us to warrant different times, so it's seven-thirty to eight-thirty."

"That makes sense. I don't really know how WU works on the student-side of things."

Belle cocked her head. "How is that possible?"

"You're the first student I've spent time with. But Jade has described WU to me, if that counts."

"It doesn't. I think during my internship here, I might have to show you how the other half lives. Could be fun, especially considering they're more your peers than most people here."

"Tell you what, let's revisit the idea once the Weatherbys are gone and we can relax, because right now we have under three hours to finish the most ridiculous scavenger hunt I've encountered since that time I was five and it was in my Nani Tanha's cardiology office."

"Oh! I had one like that too, except it was in our church's graveyard." Belle grinned at her for what had to have been a solid five seconds. It was a degree of friendliness that gave Kari an urge to escape. "Okay, we can share those stories later. Now, we hunt."

———

There were two, two-level deluxe VIP suites on either side of the bow. The first thing that struck Kari every time she walked into one was the light. A massive wall of windows extended from the oak floor to the vaulted ceiling, showcasing a pristine view of Vancouver's Coal Harbour. There was a stunning mix of boats on the calm water. Coniferous trees edged one side of the shore while sleek skyscrapers dominated the other. A VIP could also enjoy that view from their private balcony with outdoor dining area and faux-rocky waterfall hot tub.

The interior featured an entertainment area with a massive wall-mounted television in front of two cushy white leather sofas. Above the TV was the new, remote-activated theater screen for movies and virtual golf. The net for stopping the balls was bundled in a decorative curtain on one side of the screen, whereas a black lacquered coffee table in front of the sofa had a hinged top for easy access to the bright green hitting mat and various clubs. A new "end table" contained all of the Doppler technology necessary for the sport.

Kari headed to the kitchen area, which was more of a wet bar. She had reorganized the top-shelf liquors earlier to make room for the six additional bottles of requested gin. On the Siberian marble countertop, she prepared the cucumber water and arranged his charcuterie board in the shape of a pig. To finish, she headed to the powder room to add a mason jar filled with wrapped peppermint chocolates and a copy of *Atlas Shrugged.*

Kari heard the door unlock from the upper level's staff-only entrance. "How'd you make out?" she shouted.

"I got everything," Belle said, "but I'm worried about the eight votive candles arranged on a rectangular plate with one hundred coffee beans because of the fire rule."

"We can cut the wick so it's too short to light." Kari bounded up the stairs and saw Belle hanging a monogrammed

JW robe. There was a canvas bag at the end of the California king-sized bed that Kari assumed had the rest of the items. "Do you want me to handle the candles while you put the other stuff in place?"

"I'd appreciate that." Belle kneeled to reach into the bag and pulled out two glossy magazines. With a serious face, she showed Kari the cover of each. "I mean this in the most professional way possible, which one should we put on the nightstand?"

Kari's examination alternated between the close-up of an airbrushed tan butt in a thong and an airbrushed close-up of ample tan cleavage. "I'd go with whatever his former and current wives have in common."

"That's smart. I'll give the other one back to Craig tomorrow." Belle placed the copy of *Ta-Tas* on the nightstand, then placed her hands on her hips as if deciding her next move. "Are the VIPs always this needy?"

"Yes. But they're usually not this creative." Kari took the multi-tool out of her pocket and headed to the master bathroom. Using the folded scissors, she cut the wicks until they were flush with the wax. "Before I put these back, did you count the coffee beans?"

"Yes. I figured all of this is some sort of test or game, and even if it's dumb, I hate to lose."

Kari smirked and checked the list once more. Everything was accounted for. "I'd say we're ready for Mister and Mister Weatherby."

They went up to the helicopter deck to greet their guests.

Belle stepped on deck ten and gasped. "This is amazing!"

"You'll get over that feeling fast." Kari watched Henry walk over to them. He had added a pocket square that matched his tie. Double weird.

"Good morning, Karishma! And you must be Annabelle.

I'm so happy you have such a brilliant and trusted employee to show you the ropes."

Belle put her hand to her chest. "Just Belle is fine. I . . . This is such an honor Mr. Wibawa. Thank you for the opportunity to learn and serve on your magnificent ship."

Kari's eyes hurt from fighting the urge to roll them. She turned away from the scene and saw Josef. She should have known Neill's psycho-counterpart would be the security guard assigned for this VIP.

"You are so welcome, Annabelle," Henry said. "Now, the important thing is that Mr. Weatherby agrees that the *Hinewai* is as glorious as we believe it is and that every request he makes is attended to the best of your and the other VIP assistants' abilities."

"Yes, sir, Mr. Wibawa." Belle pointed at a dark dot in the sky. "I think that may be our guests."

Kari squinted. How did Belle know that dot was the helicopter? Even with perfect vision, she couldn't see it.

Henry slowly rotated to where Belle had pointed. "Karishma, you and Annabelle off to the side. I will handle introductions, and if he finds the agenda acceptable, then we can go from there; however, if he has changes, we'll need to accommodate his request."

"Understood." Kari kept her focus on the sky and, lo and behold, a helicopter soon took shape.

The chopper came in loud, whipping the looser material of all their clothes and Belle's hair. After the engine was cut, Jack Weatherby stepped out in his tailored, three-piece, pinstripe suit. Thick silver hair was slicked back away from his ruddy and droopy face. He looked down at them with a stony stare before he descended the stairs.

Jack's time-traveling twin, JJ, followed.

"Welcome to the *Hinewai!*" Henry strutted over to his

guests and extended his hand. Henry was a well-known germaphobe, so between this and the suit accessories, he aimed to impress.

"Nice of you to greet us here," Jack said in his gruff tenor, then peered over Henry's shoulder to scan the deck. "Where's your son?"

"My . . . son? Raymond?" Henry asked, surprised.

Kari joined him in that.

"Did Gabriella not mention that when she was here two weeks ago?"

Kari's surprise increased to gobsmacked levels. Gabriella Fermi had been on the *Hinewai* when she had been in Alaska? Finn hadn't said anything about that to her.

"No, Gabriella didn't mention Raymond." Henry uttered a forced laugh. "We try to avoid discussing our offspring. Brings up bad memories for each of us, especially her."

"Be that as it may," Jack said, "I'd like him here. It's important that I meet him for this process."

What kind of process needed a son Henry barely acknowledged?

"Of course," Henry said. "I'll get Karishma on it right away." He walked to her; his pace was relaxed but his eyes were wild. "Get my son here immediately. Annabelle, can you show the Weatherbys to their suites?"

Belle's eyes resembled saucers.

"You'll be fine," Kari reassured her. Now came the tricky part. "May I have your son's phone number?"

"Raymond W is already programmed into your phone. When he answers, he'll ask for proof that it's you. The code phrase is 'money boat'. Tell him I'll transfer $50,000 to his account for every day that he's here. He should contact you for transportation to the ship once he's in the Vancouver area. Questions?"

She had several questions but couldn't ask any of them. "None, sir."

While Henry introduced Annabelle—it was reassuring to know she wasn't the only one whose nickname preference he ignored—Kari kept watch on the group while she wandered to the railing and dialed. She had never once spoken to him. In fact, Henry's son had only come up in conversation twice, and both times were disparaging. But unlike Gabriella's son, who was awaiting trial for dozens of violent felonies, Raymond had only failed to meet Henry's expectations. He was a custom car and food truck painter in California.

The phone picked up on the fifth ring. "Hello, Raymond."

"What does Dad want me to do?" he asked, annoyed. "Also, it's just Ray."

After Kari provided the information, including the secret code and money, she asked, "How long do you think it'll take you to get here?"

"Let me check." After a few minutes of flight searching, he said, "About five to six hours, probably closer to six with LA traffic. Who is this, by the way?"

"Kari. I'm a VIP assistant on the boat."

"Gotcha. See you this afternoon, Kari." Ray ended the call.

Kari headed over to where Henry and Jack spoke about switching brunch into lunch and JJ gave Belle notes about each piece of luggage she had brought down from the helicopter. Kari waited for a pause in the conversation before giving Henry an update. "Mr. Wibawa, your son should be here around three-thirty pm."

"Excellent!" Jack said. "We can get settled in, tour, eat, and then go fishing. That sounds like a perfect father-son activity."

"What a grand idea!" Henry clapped his hands together. "Karishma, can you arrange that for us?"

Fishing at 3:30pm may have been the worst timing ever. "Absolutely, Mr. Wibawa. What is your target fish?"

His brow arched as if he had no idea. He looked to Jack. "Guest's choice."

"I think it would be appropriate, given the area, for salmon."

Henry beamed. "I'm sure we'll catch dozens!"

Okay, this was the worst timing ever. "Actually, salmon fishing won't be peak until the fall. I suggest halibut."

"We didn't ask for suggestions," JJ said. "We asked for salmon fishing."

Five minutes into introductions was not the time to pick a fight, especially with Henry's fists clenched at his sides. "Of course."

The muscles in Henry's face relaxed enough to unclench his jaw. "Please see to it that a boat is ready for three to . . . seven pm."

Considering it could take hours to arrive at an appropriate location, this was officially the dumbest fishing trip ever. But there was no point arguing. "Yes, sir, Mr. Wibawa. Would either of you care to have anything special on board?"

"The blonde," JJ said with his eyes locked on Belle.

Kari turned to see Belle's face with a pinkish hue. Her arms were crossed and she bit her lower lip. Kari recognized the look. Belle was embarrassed, unhappy, and feared an honest reaction would be met with retaliation. She wanted Henry to stand up for his employee, but he found adjusting his watchband more important. Such a coward. Someone had to do something. Added to the fact was that JJ's conceited grin made her want to punch it off his face. "Mr. Weatherby, the VIP assistants are tasked with providing you additional services to maximize your comfort, but that does not include allowing you to harass us in any manner. Her preferred name is Belle, please use it."

JJ guffawed. "Whatever you say, little boy."

Heat rushed up Kari's neck until her entire face warmed. "I'm an adult woman and my pronouns are she/her." Left unspoken was, 'You slimy, cockwaffle.'

"Whatever." JJ stretched his arms and cracked his back. "We'll need some drinks, she-her."

Jack cleared his throat. "I think a case of beer in a cooler and a bottle of Canadian whiskey will suffice."

The heat had started to dissipate, but the jitters from the adrenaline rush still coursed through her. "Not gin, sir?"

"Nah, I hate that stuff."

Kari gritted her teeth. What else on their requested list was bullshit? "Very well. If it's alright with you, Mr. Wibawa, Belle and I will notify Chef Jon about the change of meal schedule. Would you like to be shown to your suites now?"

"Not yet," Jack said. "We can do that once you notify the kitchen. It'll give me some time to chat with Henry some more."

"Yes, sir." Kari headed to the kitchen with Belle in tow.

"We need to talk," Belle said in a clipped tone. "Privately."

"Okay," Kari said with apprehension. Rather than go to the kitchen that had an audience, Kari took them to the VIP assistant office, which was once a walk-in storage closet. "What's wrong? Aside from that fact that JJ hasn't tripped and fallen off the side of the ship yet."

Belle's usually kind eyes took a turn for the serious. "I can stand up for myself. You shouldn't have spoken for me."

"But you were just standing there. Silent. I thought I was doing you a favor."

"Not a favor. I was mad and collecting my emotions before I spoke because my instinct of telling him to 'kiss my biscuits' would have had repercussions. And I know that you understand that, because I watched you gather yourself after he called you a little boy. Which I think was terrible, for the record."

Kari uttered an annoyed sigh. Why was she being admonished for doing a nice thing? And who said 'kiss my biscuits'? "Fine, I won't do it again."

"Thank you. All that I ask is that you give me first shot at my own rescue." Belle gave her a small smile and then took in the room around them. "Did this used to be a closet?"

"Yeah, I'll explain later. Now, we have VIPs to please and need to make a new suite for Ray. I have no idea how that's going to go."

———

After lunch, Henry and the Weatherbys settled in the lounge area with their cocktails while they discussed stocks, precious metals, and the accuracy of wealthy movie villains. Listening to Henry fawn over Jack disgusted her. So she was more than happy to check her phone when it vibrated against her thigh. Belle peered over her shoulder while she read the text from Ray.

> Just landed. I can get to the dock in about 40 min.

"Do we stay here or meet him?" Belle asked.

"Good question." Kari walked over then waited for a pause in conversation since, apparently, she was invisible. "Mr. Wibawa, your son will be at the dock within the hour. Would you like us to take the VIP boat out to meet him?"

"Can't you go and blondie stay?" JJ asked. "I'll need a refill soon."

To demonstrate she had learned her lesson, Kari turned to Belle for her answer.

The corner of her mouth ticked upward. "Sir, my name is Belle. That arrangement is fine with me, Kari."

"Excellent!" Henry pulled the olive off his toothpick with his teeth. "When you come back on the boat, Karishma, stay down on deck one. We'll leave for our fishing expedition from there."

Kari gave him a nod then dialed the VIP boat captain as she headed down. "I need to get to the dock to collect Henry's son."

"Ray's coming?" The captain shouted in surprise. "Oh, boy. I better put down the plastic in case he pukes. Again."

Once she had descended nine decks, Kari's foot paused on the final step as her mind played out the explosion, smelled the smoke and then Neill's piney aftershave while he held her. The ache in her hand was new though. She looked down to see that her hand had gripped the rail tight enough to whiten her knuckles.

Yeah, she had to start EMDR therapy as soon as possible.

"I understand the trepidation," the captain said. "I was nervous the first time I had to get into the new boat, too. I did a thorough inspection myself and promise it's safe." He held out a hand to help her on board.

The acknowledgment that her fear was shared by others momentarily surprised her, but it did make sense. Kari took his hand, trusting that he had done his job. That was progress. She settled at the bow of the covered portion and heard the pneumatic system's clicking and hissing as the boat lowered into the water. The trip to the dock was smooth, which she hoped translated into their afternoon trip.

Kari recognized Ray, not by his face, but by his clothing. No one else on the dock wore a perfectly tailored pastel pink suit. He also brought a piece of rolling luggage that could have fit an adult. As they pulled up to the dock, Kari saw he had more of a resemblance to his mother. His build was slight. His complexion darker with stubble, like he was growing a goatee. Coiffed black hair. But he did have Henry's eyes.

The captain set out the gangplank for him, but Ray didn't move.

"I'm Kari. Thanks for getting here so quickly."

"Uh-huh." He stared at the gangplank, frozen in place.

"Is everything okay?"

"I hate the water." Ray put his back to her and mumbled something she couldn't hear. When he faced her once more, he walked across the gangplank, taking his luggage with him. He took a seat in the boat's cabin, where she had been, but faced away from the water.

Kari followed.

He must have really needed the money to come on the *Hinewai*. She bit her tongue and forced a smile. "I hate to be the bearer of bad news, but I don't think you're going to like our next activity."

"What kind of idiotic hoop does my father want me to jump through this time?"

"Fishing with Jack and JJ Weatherby."

"Fishing? Are we going on an even on a smaller boat?" he asked in an ultra-sonic pitch.

"It's a little bit bigger." Kari watched as he riffled through his suit pockets for a prescription bottle. "We can lock your luggage in deck one storage if there isn't time to take it to your suite."

"Is there any way I can stay in an interior room? I don't need windows." He popped the top off the orange bottle, shook two blue pills into his hand, and swallowed them without water.

His medicine could be a lot of things, but her money was on some sort of anti-anxiety. Since pills and alcohol were never a good idea to combine, she didn't want him to feel pressured later, even if it was by his father. "Jack requested beer and whiskey on board, but we'll also have non-alcoholic options, just so you know."

"Huh?" He tilted his head. "Oh! I get it now. I don't drink, it messes with my sugars. What's after fishing?"

"Dinner." She didn't want to pry, but his 'sugars' comment raised important questions. "Pardon me for asking, but are you diabetic? I'm only asking because I can notify the kitchen staff and place a sharps container in your bathroom."

He ran his finger under his collar to pull it away from his neck. "Just tell Jon I'm here and they'll accommodate. The sharps container won't be necessary, I have a port that shoots insulin right into me when I need it."

Now the small rectangular device clipped to his belt made sense. "If you don't mind, I'll tell the other VIP assistants. Ahmed will be on duty during your dinner tonight."

His anxiety-riddled, shy demeanor shifted into a brilliant smile. It sparkled like Henry's. "Ahmed's on shift? That's great! Well, great for me, at least."

VIPs hated curiosity, but she had to ask. "How do you know Ahmed?"

"Dad doesn't like me to talk about it. Does Ahmed know I'm here?"

"No. Would you like me to text him?"

He waved off the offer. "No need. I'll do it."

Kari had to admit that except for being well dressed, Ray was nothing like how she had imagined. She thought he'd be arrogant with dashes of boorish and insulting, but, so far, he had been reasonable.

After a half hour on deck one, which gave Ray time to store his luggage, change clothes, and have several back-and-forth texts with Ahmed, she saw Belle leading the pack wearing a black baseball cap with her ponytail pulled through the back. Henry could have gone on safari with his khaki outfit. The Weatherbys wore matching long sleeve shirts with hoods and blue cargo pants. Honestly, it was the most sensible clothing Kari had seen them wear. Josef followed them all looking dangerous and evil as always.

"What took so long?" Kari whispered to Belle.

"Jack and JJ wanted to try virtual golf. How's Ray?"

"Nicer than I expected. Hates the water, likes Ahmed."

"Ah, Raymond!" Henry bellowed and took his time going over for a firm handshake. "How was your trip in?"

Ray grinned. "It w—"

"Let's do the small talk once we're on the boat," Jack said. "We're burning daylight."

"Absolutely." Henry smiled, released Ray's hand to give Jack a pat on the back. "It's time to find some salmon!"

———

"It was awful," Kari summarized in Madeleine's office. "Jack's a typical obnoxious mega rich guy, but JJ is absolute human trash. He's rude, a misogynist, a true poster boy for nepotism, and couldn't even bait his own hook."

Madeleine smirked. "What kind of bait and who ended up baiting it for him?"

"Squid and I did. It was around the same time Henry and Jack were chatting and Belle was comforting Ray as he threw up over the side of the boat." As an unintended side effect, Ray's vomit attracted more fish than the squid bait.

"What did Jack and Henry chat about?"

"They went back and forth between ex-wife and Adam Cho bashing. Apparently, Adam is working on a new angle for his 'billionaires are destroying the world' thesis. He's been after a few others since his investigation into Henry stalled a few months ago."

Madeleine gave a slow nod. "Any idea why Ray was asked to come?"

"Jack wanted him here and implied that Gabriella Fermi should have told Henry that fact." She took a moment to gather her thoughts about Ray. "I feel bad for him. He has the queasiest stomach ever, near crippling anxiety, checks his glucose monitor like every fifteen minutes, and Henry's nicer to me!"

"I've also witnessed this. What's the agenda tomorrow?"

"Father-son golf playdate. Belle and I were already told that our main job is to caddy. I'm sure it'll be just as intellectually stimulating as being a statistician and bioinformaticist at a neuroscience lab." She hitched a thumb toward the door. "Can I go now? I have a guitar lesson."

"No." Madeleine leaned forward on her desk and folded her arms. "We need to talk."

Kari groaned. "Is this about my attitude?"

"Indeed. I would suggest that you find something within this job to enjoy." Madeleine walked over to the picture frame of her family posed in front of their candy shop. "I worked here from the time I was twelve to the time I was twenty-two. Even during breaks at uni. Did I resent it the way you resent this job? Absolutely."

"Are you seriously comparing your time selling fancy chocolate to my situation?"

"Yes! Because I learned heaps about people in the shop. I learned how to spot liars and thieves. The way people act when they buy for their spouse as opposed to their mistress. If you could get it through that skull of yours with the special technology in it, you'd realize that this job you find so demeaning is an educational experience all of its own."

Considering that both Belle and Ray had put her in her place today regarding her assumptions and actions, she reluctantly saw Madeleine's point. "I'll take that advice under consideration, ma'am."

"Good. Now you're dismissed, and have a drink at the nineteenth hole for me tomorrow."

———

Was there a sport worse than golf on the planet? Kari didn't think so.

For the first nine holes of best ball play, Kari had accompanied Henry and Jack while Belle caddied for Ray and JJ. The conversation between the two titans of industry revolved around what it meant to be a man of greatness. Henry had agreed with everything Jack had said and asked about legacy. Jack believed that power was legacy.

For the second nine holes, Kari had listened to Jack act like an uncle-type figure to Ray. He provided financial advice, social circle advice, and even relationship advice. Based on Ray's tight smile and rigid posture, but lack of vomiting, she could tell he preferred golf to fishing, although not by much. To Ray's credit, he had asked the occasional question, which created the appearance he was interested.

During most of the eighteen holes, Kari would catch a glance at Belle, who seemed to be enjoying herself. She had a wide smile, clapped for shots, and had tees or balls cued. After seeing her happy face, Kari would look over to the security detail, where Josef barked orders to the golf course's team from his shaded cart.

Kari missed Neill. He would have been nicer to them.

"That was truly excellent," Henry said once they returned to the club house. They had an almost aerial view of the pristine green grass of the course and nearby river. "Karishma, Annabelle, please let them know we'll need their most competent server."

Kari followed the signs to the private room. A few of the club's platinum members already had cocktails in hand and were mingling. The bartender waved her over.

The sunlight pouring in made the dark woods of the bar seem less tavern-like. However, the stone wall fireplace with a taxidermic sixteen-point buck above the mantle did give it hunting lodge energy. "Hi, I'm—"

"Are the Wibawas and Weatherbys coming in now?" he asked while he poured a beer from the tap.

"Yes, and they've requested your most competent server."

The bartender's bushy gray eyebrows lifted. He took the beer to one of the patrons and left the bar area through the swinging double doors.

Kari leaned against its brass rail, taking in the room. The aesthetic appealed to her, even if the people didn't.

Belle cleared her throat.

Kari turned to see Belle giving her a pointed look. "What?"

"Did you really have to add the 'competent server' bit? It's not like they don't know who's coming into the room. They're on their A game."

Madeleine's words about using this as a learning opportunity to develop her people skills came back. "Did you have fun today? The reason I ask is because it seems like you did. You smiled and clapped. You did that thing where you hunched down and checked out the angles of the ground. You even offered them your own sunscreen."

Belle shrugged. "I figured I'd make the most of the day. I mean, walking in with a bad attitude sours everyone, so then that's what you get back. Take our bartender here. I would have come in and said, 'They'll be having lunch and are eager to see how your chef and servers can wow them!' That accomplishes the same thing, but spins it in a positive way."

What Belle said made sense, but it was fake nice. Like Henry's smile to Jack. "But doesn't that bother you?"

"Being positive? No. I should ask you why you're so comfortable being negative?"

Kari refrained from *tsking* because that would have proved Belle's point. "You sound like Madeleine. She made this big deal yesterday about my attitude. But I don't see it as negative, I see it as being realistic. Once you're around more of them you'll get it. Trust me."

Belle joined her in leaning against the bar. "Get what?"

"The hypocritical expectation that we have to be both by their side, pleased to serve, but also stay out of their space. It's impossible to tell what they want."

"But their body language and tone should give you that. Even their word choice is a dead giveaway. Have you ever spent time studying people?"

"No." Kari left out the part where she hadn't needed to because she could read their minds for the longest time.

Belle uttered a *hmm*. "We're going to have to fix that. Oh!" she said loud enough for the platinums to look their way. "You should play poker. Have you ever played?"

Kari shook her head.

"It's a great way to learn body language. I'm in a WU group that plays most Fridays. We have some drinks, play a few games. You should come."

Kari had never played poker but liked the concept of the game, and the outing would also give her a chance to socialize with people her own age, something she knew she needed to do. Jade and Neill were great, but they weren't her peers. "Poker sounds promising. But I can't come this Friday, I already promised Jade I'd hang out with her."

"Great! I can let the gang know to expect you next week. It's a nice group, and since we're all poor college students we don't play for money. It's also bring your own beverage."

"How many of you are there?"

"Four. There's good diversity in terms of program and year, so that helps keep conversation interesting. We meet in a club room on the same level as our dorms, which has been convenient."

Kari nodded, but the realization struck that she hadn't interacted with more than one peer in a friendly way since she was fifteen.

"What's wrong?" Belle asked. "And before you deny it, you suck your cheek in for a millisecond when you're unsure about something.

Kari's mouth—with unsucked cheeks—dropped open.

Belle's lips upturned into a grin.

"Okay, fine." It was best to be honest. "Since I was home-schooled and went to college really young, my social experiences with people my own age are very limited."

"Surely, you could have snuck into a party or something once or twice."

Her ex-boyfriend had tried to convince her to do that, but his inner thoughts alone drove her crazy, let alone a room full of insecure, horny, drunk people. However, there was another reason she could give Belle. "My moms are local celebrities, so people knew who I was, and since some people in town *really* hated my moms, that transferred over to me. Especially once Mom L was elected mayor."

Belle's smile flipped into a frown. "That's a real shame, but we're going to fix all of that. You might not be in college anymore, but you are going to get some college experiences."

———

Kari and Belle attended to the Weatherby's luggage in the helicopter as Henry walked alongside Jack and JJ to the base of the landing pad's steps.

"Thank you both so much for coming aboard!" Henry said to them.

"I had a good time," Jack said. His line of sight went to Ray in the lounge area with Ahmed. He leaned in to whisper—much too loudly—in Henry's ear, "It can't be Ray. At least in my opinion. The kid doesn't have the stomach, literally and figuratively, to have the position. Plus, the goatee is the only thing that makes him not look like a four-year-old girl dressing up like a feminist."

Henry gave him a slow nod. "But if not him, then who?" Henry said, his voice above a whisper. "He's my only child."

For a split second, Jack's eyes met Kari's before he regarded Henry once more. "Whomever you choose, they don't have to be blood. It's about potential and loyalty."

Kari knew she wasn't supposed to have heard the exchange. She stomped her way down the last few metal stairs so the metal clanged. They all turned to her. "Your luggage is securely in position, Mr. Weatherby. Would you like anything for your ride to the airport?"

"No." He shook Henry's hand and passed him a coin-sized piece of metal. It looked like copper, but it was too large to be a penny. "Keep that in a safe place and start thinking about your dig." Jack ascended the metal steps with JJ in tow.

Old coins and a dig? Kari's mind churned at the meaning as she and Belle watched the helicopter take flight toward land.

"Karishma"—Henry stood in front of her and took his necktie off—"see that Raymond gets back to land as soon as possible." He left the deck.

Kari dug out her phone and texted the VIP captain. After a few exchanges, Ray's departure was set. "I'll ask Ahmed if he can walk him down, so we can just report to Madeleine and finish our day."

"What's wrong?" Belle asked. "You sound depressed."

Kari sighed. "Are you going to analyze every gesture I make and the tone of everything I say to prove a point?"

"Are you going to be standoffish every time I ask a basic question or state the obvious?"

Dammit, Belle and her valid points. "Fine. I think it's sad that Henry doesn't want to spend any more time with his son. I'll never understand why a parent wouldn't do everything in their power to spend more time with their child." The flash of anger Kari had seen a few days ago in Belle returned.

Belle pursed her lips and folded her arms. "Probably because you have two incredibly loving parents. A lot of folks don't have that," Belle said with a melancholy note to her voice.

Tone. Body language. It wasn't difficult for Kari to deduce that Belle didn't have the loving, happy upbringing that she had.

They walked over to the lounge where Ray and Ahmed shared a laugh over JJ's need for neck tie assistance. "I'm sorry to interpret," Kari said, "but Henry would like Ray to head home now."

Ray grinned at Ahmed. "Told you." He tipped back the rest of his unsweetened iced tea, stood, and buttoned his lavender suit jacket.

"I'll walk you down," Ahmed said.

"Let's go, buddy." Ray slung his arm around Ahmed's shoulder and they left the deck looking like best friends going home from a night out at the bars. "I need off this ship."

Their relationship piqued Kari's interest, but she'd have to get their story from Ahmed later. For now, she went to Belle, who appeared to be studying the hot tub's new control panel. "Ready to wrap up this visit?"

"Sure."

After a short walk they were inside Madeleine's office. Kari took the reporting lead. "The Weatherbys are mid-flight and Ray is motoring toward land with Ahmed, ma'am."

"Those two get along really well," Belle said as she took her seat. "What's their story?"

"I'm curious, too," Madeleine said, "but I don't care enough to ask. More importantly, do you feel ready to work independently in San Diego?"

"I do, ma'am. I'm excited to learn who our guest is!"

"See!" Madeleine said to Kari. "That's enthusiasm for the job."

"Yes, ma'am. I got those memos from Belle, too." In a way, being fake nice and excited could help her in her quest to take down Wibawa Enterprises with less sneaking around. That would be safer. "I promise I'll work on my attitude."

"I'm glad we were able to get through to you," Madeleine said. "Anyway, from here to San Diego we'll have several VIPs. The first is someone called Yiz."

"The singer?" Belle practically screamed. "Oh my God!"

Madeleine sucked in her lower lip before releasing it with a pop. "You may want to reign in the enthusiasm a bit. You'll scare the VIPs and rupture my eardrums. As I was saying . . ." Madeleine listed the next several VIPs before she dismissed Belle and asked Kari to stay.

Belle stood and straightened the obnoxious pillow on the seat. "Kari, I'll touch base with you about the VIPs and poker." She closed the door behind her.

"Poker?" Madeleine asked Kari.

"Yeah, Belle says it'll help me learn how to read people better."

Madeleine leaned back in her chair. "That's actually an excellent idea. Once you learn the people part I have no doubt you'll be an excellent poker player, even without your little brain trick. But, enough of that, tell me how today went with Jack and Henry."

"Cryptic."

"How do you mean?"

"I mean, I overheard Jack tell Henry that Ray doesn't have what it takes to have some sort of job. Then, Jack gave Henry something that resembled a coin and told him to look for places to dig."

Madeleine sat straighter, intrigued. "For a body?"

"I have no clue."

Madeleine drummed her French manicured nails on the desk. "Do you know what an employee with a good attitude would do right about now?"

While Kari couldn't wait to feed Adam extra dirt on Henry, and now the Weatherbys, if she appeared eager to please or did a complete 180 with her attitude, that would be suspicious. "I think I could try"—Kari added a squirm for dramatic effect—"to look into that for you."

"Aw. Who's a positive little worker bee? You are!" Madeleine snickered. "You're dismissed. See you in a few days."

Chapter Six

Pacific Ocean

"To the end of the week." Jade clinked her glass of bourbon against Kari's juice glass of champagne. "You serve first."

Kari took a sip and placed her drink on the high shelf. Someone had finally moved them to protect drinks from paddle swinging. "Alright, coming in hot." She bounced the ball over the net.

Jade returned. "How did your first session with Dr. Egbe go?"

"That's tomorrow at six pm." Kari batted the ball back in a high arch.

"Isn't that kind of late?"

"Yeah." She went low on the opposite corner. "I have the pm shift next, so it helps the transition."

"I would hate that." Jade came up and tapped it over the net.

"I do, too. The six am to six pm shift is so much better." Kari gave the ball a light backhand. "I get the sense that Belle is more of an early bird, too, so it'll be interesting to see how she adjusts."

"What do you think of Belle?" Jade slapped the ball hard, causing it to hit the ceiling.

Kari played it anyway. "She'll be fine. A natural people-pleaser but isn't a doormat. Plus, she's got that southern charm thing going for her that people seem to like even if I think it's annoying sometimes."

Jade waggled her brow. "She's easy on the eyes, too."

"I won't deny that, but she's also *really* perceptive. Believe it or not she's convinced me to socialize with multiple people at once." Kari sent a fast forehand to the corner of the table, which then landed in dust bunnies behind a storage bin. "Point, me." Kari used the break to take a drink, as did Jade.

Jade wiped the dusty ball on her pants and tapped it over the net. "I think it's great you're expanding your social circle."

"You're not upset we'll have to reschedule next week's game?"

"Nah. Especially when I have a date . . . with Neill."

Kari gasped. The ball bounced past her. "You do not!"

"I do," Jade said with a giddy laugh, put down her paddle, and picked up her drink. "He waited for me outside the cafeteria during the time I usually get my lunch. He told me that he felt bad about how he reacted when I asked him out and, to make it up to me, wants to take me out for margaritas and fish tacos once we get to San Diego. I'm so excited."

Her clutched fists and beaming smile gave that away. Maybe Kari wasn't as terrible at reading people as she thought.

"I think I have you to thank," Jade said.

"What'd I do?"

"I don't know specifically, but he said he was talking to you in the gym and the way you reacted to what he said made him feel better."

Kari couldn't help but utter an, "Aw." If Neill ever wrote a memoir, the title should be, *Hard Body, Soft Heart*. "Well, he helped me, too. And, hopefully, the good doctor can help me further."

———

Dr. Ola Egbe's office was at the far end of deck one, past the medical center, and across from the ship's brig. That had to be intentional. She'd have to ask Neill about it later.

Like the sick bay, the exterior door to her new psychiatrist's office was unlocked. Kari went inside to a typical waiting room, where there was a door closed ahead with a message to check in on the tablet. She scanned the room. There was a plant in the corner and one check-in tablet on a lone table between two chairs. Kari sat and confirmed her health information. She had a few minutes after that so she took her multi-tool out from her pocket and flipped out the screwdriver.

The outlet by the English ivy wasn't going to check itself for listening devices.

The wall plate came off easily, as did pulling out the inner outlet's housing for inspection. Nothing suspicious. Kari was midway through reinstalling the plastic plate when the door beside her opened. She craned her neck upward to see a bald woman with ebony skin, a heart-shaped face, and a vibrant green and yellow dress. "I know this looks weird."

"I'm glad I don't have to point that out to you," she said in a Nigerian accent, "Karishma, right?"

"Kari is fine." She brought her attention back to the outlet and finished tightening the screws. "I don't know if you noticed, but that wall plate was crooked." Based on the near patronizing grin, even without telepathy, Kari knew she wasn't buying it. "So, Dr. Egbe, should I come into your office?"

"You can call me Ola and, yes, come on in."

Kari stepped past her and walked into a much more refined space. The office furniture was modern with sleek lines and ergonomic designs. Her desk was currently at a standing height, but she had a feeling they'd have their session in the seating area by the window's natural light and seascape.

"You can pace, stand, lotus position on the floor, or sit," Ola said. "However you feel most comfortable so I can get to know you."

She hated all the meet-and-greet bullshit. It'd be so much easier if she could simply say, 'I'm a genius telepath with a weird connection to birds of prey who has experienced multiple traumas. Am I allowed to put my feet on the furniture?' Although, that did raise a good question. "Do you mind if I take off my shoes?"

"As long as your feet don't smell."

Kari respected that practical answer and, given all the choices, she slipped off her canvas shoes and sat cross-legged in the cushy, club-style chair. This was how she had sat during most of her therapy sessions back home when she was younger. "How do you like to start with new patients?"

Ola took a seat across from her and smiled. This time it was broader, more genuine. "Each person is different. With you, I know that you've been in therapy for a few months now and why, but there are a few things from your past that I don't understand. I'd like to get clarity on that first, if it's alright with you."

"That's fine with me, but I don't think I can get through all my past in our hour session. I've kinda been through a lot."

"It doesn't all have to be today." Ola picked up a tablet and stylus from the side table. "This thing has unlimited pages for my notes."

The hair on the back of Kari's neck prickled. Anything

electronic could be uploaded or hacked, like her medical records that Madeleine had stolen. "I would prefer it if you didn't take notes on an electronic device."

Ola cocked her head. "Why?"

"Medical information can be hacked."

Ola took her time before responding. "That's true, but I'd like to point out that physical records come with risk, too. They could be stolen from a locked drawer or even damaged by a saucy noodle if someone were to write notes during their lunch, hypothetically speaking."

Part of Kari wanted to smile at the attempt to lighten the mood. "I understand where you're coming from, I just . . . Let's just say I have trust issues."

"Ah. I think that's a fine place to start, then." Ola put the tablet and stylus back on the table and folded her hands on her lap. "Tell me about that."

While dancing around her supernatural origin and paranormal skills, Kari told Ola about her upbringing, her moms and small extended family, her lack of friends growing up, her love of dogs, and of course, the traumas.

"I remember that God and Country attack," Ola said. "Goodness that must have been terrifying for you and your mothers."

"It was. PTSD for the whole family. Mom A still scares easily. Mom L is like me in that she has more of a hair trigger with emotional outbursts." Kari thought of how she had reacted when Belle asked about the VIP boat. She had been mindful to watch her temper during the rest of the week. "Ever since I watched Mitchell and Santos die in the explosion, I fly off the handle pretty easily."

Ola scrunched her face in a way that was both a cringe and conveyed sympathy. "You witnessed it?"

"Yes." That was the most Ola was getting. No mention of

Madeleine or Josef or the fact that the explosion was a way to cover up the fact they had been shot first. "In addition to snapping at people, I have nightmares about it."

"How often do you have nightmares?"

"About four times a week, and I want to love sleep again. I even got all new extravagant comfy things for my bed, but sometimes I'm afraid to close my eyes so I'll just stay awake. Watch an extra movie or play an entire album on my guitar. Part of me wants to take sleeping pills, but I've read enough biographies of dead celebrities to know how that goes. Plus, Mom A would go ape shit on me."

Ola gave a brief nod, then glanced out the window before asking her next question. "Out of curiosity, do you talk about this with anybody else?"

"The moms a little bit, but they worry so much, I don't want to add to their stress. My friend Neill knows and I can talk to him. He's the one who encouraged me to see you. Totally shatters the tough guy stereotype."

Ola smiled again. "He can be tough when he needs to be. I've been called in a time or two after he's brought people down to the brig."

Kari's theory about the brig was correct; that was always good for the ego. "My neighbor, Jade, has been great, too. She has a daughter around my age, so I feel like she knows how to talk to me." There was one last person Kari felt compelled to mention, too. "I used to talk to Finn, but since they left the ship, not so much. I'll text occasionally, but I don't hear back very often. That's been disappointing. I know we can't be a romantic item, but our friendship meant something to me. I thought Finn cared about me the same amount as I cared for them."

"Was this the first time you had feelings about someone to this degree?"

She had a boyfriend, Nicholas, a few years ago, but he

didn't know her the way Finn did. Kari could be herself with Finn, and she knew that they understood her better because of their empathic skills. It wasn't telepathy, but it was something. "I think . . . yes."

"How about for Finn?"

"I can't say for certain, but Finn does have a son, so that leads me to believe I wasn't their first massive crush. I'm guessing most people have extra feelings toward someone when they birth your child."

"Not always, unfortunately. However, I am inclined to agree with you, and it does hurt when that level of care isn't reciprocated. But I also need to say that we can enjoy people for the period of time they were in our lives. Circumstances change frequently in life."

Kari felt herself nodding along. Finn's circumstances most definitely had changed. From being a VIP assistant on the *Hinewai*, where they used their empath powers to further Henry's fortune, to being traded to Gabriella Fermi and living a life of luxury in Italy.

"May I offer a suggestion?" Ola asked.

"If it's to stop hoping for any type of romantic relationship with Finn, don't worry, I have."

"No, it's not that. Although, I think, given your situation, as you heal and work through this latest trauma, it's best not to seek romance. What I was going to say is that while I'm glad you have Jade and Neill, I think it may help if you try to expand your social circle. While you may work with many people, it sounds isolated."

"I'm still giving guitar lessons, and I'm going to try a game night of sorts with some WU students."

"That's wonderful. If by some—" A single beep came from Ola's watch before she turned it off. "If by some chance, you don't enjoy that game night, I can recommend a trauma support group for young adults next week."

"Next week?" Kari asked, surprised. "I assumed this would be a monthly or every-other-week thing."

"You've been through more than I think you realize. Every week is my recommendation, for now."

Kari groaned as she slipped her shoes back on. She didn't want to sit in that chair every week, but she also wanted a week of solid rest. "Alright."

"Excellent. Next week I'd like to start Eye Movement Desensitization and Reprocessing or EMDR therapy with you." Ola rounded her desk to a small filing cabinet and pulled out a stapled sheaf of papers. "Your homework is to think about positive memories and safe places that had boats, were loud, were smokey, and had fire. As someone with a neuroscience background, I'm sure you can appreciate the ability our brain has for reprogramming."

Kari nodded and took the papers from her. She read the title, *Trauma Release Exercises.*

"I think adding exercises to your self-care tool kit will help." Ola walked Kari to the door. "I can't promise you a miracle cure, but I can tell you that there is overwhelming evidence that EMDR and exercise will help you get better."

Kari stared at the faded black and white human figure doing an ankle stretch on the page while the word 'evidence' ran laps in her brain. Gods, she missed science and the way she used to be. The overly copied handout blurred in her vision and she sniffled. "I do want to get better."

Chapter Seven

San Diego, California, United States

The days cruising from Vancouver to San Diego had given Kari the opportunity to gather her thoughts regarding a variety of matters. There were the positive associations to make during EMDR, how Neill and Jade's date was going to go, had Belle mentioned her surly attitude in her WU reports to Doug, and what had caused the changed dynamic between Madeleine and Henry.

He was up to something so mysterious not even Madeleine could know. And in the strangest plot twist ever, Madeleine had given her permission to investigate why! She had no doubt Henry would kill her as easily as Madeleine had Mitchell and Santos killed if he learned about the betrayal. They'd both put bullets in her if they learned she was going to feed Adam Cho information. Which was apparently moving forward thanks to a message she received on CryptCodE that read:

Message received. Will make contact soon.

Aside from the request to have a secret meeting in-person with him, Kari had a brilliant idea how Adam could get even more information without her putting herself at risk.

Even if it was a little insane.

Kari rehearsed the words, the inflection, cadence, everything, for her speech to Madeleine. She took a steady breath as she sat in Madeleine's regular office. "I have an idea I'd like to run past you."

"Your"—Madeleine tapped her temple—"abilities will absolutely be needed for the next VIPs, so save it."

"It's not about that. I've been thinking about what Jack Weatherby said regarding Adam Cho and how he's investigating new angles. New targets. I think we should be proactive and invite Adam onto the *Hinewai*. It's just a matter of time before he circles around to Henry again. Might as well beat him to the punch."

"Interesting." Madeleine pursed her lips and swiveled in her chair.

"I'm proud I came up with that idea, too."

"No." Madeleine shook her head as she said it. "I mean I think it's interesting that you've gone from hating me and Henry to suddenly wanting to assist."

Shit. Trust a manipulator to catch a manipulator. "I think you're forgetting that Adam and I didn't get off on the right foot in Stockholm due to him assuming I was Henry's sexual plaything. I can hate all three of you and still look out for my own self-interests, which is trying to make my life quasi-tolerable on this ship, even if that means appeasing you and Henry from time to time."

"*Hmm.*" Madeleine viewed Kari with narrowed eyes. "Josef has said that the analysts have picked up blips from Adam's people sniffing around again. Have you given any thought to the timing of this invitation?"

"When we're docked for maintenance in Papua New Guinea."

Her sharp blond brows rose. "That's several months away for a 'proactive' strategy."

"But the timing coincides with a conference in Singapore where Adam's the keynote speaker. If we get him here, then he can tour the ship, interview the staff, and check out what Henry has on land there. He'll lose interest when he sees how 'normal' everything is."

Madeleine sat silent and scrutinized Kari.

Despite her heart beating so fast it was probably making the black fabric of her shirt dance, Kari said nothing. A waver in her voice or an imperfect word could have Madeleine sensing blood.

"I'll think about it." Madeleine stood and curled her index finger in a motion for Kari to follow her. After the black box ritual was completed, Madeleine said, "Have a good time on your shift. I think you'll be quite entertained when you hear about Matthew's night."

———

"Yiz did what?" Kari yelled in Matthew's pinkish, cherub-looking face. "Sorry, but I'm . . ."

"Shocked?" he asked in his British accent. "Me too. Chef Jon happened to walk out to check on dinner service and almost heaved over the side of the deck."

The sight of someone snorting a line of their dead father's ashes would do that even if that kind of behavior from a celebrity wasn't completely unprecedented. "Please tell me Yiz tossed the rest of them overboard."

Matthew shook his head and placed a comforting hand on Kari's shoulder. *Hope doesn't try to sprinkle past tiger barrier.* "Good luck and say hi to the giraffes at the zoo for me."

So her agenda for the day was taking an out-of-control pop star to the zoo. Great. "Wait!" she called after Matthew. "Did you arrange transport and the tickets yet?"

"Sorry, but no. I was too busy figuring out tonight's trip to LA with the newest rotating club. That was his priority. Details are on the VIP server." He danced backward in the hallway and then disappeared.

While Yiz and his entourage slept the morning away, detoxing whatever substances out of their systems, Kari went to the VIP office and arranged all the necessary zoo logistics. When that task was done, she learned as much about the club as she could. Their website consisted of a black screen with lime green graffiti-style script that read, If you don't know how to get in, we're not helping you.

Kari heard a yawn from the passageway and went to the source. She didn't see Yiz's face, rather his bare, lily-white ass and spindly legs struggling to keep balance.

Where am I?

She cleared her throat and he spun around. Even though she wanted to sneak a peek to learn if the rumors were true, she focused on his bloodshot hazel-green eyes. "Good morning, my name is Kari. Can I get you something to start your day? Perhaps some pants?" she asked with a perfect customer-service smile.

He looked down at his nude lower half and staggered. *The fuck?* He sniffed and then flared his nostrils along with several other facial contortions that wiggled and scrunched his nose. "Do you know why my nose feels weird? Doesn't feel like coke."

"Why don't you get dressed while I ask the kitchen to get

your brunch ready. Then, we can talk about last night and today's plan for the zoo."

His pained, awkward, hungover face brightened like a small child. *Forgot the zoo!*

———

During their four hours at the zoo, Yiz had shown the most interest in the harpy eagle. Since Kari had access to all of her mental skills, she connected with the bird at their stop. While she loved life without nonstop telepathy, she missed this animal bond. But Yiz's friends didn't share his or Kari's fascination.

When the VIPs went to the 'Staff Only' restrooms before their return trip home, she detoured as well. She was down to one burner phone that didn't have Wi-Fi. But there was a quick, easy, and morally questionable way to get one that was untraceable to her.

Kari was pleased to note that Guest Services was full of ringing phones, upset parents, and a confused bus driver. A chaotic environment was one where they'd be happy to see her leave fast. "Sorry to bother you," Kari shouted to the customer service person over a child's temper tantrum. "My client lost their phone in here. Do you have a lost and found box?"

Bus late. "Describe it for me," the young man said while running his finger down a bus schedule.

Vague was best. "Super ancient. Black. Screen is filthy."

He put the schedule down and ducked under the counter. He came back up a second later with a cardboard box. He pulled out a black phone and showed it to her. *Probably scam.* "Is this it?"

Kari saw exactly what she needed to see: a smudged finger-drawn pattern on the screen needed to unlock it. And, yes, it was a scam. "That's the one."

Dead. "This was beeping and ringing like crazy, but it finally stopped two weeks ago," he said as he handed it to her. "The battery is definitely dead."

She pocketed the phone that no one was ever coming back to collect. "Thanks." She meandered over to the lion statute—the VIP group's designated meeting spot—and waited. Her side trip to get a free phone took less time than it took for them to pee. That was efficiency at its finest.

At the end of their trip, Yiz thanked her profusely, tipped her, and headed to his cabin to nap until dinnertime. Kari went to the office to research the next set of VIPs for the hour left in her shift.

"Hey, partner."

Kari looked up from the computer screen to see Belle leaning in the doorway. She was ten minutes early. "You're very prompt for shift."

Belle came into the office and sat on the visitor's chair, which was an upside-down milk crate. *Hope not mad.* "I was bugging my roommate with my bored burpees."

"What is in the world is that?"

Belle chuckled. "Our cabin is too small to pace, so when I have pent-up energy, I do burpees. You know the exercise where you do a push-up and—"

"I'm familiar with the exercise, I just never heard . . . Nevermind. So, you came here instead of running laps around the ship."

"Right. And I thought I'd see if there was anything I could do to prep. Is there?"

"Not really, but if you want the desk to preview the details for tonight, you can."

"Sure."

In the cramped room, they switched places, brushing against one another in the process. *On the job. Can't like this.*

When Belle made it behind the desk, she clicked and scrolled on the trackpad. "No way! I'm going to this club tonight?"

Kari leaned against the doorjamb and was stuck on whether Belle's thought was related to attraction. That intrigued her. However, she agreed about the conflict. "Yiz and company are very excited to go, so I doubt the group will change their minds."

Belle nodded and read the screen a few seconds more. "Everything seems pretty clear here. It's nice there are suggestions about how to convince them to let me in."

"You're welcome. And, FYI, you can ask Neill to set you up with a security guard to come with you."

"I might do that. Safety first, right?"

"Right, which is why"—Kari took the tip from Yiz, which was a small bag of marijuana, out of her pocket—"I'm not going to partake in his 'tip' to me."

"You're not? Yiz's stuff is probably really high quality."

"I'm inclined to agree, but Moms' life lesson number 420: If you don't know where something came from, don't partake in it."

"That is true. I know someone who learned after the fact that the joint she took a hit from had heroin laced in it and the heroin had fentanyl. She almost died."

"And on that terrifying note, I'm going to hand this over to Madeleine, since we have to hand over any tip to her whether it's money or something like this."

Belle leaned back in the chair, crossed her arms, and smiled. "Are you always such a rule follower?"

Kari returned the grin. "Remember that there are cameras watching, so I suggest you follow the rules, too." She pushed herself off the doorjamb. "I'll see you in the morning." She headed to Madeleine's office for her report and deactivation, but when she arrived, Kari heard a gruff voice from inside the office.

"Come in!" Madeleine said with urgency through the door. "I can see your feet shadows."

Kari opened the door and understood why Madeleine was so eager for her to interrupt.

A man with short, silver-blond hair turned to her. He had an average build, a sunburned nose, and wore a vermillion World University polo to go with his khaki pants. He had a wrapped peanut butter cup in his hand. *There's the wonderkid.*

"So good to see you, Kari," Madeleine said in a tone that was too chipper. "This is Doug. He's the intern supervisor for WU. Apparently, we get to have once-a-week meetings about Belle." She directed her attention back to Doug. "Kari trained Belle and is her shift mate. I trust her to give you all the information you need."

Translation: Leave me alone and talk to Kari.

"I appreciate the extra resource," Doug said, "but it really does have to be you since you're the VIP Coordinator. I'll see you next week, same time." Doug stood and held out his hand for Madeleine to shake, which she did not. She looked at it though, if that counted for anything. *Mission accomplished. Like my ex-wife.* "Want a peanut butter cup?" he asked Kari.

"Sure."

He handed it to her. *This one has good taste.* "See you around."

Kari shut the door behind him. "He seems pleasant."

"He's a pain."

"Wait until he finds out VIPs occasionally tip us in autographs, used underwear, or drugs." Kari tossed the baggie on her desk. "Per the rules, here's my tip from Yiz."

Madeleine picked up the bag and appeared to examine it. "I could go for an edible right about now."

"Yet you turned down the peanut butter cup?"

"American chocolate is awful." Madeleine curled her finger for Kari to follow.

In the secret office, Kari provided her report. "Aside from major daddy issues, Yiz didn't have much in his head worth knowing. However, JonnaHa—"

"Which one is that?"

"The groupie with eyeliner challenges. She had some not so kind thoughts about her former private school, so I think that's worth researching. Yiz's producer, Bo Dop Beatz—"

"I really can't with these names, but go on."

"Anyway, Mr. Beatz is waiting for his tiger cub, which is all kinds of illegal where he lives."

Madeleine gave her a satisfied nod and placed her thumb on the box. "I'll get the team on it. Also, expect Henry to have a presence during the next VIP visit."

"Is this a mind-reading situation or not?"

"Henry made a point of telling me that you should have all of your skills available."

So Jack Weatherby's brain was off the table, but this guy was fair game. "And let me guess, you're also allowed to sit in on their conversations?"

Madeleine nodded and clicked the remote. "I'll confess that it's driving me up a wall that he won't tell me why Jack's visit was so special. You're dis—No, you're not dismissed."

"Well, this is a new, fun game."

Madeleine *tsked*. "Henry also told me that you shouldn't schedule anything personal during your up-and-coming time off because he may need you to attend an event in LA with him."

"But I have a therapy session scheduled already."

"Oh, we know that." Madeleine smirked at Kari's instinctual flinch. "Don't worry, I know you won't say too much to Ola. You've learned your lesson when it comes to that."

"Very true," Kari said through a clenched jaw. "What's the event?"

"One where you coming as a 'translator' would be very suspect, so we're working on an alternate cover. And makeup. Now you're dismissed."

Chapter Eight

Kari slept in after a nightmare-free sleep and followed through with the metaphorical dream she had all week of a leisurely breakfast in front of her TV. She allowed herself that pleasure before tending to business. She fetched the phone she had taken from the zoo to check Sky Fisher's CryptCodE messages. To limit her physical proximity to the phone, she had charged it in a club room currently off-limits for water damage and checked if it was able to pick up a Wi-Fi signal there. It did.

Thank you, Yiz entourage, and their unprotected hot spot.

Kari used the Z pattern on the screen to unlock it and recoiled at the sight of the owner's forty missed calls and 254 missed texts. She wondered if the owner had died but shook off that thought and proceeded with her plan, including using the last burner phone for the authentication code. She coughed on her second cup of French press coffee when she saw the unread message set to disappear in one minute.

Meet me at the restaurant across from the bank and running track in Playa Cantolao, Peru. Leave me another phone message with ONLY your name & the date of your visit. I'll meet you inside at noon for lunch. AC

Kari resisted the urge to respond with, 'Be careful because they will kill us both if we're not,' but Adam was smart and knew what he was getting himself into. She deactivated her CryptCodE account and cleared the zoo phone's history, which included the search, 'When should I worry about left arm pain?' After taking a moment to remember the memory of the most likely dead owner of the phone, she snapped both SIM cards in half with the pliers on her multi-tool. She'd discretely drop the pieces in the salt water when she was on the tender later in the day. After all, snacks for poker weren't going to buy themselves.

———

During the first tour she had of the *Hinewai*, WU classes had been in session. The passageways were silent.

Not this time.

Noise came from all directions. Most of the doors were closed but some were open with music or conversations pouring out. Kari walked down the passageway taking it all in before she stopped at Belle's dorm. Her and her roommate's door was decorated with cheeky bumper stickers and a world map. The southern Appalachian Mountains of the United States was circled with Belle's name in it. Vietnam was circled with Vy's name inside. Kari knocked on the area of Oregon.

A young woman with teal eye makeup and teal hair—Kari guessed that was Vy—opened the door.

Kari smiled. "Hi."

"Hi, back."

Vy stared at her long enough for an awkward silence to build. "Is Belle here?" Kari blurted.

She nodded then pounded the side of her fist against the wall beside her. "Belle, it's for you."

While Vy headed back to her desk, Kari stayed within the doorframe where she heard water running and checked out the room. Each side had a twin bed on blocks for storage underneath, a dresser, and a desk. Across from the entrance was a built-in TV that currently functioned as a faux-window for the interior cabin. The 'show' was the sun setting behind a lighthouse of North San Diego Bay.

Vy's side was decorated with a few posters—some art, some movies—and neon pillows tossed on her graphite gray comforter. Belle's side had a plain navy comforter and matching pillows. On her dresser, she had a trophy of an athlete in a spiking pose with 'Most Confirmed (Volleyball) Kills' etched in the brass plate at the bottom. There was also a single framed picture. In it, Belle wore a beige bedsheet as a toga and a petite brunette woman beside her wore a surgical mask and scrubs. They stood back-to-back with their arms folded across their chests.

"Hey, Kari." Belle appeared in the doorway of the bathroom. "Did you remember to BYO beverage?"

"Yup." Kari tapped her backpack hanging off her shoulder. "I brought some snacks, too."

"Great, and before I forget, we don't drink from cans, bottles, or clear glasses in case an RA comes in. Only Craig and I are over twenty-one." Belle turned back to her roommate. "See you later, Vy."

Kari followed Belle down the passageway. "Do the others know I'm coming?"

"They do. And I've told them not to do anything to embarrass either of us. I also kept the information about you to a minimum. They know you're nineteen and I'm working with you in the VIP world. I figured there might be things you'd rather tell people on your own, if they happen to come up."

Kari didn't want to know, but it was best to prepare. "Do they know about . . . You know . . . the incident?"

"If they do know, I wasn't the one who told them. That's your information to share."

"I appreciate that."

Belle kept walking but gave her a sympathetic grin. "You're welcome."

She led them down several more corridors before they took the corner for the last club room. She knocked twice, then once, then three times. "We don't have anything too scandalous, but it's nice to provide a heads-up before we come in so they don't think it's an RA."

The door opened and a young man, with dark brown skin, a baby face, and stocky build, poked his head out and smiled. "You're late."

"Hardly," Belle said. "Nando, this is Kari."

Kari waved. "Nice to meet you."

"And nice to have another person I can lose to," he said. "Come in."

Once they were all in the club room Nando shut the door behind him. "Kari, this is"—he pointed at each person—"Craig and Sven."

They each held up large insulated cups and said 'hello' in unison.

Kari took a seat between Belle and Nando, then took a breath. She could do this. She could socialize with people her own age. "Thanks for letting me join the game."

"Have you ever played before?" Nando asked while he shuffled the deck.

"No, but I've watched some online tutorials, so I'd like to think I understand the basics."

Craig laughed and tugged at Sven's black beanie so it covered his silver-gray eyes. "That's what my buddy here thought when he first came, but then we crushed him."

Sven fixed his knit cap. "I've gotten so much better. I know I'm going to make my uncles proud in Helsinki."

"What's happening there?" Kari nodded her thanks to Belle, who pulled out an insulated cup for her.

"There's a poker tournament," Sven said. "When I went home during the last semester break, I didn't know how to play during a family game. I bet them that I'd learn and do better than them in the tournament when I came home to visit this winter."

"Sounds like a good goal to have," Kari said. "So, Sven's from Finland, where's everyone else from?"

"Uruguay," Nando said as he poured a beer. "By a lake north of Montevideo."

"Canada," Craig said. "The Ottawa part of it. How about you?"

"United States. The Oregon part." Kari unzipped the top of her backpack, which exposed the foil and caged top of her bottle.

"You brought champagne to poker?" Belle asked with a slight smirk, then looked to the others as if she needed confirmation that this was an anomaly.

They turned to Kari in unison and burst into hysterics.

Kari took out her bottle despite the laugh track. "One, it's actually Prosecco. And two, why is that funny?" She pointed to Sven's cup. "He's drinking wine. How is that different?"

"One," Sven said with a perfect smile, "my wine does not sparkle. And two, since we're in the US, I drink what I can sneak. Today we happened to make beef bourguignon in class, so I have Pinot Noir."

"You see, Kari," Nando said, "stealing wine with plastic bags in your pockets isn't fancy, it's actually really sad. Your sparkle wine is fancy. And expensive."

"It was on sale in Vancouver!" Kari defended. If poker was only going to consist of Belle's friends giving her shit for fiscally responsible alcohol purchases, then they were not getting her assortment of mixed nuts!

"Alright, everyone." Belle pulled out a can from her bag and cracked it open. "I think we've razzed Kari enough. We're just surprised, since most of us aren't used to spending more than six bucks on a six-pack."

"I get it," Craig said to Kari. "You're just enjoying the perks of steady employment, as we all hope to do someday."

"Speak for yourself," Nando said. "I don't think working for my parents' refugee center will have me rolling in money."

"Look at it this way," Belle said, "your wallet might not be full, but your heart will be."

"Well, kiss my biscuits!" Craig said, mocking her accent. "Isn't that the most precious thing y'all ever heard."

"While I do, on occasion, say that, I don't sound like that," Belle said with a chuckle.

Since they were a group where it seemed like each person took their turn with good-natured ribbing, Kari pulled out her bottle and tin of mixed nuts.

"I think we agree that while jobs bring money, they also bring stress," Sven said. "I'm sure Kari has a lot of stress in her life."

Kudos to Sven. Kari rotated the honey-roasted cashews in his direction. "And what's your dream job?"

"I want to have my own restaurant someday, but I'm not

looking forward to the long hours in the kitchen and sleeping in an office to make it happen."

"That's why I'm picking a job where I have flexibility," Craig said. "I can work daytime, nighttime, or all the time. Inside or outside. As long as the lighting is good."

Kari started to carefully pull the cork. "And what do you want to do, Craig?"

"Sport photography."

Kari flinched from the loud *pop*. "I can't drink this whole thing, so feel free to try some."

"I might take you up on that later," Belle said as Nando dealt the initial cards.

"Okay," Nando said, "I'm the game runner and this is a breakdown of our rules. We play Texas holdem style and pull chips from the communal bowl"—he held up a white plastic mixing bowl—"so technically it's not gambling. That's why we can play and not get into trouble if we're caught. In this round . . ." He proceeded to explain the procedures of folding, calling, and raising.

"Got it." Even if by Kari's account they weren't playing by all the rules she had learned. Kari sipped her drink and glanced at her cards. As she studied the people around her, she realized she hadn't a clue what hands the others had. But like all things, if she studied, then she'd eventually understand.

After the first two rounds, Kari caught that Belle was a lip chewer, Sven sighed, Nando scratched the back of his neck, and Craig tapped. Her best guess was that these were their disappointed tells. Kari decided to test that theory after another trip around.

"Call." Kari doubted anyone could beat her three-of-a-kind of eights.

Sven mumbled something in Finnish. "Fold."

Craig chortled. "Play with some balls already. It's so early in the game and there's no actual money."

"Don't be mean, Craig," Belle playfully chided. "I'm sure it's all a part of Sven's strategy."

"His losing strategy," Nando said into his glass. "Show us your cards, Kari."

"With pleasure." She laid her five cards down, then watched Nando's pair of twos and Craig's pair of kings go down as the taste of victory filled her mouth with bubbly sweetness.

"And I have a"—Belle delicately laid her cards down one at a time in two-three-four-five-six succession—"straight."

"Hoit?" Kari shouted the unique expletive of 'how' and 'shit'. She stared at Belle, whose eyes she could have sworn twinkled.

"Because I'm that good." Belle dragged her winnings toward her while she laughed like a cartoon villain.

"You might be happy now," Kari said, "but we'll see how happy you are at the end of the night."

"Belle's always happy," Sven said as he collected the cards for the next game. "It's almost annoying."

"I can't help it if being on the boat with all of you nice folks brings out the joy in me," Belle said in a faux-saccharine tone.

Craig laughed. "Wait. Does anyone else think it's funny that a lesbian won with a straight?"

Belle closed her eyes and made a faint groan.

Kari couldn't read her mind, but it was obvious that wasn't the way Belle wanted her to learn about that fact. It wasn't a big deal, but given that Belle was from the Bible Belt and had some strong opinions about families, Kari would have bet that she had negative experiences coming out to them. Her pontification stopped at the sound of a *thwat*.

"Ow." Craig rubbed the back of his head. "Why'd you hit me?"

"Isn't it obvious?" Nando asked him.

Craig shook his head.

"I wasn't ready to come out yet," Belle said and then looked at Kari. "I guess now you know."

She gave Belle her best supportive grin. "As someone with two moms and as pansexual, I understand why it can be difficult to tell people and why each situation is unique."

"Pansexual, you say?" Sven cleared his throat. "That means everyone, right?"

"As long as they're pretty." Kari noticed Sven's perfect smile again, which suggested he knew how Nordic pretty he was. "But when I date, there are other things I look for, too."

"Such as?" Sven asked with a mischievous glint.

"Sorry, Sven, I'm not interested in dating. I just like some eye candy from time to time."

"Girls never admit that," Craig said in awe, "and I've read a lot of articles about what girls want."

"That's pornography," Nando said, "not real life."

"I genuinely appreciate the photography," he said to Kari, "and the stuff I like is highbrow, I swear."

"Craig, darlin'," Belle said gently, "*Ta-Tas* and *Badonk* aren't highbrow."

"I want to get back to Kari's situation," Sven said. "Why aren't you interested in dating? Or do you already have a special person in your life?"

Kari hated that she thought of Finn. "I don't have a person and I don't want one right now."

Sven opened his plastic zip bag of wine and topped off his drink. "But everyone likes to have someone, right?"

"Wrong." Why wasn't he getting it? "My life is complicated, and everyone on this boat has an expiration date. We're all leaving soon, especially WU students."

"You don't want to stay on the *Hinewai?*" Nando asked.

Kari coughed on her Prosecco. "No! I'm here to work toward a goal and move on."

Belle rested her chin in her hand and focused like she was studying Kari. "And what is your goal?"

Kari reflected back to before she took the job at inCog. Back then, her goal was to gain experience before going to medical school, which was primarily so she could develop a way to eliminate her telepathy. But she did that already. Now a larger life's purpose was marinating in the forefront of her brain. "As we travel the world, I see the inequity and the corruption. It can't be fixed anymore with elections or laws because governments have been bought. The only way to stop it all is to find the source, destroy it, and rebuild with community in mind. That's what I want to do."

They laughed, except for Belle. "How do you plan to do that?"

"I don't know yet, but I'm figuring it out."

———

Rules were rules. The last people to arrive had to clean, so she and Belle stayed back to disinfect and put the room back in order.

"Had that been real money you'd have cleaned us out," Kari said. "Where did you learn to play so well?"

"My friends and I would get bored at church camp." The room filled with a citrus smell as she sprayed the tabletop. "Do you mind recycling the cans and bottle on your deck level? Sometimes the RAs will take a peek in the bins."

"That's the least I could do. I had a really good time once the Prosecco shaming stopped."

"I'm really glad you liked it and weren't put off by a little teasing." Belle picked up her backpack and tilted her head toward the door. "So, do I have any tells?"

"Maybe, but me and my slight cheek sucking aren't saying."

Belle chuckled. "Want to come back next time?"

She'd have to adjust her happy hour schedule with Jade, but who knows, maybe Friday was going to be date night for her and Neill from now on. "I'd like that. Although, I'm still bringing whatever sparkling wine is on sale. I don't care if it's bougie."

"I understand and appreciated the sample you gave me. Went well with the honey-roasted cashews."

"Truthfully, if I have more than two glasses I'll wake up with a killer headache, so the samples I handed out helped the Kari of tomorrow. The idea of getting so obliterated I lose control or debilitate myself doesn't appeal to me."

Belle feigned shock. "You mean to tell me that the same person who wants to bring down corruption on a global-scale likes being in control? You've blown my mind."

"Shut up." Kari smiled at the sarcasm and noticed that Belle walked with perfect posture despite the bag on her back. Just how strict was her upbringing? The question led her to think about Craig's faux pas. "Not to make things weird, but I wanted to let you know that I think it sucks how you were outed earlier. That should have been your decision."

"Yes, it should have, but at least the response I got this time was one of the better ones. The first time was . . ." Belle's posture went unnaturally rigid. "Never mind. But it was nice that you shared what you did about yourself. It took some of the pressure off me."

Kari shot her a sympathetic look and kept walking. "If you ever want to talk about it."

"Maybe someday, but that won't be anytime soon. Trauma's still a bit too fresh."

Truer words had never been spoken. "I get it."

"I knew you would." Belle stopped in the passageway outside her dorm. "Alright, this is me. Have a good night."

Kari had such a good night, she didn't see why the next couldn't be equally as fun. "What are you doing tomorrow?"

"Writing my reports for Doug. I have a feeling I'll be spending most of the time struggling how to not sound insane. Yiz and his crew wanted me to get them roof access at Club Vex so they had UFO signals."

"And did you get it?" Kari asked. "The roof access, that is. Not the UFO signal."

"With the help of a little white lie I did," Belle said with a grin. "Why did you ask about tomorrow?"

"I was thinking about seeing the latest movie at the ship theater and didn't know if you'd like to join me."

"Tempting, but can't with that report. Definitely ask me next time though. I love movies."

"I'll remember that. Good night, Belle."

On the way back to her cabin, the muffled sounds outside Jade's door brought Kari back into reality and caused her to realize what she had been doing since she had left Belle's door. She had been smiling!

The comradery. The drinks. The jokes. It was the best evening she'd had in months.

Kari went inside her cabin and laying on the thin carpet of her entryway was something that caused her upturned lips to reverse. A white envelope. Kari picked it up and read.

Report tomorrow at 2pm. Wear clothes appro-

priate for a movie premier. You'll get makeup later (to include prosthetics).

Even without Belle, it appeared as though Kari was still going to the movies.

————

The passageways were fairly vacant for a sleepy Saturday morning, but when Kari arrived at the cafeteria, Jade nearly walked into her with a tray of pancakes. "Somebody isn't too focused this morning," Kari said with a grin. "I wonder why."

Jade giggled and bounced at the knee.

"I take it your date with Neill went well?"

She nodded and beamed with pure joy. "So, so well. Apparently, he's had a crush on me for a while."

That was news to Kari, but based on what he had told her, she knew why he hadn't acted on it. However, what he had told Jade was a different story. "Why didn't he ask you out sooner?"

"He said he didn't really know me until we spent some time together that was only us, so he had been admiring me from afar in group settings. His exact words." Jade followed her to the line where Kari picked up her order of a breakfast skillet. "Do you want to eat here and talk? Oh, never mind, you have to have your 'special coffee'."

"I already had my special coffee, thank you very much, and trail mix so I could take something for my headache, so I'm fine with eating here." They grabbed their linen-wrapped utensils, drinks, and headed over to a two-person booth with a view of the fogged over bay. "Okay, spill the details."

"He took me to this restaurant I had been hearing about through the culinary grapevine. The drinks and food were wonderful, and we talked about so many things." She smiled and sighed. "He's such a gentle soul, even if he doesn't look like it. He didn't get into too many details, but he told me a little bit about his time being military police."

A steak and veggie bite paused at Kari's lips. "He told you that?"

Jade nodded as she chewed.

"Did he tell you more?"

"He said he wasn't ready for that conversation yet, which I have to respect. I know I didn't get into all my past. Although, I had to talk about Diana."

"Did you mention your ex-husband?"

"Hell, no! You never talk exes on a first date. Plus, there's only so much you can cover in an evening, especially when a good part of that isn't reserved for talking." She winked.

Kari read that message loud and clear. "Are you seeing each other again?"

There was that brilliant smile again. "Yes, but not until next Friday. That's the only time that works for us to see the museum he wants to take me to. Is it okay with you if we move our traditional gaming day?"

"Yeah. That works out well, actually. Belle invited me to play poker next Friday, too. I had a lot of fun. Met some nice new people." Jade looked at her like how Mom A did. That reminded her that she should probably call the moms soon. It had been ages. "Why are you smiling at me like that?"

"It's really nice to hear you made some friends. Are you going to hang out with any of them tonight?"

"Can't. I have to fulfill my Wibawa Enterprise Promise, even if I don't know exactly what I'll be doing yet."

———

At two pm sharp, Kari stood in front of Madeleine in her movie premier look and disbelief that a billion-dollar enterprise's best excuse to get her on to a red carpet was a "movie premier with Henry Wibawa" contest winner. "This is literally the dumbest thing I've ever heard."

"I'm inclined to agree, but sometimes even I have to follow orders."

At least they were on the same page. "Speaking of people on screens and men I hate, have you reached out to Adam Cho yet?"

Madeleine squinted as though she debated on sharing. "We did, but we haven't heard back."

"Who reached out?"

"Matthew reached out to Adam's personal assistant. Why?"

That explained it. "Matthew's writing comes off as phony because he uses AI all the time and he never catches the discrepancies between British and American English spellings. Adam's assistant probably thinks it's a scam. I think you're better off sending something yourself."

She gave Kari a slow nod. "Thank you for the insight. Now off you go to your assignment."

"I'm sure it'll be a great time."

Seven hours later, Kari was back in the secret office.

Madeleine had her eyes closed and pinched the bridge of her nose. "Let me get this straight, Henry had me jump through hoops to have an analyst hack into your dental records so I could get someone to make fake teeth for you and arrange your prosthetic nose application with a high-end makeup artist, so he could learn what the press *really* thinks of the movie he produced?"

"That's correct." It felt so much more natural speaking without false teeth pushing against her gums. Although, she was into the wig with its short back and longer, wispy top. "He's also anxious about asking Ray to come to Chile."

Madeleine's eyelids flashed open. "What? But Ray was just here when Jack Weatherby visited!"

"Right, but Ray apparently also needs to be present for the Ricardo Rojas visit." Kari could have sworn she heard Madeleine's sharp intake of breath followed by her mouth forming a perfect O. "You didn't know about the Rojas visit, did you?"

"I did not," Madeleine said through clenched teeth. "I do know, like yourself, that Ricardo Rojas was on the Brisbane list along with Gabriella Fermi and Jack Weatherby."

Kari remembered that as well. And now that Henry was acting so secretive it was driving Madeleine to visible agitation, it was time to use that. Pitting them against each other was the best strategic move. Let their crumbling relationship take them both down while she stayed away from the falling rubble. "I should probably mention that Henry was also thinking about how Ray needed to be present for 'every one of them'. I'm guessing that's the rest of the Brisbane list: Jasi Monye, Amara Gupta, and Botan Itoi."

"I concur, but that information stays here." Madeleine left the room for her proper office. "You can clean up on your way through."

Kari stayed in the bathroom, took her wig off first, and then tossed her fake nose in the trash. The soft knock came as she was about to wash her face with hand soap.

"May I open the door a crack?"

The woman would murder people and break into medical files without question, but she made sure you were comfortable in a bathroom. A true enigma. Kari turned off the water, opened the door, and waited for Madeleine's face to appear before she asked, "Did you forget to compliment my wig?"

"No. I don't care for that style at all. It's too . . . severe. What I was going to say was that I emailed Adam Cho."

"Really?" Madeleine had actually listened to her? And it worked?

"Yes, and he'll be delighted to join us in PNG. This is also our secret for now." Madeleine closed the door, leaving Kari with another one of those natural smiles she was getting used to. Her plan was coming together.

Chapter Nine

Puerto Quetzal, Guatemala

"Sky Fisher." Kari stuck with the Australian accent, since it was the only voice Adam or his assistant had heard her use. "August fifteenth."

Like usual, she popped the SIM card out of the burner phone and dropped it in the water of the pier while she bent down to tie her shoe. She tossed the phone in the trash bin on her way to buy hair care products, snacks, good coffee beans, and sparkling wine. She had to prepare for the coming days once her pm shift was over.

This was the first time where her week off would be mostly at sea. That was a lot of time to make her own fun on board. Maybe Jade could squeeze in an extra game? Or maybe she could pick up a new student who needed guitar lessons? Or an extra therapy session with Ola to tell her that she'd had her first nightmare-free week? She knew she had to call the moms and there would be more poker, too. She had joined a second night and concluded that Craig was a little pervy but harmless, Nando would be happy penniless as long as he was helpful, Sven was sweet and mischievous just like Jade had said, and

Belle was brilliant, both in strategy and intelligence. She had evolved into a worthy adversary, as well as a solid partner when it came to work.

"Good afternoon," Kari said once she was in Madeleine's office.

"You seem . . . chipper."

Kari took a moment to think about it. "I'm in this room, yet I'm not filled with dread. It's kind of weird." When Madeleine stayed seated instead of heading back, she asked, "Are we not going back?"

"We don't need to do that today. Our guest is leaving early —Belle will fill you in—and I won't be here in the morning to reclick it."

"You didn't ask for a week off so we can pal around together, did you?"

Madeleine arched a brow. "If you must know, there's an emergency at home with one of my sisters."

"Oh. Well, I hope she's okay."

"Do you really?"

"Yes. Your sisters make candy and didn't kill my friends."

"Hmph. I suppose that's fair." Madeleine leaned forward on her desk. "I don't know how long I'll be gone, but I told Henry I'll be back before we leave Peru. You're dismissed."

"Thank you, ma'am." Kari left and, once the door was closed behind her, did a dance to celebrate what was going to be the greatest week ever. No voices in her head for a week. No Madeleine or shady business for a week. She could hang out with friends. She practically skipped to the VIP office where she expected to see Belle, but she wasn't there. Kari tried the kitchen.

"Hey, Jon," Kari said while he placed a measuring cup of a bright red sauce in the microwave, "have you seen Belle?"

"She just picked up happy hour snacks for the VIPs."

"Thanks." She turned to go.

"Wait a sec!" Chef Jon called out. "Can you try something before you go?"

"If it takes less than five minutes, sure."

"Great!" When the microwave beeped, he pulled out the cup and brought it over to a square black plate with a white chocolate dome in the center. He poured the warm viscous sauce over it. As the chocolate melted, it revealed a dark chocolate torte. Jon shoved a spoon in her face. "Dig in and tell me what you think."

This was the type of office perk she lived for. She took a bite of the dessert and her teeth ached. "That's way too sweet."

"I thought so." Jon faced away from her. "I told you all that you have to be honest with me!" he shouted into the back of the kitchen. He dug into a cabinet and took out a bag of salted, pre-shelled pistachios, which he then pulverized with a mallet. He sprinkled the crushed nuts over the dessert. "Try again."

Kari did, and the salty crunch helped balance her palette. "Much better. You know, I'm more than happy to taste test other experimental menu items for you."

"I think I might take you up on that offer because my staff has a tendency to hold back on critiques. You, on the other hand, do not."

"I am an honest soul, Jon. Thanks for the free sample. Bye." Kari took the dessert to the VIP assistant office and found it occupied this time. "I brought you something."

Belle tore her eyes away from the screen to the plate. "That's half-eaten."

"Look at you being the pessimistic one for a change. I like to think of it as half-not eaten." Kari handed her the plate and took a seat on the upside-down crate. "I hear our guest is leaving sooner than anticipated."

"There was a fire in one of the towns where several of his

workers live and he wants to go help." Belle dug into the dessert for her first sample. A dab of raspberry sauce caught on her top lip but didn't stay there for long since her tongue darted out to lick it away. "It'd be nice if there were more VIPs like him."

Kari heard the words but was more focused on Belle's lips. She hadn't noticed before that her bottom lip was slightly fuller than the top.

"I have an idea," Belle said as she loaded another spoonful. "Since I have a reduced schedule, you have the whole week off, and we're stuck on the boat, I was wondering if you wanted to raincheck that movie." Belle opened her mouth, wrapped her lips around the full spoon, and pulled it away clean.

Kari's gaze went from Belle's mouth to her inquisitive eyes. "Yeah, that sounds fun."

———

Kari opened her cabin door and made a sweeping motion with her arm. "Welcome to my humble abode!"

"Whoa!" Belle dropped her backpack inside the door as she walked inside. "This is huge compared to my dorm. Oh, you have your own balcony!" She put a hand on her hip. "I'm officially jealous."

"Before we get to dinner and our movie, do you want to—" A quick series of knocks at the door interrupted her suggestion. "One second, I think this is part of our dinner." Kari opened the door to see Jade holding a plate with foil over it. "What'd we get?"

"Hello to you, too." Jade peered over Kari's shoulder. "And to you, Belle. To answer your question, you have the Guatemalan pan dulce I made for demonstration purposes. If I were you, I'd save it for dessert. Unless you have something else planned for that?" she whispered and then winked.

Kari glanced over her shoulder to see if Belle had heard, but she was too busy admiring her guitar. She took the plate with a pointed glare. "Go bang Neill. Thank you. Bye." Kari closed the door and lifted the foil to see golden brown twisted breads that had been cut in half. "I don't think you'll be leaving hungry between this and the dinner Jon made us."

"How did you get Jon to make us dinner?"

"I volunteered to be a guinea pig and provide thoughtful feedback. Also, I gave him money."

"How much?"

"Don't worry about it. These things have a way of working themselves out."

"Thank you. My internship paycheck is pretty minimal." Belle walked away from the guitar and to Kari's sliding door. She paused at the glass while she peered out at the water.

"You can step outside if you'd like."

Belle shot her a giddy smile, opened the slider, and walked out on the balcony. "Absolutely breathtaking. You must get stunning views from all over the world here."

"I do. The best part about the ship is that on days like today I can watch the sunrise with my coffee. Feels like I'm in a commercial."

"Want to have sunset with another drink? Madeleine told me to keep the bottle of guaro Señor Coffee Tycoon tipped the VIP staff."

"Isn't that stuff like fifty percent alcohol?"

"This is thirty and I'm not drinking it straight. I brought club soda and some limes with me to make it more palatable."

"I'll try it. Since you're my guest, I'll give you the glass-glass and I'll drink out of my coffee mug."

"You don't have more than one glass?" Belle asked, completely perplexed.

"The only person I socialize with in my cabin is Jade and she always brings her own."

"That's kind of amazing." Belle took the soda and limes out from her backpack and put them on the kitchen table. "You really didn't do anything except for work last year, did you?"

"I mean . . . I went to the cafeteria and gym. Not sure if that counts." Kari took the ice cube tray out and dropped a few cubes in the glass and mug.

"Oh, less ice for me, please. Hurts my teeth."

Kari tipped the glass so two extra cubes fell into her mug. Then she stared at the bottle of clear liquor on the counter. "I have no idea what this is going to taste like."

Belle took the bottle, unscrewed the cap, and sniffed. She followed up that test by using her pinky finger to trace around the inside of the bottle's neck. She delicately sucked the liquid off its tip. "Like a rum-vodka hybrid. I'd do two shots."

"I don't have shot glasses," Kari said as she tried to get the image of Belle's lips and the wet sound of finger-sucking out of her head.

"What are we going to do with you?" Belle mock chastised and poured the liquor into her cup until it was level with the ice cubes. "Problem solved. You can pour your own after you do your own test."

Kari did so and finished off their drinks with fresh lime juice and club soda. "Cheers." The sound of her ceramic mug against the glass made a unique clink sound. "Let me grab a chair for the balcony. You can have the lounger."

Due to the position of the ship, they had an unobstructed view of the Pacific Ocean. The breeze off the water cooled the summer air and blew strands of Belle's hair that had escaped her ponytail.

"I don't think I've been this comfortable in months," Belle

said, her long, lean body stretched on the lounge chair. "Do you ever sleep out here?"

"I may have taken a nap once or twice."

"I wouldn't have believed you'd had time to nap with how much you do. How many of those extra translating assignments have you been on?"

"Last year, I was kept pretty active on most weekends, sometimes during the week, too. Now, it blends into the VIP job."

Belle adjusted the seat so they faced one another more easily. "What's been the most interesting or difficult assignment?"

Kari could answer honestly while being mindful of the details. "Stockholm was up there, but honestly, I think I saw crazier stuff at this birthday slash costume party for this rich guy in India. There was all kinds of debauchery. Wall-to-wall drugs and naked people. I ended up staying in a corner and speaking to one of the waiters for the majority of the party."

Belle smirked. "Were you naked, too?"

"Ah, no. There was a theme, so I had to dress as a go-go dancer. Henry was Andy Warhol."

"That is so wild on so many levels. Like, no offense, but I would think there are tons of people who are professional translators that Henry could have hired, but he wanted you there."

Kari sipped her drink. "I'm good at remembering people's names and facts about them, too, so he finds that helpful. Maybe I should suggest you the next time he needs a go-go dancer? You have a great memory."

"And I do look good in boots. But I'm not like you with all those languages, and I don't think Henry would like me in that type of role. He treats you like you're his golden child, except you're not related."

So even people outside the secret circle knew she was

special to him. Dammit. Kari shrugged, focused on a point out in the horizon, then took a drink. "I guess he does."

Belle stared at her in that thoughtful way she did at poker sometimes. "Even though millions of people in the world would die to be in your position, you really don't want to be considered Henry's right hand, do you?"

Kari shifted the ice cubes and lime wedge around in her mug. "Absolutely not. But . . . it helps me."

After a moment, Belle nodded. "I see. This comes back to your big goal. Your purpose. You need to get close to him to right those wrongs you were talking about." She didn't say it as a question. Belle knew right then and there Kari wanted to bring down the Wibawa Empire.

And because of it, Kari was in trouble. So was Belle.

"Hold on!" Kari blurted. "I should rewin—"

"Kari," Belle said in a gentle tone, "I won't tell. I'm not naïve enough to think that a man as powerful as Henry has gotten that way because of luck or charity. I'm sure he has plenty of skeletons in his closet."

The invisible vice that had started to squeeze her chest released its pressure. But then it hitched again. "I'm glad you understand, but I mean it when I say you can't talk about this. People like us disappear from the world when we don't play by their rules."

"Oh, I know, which is why I promise I won't say a word." Belle touched her cross at the edge of her T-shirt's neckline. "Swear to God."

"Thank you." Kari collapsed back in her chair and breathed easier once more. Belle had taken what she had said seriously and even brought in her god. That meant something coming from her. "I can't believe I told you what I did. Except, I didn't really tell you, you figured it out and then I confirmed it. I'm such an idiot."

"Don't beat yourself up." Belle gave her a soft smile. "Maybe you couldn't keep it inside anymore and you needed someone to talk to? No one else knows, do they?"

Neill knew they were criminals, but she had never discussed her plans with him. "Finn and I talked about broken society when they were here."

"How about now?"

Kari blew a raspberry. "We don't even talk-talk anymore. I've accepted Finn's left for good and are happy with their new life. And lover," she muttered into her mug.

"Lover? Did Finn get serious with someone?"

"That's putting it mildly." Kari took her cell phone out of her cargo shorts, opened her texts, ignored the one from Mom L —shit, she needed to call—and went to the text Finn had sent her earlier in the day. Kari handed her phone over to Belle so she could see the picture where Finn—with their wavy, flaming red hair as fabulous as ever—had their arm around the waist of a young woman with classic Mediterranean features. She had her left arm extended to show the diamond ring on her ring finger. The text that accompanied it read:

> Declan really likes Renata (excited to have a mom), so does Gabriella. No date set.

Belle grimaced. "This is . . . That's gotta hurt. When did Finn leave the ship?"

"Not even six months ago."

"Ouch. How are you taking the news?"

Kari used the moment putting her phone away to think about the answer. "The news is still fresh, but my initial reaction is that I'm jealous, even if that's stupid."

"Why would that be stupid? You dated."

"Eh. It was one date, so I don't think that counts as a real romantic relationship."

"But I'm sure there were feelings that led up to that one date, so I think it's okay to admit you're jealous." Belle took a sip and then gestured to Kari with her glass. "And, deep down, your jealousy might not be because of romantic reasons. Maybe it's because Finn seems happier in that picture than you feel right now? I don't know."

Kari didn't know if she agreed but found herself nodding anyway. "It doesn't help that she's hot."

"In the spirit of female friendship, I was going to say something to the effect that you're more attractive, but I was trying to phrase it in a way that wasn't disparaging to her and didn't make it sound like I was hitting on you."

"That is a tough line to walk. How about you say that I'm probably more interesting than she is and we leave it at that?"

"Sounds good," Belle said with a chuckle, then tipped back the rest of her drink and shook the ice in the glass. She peered over the arm of the lounger to peek inside Kari's mug. She looked at Kari with a quirked brow. The universal expression for 'really?'

"I'm nursing mine. You go make your own drink if you want one."

"I don't need to be told twice."

Kari watched in amusement as Belle struggled to stand from the lounger and headed inside. "If you wanted to bring out the pan dulce, I wouldn't say no!"

Belle came out a minute later with another drink and the ceramic plate of sweet breads.

Kari held up most of an intricately cut and oblong roll. "Being Jade's neighbor is another perk."

Belle bit into a roll and moaned. "I'm so envious of you. You have a great neighbor, get quiet time whenever you want, and have views like this every day. Quite the life."

Kari knew what Belle meant, but if she knew the whole

truth, she'd run away from the life screaming and praying, not toward it. And because Belle was as inquisitive as she was bright, Kari knew she'd have to take steps to steer Belle away from those aspects of her life. "I feel like I've talked a lot about me. Tell me something about you."

"Like what?"

The go-to question most would ask would be about family, but given Belle's comments about coming out she steered away from that. "Like there's a photo in your dorm room—I'm guessing a Halloween party—of you in a toga and someone ready to perform surgery. Who is that? Sister? Girlfriend? Teammate? Hopefully, not all three."

Belle snickered, but then a sad smile took over her features. "That's Tess, and she passed away before I started at WU. We were a lot of things to each other, but I think friend encompasses it the best." Belle reached under the top of her shirt then pulled out the cross necklace. "She got this for me when I misplaced mine. I like to think she's watching over me, acting as my guardian angel." She kissed the cross and placed it back under her shirt. "Gives me comfort."

Kari sipped her drink in silence, while the red-orange sun finally started to make its descent. Maybe someday the spirits of Mitchell and Santos would visit her.

"Tess would have liked you." Belle kept her eyes focused on the sunset. "You're what she would have referred to as 'one boss bitch' as opposed to Madeleine, who is just a boss and a bitch. I swear sometimes I just want to tell her to kiss my biscuits."

Even with tears threatening to fall, Kari laughed so loud the people on the balcony five cabins over must have heard her. "I'm sorry, it's just nice to hear my thoughts said by someone else. And aren't you supposed to love your neighbor as much as yourself?"

"I'm supposed to try, but I'm human and have feelings for

myself and others. Madeleine's just . . . cruel. She completely freaked out on someone in the office for burning toast. Like, get a grip, lady." Belle shook her head but then perked up, excited. "And for reasons I don't understand at all, she has a fake nose."

That got Kari's attention fast. "What do you mean?"

"She let me use her bathroom about a week ago because I had cilantro in my teeth and she insisted that I remove it before we continued our conversation. Anyway, when I went in, there was a fake nose in the trash."

Kari drank to obstruct her face from any reaction that may give her away. How had Belle found the nose from the movie premier? It wasn't as if the prosthetic was on the top; she had thrown balled-up tissues on it. The trash either had tipped over or Belle had been searching in Madeleine's bathroom garbage. "That's really, really weird."

"Yeah, and it wasn't even her skin tone, it was closer to yours."

"Maybe she went to a politically incorrect costume party?"

Belle *tsked*. "I hope not, but I wouldn't put it past her. But that's weird, right? Or is she an actress in plays on the ship?"

Kari lifted her hands in a 'who knows' gesture. "All I can say is that we live in a crazy world filled with fake noses, really good bread, and movies." Kari pointed to the dark orange and purple horizon. "The sun's almost gone. Want to go inside, eat something other than bread, and start the show? I added a new action movie the ship has to my list."

"Bring on the food and fighting."

Clad in her underwear and an old T-shirt, Kari groaned at the ring of her cell phone. Speaking to whoever called was the last thing she wanted to do. What she actually wanted to do was go back to sleep, but to do that it was imperative she find the phone. Once found, she could put it on mute, since ignoring the ringer hadn't worked. The caller was persistent.

She just knew it was one of the moms.

The sound became clearer and louder once she was in front of her loveseat, but the phone was nowhere in sight. She got on her hands and knees—the sudden change of motion made her head throb and stomach roll—and saw her phone along with some dust bunnies and a moldy piece of granola. Her stomach contracted, the taste of Jon's experimental chorizo-stuffed wonton soup revisiting her mouth. Kari jerked back to sit on her heels, took a deep breath, concentrated on unmoldy thoughts, and bent down again to quickly snatch her phone from underneath. The caller was Mom L.

Shit. There was no fooling that one. "Hi," Kari croaked out. Gods she needed water.

"Well, that answers my question if you're alive, but you sound like death. Are you sick or hungover?"

"I love how we have such an honest relationship that you can ask me these questions." She went to the kitchen with Belle's glass and rinsed it.

"A question you didn't answer."

Kari filled her glass from the tap and grabbed the last pan dulce. "Hungover. I shouldn't have had that last drink."

"Famous last words. How many drinks did you have?"

"Only three, but I thought having all the electrolytes in the wonton soup and corn chips would have helped."

"Food in your stomach did help, even if that combination sounds bizarre."

Kari took her pre-breakfast bread to the loveseat, tossed her pants from the night before to the side, and sat. Yeah, not moving was the way to go. There'd be more of that today. "So, is this a wellness check or is there something going on?"

"Believe it or not, sometimes it's nice to talk to my daughter and know what you're up to. We haven't spoken since you left Anchorage and that was over two months ago."

"I've texted once a week." She bit into the bread.

"I know, but *hearing* your voice is important. It's really bumming out your mom A," she said in a whisper. "Can you please call or leave a message—that counts—every two weeks? It would mean a lot."

Kari sighed. "I can do that."

"Thank you. We don't want to be nosy, especially now that we know you can enjoy a social life, just let us know where you are and what you've been up to."

She took a large gulp of water to wash down the bread and put Mom L on speaker to open the *Hinewai* app. She went to the course map option. "Right now, we're off the coast of Ecuador. We should get to our Peru stop in a few days. And as far as what I've been up to . . . The consequence of this morning was a fun night with Belle."

Mom L snickered. "Usually, people only phrase it that way when they wake up with their pants off."

"Actually, I did."

"Oh."

After a long pause, Kari had to ask, "Is that really all you're going to say?"

"Well, it's tough, because my mom-side is a little concerned you sound so casual about it, but my lesbian side is very proud."

Kari had enough energy to grin. "Calm your sapphic self. It was nothing like that, even though she does identify as a lesbian. She has a lot of the ex's features, actually." Kari thought of an even better trait than her attractive, tall blondness. "Except she's smart, too."

"Wow. I think I can count on one hand the number of times

you've called someone else smart. Next thing you're going to say is that she's funny."

Kari chewed another delicious mouthful. "She is."

There was a long pause before Mom L said, "Be careful, chickpea."

"I promise no more guaro. I'm sticking to my two glasses of champagne from now on."

"That's not what I mean, but I won't say anymore because it's your Mom A's territory. But do me and yourself a favor, finish eating whatever it is you've been eating—"

"How did you know?" she mumbled around the bite.

"You've always been a loud eater. But finish your snack and water, take a pain reliever, go back to bed, and call your mom A."

A sense of dread filled Kari. Mom A always became too excited about friends and read into every detail. "Are you going to tell her about Belle?"

"I will if you don't call her by the end of today."

"Deal," Kari said with a lack of enthusiasm.

"Thank you. I love you, chickpea."

"Yeah, yeah. I love you, too." Kari ended the call, finished her bread and water, and took a pill. But before she turned in for sleep round two, she took her cargo shorts to the wardrobe closet. And stopped.

Normally, she kept her guitar pick wedged between the strings of the second fret of her guitar, but now it was tucked in between the second and the third. Had she played a song last night and forgotten?

Kari ignored the possible memory—real or false. She was in no state to second-guess anything. She was in the state to sleep a few more days until they arrived in Peru for her meeting with Adam Cho.

Chapter Ten

Callao, Peru

Kari chuckled at Belle's text.

> Feeling any better?

> Much. And I shook off my hangover before I had to talk to Mom A, which was good because alcohol makes her uncomfortable.

> Then I'm glad to hear you dodged that bullet. I'm going into town later this morning, want to come with me?

Shit. That meant Belle would be on the tender and she absolutely could not know about the meeting with Adam. She'd either have to disguise herself or hide for the trip to shore. Probably both.

> I wish I would've known sooner, I have a guitar lesson. Then, gaming with Jade.

No worries. I'll see you at work tomorrow. (I hate the night shift.)

Sounds good. Have fun in town!

It was mostly a crisis averted.

Now she had to choose an outfit Belle had never seen her in. Because of work and only low-key hanging out, Belle had only seen her in either her black VIP uniform or her super casual and—per Mom L—'super gay' combo of cargo pants and a tank top. So jeans it was. There was a chance of rain, so she'd add her black rain jacket with the hood up. And, just in case the weather moved out faster, she tossed a baseball hat into her day bag. Like her past shady land trips, she'd leave her digital devices behind.

Once on dock one, she settled on a bench opposite the passenger loading area while her knee bounced. What would Adam's reaction be to seeing her? Would he be disguised in some way, too? How would he react to what she was going to tell him? Would he understand the danger?

She was deep in thought, mentally reviewing all that she needed to tell him, when she caught Belle in her periphery wearing a light jacket in the brightest crimson imaginable. At least Kari would be able to track her wearing that. Belle took a seat at the bow. Therefore, when Kari boarded, she took a spot at the stern where she knew the captain-crew area would block her.

The ride to shore was short. Kari stayed on the tender until Belle set foot on the dock, dropped some cash into a disheveled man's charity cup, and moved on in the direction of one of the plazas. Kari had given herself plenty of time, so she waited until there were only a few passengers left on board to leave. From there, she hailed a taxi. In a card-only payment system, she held up enough cash to make it worth the driver's while. "Playa Cantolao?" she asked.

He nodded and drove them down the industrial streets until they reached the beachy area of the peninsula.

Kari looked out the windows on either side. Looming dark clouds hovered over the ocean and the buildings. She hoped that wasn't a metaphor for what was to come.

When the driver stopped at the beach's road marker, she asked for the general direction of the running track and bank. He provided them, pointed, and went on his way. Now it was time to find the restaurant.

At a busy street corner and across from an international bank chain and running track, there was a window with a neon sign advertising a local beer. The good news was that she had found the meet-up location. The bad news was that a bank that size was destined to have several security cameras. She put her hood up and kept her head down as she walked to the restaurant.

Kari opened the door and her heart skipped a beat as the bell at the top jingled. She assumed Adam would have picked this location because it was quiet. No. Of the eight tabletops, six were occupied.

A waitress busted out of the double doors holding a circular serving tray with several steaming dishes and told Kari to have a seat as she went to a table of men in suits.

Kari took her seat, kept her back to the wall, and rested her head in her hand to obstruct her face. From there, she locked into a state of hypervigilance. Her fingertips tapped the rhythm of the Latin music coming through the speakers as the scent of roasted chili peppers, cumin, and oregano wafted her way. Across from her was a print of *The Last Supper* and table full of people, including a jabbering toddler. Over the swinging doors to the kitchen was a sign reminding people to wash their hands. The bell chimed, and she inhaled sharply. This was it. Kari's head whipped back to the door only to see two police officers. They had a conversation with each other wondering whether or not their to-go order was ready.

This was not how Kari pictured the meeting. In her mind, it was supposed to be only the two of them. She checked the time on her analog watch and saw the minute hand had passed twelve. Why had Adam chosen this spot and why wasn't he here yet? Had Henry gotten to him and this was a trap?

The same waitress who came from the swinging double doors hustled to the police officers, holding a large paper bag. They left with their thanks and, with the door still open from their exit, a man with a muscular build wearing a generic track suit, a few days beard growth, sunglasses, and baseball hat snuck into the restaurant.

Conclusion: Adam looked like a regular guy when he wasn't in a suit.

He saw her and his mouth dropped. Adam headed her way and took off his sunglasses. "You?" he whispered as he took a seat across from her.

"Surprise," Kari said.

"I can't believe it's you." He was stunned but kept his cool and volume down. "You're not Australian and you're Aurora's daughter."

"Those are both true statements. When I was in Alaska with the moms, I heard about an ENN dinner you went to with them. That's when I realized you were the person I could talk to. Who I needed to talk to."

The swinging doors opened as a server came out with two menus for them. She rattled off the specials and asked for their order before they could continue their dialogue.

Kari ordered the seafood and rice with an iced tea while Adam went for the ceviche and a bottled water. Once they were as alone as they were going to get, she asked, "Why are we meeting here? There are tons of people."

"You're not my first inside source, so I know how to be cautious. This makes us forgettable."

"Fine, but this is my first time and I'm freaking out right now."

He placed a hand over hers, which had gripped her napkin-wrapped utensils like a weapon. "I get that, so please know that the only person who knows I'm meeting Sky Fisher is my assistant slash camera person, and she's spending the day in Lima getting B-roll for an interview I'm doing tomorrow. That's why I chose this location; it was the only time my schedule and the *Hinewai's* course aligned." He released her hand. "Do you have anything electronic on you?"

"No. I left all that in my cabin."

"Good. Because it's not just your ass or your family's asses on the line here. Henry fucking hates me and I have no doubt he would plan my murder if I got too close."

At least he understood the gravity of the situation. "Then why do this?"

"Because someone has to expose him and people like him. He hasn't gotten where he is legally or ethically, and because of that he's left a damage path in his wake that he hasn't taken responsibility for. Also, as we speak, he's trying to buy ENN."

If Henry succeeded, then not only would he have control of a major news network and could craft the stories in his favor, but Mom A would be under his thumb, too. "Okay, what I'm going to tell you . . ." Adam was right. Henry would kill him if he found out. And her mothers. And her, no questions asked. She stood to leave. "I'm sorry. I can't—"

"Hold on." Adam grabbed her forearm this time but loosened his hold quickly. "I've spoken to scared informants before and I understand why you're frightened. We can start with little things. Doesn't have to be ground breaking, just give me enough to start."

She wasn't relaxed, but she found the nerve to return to her seat. "Okay."

"Good," Adam said. "Let's start at the beginning. How did you get so close to Henry so fast?"

Kari told him about inCog and the Wibawa Enterprise Promise. "Being a polyglot and a young woman allowed me into some unique situations, which caused me to see more than most do."

"Like what?"

"The first incident was with Robert MacDonald. I don't have proof, but I know they paid off the coroner to change the report."

"How do you know that?"

"Because he was a handsy cockwaffle and I broke his nose because of it. The final coroner report had no mention of that." A woman at the toddler table took out her phone and started taking pictures of the food-covered child. Kari shifted her chair and rested her head in her hand once more. "It's similar to how Henry acquired the movie studio in India. Henry and I went to Pawar's birthday party in Mumbai. One of the waiters was an open book about him. I told Henry everything and the next thing you know, Pawar is dead and Henry has taken over the movie studio."

"*Hmm.* Just like MacDonald's business. Why those people and businesses though?"

Their waitress arrived with their lunches.

Kari nodded her thanks and waited until she disappeared behind the double doors again. "My theory is that I think Henry has to meet a financial threshold to get into a powerful group. That night the two of us met in Stockholm was specifically so he could buddy up to Gabriella Fermi. She's on that Brisbane list."

His forkful of ceviche stopped midway to his lips. "How do you know about that list?"

She took a deep breath. "Because I'm the one who went into your source's office and saw it." Kari ate a mouthful of rice even though the situation made her want to throw up.

"You broke in?" he asked, astonished.

"The door and drawers were unlocked, but"—Kari leaned forward—"if I don't do what they say, I have no doubt that they will kill my mothers. They already . . . They killed my friends in that VIP boat explosion."

"The one ruled a 'freak accident.'" He used quotation fingers as he said it. "I wondered about that."

Her flashbacks started, but the intensity of her fear had dulled in her almost two months of therapy with Ola to the point where she could speak about it without shaking. "I watched it happen. Madeleine described them as 'loose ends' and gave the command for Josef to detonate."

"Whoa." Adam took a pull off his water bottle. "I knew Henry and Josef were dirty, but I didn't think Madeleine was a part of this."

"Madeleine is Henry's lieutenant. She knows everything or, at least, used to know everything. He's up to something lately and keeping her out of it." The door of the restaurant jingled again. Kari automatically turned her head in that direction and promptly dropped her spoon against her plate with a *clang*. Grains of rice fell onto the table top.

"I thought you said you had a guitar lesson," Belle said as she walked toward the table with a paper shopping bag. She didn't look mad, but the furrow in her brow suggested she was confused. Then, she made eye contact with Adam.

Kari could see her metaphorical wheels spinning; Belle recognized him but didn't know from where. Belle's hand shot up to cover her mouth and she backpedaled. Kari scrambled out of her seat and went to Belle. She put a hand on each of her shoulders. "Please don't make a scene and sit down."

Belle stared at Adam the entire time she pulled out her chair and sat. "You're Adam Cho. I'm such a fan of your work. The exposé you did on collection fraud after natural disasters really changed the way a lot of congregations handle fundraising."

Adam suddenly found the floor interesting and Kari knew why. He didn't know Belle or what consequence there would be to her discovering their meeting. "This is Belle. She's a WU intern who works with me and the other VIP assistants."

"Kari's been so helpful in teaching me the ropes." Belle pointed to their two plates. "Are you two having lunch together?"

"We are," Kari said. "My guitar student canceled and Mom A let it slip to Adam that I was in the area, so we thought we'd get together for lunch. He's thinking about doing a story on geniuses."

Belle skewed her mouth. "You are both a genius and an awful liar." She shifted in her chair so she faced Adam. "We play poker together on the ship and she still hasn't fixed her tells yet."

"Interesting," Adam said and cleared his throat. He folded in his lips and tapped his fork all while staring at Kari.

Kari shrugged. She didn't know what their next move should be either.

"I guess now that you're here," Adam said to Belle, "would you like to join us for lunch? It's on me."

"Maybe just a soda. I am parched."

Adam waved over the server, ordered, then directed his attention back to Belle. "So, what's WU like?"

Belle's starstruck smile disappeared as she launched in full chat mode. She talked about WU's programs, how she got her internship, and her observations so far on the ship. "It's been amazing! I've seen a lot of powerful people come by in only a few months of my internship."

"Such as?" Adam asked, his posture more relaxed than when Belle had first arrived.

Belle took a sip and picked at her fingernail with her thumb. "I would say the most powerful was Jack Weatherby. Unfortunately, his son, JJ, was there, too. If you want a news story Mr. Cho, you ought to investigate them. They're dirtier than the floor of a chicken processing plant when the inspector is on vacation."

Adam grimaced. "I'll consider the Weatherbys for a piece."

"Good. I feel like I could write my own book after just a few days with them. JJ's misogyny alone is several chapters." Belle looked at Kari. "Do you disagree?"

While Kari's focus today was to report Henry and Madeleine's activities, she couldn't deny what Belle had said. "Actually, no. They're scum. JJ is especially awful." While Belle had only reported well-established facts, she had to stop Belle before she said something that could be traced specifically back to her and the ship. But since Belle would question a sudden request for her to leave—and it would hurt her feelings —Kari had to get rid of Adam.

Kari gestured to Adam's empty ceviche dish. "Well, thanks for meeting me here, Adam. I know you have to get back to work."

Adam squinted as though confused, but then nodded and stood. He dug into his pocket for a stack of bills held with a money clip. "I appreciate the time and I guess I'll see you both of you in Papua New Guinea for my *Hinewai* tour. Please tell Aurora—I guess that's Mom A—that I said hi." He laid cash on the table and left.

Belle scraped her fingernail with her thumbnail and looked at Kari as though her brain were only filled with questions.

"Fun fact," Kari said, "Mom A works behind the scenes on environmental news pieces for ENN and knows Adam. It's such a small world," she said with a nervous laugh.

"Uh-huh. Kari, why are you having clandestine meetings with celebrity journalists in Peru?"

Shit. "Trust me when I say that it's safer for all three of us if you don't know. Please don't push me on this."

Belle leaned back in her seat while she studied Kari. "*Hmm.* This has to come back to your goal." She took a drink and tapped her trim nail against the glass soda bottle. "You've seen something that has made you too scared to go to the authorities, so you're going to him instead."

How was Belle so good at this? "Please stop," Kari said in a whisper, "and keep your voice down. But you're right, I have seen things."

Belle gave her a lopsided grin. "Kari, I get that these VIPs are major pains, skirt the law, and could have us fired simply for cutting their cigar the wrong way, but I don't think it's worth the cloak and dagger routine with Adam Cho to make an exposé episode of television."

Kari shook her head and watched the people from the toddler table leave. Dammit. Now there would be less noise to cover their conversation, but at least the picture taking was over. "You don't understand, people have been murdered."

Belle sat straighter and then leaned forward. "What? Who?" But as soon as she asked, her eyes grew wider. "Mitchell and Santos?"

Kari hesitantly nodded. "If the wrong people find out I'm

talking to Adam—including the authorities who have no doubt been bought by Henry—my mothers are next. Then, me."

Belle's hand covered her mouth.

Kari understood the shock and gave her a moment to process it all. "That's why this meeting has to remain between us. You cannot tell a soul about today. Do you understand?"

A myriad of expressions crossed Belle's face. "I do, but Kari, please tell me you won't do this again if it's this dangerous."

"I've been smart about it. I haven't left a digital trail and I avoid cameras. I even left my TV on in my cabin, which I never do." Wasted energy lectures from Mom A ran deep within her.

"I'm glad to hear you're taking precautions, but what if it had been Josef walking in here today and not me?"

Belle had a good point, also . . . "How did you know that Josef is bad news?"

"That's just insulting. Josef's like a big, ominous puppy with a soul patch who follows Henry around."

The conversation had been about lies and murder, but Kari found the image comical. "I promise I won't meet Adam like this again and I'm sorry that I lied to you this morning. How'd you end up on this side of town anyway?"

"I wanted to withdraw some cash from the bank and I could smell everything from the ATM. Very tempting."

Kari pushed her plate over to Belle. "Help yourself to mine. I still feel like throwing up."

"I'm guessing this time it's because of stress and not guaro. Can't say that I blame you though." Belle took Adam's unused spoon and pointed it at Kari. "This past year has been a whirlwind of emotions for you, hasn't it?"

"You have no idea."

Belle studied her for a moment with a small shake of her head. "How have you held yourself together?"

"I have regular therapist appointments again, which have

really helped. I have less nightmares and I can go on deck one without paralyzing fear. I also try to stay busy and spend time with friends." Kari gave Belle a pointed look as she ate a mouthful. "Even if I thought that some of those friends had a bit of toxic positivity to their personality when I first met them."

"I may have been told once or twice that I need to tone that down," Belle said with a smile. "I hope you know that, as your friend, if you ever want or need to talk to me, you can."

"I might take you up on that offer." Kari could feel in her bones that Belle could keep a secret better than anyone else and could keep her cool better than Jade.

———

"We're going away together!" Jade announced.

Kari flinched at the scream and missed the ball. "What do you mean you're 'going away'?"

"WU has a break in between semesters, so I asked Neill if he wanted to take a few days in Concepción. He said yes!"

There was no way the WU break had anything to do with Ricardo Rojas's visit, but there was something else that struck Kari as interesting. "This must be getting serious with Neill." She tossed the ball back.

"I think it is. Every time I see him, I learn so much more about him. He's just the sweetest man and so attentive. He remembered a stray comment I made about walnuts back in San Diego."

"You mean, how according to you they're the best nut?"

"Yes! And Neill asked our waiter if they could add some to our dessert while he held my hand." Jade placed her paddle over her heart.

Kari had never considered hand holding while reciting nut facts to be the height of romance—in fact, it sounded really basic—but she wasn't going to rain on Jade's parade. "I'm very happy for you. Where are you staying for your getaway?"

"Don't know. Neill said he'd ask you."

"Why me?"

"Because you have resources for that kind of stuff. Consider it a special project you can do when your VIP is sleeping."

"In that case, I'll ask Belle."

Jade smirked. "You'll just hate that."

Kari could hear the sarcasm dripping off the comment. "What's that supposed to mean?"

"You like her, which if you recall, I knew you would. That girl's pretty."

"Yes, she is. Denying that would be stupid, which I'm not. And, of course I like her; she's my friend."

Jade chuckled deep in her throat. "I think you left that territory and have entered the crush zone. You talk about her more than you did Finn, and you had a tropical waters make out session with them."

"It wasn't . . ." Kari scoffed. "I didn't make out with Finn. Lips never went off lips and hands never strayed off the waist-hip region."

"Okay, I'll give you that, but it doesn't change the fact that you bring up every single fact about Belle whether it's interesting or not. That's only something people do when they are crushing hard on someone."

"I don't do that."

Jade put her hand on her hip. "Kari, the fact that she has sensitive teeth is not interesting unless someone has commissioned me to make an ice cream cake for her, which no one has."

The observation gave Kari pause. Did she have a crush on Belle? Sure, she could understand why someone would. Belle was kind, intelligent, fun, sympathetic, was a great listener, she had the accent, smelled a little like sandalwood, had an athletic figure, and when Belle stood close to her she towered over her in a way that was kind of sexy—

"Shit," Kari drawled.

Jade gave her a crooked smile and resumed their play. "Look at it this way, you're officially over Finn."

Chapter Eleven

Bay of Concepción, Chile

"Hey, Kari!" Neill jogged down the passageway after her, his heavy steps making a thud with each impact.

She paused outside of the VIP office where Belle arched her back in a stretch. "What's going on, buddy?"

He took a step closer. *Talk in private.* "Could you help me with something really quick? You don't mind, do you, Belle?"

"Go ahead," Belle said with a yawn and a shooing motion.

Kari followed Neill to a new room: the security office. Instead of scanning his thumb, he leaned forward for a retina scan, entered a ten-digit code, then pushed open the solid, gunmetal gray door and gestured for her to come inside. Kari entered and stared at the twenty-five color monitors in a five-by-five configuration that showed alternating views of every deck on the ship. There was a charging station for the walkie talkies, gas masks, and night vision googles. Then, there were the weapons.

"Whoa," was the best summary she could muster.

Behind two layers of crisscrossed, locked metal fencing was an arsenal. Automatic rifles with banana clips that were illegal in many countries, handguns, tactical gear, and something in a rectangular olive-green case on the floor that she had only ever seen in the movies. "Is that a rocket launcher?" She caught a glimpse of her own awed expression in a security monitor.

"She should not be here," a guard watching the screens said.

Privacy. Embarrassing question. "She's fine, Dmitri. Do some laps around the decks."

"You're the boss." *Josef dislikes her, I see why.* He buttoned his black suit jacket and left the room.

She asked the unanswered question. "Is that a rocket launcher?"

Baby. "It's just a little one."

"Why do we have a rocket launcher?"

"Pirates," Neill said, like it was a no-brainer. He unbuttoned his jacket, which showed his dual shoulder holsters, one for a 9 mm and another for a taser. When he took a seat in the rolling chair across from her, his black pant leg raised enough for her to see an ankle holster with a revolver and socks with bicycles on them. *Romantic time.* "I want to ask you about this weekend."

The man wanted to discuss his romantic weekend getaway surrounded by enough firepower to overthrow a small government. "Okay."

"Do you think I should tell Jade that I love her when we're at the restaurant or in the hot tub at sunset?"

"That's not a question I'm prepared to answer!"

Confused. He cocked his bald head. "Why not?"

"Because . . . I have no experience in that department."

"But I thought that since you're a woman you'd have a romantic perspective."

"That's so sexist!"

Maybe right. "Could you at least please try to help? I'm really nervous."

Kari groaned. "I can help you think about it logically." She did a quick review of her favorite love declaration scenes in books, movies, and real life. That didn't help. "Okay, let's start with this. In your dream scenario, how do you want her to react when you say it to her?"

Good question. He exhaled a breath and nodded. "Well, it'd be nice if she said it back, but I can't expect that because we may be in different emotional places. So, if she doesn't return the sentiment, I at least want her to feel free to express herself openly and not worry about a crowd." *That's answer.* "I guess I shouldn't do it in the restaurant."

"I agree. Plus, sunsets are very pretty and classically romantic."

Hot tub sex. "Thanks, Kari, I needed to talk that out."

"Happy to help." Kari went to leave and saw Belle on the security monitor doing push-ups with perfect form. "I hope you two have a wonderful trip. Jade's a lucky lady."

"Thanks, Kari. I'll see you later when Rojas comes aboard."

Kari left and headed back to the VIP office where Belle was mid wall-sit. "Trying to stay awake?"

Feel dead. Belle gave her a sleepy smile. "My roommate kept me up packing for her break while I attempted to sleep through it. The disadvantages of having the night shift."

Kari sympathized despite the fact that she'd never had a roommate once in her life. "Is Vy gone now?"

"Yes!" Belle said with much more energy. *Privacy.* "For two weeks."

"Well, get your rest tonight. Anything I should know before I start my shift?"

"VIP is fine as long as you remember to disinfect everything you touch. The kids are what you'd expect. It's so weird seeing children on the ship, though."

Kari understood what she meant. Because of the ships' limited in-person health care, residents who were more than twenty-four weeks pregnant weren't allowed on the ship. They also weren't allowed to bring on children under sixteen.

Almost forgot. "And Henry's son confirmed his arrival on Monday."

"But Rojas doesn't come until Tuesday."

"I think he and Ahmed want some pal around time. It's cute. Well, let me get out of your hair." She came from behind the desk and shimmied in front of Kari. *Don't be too eager. Sound cool.* "Hey, since most of WU is away and we can't do poker, I was wondering if you wanted to get together again at your place?"

Kari hovered in an awkward position above the chair. But it wasn't the question that had paused all motion, it was Belle's anxiety before asking it. Was the crushing mutual? Regardless, it would be good to unwind before the Rojas visit. "I'd like that, but no guaro this time. Let's stick to dinner and a movie."

"Don't forget the sunset." Belle winked and walked away.

Kari finally sat, stunned. This was new territory and, as much as she didn't want to, there was an expert she could consult.

———

"Hi, Mom A!" Kari waved to her computer screen.

"Chickpea, this is such a pleasant surprise. Where are you in the world right now?"

"We arrived in Concepción yesterday. We'll be here a week and then it's off to Tierra del Fuego."

"It's so neat that you get to experience new places this time around. You'll have so many stories for when you come to Michigan."

"Subtle reminder. I have my tickets booked for flying out of Rio and back into Cape Town. And before you ask, I already had a conversation with Madeleine that I absolutely can't miss this visit."

"That's what I like to hear. So, what else is going on?"

Quick, like taking off a bandage. "I may have developed a crush on someone and I'm unsure how to navigate it."

Mom A bounced on the couch at home. "I love it when we girl talk! Who is it?"

All of Kari's muscles tensed at once. "It's Belle."

"Belle? As in the intern Belle?"

"The same one."

"Oh, this is risky territory. You work with her and that gets messy."

"But we don't really work together," Kari said. "I'm an employee of the ship and she's a student of WU. Plus, our working interaction mostly consists of information hand-offs because we're on opposite shifts."

"Sounds like you're stretching to justify it."

Was that what she was doing? The answer was no, she was simply stating facts. "Logically, I know it's a bad idea it's just . . ." Kari sighed. Her chat with Neill about romance had lingered with her. "Seeing someone in that way seems nice, even if I've told people that's not what I want."

"Oh, chickpea." Even through the laptop screen, Mom A's gaze softened. "I've been in your shoes and remember that feeling of being the only single person in the group well. Between Finn getting engaged and Jade and Neill seeing each other, I can see why you might feel like you're missing something. Or someone. Have you talked to Ola about it?"

"Only in the sense that she says she recommends healing as

much as possible after trauma before attempting a romantic relationship, but that wasn't directed at me specifically. Having said that, she has said that she's happy about my progress and that I've made extra friends."

"I'm really happy about both of those things, too, but friendship and romance are different forms and levels of intimacy. Maybe you and Ola can make those two things a topic for the next time you have an appointment, because I'm assuming you don't want to talk about the details of that with me."

"You are one-hundred percent correct." Kari knew she might regret asking, but she did want to know. "But what should I do if Belle feels the same way?"

"I think that depends on how honest you've been with her about what you've gone through. If she's aware of the boat accident and your work with Ola, then I think it's completely fair for you to say that you're not ready for a relationship yet."

"That sounds like such a cliché though."

"Maybe it is, but if Belle's the person you say she is, then she'll respect it. And over time, you'll heal more and you won't work together, so maybe you can explore something then. But right now, I want you to focus on getting better."

Mom A was right. She had no idea how amazing Belle was, but she was still right. "Thanks for the talk, Mom A. I love you."

"I love you too, chickpea."

———

"No backpack this time?" Kari asked as she ushered Belle inside her cabin. "Although, you certainly didn't forget to bring layers."

To go with Belle's jeans, she wore a thick indigo cardigan over a white shirt. "There was nothing to bring since you said you'd take care of everything. And you're one to talk about layers."

"It's chilly out on the balcony!" Kari had determined that a way of insuring a platonic fun time was by down-playing her own sex appeal with gray sweatpants and an oversized orange hoodie. "But enough of weather talk, what would you like to drink? You'll be pleased to know that since the last time you were here, I purchased a second glass."

"Someone's getting fancy. I'll just drink whatever you're making yourself."

"That'd be herbal tea." Also not sexy.

"No champagne for your guest? I'm surprised."

With that question and comment Kari realized she was being stupid. It wasn't as though opening a bottle of champagne meant her sweatpants would be thrown to the floor and Belle's head would land between her thighs. "You make a compelling case. I'll open a bottle."

"Wow, I really had to twist your arm." Belle studied her guitar while Kari dealt with the bottle's cage and foil. "It's a shame I've never been able to hear you play." She stuck her lower lip out in a perfect pout.

Kari put the bottle down and walked over to her guitar, giving Belle a faux-annoyed scowl along the way. She picked her baby up from its rack then sat on the loveseat, placing the waist of the guitar over her thigh. "What would you like to hear? Also, I do not sing."

Belle clapped quietly and sat beside her. "Um . . . It's old, but do you know *Mountain Home?*"

"Okay. One, the classics are never 'old'. Two, yes, I know it. Mom L loves it."

Kari removed the pick between the strings. She'd fingerpick rather than strum the beautiful but sad country song. Next, she placed the capo lower on the neck to give the strings a higher frequency. As she started to play, Belle sang. There was a slight twang to her voice, but there was also a rasp—gritty and mature. It also sounded like despite Belle's almost twenty-two years on this earth, she had seen far more than most.

At the second mention of the uncle in the song, Belle's voice cracked and she stopped singing. A single tear escaped and fell down her cheek.

Kari stopped playing and rested her hand on Belle's knee. "Are you okay?"

Belle sniffled and used her cardigan sleeve to wick away her tear. "I'm sorry. You know how songs can really take you back?" She took a deep breath, her chest visibly expanding as she did, and she released it as a loud exhale. "I promise I'm fine."

"Okay." Kari followed Belle's line of sight to see that her hand was still on Belle's knee. She returned it back to the guitar's strings. "But if you want to talk about it, we can."

"That's hard. The concept of home, that is." Belle seemed to look all around the cabin and picked at her fingernail with her thumb. "I suppose the easiest way to explain it is that that song reminds me of my chosen family, and I don't think I realized how much I missed them until right now. It's been almost two years since we've seen each other."

Kari's eyes bulged. She couldn't imagine what it'd be like going so long without seeing her family. "Will you be able to see them when you go home in November for Thanksgiving?"

Belle smiled. "Yes. It'll be great. I've been promised a birthday celebration, too."

She found herself smiling, but she wanted to know more. What were their names? How did Belle meet them? But with a topic so sensitive, it was best if Belle volunteered that information when she was ready.

Kari gestured to her guitar. "Do you want me to play anything else? Something happier perhaps?" She strummed an upbeat progression of chords while wearing a manic smile.

Belle chuckled. "Maybe next time. You might inadvertently play something else that reminds me of something and has me crying again. Besides, we have champagne on the counter getting warmer as we speak."

"We should fix that." Kari took her guitar to the stand, popped the cork, and poured their glasses. Someday flutes would be purchased. "You have a nice voice. Did you sing back home?"

"Many years in the church choir. You don't know any gospel songs, do you?"

"Believe it or not, since Mom L is pretty much agnostic and Mom A follows Anishinaabe spiritual practices, they didn't take me to many churches growing up." She handed Belle a generously poured glass.

"Have you ever even been to a church?" Belle opened the sliding door.

"A few times." Kari indicated with a wave of her hand for Belle to take the lounge chair. "Mostly for weddings and once for homeschool. Mom L and I would sit in on different religious services and then I interviewed the clergy. The rabbi was my favorite. She was sassy."

"Coming from you, she must have been a pistol," Belle said with her eyes on the darkening horizon. The city lights flickered in the distance. "Are we facing south?"

"Yeah. It's a cardinal direction crap shoot as to which direction I face. We lucked out last time." Kari thought of the sunset and wondered if Neill had declared his love to Jade yet.

"What are you smiling about over there?"

"I can't say because Neill probably wouldn't want me to tell, but let's just say, I hope that things are going his way right now."

"Is that why he asked to talk to you the other day in private?"

"Yep. Oh!" Kari yelled so loud she made Belle jump. "Sorry, but I forgot to tell you the craziest thing. Neill took me into the security office. You wouldn't believe what they have in there!"

"Guns?"

"And a rocket launcher."

Belle's eyes widened. "That's . . . a big gun."

"Neill said it's for pirates."

Belle took a long drink of champagne. "Hopefully, they're all trained to use them properly."

"I know Neill is."

"You know his story?" she asked, surprised.

"Some. He's former military and an incredibly sweet man. He um . . . He was with me during the explosion. I was a sobbing mess, so he carried me here and took care of me until Jade came home."

"You poor thing." Belle's hand covered her heart. "I'm glad to hear he's a good soul."

"He is. Jade, too. Honestly, between them and Ola they've helped me start to feel like me again."

"You don't feel like you yet?"

"No, but I'm getting there." Kari sipped her drink, appreciated the friend at her side, and admired the transition of the orange sky to shades of violet. In minutes, the stars speckled the darkness with their celestial light.

"That was the shortest sunset ever," Belle said with a frown.

"Pretty much. Do you want to stay out here or go in? I should note that I'm excited about Jon's feast."

"I'm kind of afraid after last time. Chorizo wonton soup was a miss for me."

"That was noted in my report back to him, but that conversation led to me to learn that he'll make whatever in exchange for a little more money. So, I asked for something relatively basic: cheeseburgers and chips. Or rather, I have the different ingredients and instructions to put them together in the way he envisioned." Kari pulled open the door and went inside. "I asked him to make one traditional and the other spicy. We can split if you want, so we can try each."

"Sure. I can get the movie started while you do that."

Kari gave her a thumbs-up and headed to the kitchen. Jon had placed every element of their burgers in cardboard takeout boxes. The chips were in a paper bag splotched with grease from the fresh fry. "Do you remember how to navigate my TV?" Kari asked as she watched the burgers rotate in the microwave. When there was no answer, she turned to see the TV cued where it needed to be. Considering there were about a dozen non-intuitive steps needed to reach the movie and Belle had only ever seen the process once, Kari was impressed. "I guess you do."

Belle shrugged. "I paid attention. Do you need help?"

"Nope. I got it." Kari placed the burgers with melty cheeses on top of the split rolls, divided the veggies, and spread the different sauces. To make the plates more decorative, she lined the chips down the middle and placed half a burger on either side. She balanced the plates on one arm so she could grab the bottle of champagne with her free hand.

"Bon appétit!" Kari presented the plates in front of Belle. "A little help please."

Belle took the plates. "This looks pretty amazing. I don't

know if I'll be able to say the same about our feature film, *Lieutenant Streets*."

"O ye of little faith. Besides, I didn't say it looked like a good movie. I said it looked like—"

"An entertaining movie," Belle finished for her. "Yeah, yeah."

Belle's memory impressed Kari once more. A single word she had used weeks ago had stayed rooted in her brain.

They started the movie and their dinner. After the first juicy bite, Kari went to the kitchen for more napkins and pushed up her sleeves. Even though she wasn't going to flirt, she also wasn't a slob who would tolerate food juices on her clothes.

"That's a good idea." Belle unbuttoned her cardigan, which revealed the sleeveless white shirt she wore underneath.

Kari tried not to ogle Belle's well-defined arms. Her triceps flexed with a slight indentation as she reached forward for her glass. The shadows of her deltoids shifted as she lifted it and her biceps contracted as she brought the champagne to her lips.

Belle turned toward her, brow raised. "What?"

Kari noticed something else aside from her musculature. "The scar on your shoulder. Was that from your volleyball surgery?" The blemish was several inches long and branched toward her armpit in an irregular way.

"Sure was."

"I would have thought they'd go in arthroscopically."

"I didn't ask questions. Figured the doctors were doing what they thought was best." She munched on a chip, then her eyes rolled back. "These are heavenly. I think Jon used that fancy truffle salt."

Kari tried a chip. Belle was right.

They started the movie, loving the action and terrible dialogue. When they finished their food and champagne, Kari took their plates to the sink and started the electric kettle for tea. She caught the action on the screen, and the utter ridiculousness of it made her break into hysterics.

"I missed the part where the man's arm being broken at the elbow was funny," Belle said.

"It's because that's not how physics or the human body works."

"Oh, and you're an expert in both, I suppose."

"I'm not an expert, but I know enough about anatomy and grappling to know that's not how you'd take someone down."

"Grappling?"

"I took jiu-jitsu for a little while. It served as my homeschool physical education credit."

Belle nodded as though the dots of a puzzle had just connected. "That's how you knew how to put the wrist lock on the perv in Stockholm."

"Exactly." When Belle continued to stare at her while crunching on a chip, she added, "If you're curious about it, I'd be happy to show you some basic self-defense maneuvers. One can never be too careful." Especially on the *Hinewai*.

"That's a nice gesture, but I was actually thinking about your hair from the viral video of that incident. It was nice long, but I think it looks better short."

Kari ran her fingers through her hair. "I'm growing it out more, but I think I will keep it on the shorter side from now on. It's safer from a self-defense point of view that way, too."

Belle pursed her lips and then nodded. "Because of hair pulling?"

"Correct. This is unpullable."

"I don't know about that." Belle paused the movie and strode over to Kari with a wry smile. She gently placed her hand on the device-less side of Kari's head and gripped her hair. "It appears as though you're not immune from a little pulling after all."

The nerve ending in Kari's scalp made an electric connection to her lady button. Was this a kink she had now? "I stand corrected."

Belle smirked. "Now, give me a tutorial. Tell me how you'd get out of this."

Kari swallowed the lump that suddenly lodged itself in her throat. "There's two ways I've practiced. One, I would put my hand over yours, like this"—Kari demonstrated—"and press down until it became too uncomfortable for your knuckles and you lost your grip."

"Then, you'd take me down?"

"Then, I'd run away."

"But Lieutenant Streets doesn't run away," Belle said seriously. "Lieutenant Streets takes down the perp."

The lump would not go away! Kari cleared her throat to assist its removal but failed. "In that case, I'd put my closest leg behind yours, tuck my arm in, and do kind of a backstroke to catch your arm in an elbow lock"—Kari followed through, trapping Belle's arm—"and then keep rotating until— Ah!"

They both fell with a thud, causing Kari to land on top of Belle with her knee between Belle's thighs and her hands on either side of Belle's arms. Neither of them moved or spoke. They locked eyes and matched breaths.

"That was an effective technique," Belle said and then licked her lips. "Kari . . ."

The heat from Belle's breath brushed against her. The scent of sandalwood enveloped her. They were so close. Mere inches away. But as much as she wanted to kiss Belle, she couldn't. Not while she still had to research movie spoilers to learn if they had explosions or murdered scientists in them before choosing her entertainment. "I don't think we should."

Reluctantly, Kari pushed herself off then offered Belle a hand to stand.

"You're right," Belle said, and straightened the shirt that had risen above her navel. She had abs! How often did she work out? "I agree we should remain friendly but professional given our circumstances."

"I'm glad you see it that way." The tension in Kari's shoulders left even if other places in her body were tighter than her guitar strings. She returned to the kitchen to prepare their tea. "Maybe it'll help our situation if we talk about how we feel. What do you think?"

Belle was back on the loveseat with her cardigan on and picked at her fingernail with her thumb. "Can you go first? I'm really nervous."

Having to articulate the level of her infatuation directly to her crush made Kari squirm and twitch. But she was an adult and could do this! "Okay. Um. I guess there's a few things I should say. The first is that I really, really value our friendship. You're the first person since I was twelve who I've hung out with who's my age—mostly—and can keep up with me. Intellectually speaking."

"Oh, dear." Belle looked completely crestfallen. "Since you were twelve?"

"Yeah. So, what we have, as stupid as it might sound, is really special to me, and I don't want to mess that up. And the second thing is that I don't think I can handle romantic intimacy yet."

"Oh, my."

Kari nodded vigorously. "Yeah, it wouldn't be fair to you—to anybody—really." Kari paced the kitchen and stopped. "I have this new fear where I do sleep with someone and I have a nightmare where I wake up screaming and crying and the person I've slept with runs for the hills and never wants to see me again."

"Oh, my. That'd be extra traumatic for sure. I can understand why you wouldn't want to put yourself through that. Or, you know, the person you're with."

Kari could see it in Belle's eyes that she understood, and that encouraged her to keep going. "And to be brutally honest, those two things are coming from my brain, but my body . . ." Kari uttered a nervous laugh. "At times I feel a lot of sexual tension between us."

"Like when you fall down on top of me?"

"Correct."

"I understand. I won't ask you to show me any more grappling moves."

"That's a good idea." Kari stood astonished. They had a mature conversation about a complex and delicate issue. "Is there something I can do to help? Or is there anything you want to tell me?"

"Um. Well . . ." Belle bit her lip and picked at her nails. "Regarding the tension, I'll be mindful not to do anything that might be construed as flirting. But, just so you know, I'm not one who jumps into bed with someone just because of some intense feelings."

"Are you one of those wait-until-marriage types?" Kari thought that species was nearly extinct.

"No," Belle said with a light chuckle. "That didn't quite work for me. Just like you, I have a past with some dark spots, and it takes a lot for me to feel comfortable enough to share all of it with someone to go to that place. It's not true intimacy if they don't know the real me."

Kari leaned back on her counter and folded her arms. What in the world had happened to Belle? There was so much more to her than a family who had rejected her. "If you ever need to—"

"I know. If I ever want to talk about it, I can come to you. And part of me"—she took a deep breath—"really, really wants to, but this isn't the time."

"But maybe someday?"

"Yeah," Belle said with a smile, "maybe someday. But for now"—she stood, walked over to Kari, and outstretched her hand—"friends and partners?"

Kari took Belle's hand and gave it a gentle squeeze and shake. "Friends and partners."

Chapter Twelve

"Reporting for duty," Kari said as she entered Madeleine's office. There was a thin, white, rectangular box on the corner of her desk with the embossed gold script of Coultier's Candies. A note with Kari's name was taped on top. "I get chocolate?"

"It's a small reward for your ideas. My sister insisted on making you a key. Nut allergies and whatnot."

"That was very considerate of her. Eat one."

Madeleine looked as though Kari had sprouted another head. "I'm sorry."

"Eat one. In front of me. Right now."

Madeleine *tsked*. "They aren't poisoned."

Kari glared at her.

"Fine," Madeleine said, exasperated. She took one from the middle, not bothering to use the key, and bit it in half. A string of caramel stretched down her lip as she struggled to chew it in a dignified way. "Satisfied?"

"Very." Kari didn't bother holding back her smirk as she took the box and sat in the visitor's chair.

"Ray arrived yesterday while Ahmed was on duty. If you could, find out what their relationship or their history is for me. But, more to the point, Henry has prepped Ray better for Ricardo Rojas's visit, so you and Belle shouldn't have to manage his anxiety like last time. And like last time with Jack Weatherby, Henry doesn't want you to be able to mentally eavesdrop, but I still want a report from you at the end of shift. Dismissed."

"Thank you, ma'am." Kari left and headed to the VIP assistant office.

"Right on time," Ahmed said from behind the desk. The five o'clock—or six o'clock—shadow of his beard had come in more like midnight. An almost empty coffee cup with dribble stains down the side was on the coaster in front of him.

Now that she was sure the chocolates weren't poisoned, she opened the box in front of him. "I hear chocolate helps get over rough nights."

Ahmed studied the key and shook his head. "It wasn't rough. Ray just likes to make up for lost time. After dinner, we went into town and then played virtual golf until three am."

"Sounds like it'll be a quiet morning for me."

"You got that right, and Henry, Ricardo Rojas, and his daughter, Raquel, won't be here until four."

That was new. Henry never spent time with a VIP before they came onboard the ship. "Henry is already with him? Why?"

"I thought that was weird, too. But when I asked the Rojas's assistant, he said that Ricardo wanted Henry to go on an expedition of sorts before they all came here." Ahmed stood from behind the desk and took his coffee with him. "Enjoy your next few days with them. I have a feeling it'll be interesting."

Kari did the VIP shimmy to switch places behind the desk. "Do you know if you'll be able to hang out with Ray more?"

"Probably not. It's a shame, too. I really like spending time with him."

She was never going to get a better opening than that to ask. "It sounds like you two go way back. How do you two know each other?"

A sad smile crossed Ahmed's features. "Henry doesn't like me to talk about it, but I'm Ray's half-brother."

At the revelation, Kari practically heard dramatic soap opera music in her head. "Get out!"

He chuckled. "We share the same mother, but not father, which is why I'm the assistant to the rich and Ray gets to be periphery rich, even though Henry still treats him like garbage."

"How many people know this about you two?"

"On the ship?" He bobbed his head about as though he were thinking about it. "Only you, I think. You're the only one who ever cared enough to ask."

A sympathetic sound escaped her. "If you don't mind me asking, why do you stay on the ship? Why don't you live near Ray?"

"Henry doesn't want us seen together. The press hasn't caught on to me and that's the way he likes it. But I like the ship for the same reasons a lot of others do."

"Food and exotic locations?"

"Absolutely. I might do something else when I have enough money saved."

"Like help Ray build his business? Maybe expand to murals on rockstar tour buses?"

He returned her smile, showing his slightly coffee-stained teeth. "Maybe. I hope you and Belle have a good week." He held up his cup as a goodbye gesture.

The mysterious pieces of Henry Wibawa kept showing up on the game board. Kari had known Henry was divorced but had never bothered to learn about his ex-wife. Since Ray was still sound asleep for the next several hours, she had plenty of time to resolve that issue.

It was internet rabbit hole time!

Ray and Ahmed's mother, Duni, was born in Nairobi to a wealthy banking family. Her second year at university, she met her first husband. They married and moved to Jakarta, where Ahmed was born shortly thereafter. Tragically, Ahmed's father died from bile duct cancer when he was eighteen months old. While raising young Ahmed as a single mother, Duni went to work for the largest banking institution in Indonesia, which was where she met Henry. They married four months later and Ray was born five months later. When Ahmed and Ray were both teenagers, they divorced. Henry didn't fight for any form of custody.

Kari's curiosity piqued further. She went to the employee management cloud, where she could see the hierarchy and divisions of roles. Under Madeleine's VIP Coordination were the VIP assistants, kitchen staff, and housekeeping staff. She clicked on the VIP assistants, and then Ahmed. He had gone to university for a year, worked odd jobs, and eventually landed on the *Hinewai*.

Next, she clicked on Madeleine.

Her biography was scant, but it was there. Madeleine had come to the US for an Ivy League undergraduate and back to Australia for her law education. After obtaining her solicitor license, she had worked her way up the ladder at a legal firm based in Japan in their international trade division. She had written dozens of articles in well-respected publications. She had given speeches at numerous high-profile conferences. Madeleine was nearly at the pinnacle of her career when she bounced over to Wibawa Enterprises. Henry must have offered her a shiny carrot for her to take that leap.

Kari crossed her arms and leaned back in the chair. People made so much more sense when she understood their past.

———

A little after ten am, Kari's work phone buzzed with Ray's request for breakfast. She appreciated that he included "please", since VIPs rarely did that. Fifteen minutes later, she headed in the direction of the kitchen for pickup and ran into Neill. "Hey, how'd it go with Jade?"

His all-business, mean mug was replaced with the kind of joy that she assumed only came from playing with dogs. "It couldn't have gone better! She told me that she loves me too."

"That's great!"

He grinned and looked down at his shiny black shoes. "I've never been happier, but I know I need to tell her the details of my past. I just don't know how."

She exhaled a long breath. "I wish I could help you there, but you should trust yourself to know when the time is right."

"Maybe when we're anchored off Cape Town?" he mused aloud. "Okay, I have to go. The security cameras are fritzing on deck seven."

"That's where my cabin is, so, yeah, you should go check that out."

"Will do. See you on deck for the Rojas."

"Really?" she asked, surprised. "Josef isn't the security detail for these VIPs?"

A thoughtful expression passed over his features. "Interesting you should ask that. He was, but he picked up a virus and Henry insisted that he follow quarantine procedure and stay in his cabin." He lumbered away and down the passageway to tend to his task.

And so did Kari, but without the lumbering.

Kari pushed Ray's meal cart, complete with a tea set and silver cloche, to his windowless cabin.

Ray opened the door in his no-frills pajamas, took the cart from her, and wheeled it in front of the TV. "Thank you so much. I've been craving this meal all week and my phone finally gave me the go-ahead."

"I'm sorry, but your phone told you that you could eat?"

He laughed as he lifted the cloche to display some sort of pancake and half a pig's worth of crispy bacon. "I have a sensor that tracks my glucose, which 'talks' to my insulin pump through my phone. I don't know how they work in tandem, but it's amazing."

"Sounds like. Do you need anything else before I go?"

"I don't need anything from you, but do you know when I have to start behaving like a loyal son and what I'll have to wear?"

"The last I heard was Henry and the Rojas's are returning around four, so if I were you, I'd be ready at three. I haven't heard of any fishing or hunting trips, so I think you'll be safe wearing a suit of the boring color variety."

He focused on smearing peanut butter over his pancake. "Will do. Thanks, Kari."

"You're welcome." She turned to leave but stopped and faced him again. "I wanted to let you know that I appreciate the 'pleases' and 'thank yous'."

"You have Mom to thank for that. Dad's never really been known for showing gratitude." Ray sipped his hot tea. "I remember when I was six, I made everyone I loved a necklace made of macaroni. I decided to go next level with that idea and painted each one special. Paint is my love language. It really hurt my feelings when I found Dad's in his office trashcan the next day when I was playing hide and seek."

Had she made a macaroni necklace for the moms, they

would have worn it every day until it grew mold. Since she couldn't relate at all, his tale left her without words, so she gave him a sad nod and left to prepare for Ricardo and Raquel Rojas.

———

Kari shielded her eyes from the sun as she watched the helicopter touch down. It was then Ray—in his blue suit and gold necktie—stepped out from the shadows with Neill. Once the blades stopped whirling overhead, Henry descended the stairs with the two guests close behind and a megawatt smile.

"Ricardo, Raquel," Henry said once all of his VIP guests were on deck, "this is my son, Raymond."

Ray shook their hands. "It's wonderful to meet you."

Henry watched them shake hands, then gestured to Kari. "And this is Karishma. She'll be your VIP assistant during the morning to early evening hours of your visit. Annabelle will attend to the others."

Kari smiled and extended her hand. She didn't stare at the mole on Ricardo's cheek or the bountiful cleavage that plunged into Raquel's bright blue neckline. "It's a pleasure to meet you both. Do you have bags on board?"

"Yes, one for each of us," Ricardo said with his Venezuelan accent. "Mine is the brown bag. Hers is the trunk that weighs one hundred kilos."

Raquel batted his arm. "Papa's a kidder. It's only fifty kilos. I don't know what that is in your American pounds."

"That would be 110 pounds."

Henry placed a gentle hand on her shoulder. "Karishma is as much of a whiz with numbers as she is languages."

"Do you speak Spanish?" Raquel asked.

In her periphery, Kari caught Ray spin away from the

group, but she smiled politely and asked her next two questions in Spanish: Would you like me to give you the VIP suite tour? Or would you like to stay here to have happy hour with Henry and Ray while I drop off your luggage?

"I would say that after our excursion to the mountain retreat this afternoon," Ricardo said in English, "we shouldn't delay happy hour any longer."

Mountain retreat? That didn't make sense. When she had researched the VIPs, she learned Ricardo had a cabin near La Paz, Bolivia, but that couldn't be where they went. La Paz to Concepción was an airplane trip, not a helicopter one. What other 'retreat' was there?

"Karishma, please handle their luggage and bring us a bottle of the Bordeaux in the top rack of the special wine refrigerator. Neill will need to show you. Oh, and round up some appetizers."

Kari led the way and left the weekender bag in the master bedroom. Neill dropped off the trunk in the smaller, but still impressive, second bedroom.

"I'm surprised they didn't want separate suites," he said.

"She's a licensed physician and he has health issues, so she likes to be nearby. The majority of her trunk is probably monitors of sorts." Kari respected the fact Raquel sought achievement outside of the family business but also recognized that she was probably still a pain in the ass. "I have hope that they'll be better behaved than the Weatherbys."

"They seem lower maintenance. He's not wearing a tie and she's wearing modest shoes."

"I would still bet those shoes cost both of our next paychecks combined." After they dropped off the belongings, she placed a request for the appetizers. "Okay, so, where's this special wine? I thought I knew everything when it came to VIP stuff."

"That's because it's not VIP. He's referring to his personal stash in his cabin."

"No way! We're going into Henry's cabin?" He nodded, and she followed him to the stern of deck eight, where all of the upper-level executives and ship personnel lived. Neill was about to place his thumb on the scanner when she darted her hand out to block it. "Wait. Can I try?"

"Only Henry, myself, and Josef have permissions. Even housekeeping needs either myself or Josef present to clean. Same thing with Madeleine's cabin." Neill placed his giant thumb on the scanner, typed in a code that was easily fifteen digits, and pushed the door open.

The fact that she stood inside Henry's personal space didn't dawn on her until she had gone passed the marble tiled floors of the foyer. Her feet stopped and her eyes darted around the cabin. "Oh my Gods."

It was more than the extreme opulence that made her say that, it was the oil paintings and statues that depicted different deities. In the open expanse of the living room area, she saw Buddha's calm face and lotus pose, Jesus Christ's beard and crown of thorns, Ganesha's elephant head and multiple arms, and the sun over Ra's falcon head.

"I find Henry's taste to be a bit garish," Neil said from the kitchen.

Discovering that her feet worked again, Kari followed him into the top-of-the-line chef's kitchen that Henry, no doubt, had never used. There were no Gods depicted in the room, but the refrigerator did have a collection of magnets that centered around power. She read the nonsensical string of words: *force, capability, strength, aggression.*

"I think that was Madeleine's birthday present to him last year." Neill went to an oak door with grape vines carved at the top and opened it to reveal a massive refrigerator divided into fourths. Red wines were racked on the top and sparkling wines were at the bottom. Lighter red and whites were nestled in the middle. Neill plucked a bottle from the top, read the label, and punched in a serial number on a nearby touch screen. "Okay, let's get back."

Every part of her wanted to take an extra minute to tour his cabin. She knew it was two levels and there had to be secret passages, but Neill was already halfway to the main door. Instead, she committed everything to memory. Everything from the god aesthetic, to the dark cream leather dining chairs and gleaming walnut table, to the chocolate-brown leather seating area in front of a stone wall that had an ornately carved mantel above its . . .

"He has a fireplace!" she yelled in disbelief. "Wait, it has to be fake."

"No. It's a real gas fireplace."

"Seriously? No, fire is like the number one rule on the ship! There isn't even a no murder rule, but there's a fire rule." It was the reason why she let everyone believe her necklace was just that. A necklace.

"If it makes you feel better, the firewalls to his place are three times the thickness of everyplace else on the ship. That also helps with his secret passage access in the powder room."

Kari made a small fist pump in victory. She knew she was right! As they made their way back to the happy hour area, she thought about the fireplace. The logistics gnawed at her. "Where's the propane tank?"

Neill shrugged his massive shoulders. "Don't know."

She brainstormed the possible location as they walked. It had to be outside since it would be too hazardous to have it inside the firewalls, even if they were thicker. Then, it dawned on her. Through the glass wall of his living room, she had caught a glimpse of a statue of Prometheus, the Greek god who stole fire from Olympians and gave it to mortals. Because of the privacy wall and pergola of his balcony, she had never seen it from outside the ship before.

Henry had kept a lot hidden, including how deep his obsession with power went. Did he have a God complex to pair with his narcissism? Probably.

As they walked around the corner in the passageway, she caught the round black lens of the security camera. "Hey. Were you able to fix the security camera issue on my cabin's deck?"

"Yeah, we were. It kind of worked itself out."

Kari uttered a hmph. "Any idea what caused it?"

"No, but I wouldn't worry about it." He pointed to the large pitcher on the center of their low table in the lounge. "I'd be more worried about the state of your VIPs tomorrow morning."

Ricardo looked at her and held up his small glass. "We couldn't wait to get started. We've introduced Henry to the pisco sour."

Since Kari was happy her guest was happy, she gave them an enthusiastic thumbs-up. "Very good, sir. I'll get your appetizers now."

———

For two hours, Kari watched four people genuinely have fun with each other. It was odd. Nice, but odd. Even Ray seemed to be having a good time. The conversation had more to do with art than industry takeovers. And the Rojas's were courteous to her and the other service staff as well. Overall, Kari didn't get the sense they were evil, but there was still time.

"Hey, you," Belle said from behind her.

Kari turned to see her pleasant smile. "Welcome to the party. They've already polished off a pitcher of pisco and a bottle of wine, so this evening ought to be interesting."

"Thanks for the heads-up. Any changes to their schedule or requests that I need to be aware of?"

"None."

"Sounds simple enough." Belle waved to the group. "I guess I should go introduce myself now. Have a good night, Kari. I'll see you bright and early."

"Yep, see you then." Kari glanced at the foursome as they waved goodbye to her. She returned the gesture, then left the deck to pick up her chocolates and give Madeleine her report. When she reached administrative cubicle land, her door was cracked open and she heard Doug's voice.

"I really need your input on Belle's progress," he said. "If I don't get it, they may not continue with the internship program. Think of the kids!"

Madeleine saw Kari and beamed. "Your report has arrived! Kari, describe Belle's progress to Doug here."

"I would say that she's punctual, a self-starter, proactive, thinks outside the box, and knows how to be a team player."

He scoffed. "Those are all buzz words."

"If you need something more detailed, I can write a summary for you and email it."

"Please. Something is better than nothing," he said and then stood. "See you next week, Madeleine. With a report, I hope." He left, closing the door behind him.

"You"—Madeleine pointed to the closed door—"are a godsend. Can you write one of those emails every week for me?"

First there were secret favors, then chocolates, and now this. Kari could feel Madeleine inching closer and closer to her side. But she still couldn't appear too eager to please. "I guess so," she said as she took her seat and placed the chocolates on her lap.

"It's appreciated. How are Ricardo and Raquel fairing?"

"They seem to be enjoying themselves, but no significant shop talk that I've heard."

"Any idea what their earlier trip was about?"

"Not much except that I think Ricardo must have property near here based on a 'retreat' comment he made. I'll ask Belle if she heard anything else about it tomorrow morning."

Madeleine steepled her fingers. "I was wondering why he came to this port and not when we were farther north. Anything else to add?"

"I learned the answer to the Ahmed-Ray question."

"Really?" Madeleine asked with a surprised lilt. "How did you manage that?"

"I asked him."

Her excited expression settled into one of boredom. "Oh. Well, that was rather anti-climactic. What's their story?"

"They have the same bio mom. They're half-brothers."

"Bloody hell!" Not only was Madeleine so shocked that she used slang, but her face went as red as a painting of a bloodied hell. She stood from her desk and faced the wall with her arms crossed, seething with anger. After several moments to collect herself, she faced Kari again. "I need to find Henry's will and see how his assets are split."

"Okay," Kari drawled. That was an unexpected leap, but she'd go with it. "My gut tells me that he hasn't left a dime to Ahmed. I mean, he barely acknowledges his existence."

"No, no, no." To add to the negativity, Madeleine waggled her index finger side to side. "Henry's been talking to his estate attorneys a lot more lately. Between that and this secret VIP nonsense, I have to find out what's going on."

Kari had never seen Madeleine like this before. She was incensed. But not in the way she was when she blew up boats. This was personal. Henry had pulled the rug out from under her so hard and fast she was left tumbling and flailing. This had to have Madeleine questioning her place in the ranks even more than she was before. That was good. That was the instability Kari needed to add a little push to topple it all over.

"I can try to look into that for you," Kari said. "It would help if I knew which law firm because that information is most likely kept with them and not anywhere here."

"Good point. I'll give you the information at the end of your shift tomorrow." Madeleine pointed at the chocolates. "You just earned another box."

Chapter Thirteen

Ushuaia, Argentina

Kari pushed the plastic-wrapped chocolate box in the center of the poker table. "Wrapped for freshness. Enjoy!"

Sven put down his soda—probably with smuggled rum in it—and reached for one. "Thank you."

Nando stopped whatever he was searching for in the room to study the chocolate map.

"Great priorities, Nando," Belle said. "It's not like we need poker chips to play poker or anything."

"I gave up," Nando said as he chose an orange cream. "I don't know where they are, so we'll have to play using something else. Does anyone have any doubloons laying around?"

"Henry does," Belle said.

"What do you mean?" Kari asked.

"When Mr. Rojas left, he gave Henry this really old looking coin."

That sounded a lot like what Jack Weatherby had given Henry when he had left. "Was it made of metal or wood? Did it have something engraved on it?"

"Sorry, detective," Belle said with a smile. "I only saw it from a distance."

"As fascinating as your jobs of catering to rich people are," Craig said, "can we play something?"

"We still have the cards." Sven gestured to the deck then reached in the box for another chocolate. "We could play kings?"

Nando, Craig, and Belle groaned.

"Or not." Sven bit into the chocolate and then moaned. "That is delicious. The raspberry was good, but this pecan caramel is just . . ." He moaned again.

Kari's ears perked. She didn't hate that sound.

"How about Never Have I Ever?" Nando asked. "We haven't played it with Kari yet."

Craig put his beer down. "Oh, I like that idea."

Kari shifted in her seat. "I'm really not that interesting." Or at least the parts of her life that weren't based in paranormal ability or her work as a billionaire blackmail gatherer weren't interesting. Yep, she was just a regular person.

"I think we should be the judge of that," Belle said with a mischievous smile. "Unless you're uncomfortable, then we—"

"No, it's okay," Kari said. "I'll play."

"Great!" Craig rubbed his hands together in anticipation. "Never have I ever"—he stared at her while he contemplated—"fired a gun."

They went through a dozen more questions that included fighting, sex in cars, skinny-dipping, shoplifting, karaoke, and getting stitches before the next juicy round.

"Never have I ever been in love," Nando said.

Everyone drank except for Craig and Kari.

"I'm surprised," Belle said. "How about your ex?"

Kari's feelings about Nicholas had evolved over the past two years. "I think I thought that I loved him at the time, but in retrospect, I think I was more in love with the idea of him. The idea that someone could want me in that way."

"Did he love you?" Sven asked.

Thanks to her handy-dandy brain, she knew Nicholas had wrestled with this emotion, too. "He said he did, but . . . I held back in a lot of ways, so since he didn't know me, I don't think he could have loved me."

"How did you hold back?" Nando said.

Kari remembered something Belle had told her back in Chile. "I couldn't tell him some important parts about me and the traumatic things my family went through. I think that if I had loved him, I would have found a way."

"I think you can still love someone and not tell them every single thing about yourself," Craig said.

Sven scoffed. "Says the guy who has never been in love. But, Kari, you wouldn't have gone to the edge of the Earth and back for Nicholas?"

Kari stifled a laugh. "I wouldn't even visit him when he went away to art school, and I could have since my grad school was online. I'm not even mad at him anymore for cheating on me. Just wasn't meant to be." The eight eyeballs looking in her direction all had a trace of pity in them. She had to turn that mood around. "Which is why I never should have had sex with him in a car. Not comfortable at all."

"You're next, Belle," Nando said. "You've been unusually quiet. Who have you loved?"

She bit her lower lip and looked down at the table as if she didn't want to answer. "I loved Tess. Love Tess. I don't know the best way to say it when that person is no longer with us."

Craig's boisterous expression vanished. "What happened?"

Belle continued to focus on the table. "Army. KIA."

Sven pinched his brow. "What is . . ."

"Killed in action," Kari answered softly. She hadn't

consciously placed her hand on Belle's shoulder, but it was there. "I'm so, so sorry."

Belle finally looked up from the table to her. "Thank you." There was a haunted look in her eyes but then she blinked it away. "Next," she said as she pointed to Sven.

"I've loved all the women I've dated," he said, "but I know they have not all loved me. That's the part that hurts."

"Not to sound like a jerk," Craig said, "but it sounds like you love pretty easily."

"I guess I do," Sven said. "But I don't know how not to be passionate."

"So, it's all or nothing for you?" Nando asked.

"Maybe. But that also makes me an excellent lover." Sven grinned at Kari. "What'd you think about that?"

"Pass for now," Kari said. "Okay, never have I ever witnessed or found evidence of my parents' sex life." She drank and waited for the rest to catch up.

———

"I'm surprised how you responded to Sven's proposition," Belle said as they left the club room together.

"What do you mean?"

"He clearly wants to go out with you and you responded 'pass for now' which implies that you might want to later."

"That's because I might. He has a pretty face, is nice, possibly has culinary skills, and likes me. That's more than a lot of other people have going for them." Kari glanced over and saw Belle's neutral face, which meant she had feelings about it. Had that response hurt her feelings? It was times like this when mind reading would have been a nice tool to have. "What do you think?"

"I think that if your mental health is at a point where you feel ready to date and want to, then you should."

The response was too perfect. Almost like it had been tested in a focus group. "Would that make things weird between us?"

Belle kept her eyes locked forward. "It shouldn't. We had a very clear conversation where we mutually decided that it'd be a bad idea if we pursued that. Having said that, you still may want to think twice about Sven. It sounds like he develops feelings fast and, based on what you've told me, that might create complications down the road."

The rest of their walk to Belle's cabin was filled with awkward silence. Which was a first.

Belle stopped in front of her dorm. "I almost forgot to ask you why you were so intrigued by the Rojas's coin?"

Kari was torn whether or not to tell her, but Belle could be her eyes and ears when she was off shift. It was low risk intel gathering and that was worth Belle knowing. "At the end of the Weatherby visit, Jack gave Henry an old coin, too."

"Really? That's a weird coincidence."

"Agreed, so I'm starting to think that it's not a coincidence. If you see any other VIPs give Henry something that looks like that, can you tell me?"

"Why?"

"You know why?"

Belle's jaw muscles twitched. Then, she opened her cabin door, grabbed Kari's backpack strap, pulled her inside, and shut the door behind them. Vy wasn't there.

"What was that about?" Kari asked, shocked by Belle's behavior. Although, she didn't hate the rough handling. Add that and hair pulling to her turn-on list.

"You need to be careful," Belle said. "Per your own words,

there are dangerous people here, and trying to be sneaky to send Adam Cho information is not being careful."

Kari readjusted her pack. "I'm only asking for the sake of my own curiosity."

"Do you promise that's why?"

Kari gave a dutiful nod. "I have no plans to contact Adam." She left out 'at this time'. Belle had no idea—and would never know—how she covered her tracks. "Does that make you feel better?"

Belle glanced over to her dresser where the picture of Tess was, then sighed. "I don't know. I suppose. But I still don't like what you're doing."

Kari saw annoyance mixed with something else. Was it fear? Were the risks she was taking reminding her of Tess? "Can I ask if the reason you're so worried is because of something else that's happened to you?"

Belle looked everywhere but at her. "I can't talk about it now."

"I understand. But maybe you'd feel better if you t—"

"Kari," Belle said, her voice firm, "please be careful and good night."

She hadn't been reprimanded, but the new tone that was both severe and concerned caused Kari to backpedal. "Okay. I promise. Good night to you, too."

Kari walked down the passage and stairways while the same but very different questions bounced around her head. Was Tess the dark spot in Belle's past? Had Belle seen a therapist to work through her trauma like Kari had? And why was Henry getting coins?

She recycled the champagne bottle, went to her cabin, and turned on her electric kettle. After changing into her pajamas, she settled on the loveseat with a cup of orange spice tea, and grabbed her new tablet—courtesy of the lost and found at the

Penguin Watching Tour—to continue her next activity: The search for Henry's will.

Her search was interrupted with a buzz from an incoming text. Kari brought the screen to life and did a double-take when she saw the message was from Finn.

I thought you'd like to know that Gabriella is happy to hear the visit with Ricardo went so well. He mentioned how much he likes you. Thinks Ray is a bit of a pushover. Good luck with JM.

Earlier questions about Tess, therapy, coins, and wills were replaced by much larger and more urgent questions. Her thumbs hit the letters in rapid fire for her text back.

Why does Gabriella know about the Rojas and Weatherby visits? And by JM, do you mean Jasi Monye?

The blinking dots that indicated Finn was returning her text went on for far too long considering the message she received.

Never mind.

Kari waited several more minutes for a follow-up message, but there was none. The idea that Finn knew about a possible future guest—a guest on that Brisbane list no less—itched at her brain. And in order to scratch that itch, she needed to get to the VIP computer.

She slid on her flip-flops and left her cabin, not caring that she only wore faded starry pajama bottoms and her orange hooded sweatshirt. She strode into the VIP assistant office.

Matthew stopped typing and looked away from the

computer to her. "This is a surprise. What do I owe the pleasure of this visit?"

"Can you check our upcoming VIP list and tell me if you see anyone who was recently added?"

"Sure thing." He clicked and scrolled until he gave her a smile with those impossibly thin lips of his. "Here we go. Jasi Monye and his son will be our VIPs when we get to Cape Town. They'll be using both suites." Matthew went back to his clicking and scrolling. "Well, that's interesting. They were both added this morning by Henry. Does that seem weird to you that Henry added them into the system and not Madeleine? Because it does to me."

"Yeah, that's weird," Kari said, even though to her the pieces were falling into place. "Can you see if Henry's added other people?"

"The whole history? Or just after today?"

"Just after today."

More clicking and scrolling. "There are three more after Cape Town. Henry added Amara Gupta and daughter for Dubai, Gabriella Fermi and her sister when we're in the Maldives around New Year, and then Botan Itoi and associate after our PNG stop. Fermi, Gupta, and Botan are listed as tentative."

Finn must not have known about the potential Fermi visit or they would have said something. "Is Ray listed for those visits?"

"Um . . ." Matthew squinted as he scanned the screen. "Yes. He has the same status as those VIPs."

Everyone on the Brisbane list was accounted for, but their presence wasn't definite. That was curious. "Thanks, Matthew."

"Sure thing. Can I ask why the sudden urgency to ask?"

"Um." Kari shifted from side to side in her flip-flops. "I'm visiting my family soon and want to prep Belle with the people who may be coming. As her mentor, I wanted to create an extension of learning activity for her."

"Oh, I get it. I have no doubt she'll ace it. Belle's bloody brilliant."

"Yes, she is, and thanks. Have a good rest of your shift." Kari put her hands in her hoodie pockets and headed back to her cabin.

Once Kari arrived, she reheated her tea in the microwave and paced while she mulled over the new information. Fact one, all of the In Virtute members on the Brisbane list had either visited or were planning to visit the *Hinewai*. Fact two, Henry's name had also been on the Brisbane list but with a question mark. And fact three, based on what Finn relayed, Jack Weatherby and Ricardo Rojas had spoken to Gabriella about how the visit went.

The microwave beeped as Kari reached her epiphany.

Henry was essentially in the tryout process for In Virtute with coins being given out for a successful visit. But why was Ray on board when Henry wanted nothing to do with him? Kari pulled out her tea while the question steeped in her mind. Fact four, the In Virtute VIPs always had someone else close with them. Most had a child.

The next light bulb moment struck her so hard that she had to sit on her bed. These seven people, including Henry, were the most connected, influential, and powerful people on the planet. Especially if they worked together.

So much for what she had promised Belle.

Kari needed to tell Adam. But without a burner phone, she'd have to wait.

Chapter Fourteen

Rio de Janeiro, Brazil

Due to a once-in-a-century storm, Kari never made it ashore in Montevideo. Nando couldn't even visit his family or the refugee center for a school project he had been working on. Fortunately, the *Hinewai* did have another major stop before her trip to Michigan and the transatlantic trip to Cape Town to contact Adam. And take care of a few other things.

The knock startled her, but Jade was right on schedule. Although, she looked as though to be on time she had to skip sleeping. Jade had bags under her eyes that were so pronounced her pink glasses were practically resting in them. "What's wrong?" Kari stepped to the side to let her in.

"My energy is zapped."

"You're not sick, are you? Because I can text or email you the pictures."

"I don't have a fever or cough or anything. I just feel blah."

"I'm sorry to hear that. We should probably cancel our game play for tonight, even though I don't want to. I miss you."

Jade nodded and pushed up her glasses. "I miss you, too. I

promise once I get my energy back, table tennis with you is the first priority. Banging Neill is second."

"I appreciate where I land in that order." Kari waved her over to the small table and shifted the laptop so it faced both of them. "These are the haircuts I've narrowed down based on my ultimate haircut goal."

Jade stifled a laugh. "Only you would say it that way. What's the ultimate goal?"

"Cool, fun hair." Kari showed her the collection of stylish short haircuts and noted Jade's honest opinion of each. After the show and tell, she shut her laptop. "Now, take it easy this weekend. Watch some movies or call Diana before the time zones really start messing with us."

Jade smiled as she stood. "Both are good ideas. I need to find out how my lovely daughter did on her LSATs. I'll see you later."

Once Jade left, Kari grabbed the few items she needed for her day trip. But unlike other trips, this time she was going with her friends. Nando spoke Portuguese, so he'd offered to act as a translator, if necessary, in exchange for lunch. Craig needed to take pictures for class. Belle simply wanted to take advantage of land before the eleven-day voyage. Sven wanted a haircut, too. Although, because of his beanie, she had never seen his hair and had no idea what kind of style he could get.

As Kari boarded the tender, she could make out dozens of interesting and famous landmarks of the port city. There were strips of the famous Copacabana Beach, hundreds of high rises, the massive grass-covered land formations that jutted out of the harbor like tall islands, and the famous statue of Christ the Redeemer where Jesus's arms were outstretched to form a cross. Belle leaned over the stern and pointed to something on shore.

"Whatcha doin'?" Kari asked as a way of announcing her presence. "Checkin' out Jesus?"

The three friends turned to her in unison, but Nando answered, "Craig told us this was a nude beach, but we don't think it is."

"I had a great idea for a picture," Craig said. "I think it would turn out tasteful."

"Speaking of pictures, but not pervy ones." Kari aimed her phone's camera at the scenery and snapped the photo. "This will function well as my check-in with the moms."

"You don't want us in it?" Sven exclaimed in mock outrage.

"They do get really excited when they see my friends." She directed them how to group together to capture the scenery. For the five of them to fit inside the frame, Sven and Nando squatted in the front while Craig and Belle stood on either side of Kari. The Jesus cross rested on Belle's head, which was appropriate.

Kari sent the pictures to her moms and listened to the chatter among her friends as they went into shore. Her hair appointment wasn't for another hour, so she went to the shops with the others and bought a few snacks, items at the pharmacy, and, when the others lingered in a tourist trap, she left for the corner store and bought a burner phone. Also gum in case someone asked.

"Where'd you go?" Belle asked, alarmed once they met outside. "There's a buddy system in a big city. I'm your buddy! Even with your self-defense moves, you can't wander off like that."

Kari had no idea Belle took that system so seriously. "I told Nando, but I promise I'll tell the whole group next time." She pulled a pack of gum out of her day bag. "Want some?"

"Oh, yes." Sven took a piece while the others declined.

"We should head down to the stylist now. We don't want to be late."

Kari plugged the address of the salon into her phone. "We'll meet you at the restaurant when we're done."

———

After a luxurious shampooing and conditioning, Kari watched the show—via the mirror—of a man receiving an old-fashioned straight-razor shave while her hair was cut and sculpted to deliver the messy pixie haircut she wanted.

"Your hair is very cute," Sven said from behind her at the register. "Like a fairy girl or something."

She spun to him and tried not to gasp. Or drool. Hair like corn silk fell slightly past his shoulders. "You have long hair?" How could he have kept such an important detail away from her?

"Partially." He gathered his hair into a ponytail—the bottom half had an undercut—and finished putting it into a bun before he pulled the beanie back out of his pocket and pulled it over his head. "Every time I ask someone to do it on the ship, they either screw up or shave bad things in it."

"Why do you have long hair if you hide it?" That was a Greek tragedy starring hair.

"Long hair makes me feel like a Viking, but I also keep it up so it doesn't get in the food I make." He laughed and pointed at her. "You think my longer hair is sexy. I can tell."

Oh, it was going to be like that, was it? "It looks nice, that's all. Also, the Vikings weren't from Finland."

"Ah, ah, ah," he taunted and booped her nose with his index finger. "My mother is Swedish."

The nose boop was equally cute as it was annoying.

"Alright, Viking explorer, lead me to that purple-sequined octopus restaurant."

As they dodged other tourists on their way to the gawdy beachside landmark, they chatted about Sven's self-described mastery of challenging culinary techniques. Nando, Craig, and Belle were at a table on the patio, each with clear drinks garnished with slices of lime.

Belle beamed behind her sunglasses. "I love your haircut!"

Sven took off his beanie. "And me?"

Nando and Belle shrugged.

"I liked it more when there was a dick shaved into it," Craig said.

"Well, Kari likes my hair." To show his appreciation, Sven pulled out Kari's chair. "What are you drinking?"

"The waitress suggested the caipirinhas," Belle said. "Which, after waiting for this table in the heat for forty-five minutes, wasn't a hard sell."

"She'll be coming back with menus, too," Craig said.

"Excellent." Sven rubbed his hands together. "I can add to my collection."

"You steal menus?" Nando asked

"No! I take as many pictures related to food as possible and then place them in my inspiration folder. I think about the details of my future restaurant a lot and what the food or even the menu looks like is an important part of that." Sven took a series of pictures of the front and back of the menus.

"I could give you some tips when it comes to that," Craig said. "Lighting, filters. Stuff like that."

"That would be great! Thanks. And it would make up for the time you shaved genitals on my head."

Kari thought more about Sven's dream and the steps he was taking to reach it. She didn't know the long-term goals for her other friends. "Where do the rest of you see yourselves in five years?"

"You know mine already," Belle said.

"I know that someday you want to manage your own ski resort in the Smoky Mountains, but do you really see that happening in five years?"

"Point taken." Belle leaned back in her chair and crossed her arms. "Then . . . probably holding different positions at a ski resort to learn the ropes."

"How about family?" Nando asked.

Belle's brow knit together. "Do you mean like married and kids?"

Nando nodded.

"Not really. I want to focus on my career. How about you, Nando? What's your five-year plan?"

"I've actually been thinking of turning the information I've learned about hospitality and living on the *Hinewai* and putting those two things to use in a way to help people in need, like refugees or people affected by coastal disasters."

Sven's eyebrows disappeared into his beanie. "That's a great idea!"

"It really is," Belle said. "How do you see that working?"

"I'm not sure yet, but there's a lot of overlap, like rooms, shelter, food, transportation. I still need to work out the details. How about you, Craig?"

"I'd like to land with a company that does extreme sports photography. I really love the idea that I can capture an image that'll stick around for centuries. It's like being immortal. Probably meet some cool people, too." He finished his drink, the suction from his straw making it obvious. "How about you, Kari?"

"Me?"

Sven gave her a friendly nudge. "That's true. You can't ask us and not answer it yourself."

Belle shot her a look over her drink that said, 'you don't have to tell the whole truth.' "Come on. Surely, you have some idea."

"Okay, then." Kari pursed her lips as she thought about the safest and most truthful answer she could give. Despite lingering fears about Henry, Madeleine, and Josef, deep down she knew she could outsmart them. She would win. She would have a well-adjusted, happy future in five years. "I know I'll be off the *Hinewai,* but what I want to do . . . My number one goal used to be to go to medical school, but it's not anymore."

Sven leaned his elbow on the table and placed his chin in his hand. "Why not?"

"Well, as selfish as it might sound, I wanted the skills to get rid of my seizure issue, but I was fortunately able to do that last year. Like Nando, I do want to do something to improve society.

"As for family, I'd like to live an hour or so away from my moms or my grandparents. Then, I don't have to hear Mom A bitch about the fuel it takes to fly. It is a valid point, but it's really annoying the way she does it." For the other part of the future that she wanted, she braced herself for the anticipated mockery. "And I don't see myself married or with kids ever, but I do see myself with dogs."

"Really?" Belle's eyes sparkled with her bright smile. "What kind of dogs?"

Kari knew her own expression matched Belle's. "I've always wanted something like a golden retriever mix." She smiled even wider as she pictured a reoccurring daydream. "It's like I see an image of me from above—"

"Are you dead?" Craig asked.

Nando slapped his arm. "Please continue, Kari."

"Anyway, I see this image of me where I'm sitting in a rocking chair, playing my guitar in front of a fireplace—no, make that a wood stove—and there's a big, sleepy, yellow dog at my feet. On the couch, curled on a blanket is a smaller, ugly but cute dog. I think that's enough companionship for me."

"No people?" Sven asked.

"I'll have my family and I'll see people at work—whatever that is—or when I need to get supplies for my little cabin in the woods."

"That sounds so lonely," Sven said.

"No, it doesn't," Belle said without taking her gaze off Kari. "I think it sounds lovely. I hope you get that someday."

After a few moments of quiet, Nando broke the silence by blowing a raspberry. "That conversation went deep. I thought we'd people watch and rank their swimwear or something."

"We can still do that!" Craig said.

"Yeah", "totally", and "if you want" followed.

With the beach fashion show a focus of conversation, they took their time enjoying their drinks and plates of local favorites. Once they sensed their waitress getting annoyed they weren't ordering more food, they headed back to the tender. Despite not ordering more, Kari was stuffed to the gills, so she stood by the railing in case her meal tried to make a hasty exit.

"You look queasy," Belle said as she sidled beside her.

"I shouldn't have had that last codfish ball."

"I'll try to take your mind off it then." The engines of the tender started and created a loud rumble under their feet. Belle leaned back with her forearms on the railing. "Are you excited for your trip to your grandparents' house?"

She could answer a simple question. "I am. My other grandmother, Nani Tanha, is coming too and flying in with my moms. Then, my uncle River and my two cousins will be there at times." She was excited to see her cousin, Logan, at least.

"That sounds like a lot of family. Do the two sides get together often?"

"Not really, but with my travel schedule now, Nani Tanha thought it'd be easier to see me this way. She's the only one on my Mom L's side I see now that Nana Sid died a few years ago."

"That's . . . It's pretty amazing you have family that loves you like that."

Kari had her vision locked on the beach but rotated her head to see Belle staring off into the distance and picking at her fingernail. Belle didn't dream of a family in the future, probably because her one from the past was so awful. "I know I lucked out in that department."

"That's good." Belle sighed again and shook her head. "I have no idea what I'm going to do while you're gone. After Rio, there're no new VIPs and we'll be at sea for over a week. I'm already bored thinking about it."

Kari sympathized with her. "Want to start a movie and book club? We can share our thoughts via text since time zone differences will be an obstacle."

"That sounds promising." Belle bobbed her head as though she were thinking about it. "Okay, I'm in."

"Great! And that'll give me something to do if I have an unexpected layover or something."

Chapter Fifteen

Upper Peninsula, Michigan, United States

The TV show Belle had described as 'queer historic fiction' proved to be an excellent use of time during her five-hour layover in Miami. But, then again, so was her call on her way to the Rio de Janeiro airport to Adam's assistant, where she had said, "Sky Fisher. R. Rojas visited. Next visitors J. Monye, A. Gupta, and B. Itoi. No need to contact me back."

After an almost twenty-four-hour journey, Kari arrived after midnight, and while she had been able to secure a hotel, she didn't have the energy to watch the northern lights from its parking lot. That was a first. She'd cross her fingers the sun had particles to shoot at Earth the following night and get a report about the night's astronomy show the following afternoon when the moms picked her up.

"Chickpea!" Mom A rushed her in the hotel's lobby, knocking Kari off-balance with her hug. "I love your hair! It's so cute."

"I missed you too." Kari disengaged from the contact. "Where's the other one?"

"I think you mean the other two."

"Nani Tanha's here?" As soon as she'd asked, Kari watched her eighty-plus-year-old grandmother through the glass of the lobby windows with Mom L in position close behind to catch her. Her grandmother used her cane to push the large blue square button to open the automatic door. Kari abandoned her luggage and went to them. "Nani Tanha!" She hugged her in the gentlest way she could, even though she wanted to squeeze her to pieces. It had been eighteen months since they had last seen each other. "I missed you so much," Kari said and immediately heard the crackling of the feedback from her grandmother's hearing aid. "I should have flown down to Portland for a visit when we were in Vancouver."

"Quite alright." Nani Tanha gave Kari soft pats on the back. "It's easier for me to go to others, even if that means I can't have any peace when I do so." She dropped her voice to what she believed was a whisper. "Leela has not left my side. She thinks I belong in a convalescent home."

"It's just because I'm worried some hurried traveler or a stiff breeze will knock you over," Mom L said. "Come here, chickpea."

The scent of warm citrus enveloped her as they hugged. "It's great to see you, Mom L."

"We're really glad you're here to join the circus." Mom L released her but kept a gentle grip on Kari's hands. "Things have been a little crazy."

"She means me and this visit," Nani Tanha said. "But it's been ages since I've seen you or Aurora's side of the family. It's important to me that I maximize my time with loved ones before I die."

"What?" Kari took a step back as her heart sank. "You're sick?"

Behind Nani Tanha, both Moms shook their heads.

"You don't have to be sick to die," Nani Tanha said, "especially with my ticking clock."

"And on that note," Mom A said, "let's get in the car and head off to see your other grandparents. They're pretty excited to see you, too."

The drive from the airport wasn't filled with the usual chatter of what sorts of activities they could do as a family. Rather, they had a philosophical discussion of life and death, courtesy of her grandmother. Nani Tanha was a daughter, sister, mother, wife, ex-wife, in-law, and friend. She was an immigrant who battled misogyny and racism to become a top cardiologist in Portland. She had saved lives and also watched many literally slip from her fingers.

"And it's not just about spending time with my loved ones," Nani Tanha said from the front passenger seat, "it's about checking items off my bucket list. I spent eighty-four years of my life studying, educating, saving lives, trying to be a good mother, trying to be a half-decent wife. I never did mushrooms and now, I fear, it's too late."

"You've had some real interesting epiphanies about mortality," Kari said as she watched the trees on the highway whiz by.

Nani Tanha twisted the best she could to face the back. "You need to do these things now while you're young!"

"Or maybe not," Mom A said. "Doing mushrooms outside of a ceremony and not knowing sources can be incredibly dangerous."

"Not to mention the fact that it's illegal in a lot of places," Mom L said.

Nani Tanha waved her hand in a dismissive motion. "Such a dumb law. It's right up there with not being allowed to drive your car backward."

Mom L gripped the steering wheel with both hands. "That was dangerous!"

"And so is driving forward with a shattered front windshield courtesy of a construction vehicle," Nani Tanha reasoned. "I performed cardiac surgery once during a power outage without a generator! I can drive a car down a few straight streets backward and pull it off to the side of the road for the police with their obnoxious lights. But the point is this: I need to spend more time with my only granddaughter before she leaves again. Even if that means I have to share her with others."

Her grandmother wasn't the most sentimental, but her words made Kari smile. "I'm excited to spend time with you, too. Also, tell me about that surgery! Sounds wild."

After hearing the details of that story, Mom L parked along the curb in front of her other grandparents' home. "Are you ready for round two, chickpea?"

"As ready as I'll ever be. Am I still sleeping in the basement? Or does Nani Tanha have it?" Kari asked as she got out of the rental car.

"You have the basement. Tanha has a hotel close to here." Mom A met her at the trunk and then hugged her again. "It's so good that you're here. It means a lot to everyone."

"I said I would come."

"Yeah, but a lot of people break promises like that."

"Chickpea!" Noko Ani, her somewhat more vibrant seventy-year-old grandmother, walked a fast pace out of the home and hugged Kari with the sway she always added. "It's so good to see you! How was your trip?"

"So, so long. I'm glad I gave myself a buffer day for traveling back."

"Let's not focus on you leaving when we're so excited that you're here," Noko Ani said. "We need to get caught up, and we can start by chatting while we make dinner."

It was nice having three grandparents, two parents, an uncle, and the non-evil cousin together. However, squeezing everyone into the small dining area had an unintended consequence. Between the body heat, the wood stove, wild rice and vegetable soup, warm bread, and the collective pressure of two grandmothers insisting she wear a sweater, Kari thought she would pass out.

"I have to get out of here or I might die from heat stroke," Kari whispered to Mom L, who had shared with her earlier that she was still having hot flashes.

"I died an hour ago and this is my ghost speaking. You go. Save yourself."

Rather than interrupt the boisterous conversation of memory lane between Mom A and Uncle River, Kari picked up her dishes and headed to the dishwasher. After her dishes were loaded, she made a beeline for the back door. Sweet, cool air struck her face and began to bring her core body temperature down to a medically acceptable level. Kari breathed the crisp, early night air in deeper and exhaled to make a cloud. The wispy haze combined with the electric colors in the sky from the northern lights made her wonder if this was the magic mushroom experience Nani Tanha wanted.

"You escaped, too, huh?" Logan asked from the side of the house. He had started a small fire in the pit in front of him, where a pile of fallen leaves had been raked a safe distance away from the flames.

Kari approached her eldest cousin and smiled. When she had been growing up, Logan could do no wrong. He was brave. He was street smart. And he couldn't stand his younger brother, Wade, which was something they continuously bonded over. Now the idolization was replaced with respect for how Logan had made his own path. After high school, he had enlisted in the Army and spent four years there. He followed that by earning his bachelor's degree in history education. Now he was a teacher and hockey coach at a local school.

Who was currently smoking a joint by the fire pit and watching nature's light show.

"Care if I join you?" The smoke from the logs and the marijuana became more noticeable as she neared.

In response, he held the joint out for her.

"I was referring to sitting in one of the chairs, but sure. Don't mind if I do." She plucked it from between his fingers and took a hit before handing it back.

"I'm surprised you know how to do that given your refusal to go to parties."

She kept the smoke in her lungs a few seconds before exhaling. "I had to look it up online after I had pinched enough of the moms' stash to try it myself."

His cheeks became even fuller when he laughed. "I'm surprised they didn't teach you themselves."

"They walk a tight line with culture and the law, especially since Mom L got into politics." She took the seat beside him and lost herself in the shimmering neon green light above. The colors would really pop closer to midnight. "So, how have you been?"

"You were at the same table I was when I gave my report."

"Yeah, but it was the safe response you give relatives when they ask. How are you really?"

He shrugged and took another puff before passing it back to her. "Still trying to figure out my place. Every time I go somewhere new, it's like I have to change in some way. My biggest challenge used to be not pissing off my CO or stepping on an IED, but now it's to be more interesting than a phone or a sketch of a dick. Student teaching was bullshit compared to this. It's so much harder and there's no one at my school to vent to. When I bring up how frustrated I am, they laugh at me like, 'Yep. That's the way it is. Welcome to the club.' They're so complacent it makes me sad and pisses me off."

"Do you have friends that are still here you could talk to about it?" she asked in a strained breath before exhaling.

Logan winced. "The friends I have here are the ones that never left, so this town is all they know and it shows. I tried hanging out with them a few times, but it's not the same. I'm thinking of moving."

"To where?"

"I don't know. You've seen the whole world, do you have any suggestions?"

"Not the whole world, but from what I've seen . . . The Maltese Islands are gorgeous. Osaka had everything plus infinity. Food in Barcelona was phenomenal. I was just in Rio and . . . that Jesus is big."

He doubled over with laughter. "You sound like a damn tour guide. Forget that doctor business."

"Yeah, I'm not doing that anymore. Don't tell Dr. Tanha Mitra in there."

He took another hit. "I won't. You're allowed to change your mind. So am I for that matter."

"Hey, kids!" Mom L yelled from right outside the door and then walked toward them with a smirk. "I smell the devil's lettuce."

Logan held out the joint to her. "I swear it's not mine, officer."

"That's mayor, not officer, and no thanks. As much as I'd love to partake, I have to drive Mom back to her hotel. She's getting pretty sleepy."

"It's seven o'clock!" Kari said.

"Today was a busy and emotional day for her and, much

like a child, if she doesn't get enough sleep, she'll get cranky. I'll be back before you know it. In the meantime"—Mom L shifted her attention to Logan—"I'm supposed to tell you that the desserts are out, which I'm thinking you'll both"—she leveled her gaze to Kari—"really appreciate soon."

"I would never," Kari said in her most serious voice.

"Oh, you absolutely would." Mom L started to walk away, but then stopped and turned. "Honestly, it's nice to see you two bond over something that isn't hating Wade."

Kari shook her head as her mom left. "She had to ruin the moment by bringing up that cockwaffle."

Logan broke into a laugh, complete with snort. "Oh, there's a new story about him, but Dad tells it the best." He tossed the roach into the fire pit and looked up at the night sky once more. "Do you believe in aliens?"

"One hundred percent." Given the expanse of the universe, it just made sense to her. Kari took out her phone, chose the right filter, and hit record to capture the fleeting beauty of the northern lights.

"Hoping to see intelligent life?"

"I think my friend, Belle, would like to see it." She stopped the recording and sent the clip.

"You have a friend? Wow, smoking pot and now this. You have changed!"

"Shut up." She stood with a grin and put away her phone. "Come on, let's eat some fry bread."

———

Muffled laughter from the floor above woke Kari, but a peek at the window showed complete darkness outside. She groaned and rolled over to check the time on her phone: six am. She also had four texts from Belle. Kari found the energy to quickly sit up and read them.

> That video you sent is amazing! I wish I could have been there to see the lights with you.

> Did you know they're making a Lieutenant Streets 2? How can they top the perfection of the first?

> I will never forgive you for recommending 50% Lungs, 100% Heart. I ugly cried for hours. Vy was concerned.

> Starting the second book rec today. Did you read or watch any of mine yet?

Kari texted back.

> You were there in spirit. I watched Daughters of Saratoga in the airport and finished the first book in the Dr. Adams series. I have a lot of thoughts I'll send after coffee.

After she sent the reply, Kari added a second text.

> Do you believe in aliens?

Kari headed up the stairs, phone in hand, and identified the giggles as belonging to her grandparents from the Mom A variety. "You two are having fun up here."

"Good morning." Ata Niq gave her a side hug from his seated position. "There's coffee on, if you'd like."

"Oh, I'd like." Kari went to the mostly full carafe and poured herself a cup of what she anticipated to be mediocre coffee. Her first sip confirmed it, but when most of the family drank tea, this was to be expected. She joined them at the dining table. "It feels like I was just sitting here."

"I can get you a snack if you can't wait for the big breakfast," Noko Ani said.

Kari could swear the elastic on her pajama pants was already tighter than usual. "If you give me more food right now, I might roll around instead of walk today. I ate way too much last night."

"I wonder why?" Ata Niq snickered. "We don't know what was funnier, you and Logan talking about the lights or when Tanha and Leela were on the same charades team. They were such a hoot. We were just laughing about it before you came up. I'm sorry if that's what woke you."

"It's fine. The travel is the biggest culprit. I am not looking forward to the time zone leap when I get to Cape Town," she said into the blackness of her coffee.

"Where do you suppose that ship of yours is right now?" Noko Ani asked.

"That's an easy question to answer." Kari went to the *Hinewai* app's navigation tab. A map of the world appeared with a red dot off the coast of South America. She flipped her phone around so her grandparents could see. "They're here."

"That's so nifty!" Ata Niq looked at her with pure delight. "Does it tell you how fast it's going?"

Kari should have known her grandfather would have had follow-up questions. He loved all things mechanical and engineering. "At sea we average fifteen knots." She clicked on the gear icon of the ship, and then uttered a, "Huh," when she saw the speed. "That's weird. It's going twenty-five knots. I don't think we've ever gone that fast."

"Maybe it's trying to outrun bad weather?" Ata Niq suggested.

"Maybe." But if weather were the case, usually the ship

steered around it, slowed down, or drifted a bit to save fuel, like when they approached Montevideo. She'd text Belle and ask as soon as she had the opportunity.

"Do you still like working there?" The skeptical squint Noko Ani directed at her was impossible to miss.

She needed to focus on the question and not worry about the ship. Kari took a drink and wrapped her hands around the cup. "It's not the most intellectually stimulating job, but I enjoy the ship. And the people. My therapist is great and I've made a lot of progress. Case in point, I didn't have any nightmares last night despite the fire pit time with Logan. I have friends—plural—for the first time ever." Kari opened her photo gallery and handed it to her grandmother, who held the phone away from her at various distances to focus the image.

"You do have a lot of friends!" Ata Niq said, who always had his reading glasses ready.

"I'm so happy for you, chickpea, but it does still bother me that you silenced your gift. The Creator gave that to you for a reason."

Kari knew from experience that eye rolling was the most disrespectful reaction, so she converted it into a frustrated groan. "You know my stance is that by that logic, the Creator also gave me the intelligence to solve the problem I had of not having healthy relationships and hating most people."

Her grandmother skewed her mouth, which Kari knew meant disappointment. Fortunately, the creaking of floorboards that came from the direction of her moms' room in the house provided the distraction necessary to change the topic.

"Sounds like we've woken the stragglers." Ata Niq stood with a grunt and filled the kettle. "Do you think I should get the maple syrup out for Aurora's tea?"

She didn't want Mom A to develop the issues Ray had.

"You should probably let that temptation go. Since her last blood work, she's watching her sugar like a hawk."

As the creaks became louder, her grandparents fussed in the kitchen for the new arrivals. Kari used that time to text Belle.

> Do you know why the ship is going 25 knots?

The blinking response dots were immediate.

> What?!?!?! I'll go see what I can find out.
> Also, I absolutely believe there are aliens.

> If you find out about the ship, please let me know.

The hand on her shoulder made Kari flinch.

"Texting Belle, huh?" Mom A said, then followed it with a low chuckle.

"You know what"—Kari grabbed her coffee—"I'm going to get my shower while you all chat about our extended family adventures for the day."

Kari went back down to the basement to collect her clothes and toiletries before heading into the bathroom. The room was as modest as they came, but, oh my, was that shower spacious compared to hers on the ship. She hadn't been planning on it, but she had to take advantage of the roominess to shave her legs.

When she returned to her sleeping quarters to ditch her pajamas and hang her towel to dry, she checked her phone. She had several texts from Belle and three missed calls from 'Restricted Caller'. No voicemails were left, so she went straight to reading Belle's texts.

We weren't the only ones who were surprised.
Madeleine had no idea.

There's a change of schedule with the Monye
visit. It's been bumped up.

Shit. Kari had a feeling she knew who the unknown caller was, but she was on approved vacation. She was not calling back.

With her phone tucked into her cargo pants, she took her empty coffee cup with her up the stairs for a refill. "And what activities did you all decide while I was freshening up?"

"There's a trunk-or-treat for the five and under crowd at the community center this afternoon," Noko Ani said. "It's on the way to Tanha's ho—" The cordless phone on the wall behind her rang. "One second. Let me get that."

"I can't believe they still have a house phone," she whispered to Mom A.

"It's the only way Dad can get a phone book," Mom A whispered back.

"Oh, yes, she's here," Noko Ani said into the phone. "May I ask who's calling?" After a period of silence, Noko Ani nodded and cupped her hand over the bottom portion of the phone. "Chickpea, Madeleine wants to speak to you. She sounds agitated. Also, British. I thought she was Australian."

Kari groaned. "She has the fanciest of Australian accents, so it sounds British to our ears." She took the phone into the living room. "Can I call you back on my cell phone?"

"Of course, I want you to do that! That's why I called it three times! And call from the yard where you enjoyed smoking with that young man."

The hair on Kari's neck stood on end, but she shouldn't have been surprised. Madeleine had spied on her before she worked for inCog, when she had visited home in Oregon last winter, and she was spying on her now. "Understood, ma'am." Kari hung up and took the phone back to its charging station.

Mom A stared with her brows knit together.

"I'll call her back from the yard, so I don't wake Mom L."

"Take a sweater with you," Noko Ani said. "I don't know if you saw, but we got a little bit of snow last night."

"I'll put on my hoodie." She grabbed the garment on the way outside and called Madeleine back.

"Hello, chickpea," Madeleine said in a saccharine voice.

"I'm on vacation, which you approved."

"Yes, I'm aware of that, and had I known Henry was going to have yet another surprise thrown our way, I would have declined it."

"What's the surprise?"

"Apparently, Jasi Monye wants to meet earlier than planned, and since we are literally in the middle of the Atlantic, flying out to us with either his or Henry's helicopters isn't feasible."

Kari faced the combination of leafless and full-needled trees. "I still don't understand why you called me. He hasn't wanted me 'activated' for these types of VIPs, so it's not like the other assistants can't handle it. Plus, they're the ones on the clock."

"I understand your point and I'd give you a better reason if I could, but all I know is that it's Jasi Monye who has requested your presence."

"What?" Kari shrieked. "The richest man in Africa—whom I've never met—and not Henry wants me there?"

"Correct. While Henry does love his *Karishma*," she said her name in a breathy, ominous voice, "others seem to have taken an interest in you as well. Therefore, you need to be here."

Kari knew where the direction the conversation was headed, but hearing the words still made her yell, "Dammit!"

"I'd be upset too if I were in your position."

"Upset doesn't begin to cover it." Her skin was hot with anger, stomach in knots from disappointing her family, and her temples throbbed with the incoming telltale sign of a stress-induced headache. Wait. No. This was stupid. "I'm not doing it. Someone who isn't my boss is requesting my presence, which would force me to leave a family vacation early, on a different continent, for mysterious reasons. And because one of my bosses—meaning you—understands how absurd this is, I should be able to say no to this without any consequences."

"Kari, you're too smart to say something so dumb. These new friends of his do not take 'no' for an answer, and while you have experienced consequences from me, you have never experienced Henry's wrath. He is not the jovial eccentric the media makes him out to be. Don't be naïve."

Deep down, Kari knew Madeleine was right. Her family would be heartbroken she had to leave and she couldn't even be honest as to why. "When do I need to leave?"

"Three days. Cancel your old flights, I'll set up new ones and forward the details. Do you have any questions?"

Kari's chin quivered and throat burned. "No."

"Then I'll see you soon. And thank you for alerting Belle about the ship's speed. That's how I learned about this entire charade."

The call ended and Kari tucked her phone away and dabbed at the tears with the thick fabric at her wrist. How could she break this news to the family? Or the better question, what lie was she going to tell? She kicked the snow-covered, rust-colored leaves at her feet.

"I don't think they're what you're angry at," Mom L said from behind her.

From bad to worse in less than five seconds. Kari squeezed her eyes closed and kept her back to her mother. "How much of that did you hear?"

"The talking in the kitchen woke me. Then, because we keep the window cracked at night, I heard you yell 'dammit'. The word 'consequences' is what piqued my interest. Finally, I heard you say, 'When do I need to leave?' And since you still have your back to me, I know you're really upset because you don't want me to see your face."

Kari used the other, drier sleeve to dab at her eyes again and clenched her jaw. She hated that her moms knew her so well. "I'm sorry." She heard the leaves rustle behind her.

"Please, please tell me that you aren't leaving early because of work."

"I'm sorry."

"No." Mom L appeared in front of her. "There is no 'I'm sorry' because you can't do this."

"I don't have a choice."

"Of course, you have a choice! It's a job. People quit their jobs all the time. Even I did, and I liked the work!"

"Please. I . . . I can't talk about this." Kari walked away from her and closer to the tree line behind the house. With Mom L's volume, it was bound to get the attention of the others in the house.

"Oh, we absolutely can talk about this!" Mom L's comically large and fuzzy goat slipper-covered feet crunched the leaves behind her on the trail that went deeper into the woods. "We see you twice a year now. You see Ani and Niq once a year. You haven't seen my mother since Dad's funeral and that was over two years ago! This will break her heart. And will you stop walking?" Mom L put her hand on Kari's shoulders and spun her so they faced each other. Neither mother had ever done that before.

"You don't understand," Kari said with a crack in her voice. "I have to do what they say."

Finally, Mom L looked at her. Really looked at her and crossed her arms. "And what if you don't do what they say?"

All Kari could do was shake her head. She wanted to say, 'Or they'll kill us all' but she knew she couldn't. At the same time, Mom L would not let this go without some kind of explanation.

The gears in Kari's brain rotated until they clicked into position. When she was on the phone with Madeleine, she had referred to her smoking but didn't reference any of the conversation. If Madeleine had that information, she would have added that twist to the knife.

Conclusion: They could see Kari, but they probably couldn't hear her.

The *Hinewai* app had the perfect explanation to show Mom L, but she couldn't stop the trembling in her hand as she put up her hood. After all, seeing meant potential lip reading. "I'm going to show you something, and it's important that you keep your head down and not visibly react."

"Oh, what is the great and power—"

"I mean it!" Kari had never used such a warning tone with either mother before.

Mom L must have detected the gravitas because her anger-filled, crinkled forehead softened into worry. Then, she nodded.

Finally, she had broken through. "Walk with me a little farther."

They matched strides, despite Mom L's fluffy footwear, and Kari opened her banking app. To anyone watching from above, it looked like she was showing her mother a text or picture. But it was her payment history, which showed over $250,000.

Mom L turned to her with eyes larger than Noko Ani's soup pot. "That can't be right."

"It is. Also, look at the ground when you talk. They're watching us."

"Watching?"

"Yes, they're spying on me right now and there's lip reading software out there, so look at the ground when you talk." The change of surprise to terror to then focused on the ground made Kari believe Mom L finally understood. "Thank you."

"How can you have that much money?" Mom L asked. "I know what starting scientists and assistants make."

Kari placed a gentle hand on Mom L's back and nudged her down the trail until they were at the bend in the stream. The tree cover of the evergreens was denser down there. Not to mention a gigantic granite boulder. "I think it's safer now."

Mom L's eyes bore into hers. "What are you doing on that boat?"

As Kari was about to answer, the words caught in her throat. Rather than speak, she hugged Mom L and looked in the direction of the house.

Mom L cooed in her ear, which only made Kari hug her tighter. "Take your time, chickpea."

Kari took a breath and dug deep for the courage to tell her mother the bare minimum. "They pay me extra as a part of my Wibawa Enterprise Promise. I've become Henry's favorite employee, but I have to do what they say or . . ." She couldn't finish.

Mom L held her tighter and rocked her back-and-forth. "Have they threatened to hurt you?"

"No."

"Are they making you do anything illegal?"

Thankfully, she hadn't had to break into that office in Brisbane, but it was only a matter of time. "No."

"Then, what? I'm sorry if I'm acting dense, but I still don't understand why you can't quit. You don't need the money."

"Because if I quit, it won't be me who suffers the consequences."

Her mother broke the hug, took a step back, and nearly put her foot in the stream. "They've threatened us? Mitchell and Santos?"

Kari nodded and wiped her tears away with her hoodie sleeves. "I don't think you can really call it a threat when they follow through with it."

"Oh, my Gods," Mom L muffled through the hands that covered her mouth. "We have to go to someone. We have to report this to the authorities."

Kari's eyes watered further as she shook her head. "Do you really think Henry hasn't bought them all?"

The shock disappeared from Mom L as the reality of Kari's situation landed. "Shit."

"Yeah, shit." Kari pushed up her sleeves and, even though it would be near freezing, cupped her hands in the water and splashed her face. The puffiness around her eyes had to shrink before she returned to the house. "You can't tell anyone, especially Mom A."

"I figured you were going to say that, but . . . is this the rest of your life?"

"My contract says two and a half more years, but contracts tend to disappear or change on the *Hinewai*." Kari wanted to say that she was working on a way to end them all, but she had already shared too much.

Mom L circled with her hands on her hips. "I'm going to find a way to get you off that ship. There has to be a way to appeal to Henry."

"Mom L," Kari said completely resigned, "just stop. Let this be my fight. After all, you're the one who told me, 'you've made your bed, now lie in it'."

"That was about a subscription music service, not when I found out you were entangled in the web of a manipulative billionaire!"

"At least it sounds like you grasp the situation now."

Mom L nodded the way she did when she was deep in thought. "We need to come up with a damn good reason why you have to leave early because 'my boss wants me to' isn't going to cut it with this crowd. We're really going to need to pull at the heartstrings."

———

"To Kari's last night with us," Nani Tanha said with her glass of red wine raised. "Her visit was shorter than she had planned, but the physician in me understands."

A round of 'absolutely', 'here, here', and 'such a good friend' carried through the dining room as Kari's family toasted her with their wine, water, or tea.

"I'm so torn about how to feel," Noko Ani said, holding her tea cup for added warmth. "On one hand, I'm sad and disappointed you're leaving. But on the other, it's so good that you want to be there, holding your friend's hand when she gets her biopsy results. I've been there and it helps having that physical connection."

"That's what I keep thinking, too." Ata Niq took a sip of his hot tea.

"And the biopsy could be negative," Mom A said, her eyes unfocused. "I hope."

Mom L focused on drinking her wine.

"You'll have a much better bedside manner than I did," Nani Tanha said. "Have you given any thought to which medical schools you'll apply to? This time next year you should have your materials submitted."

Off like a bandage. "This might be tough to hear, but medical school isn't what I want to do now. There are so many other ways I can help or make an impact in the world." Kari locked eyes with Mom L. "I think the best way I can contribute to society is to learn about the power structure that currently exists, get inside of it, and then blow it up. Metaphorically speaking."

"That's a mighty big goal you have there." Noko Ani drank from her mug of hot tea. "But that is needed. A lot of things are broken out there."

"But as a doctor, she could put a splint on what is broken," Nani Tanha said.

"I look at it like this," Kari said. "If I became a doctor, the kinds of procedures I could do would be dictated by the equipment my institution has, and, depending on where I am, I might be limited with what kinds of treatments I could offer. Patients might not even see me, because my practice isn't allowed per their insurance. Therefore, I can't be the best doctor I could be until the system that oversees the medical industry is fair and just."

Nani Tanha gave her a slow nod. "Ah. You're seeing yourself in some sort of policy role?"

"In a way, yes." Kari tipped back the rest of her iced tea. "And the ship is a great place to learn that. I've spent a lot of time with powerful people and, by doing so, I'm learning how they think, what their motivations are, what their challenges are, and what I can bring to the conversation. I think I can bring a lot. Even Henry and his friends have seen it."

Chapter Sixteen

Cape Town, South Africa

Madeleine squeezed lemon into her Earl Grey. "How was your vacation?"

"Full of family fun." Kari adjusted the pink pillow on the chair before she sat. "I'm sure you saw that from your lovely surveillance."

Madeleine smiled, but not in the way she normally did, like she derived pleasure from Kari's discomfort or inconvenience. This time it was almost sad. "I'm curious what you told them as to why you had to leave early."

"That Jade might have cancer."

Madeleine dropped her juiceless lemon sliver on the saucer. "That's dark even for me."

"Well, I had to tell them something that would make them feel bad if they gave me a hard time about it. Nani Tanha was a doctor, Noko Ani had breast cancer, and both Moms are hyper-vigilant about mammograms. It made sense."

"Hmph. I see your point. Now"—Madeleine slapped her desk—"as to why I called you here before your shift. You don't

203

need to try to find Henry's will any longer. I put an analyst on it."

Kari was always a fan of less shady work, but that sounded like a major risk Madeleine was taking. "Aren't you worried they'll tell Henry?"

"You're not the only one on this ship with looming threats over their head. Also, Henry is in his own world right now. I honestly don't know what he wants to focus on anymore." Madeleine folded her delicate hands into her lap and shook her head. "Dismissed."

Kari left, pleased that she didn't have to change her lazy morning plans.

On the stairway landing to her cabin's level, Jade walked from the deck below wearing her WU teaching apparel. Her eyes were vacant, like she was in a trance. Kari stopped and waited for her. "Are you playing hooky today?"

Jade jumped back, like Kari had leapt out at her wearing an old school hockey mask and wielding a machete. Instead of scolding Kari for the fright, she sobbed into her polo shirt.

"Hey, hey, hey." Kari ran to her crying friend and placed what she hoped were comforting hands on each shoulder. "What's wrong?" When Jade didn't respond, a sense of dread started to coalesce in the pit of her belly. "Are you hurt?" Then, dread's mouth opened and swallowed Kari whole. "You don't have cancer, do you?"

"No," Jade said, barely audible. "I . . . Ah!" Jade hugged Kari and wailed in her ear. "I'm pregnant."

Based on her reaction, Kari didn't think 'congratulations' was what Jade wanted to hear. "Oh, my."

"I don't know what to do. I don't know how to tell Neill. Or my bosses."

"So, you found out like a minute ago?"

Jade nodded, took off her glasses, and wiped tears on her shirt. "I don't understand how this could have happened."

"Are you sure about that?" When Jade looked at her with her face twisted in horror, Kari realized her misstep. Plus, she herself was the product of a magical conception, so who was she to judge. "I'm sorry, that was insensitive. How far along are you?"

"Two months, I think. I have to go to a doctor on shore for a more thorough checkup."

Kari did the travel math in her head. "The conception was in Concepción?"

Jade cried harder. "I didn't even think of that."

Kari led Jade to her cabin, then to her recliner. She went to her small kitchen and poured a glass of water.

"Thank you." Jade took greedy swallows, then held the cool glass to her temple. "Seriously, how am I going to tell Neill? Not only is this an unplanned pregnancy, but he'll hardly be able to see his child given his contract with the ship, and that's assuming everything goes the way it's supposed to since I'm a 'geriatric pregnancy' with extra risks. I could be a grandmother soon!" She shook her head. "Diana's going to freak out!"

It was important to stay positive. "If you're worried, it's legal at this point in development to terminate in South Africa."

"I can't do that!"

Okay, a different form of positivity. "Diana will be surprised, but I'm sure she'll be happy for you, and Neill will do everything in his power to shorten his contract since he'll want to be involved as much as possible."

"I know you're right about that." Jade took another drink of water. "We have a date Wednesday night, I'll tell him then. He'll know something's off if I don't." Jade sniffled as her crying ceased and she looked at Kari with uncertainty. "My life was drastically different an hour ago. Now, my twenty-one-year-old daughter has a sibling and, in the next four months, I'll be unemployed."

Kari hadn't even thought about Jade's job and the rules of the ship. Once she started her third trimester, she would no longer be allowed to work or live on the *Hinewai*. Kari kneeled and hugged Jade. "I'll help you in any way that I can, whether you're on the ship or off it."

Jade returned the embrace. "I appreciate that, but now, I think I'd like to be alone for a little bit."

"Of course. I'll be there until I leave for work. I have the night shift for the next four days. If you need someone when I'm gone, maybe you could call Diana. From what you've told me, I think she'd have a kind ear."

"Yeah, she does want to be a family court attorney."

"See, she'll be a good listener." Kari walked to the door, but before she left, she added, "There's a lot of people who have your back. You're not alone."

Two loads of laundry and a power nap later, Kari donned her black uniform and headed to work. Of course, the first person she saw was Neill.

"Hey, Kari. Did you have a nice vacation?"

"I did. I didn't like that I had to cut it a few days short, but it was great seeing some family. Has anything interesting happened while you all were at sea?"

"Aside from the fact that we went the fastest we've ever gone? Not really." He rested a hand on Kari's shoulder. "I wish I could stay and catch up more, but I have to check another camera."

"Another one?" What was with the cameras these days? "I hope it's not on my deck again."

"No, this one's by the VIP boat."

"Gotcha. See you later, then." Kari continued her path to the VIP assistant office, but Belle wasn't behind the desk. She detoured to the outside lounge area where she overheard the conversation about ice preferences between Belle and the bartender.

As soon as Belle saw her, she strode toward Kari with purposeful steps. The sun behind her had her figure in near silhouette. "Thank you so much for coming early," Belle said.

There was a desperation in Belle's voice Kari hadn't heard before. "What's going on?"

"Henry, Ray, Mr. Monye, and his son have been talking, but it's really uncomfortable and tense. They keep asking Ray questions about his opinions on geopolitical issues and he's wildly unprepared for that. To make matters even stranger, a few times Mr. Monye has asked for you, specifically. Do you know why?"

"I wish I knew, but I have a feeling I'm going to find out very soon."

"Well, good luck, and I'll see you in the morning." Belle left for the inside of the ship but stopped. "We need to schedule our movie-book club discussion."

"We can add that to our morning debriefing." Kari grinned as Belle left the deck then walked over to the party of four. As Kari approached, she heard Mr. Monye's bass voice report the latest advancements in Central African agriculture.

Henry's slight scowl vanished. "Here's Karishma!"

Ray made eye contact with her, but then brought his attention back to his club soda.

"Hello, gentlemen."

The Monyes rose from their seats to greet her. "It is lovely to meet you, Karishma. I'm Jasi, and this is my son, Ise, who's the fifth of the great Jasi Monye line." Both Monyes extended their hands with such identical timing it seemed choreographed.

"Ise is five in Igbo," his son said with a congenial smile.

"It's a pleasure to meet you both." She watched her hand disappear in both of theirs. Even without their identical charcoal-gray suits, the resemblance between them was uncanny. The only obvious differences was that Ise's hair had less white and his earlobes were adorned with impressive diamond studs.

Ray stayed seated and chewed his crushed ice.

"Can I get you gentlemen anything?" Kari asked once they returned to their seats.

Henry appeared to assess everyone's glasses. "I think we are good for now, but you don't have anything. Why don't you get yourself a cocktail and join us?"

If she didn't look surprised by the question, Ray certainly did. He turned to Henry with his mouth open.

Kari flashed what she hoped resembled a genuine, and not baffled, smile. "I'd love to. I'll be right back."

As she made her way to the bar, an uneasiness coursed through her. This was beyond peculiar, but it could have been related to what Belle had told her. Maybe she was being asked to join to make the conversation livelier?

The bartender poured her a glass of champagne, and she went back to the lounge. In the brief period of time she was gone, someone had arranged the chairs so that she had a seat between Henry and Ray. She was literally coming between father and son. "Cheers, gentlemen." Once they clinked their glasses, she asked, "What's the topic of discussion?"

"The current state of affairs in an area where I have invested in several different farms," Jasi said. "Tell me, how do you feel about militias?"

Kari didn't see the connection between crops and civilian military, but she was sure she was going to find out. "I think that depends on the state of the current government and what crops you're referring to."

"Interesting," Ise said and crossed his leg at the knee, displaying both his fine Italian leather shoe and argyle sock in the process. "Can you expand on that?"

Kari didn't believe her response was interesting but was happy to add more details, like her thoughts on self-governance and how while militias may be well-intended, it's a slippery slope that can bring new forms of totalitarianism. Also nutjobs with assault weapons. The VIPs had a few basic follow-up questions and comments, so overall Kari assessed the conversation as terribly boring and hoped it would be over soon.

"How would you respond to those who say that democracy is full of flaws?" Henry asked. "That people who have no awareness of current affairs still get a vote?"

She bit her tongue so she didn't say, 'Like billionaires who have never been working class?'. "It comes down to access to education for the public and electing honest, well-rounded people. And I'm not just saying that because one of my mothers is the mayor of my hometown." Kari released a polite-society chuckle.

Jasi grinned. "Your mother is a politician?"

"She is now, but, in her heart, she's still a goat farmer and businesswoman."

"Her other mother is an environmental activist who is often featured on"—Henry leaned forward dramatically—"ENN."

"That's Adam Cho's network, is it not?" Ise asked.

"Indeed it is," Henry said with an edge to his voice. The powerful trio all shook their heads. "But I'm making steady progress on purchasing it. Then"—Henry waved—"bye, bye, Adam."

Jasi and Ise laughed.

Ray tipped back the remainder of his club soda. He turned to Kari and shook the ice in his empty glass. "I'm out."

Kari hadn't forgotten that she was there to work, but for Ray, of all people, to remind her of her service role was a surprise. She placed her flute on the table and stood. "I'll check in on dinner service while I'm gone." Ray didn't bother to look at her when she took his glass.

As Kari walked away, she heard Henry admonish Ray for his rude behavior and saw an uninvited guest turn the corner with her martini glass. Kari placed Ray's tumbler on the bar and asked for a refill before she blocked Madeleine's path to the lounge area. "What are you doing here?"

"Ah, there's my mate," Madeleine garbled in a more general Australian accent.

It wasn't only the slurring that raised Kari's eyebrows, it was being called 'mate' and the accent shift into something almost brogan. Intoxication had reverted Madeleine back to her roots. "Are you okay?"

"I'm fan-bloody-tastic. I'm on my third cocktail, which has helped dull the pain from realizing the last decade of my life has gone right in the bin."

"Club soda's ready!" called the bartender.

Kari pointed a finger at her. "I'll be right back, but stay here," she said firmly.

Madeleine gave her a quick nod of understanding and a salute.

Kari picked up the refill and went back over to the party of four. "My apologies for neglecting your empty glass, sir." After she handed the glass to Ray, she looked at Henry. "On my way to the bar, I noticed a loose grate. If it's alright with you, I'd like to alert maintenance before I go to the kitchen. I would hate for someone to injure themselves."

"Yes, of course, and get a refill of your champagne while you're at it."

Kari took her flute and placed it on the bar. She went to Madeleine, placed a hand on her back, and led her to the VIP elevator. "I think we should go to your cabin where you can tell me what's going on."

Even though Madeleine didn't resist leaving, she said, "But I'll miss the party."

"It's not much of a party. They're talking about basic political ideas and thinking it's deep." The sound that came next shocked Kari.

Madeleine erupted in a full belly laugh without the faintest trace of evil, spilling some of her martini in the process. "You are funny."

"That's nice of you to say." Kari carried her martini the rest of the way to her cabin. "Okay, I hope you remember your code."

Madeleine wiggled her thumb before she placed it on the scanner, then proceeded to type in the numbers. "I've been using this code since I was in uni and it was my combination to my swim locker. Eight-hundred-meter backstroke was my best event. I was very lean despite the chocolates. Looked great in a cozzie, but I hated shaving all the time." She gestured to her pubic area, then pushed the door open. "Home sweet home."

Kari was struck by how different Madeleine's cabin was compared to Henry's. Her style was modern with only abstract art decorating the walls. No Gods in sight. Her furnishings were sparse, but what was there were pieces done in black, white, with a few pops of color here and there. Whether it was a crimson throw pillow on the white couch or a cerulean vase on the glass end table.

It reminded her of the Portland skyrise apartment Nani Tanha used to have.

"Would you like a martini?" Madeleine pointed a stern finger at her. "It's important to always be a good host. Always. Remember. That."

"I'll take a rain check on the martini and, per being a good host, I really should check in on the kitchen for dinner service." But as much as Madeleine asphyxiating on her own vomit appealed to her, Kari didn't want to be responsible for it. "Are you going to be okay by yourself?"

"Short-term, I'll be fine. Long-term . . . I don't know." Madeleine slipped off her mossy green heels and plopped down on the couch, spilling more of her drink in the process.

While Kari couldn't stay long, she was curious what news had caused Madeleine to self-medicate into a drunken stupor and existential crisis. Kari sat in the matching chair, catty-corner to the couch. "What happened between now and this morning?"

"My analyst cracked the code when it came to Henry's will." Madeleine shook her head, then directed her glassy eyes toward Kari. "I gave up my life for that man. I left my law career because he promised me power with partnership. Yes, it's his name in Wibawa Enterprises, but he promised me that I would be his partner until the day he died. Then, his empire would be left to me. He promised me!"

Kari was afraid to ask, but she needed to know who had inherited the keys to the kingdom. "Who did he leave it to?"

She bit her lip, then brushed away a tear with her thumb. "Back in June, Henry changed his will so that all of his assets would be split equally between Jack Weatherby, Ricardo Rojas, Gabriella Fermi, Jasi Monye, Amara Gupta, Botan Itoi, and someone listed as 'fidele'. Whatever that means. Leonarda Fermi acted as a witness."

The weight of these new facts pushed Kari farther back into her chair. This explained why Gabriella had been on the

Hinewai in June. "How do you know you're not this 'fidele' person?"

"You only do that if the holder of the title is to be determined. I have a name, Madeleine Evelyn Coultier. Some even call me Mad."

"You don't say."

Madeleine nodded and finished her drink. "On the bright side, at least now I have a strong idea as to why he doesn't want you to be able to read their minds during these meetings. He knows you report to me, and, despite you hating me, he knows that you tell me everything."

Points to her for understanding Kari's feelings. "Speaking of reporting, did you know that Henry has Amara Gupta, Gabriella Fermi, and Botan Itoi booked as 'tentative' on the VIP calendar?"

Madeleine's thin lips frowned, which made her glassy, bloodshot eyes even sadder.

"I guess you do now."

Madeleine's gaze went to the painting that looked like a five-year-old had a field day with primary colors. "I don't think I need to say this, but keep the information about his will between us. Please."

She absolutely would not. Adam was getting this info as soon as she was able. "Of course, ma'am, and I'll see myself out."

"Excellent." Madeleine struggled to stand. "I think I'll take a long bath while I sip some apple juice. I do love apple juice. So tart and sweet. Just yummy."

That was a new fun fact about her boss to go with the flood of new things she had just learned. "Okay, but don't make the water too deep in your tub and use a silicon cup. I'm a little worried at this point you might drown or cut yourself."

"Duly noted." Madeleine walked on unsteady legs through

the dining area, past a ticking grandfather clock, and to her stairs. "It just occurred to me that you're more my ally now than Henry is. That's wild." She gave Kari a sad smile and proceeded up the staircase.

Kari took a moment to gather herself. Her plan of gaining Madeleine's trust had worked, yet she couldn't bring herself to celebrate.

———

Per Jasi's request, Kari saw him and his son off the *Hinewai*, even though Belle was present. Kari watched Henry say his farewells, and lo and behold, Henry received a coin.

"Annabelle," Henry said once the helicopter was up and away in the sunny morning sky, "tie up the loose end of this visit and see to Raymond's departure."

"Yes, sir. I'll see you later tonight, Kari." Belle left the deck.

Next, Henry turned to Josef. "You won't be needed at this time. Please do some security rounds." Once he left, Henry gave his attention to Kari. "I know you're tired from your shift, but I'd like you to come to my cabin with me. I won't take up too much of your time."

It was tempting to say that she had never felt so exhausted in her life. The Monyes had kept both her and Belle on their toes twenty-four hours a day for their four days on and off the ship, which included a shark cage excursion.

Kudos to Belle for being an all-star on that underwater adventure.

Kari followed Henry in silence. This time she wasn't thrown by the décor; however, she was surprised by his indication for her to sit at one of the heads of the dining table where there was a place setting with a scone, clotted cream, and fruit.

Henry unfolded the white linen napkin shaped like a boat with a quick flick of his wrist. "I know you want to get to bed, but feel free to have some breakfast while we talk." He placed a napkin on his lap with a frown. "I was very upset to see the way Raymond treated you, as were our guests, and I would like to apologize on his behalf. Having said that, you handled his attitude with grace and didn't create extra tension because of it. I wanted to thank you."

"I appreciate you saying that, but you should know that Ray did apologize to me in private the next day."

He nodded while he spread the cream on his scone. "I don't know why he acted like that to begin with."

Even her rudimentary people skills knew why, but she threw him an explanation that he could accept. "He said he doesn't understand what you want from him in these visits and he feels as though the two of us are in competition."

"Well, in a way, you two are." He used a fork and knife to slice pieces of cantaloupe. "Karishma, I will be brutally honest with you. I have not reached my next goal in life, but I am close. So close, I can taste it." He snatched the cantaloupe off his fork with his teeth and regarded her intently as he chewed. "As you are aware, those individuals who make it to the top have a strong support network and a person by their side who has their best interests in mind. A *fidele*, if you will. You understand the Latin, right?"

She stopped chewing the scone at the mention of the mysterious word in Henry's will, then swallowed hard. "Fidelis means loyal. Faithful, even. That's where Madeleine comes in for you, right?"

"Not in this scenario. Not in these rules." He put down his utensils with a *clang* and picked up his scone. "I need to rely on my fidele in a unique way. I don't know if I trust Raymond, but

I do know that I cannot rely on him. He's a man-child. He is ignorant to the world around him. He has no ambition. When confronted with fear, he literally pisses himself. For a man such as myself that poses certain risks."

"I'm sorry, but how can Ray pose a risk? He's a painter." She wanted to add that being surprised by a breaching great white shark while you were in a rather tiny boat was a urine-evacuating occasion. At least that's what Belle had told her had happened.

Henry chewed with his eyes focused on Ra. "Let me put it this way: Every time Raymond has been aboard for a VIP visit, those VIPs have pointed out certain traits of his that could jeopardize my chances of greatness. Therefore, they have all suggested I start looking elsewhere for a fidele. Karishma, I'm thinking of you."

She stared at him, scone at her lips, stunned. "Me?"

"Yes, and I would appreciate it if you kept this between us. I don't think Madeleine would care for the news."

The questions flew into her mind at an exponential pace. "Why wouldn't you choose Madeleine? Or even Josef? They've been with you so much longer and know you better."

He winced. "He's the right age and loyal but too . . . We'll say emotionally immature. She's too old, per the rules."

Kari had no idea how old Madeleine was, but she was far from being ancient.

"There is an age requirement, you see. My fidele must be at least twenty years my junior and at least twenty years old. They call it the twenty-twenty rule, and it's been around for centuries. Even before that eye test."

"But I'm not twenty."

Henry grinned. "You will be in April."

More questions popped into her brain while Henry nibbled

on his breakfast. "If I was your fidele, what would that mean for my service on the ship? To Madeleine?"

He dismissed the questions with a wave. "I think you're forgetting that I am the one in charge." He poured himself a cup of coffee from the silver carafe. As he stirred in his cream, he looked at her. "What do you think? Is this something that interests you?"

"Um," she prolonged the sound. "I'm not sure what I think or even know what the responsibilities of a fidele are, but you said 'they' created the twenty-twenty vision rule. Who are 'they'?" She knew the answer was In Virtute but had to ask for the sake of appearing ignorant.

"Those details will come if you are interested, but the general idea is that you would be my sounding board, my 'go-to' in difficult situations, and work on the most critical projects."

"Okay. I guess that makes sense. But I'm still stuck on why you want me of all people."

He hmphed, but with a smile, and averted his eyes. He smoothed the napkin on his lap. "Do you believe in visions?"

As a telepath who saw herself in the future playing guitar to dogs in a cozy cabin, yes, she did believe in the possibility. "I can't explain it, but I do."

"Good. Then, I'll let you in on a secret. I've had a reoccurring dream most of my adult life. In it, I'm in a dark room made of marble with a tremendous fire. I'm not scared, even though I'm staring down an elephant. I feel powerful. More powerful than I've ever felt before. Beside me, there is a young woman. In the dreams, I have never seen her face, but she wears a necklace much like the one you do. Do you know what that means?"

"What?" she asked, despite the fear of learning his answer.

"That is fate. The Gods"—he used both hands to gesture at the artistic renderings in the room—"have brought you to me to help me see this power realized."

Goose bumps sprung on her arms. She had to admit his vision did sound prophetic; however, he had it flipped. He saw the vision as her bringing him greatness, she saw it as his demise.

"And that isn't the only time I've had visions. I had them as a boy, too. It's what led me to the *Hinewai*. The only people I ever shared that with was my mother and Madeleine."

Henry saw himself as psychic. But if he truly was, would he eventually know what she had planned? "I'm . . . I'm at a loss for words at the moment but I think I understand the fidele question better."

"Good. Take some time to think about it, but not too much time. If you decide that you're not interested, I will have to find another." He gave her a warm smile. "Thank you for your time, Karishma. You may stay and chat or take your breakfast with you. I understand that you're tired and probably overwhelmed right now."

"I appreciate your understanding, Henry." She rose from her chair and took her plate to her cabin, where she hoped to sleep without dreams of Gods, prophecies, or great whites.

After that, poker with the gang was bound to be less dramatic.

———

"Picking up an order," Kari said in the chef's kitchen.

Chef Jon poked his head around the corner then came to the other side. "Let me nudge the staff in the back and see where your pizzas and cake are. I hope not all of this is for you and Belle."

"Nope. This time I decided to treat my other friends, since it's the last time all of us can get together for a while. Belle's going home for Thanksgiving and her birthday. Then, WU has their finals. It's quite the logistics puzzle."

"Sounds like." Jon left for the back and came back out a few minutes later with a stack of three pizza boxes and a dessert box. "I'm surprised you didn't ask Neill's girlfriend to make the cake. She lives for that!"

"Normally, I would, but she's a little busy right now, but she knows I asked you so no feelings were hurt."

Kari made her way down to the poker room where she was greeted with a chorus of appreciation that she had arrived with food. "It's nice to see you all, too. Where should I put all of this?" After some brief direction and furniture shifting, Kari went to the far side of the room and observed her friends. She focused on each interaction. Nando spoke to whoever would listen with a hungry smile as he decided what to try first. In exchange for Sven plating Craig's pizza, Craig opened Sven's wine—an actual bottle—and poured him a healthy glass. Belle watched her with a slight grin. "What?"

"You look really happy right now."

"That's because I am. Now stop staring at me, you creeper, and get some dinner."

After they all settled with their pizza and drinks at the round table, Craig raised his can of beer. "To the last full gathering of the calendar year and Belle's birthday!"

They clinked cans and cups in their toast then dove into their pizza with ravenous bites. All gave their compliments to Jon.

"I can't believe it's almost over," Craig said. "After the spring semester, I'm done."

"Do you have any leads on where you're going next?" Nando asked him.

"I found some adventure tourist places in Whistler, but I

know I have to make an appointment with the career counselor soon to go over my best options. Have you done that yet, Belle?"

Logically, Kari knew that Belle graduated in May, but hearing it said aloud made it more real and her pizza less tasty.

"I haven't," Belle said. "But I'm flexible with where I go."

"Do you think I can have your intern spot?" Nando asked Belle. "I think I'd like it and it'd be nice to add to my resume."

"I can put in a good word with Doug for you. Also, it might be helpful if we knew someone who worked in the VIP program." She batted her blue eyes at Kari and gave her a sly smile to go with it.

"I may be able to pull a few strings. I just hope Nando is up to the challenge. You may have to get into a shark cage."

The three young men turned to Belle in shock.

"Okay, let's set the record straight," Belle said. "I wasn't required to get into the shark cage. I volunteered because I've always wanted to do it, and when I came out of the water alive, it put our VIP guests and Henry at ease. Henry's son, not so much."

"Why in the hell would you want to get into a shark cage?" Craig asked. "Even I wouldn't do that to get a perfect shot."

"I like adventure, and getting into the water with a great white shark is pretty adventurous."

"You can have it," Sven said. "I'll stick to cooking where the elements won't eat me."

Kari swallowed her mouthful of pizza. "But they can cut or set you on fire."

"That's still less terrifying than all of those teeth."

"How about you?" Belle asked Sven. "What does the next calendar year bring?"

"I'm going to start by making my family proud with my poker tournament victory. After that, I don't know." Sven scratched at his light beard while he thought. "More school, more light flirting with Kari. Maybe I can even get her to flirt back."

"If by some miracle, your charm cracks my heart of stone, then I'm just going to be direct with you. No passive flirty stuff."

Sven's eyebrows raised.

Belle nodded. "I believe that one hundred percent. If Kari wants you to know something she'll tell you."

Chapter Seventeen

Port of Zanzibar, Tanzania

"She thought the reason why the Earth's core is hot is because of Hell."

Madeleine chortled. "Well, I don't think Mr. Precious Metals brought her on board for a stunning geology-based conversation, even if Henry did ask one thousand questions about his mining operation."

"Oh, I'm aware of that. Or rather, Matthew is since he walked in on one of their rather more athletic 'conversations'."

"Good for them."

Kari shrugged. "I guess."

Madeleine leaned back in her chair and folded her hands in her lap. "Have you dated anyone but Finn since you've been on the ship?"

"Why do you care?"

"Just curious. I'm not planning on using anyone to make a 'point' if that's what you're worried about."

"That's exactly what I'm worried about, but, no, I haven't dated anyone."

"No sex workers either?"

"That's also a negative."

"Are you just not interested in dating or sex? Which is fine, by the way. One of my sisters is asexual and quite happy with her life."

"I really don't think you're supposed to be asking me or telling me these things."

"I'm also sure HR wouldn't approve of the fact that I have a remote control that turns your brain on and off, but here we are. So"—Madeleine directed a pointed stare at her—"which is it?"

Kari took a deep and annoyed breath. "I don't want to complicate my life further with a relationship."

Madeleine chuckled deep in her throat. "I'm not talking about a relationship. I'm talking about fun. Even though your work for me and Henry is stressful, you don't have to deprive yourself of life's pleasures."

"I appreciate the note, ma'am, but I can assure you that I have fun when I can. Is there anything else?"

"No." Madeline took out the remote and clicked it. "You're dismissed to have whatever sort of 'fun' you'd like to have."

———

"So, what's your plan?" Kari returned Jade's serve in the back corner of the table.

Jade volleyed, but the ball soared over the table. "My supervisor says that while I have to leave the ship, I can still remain an employee of WU as long as I do online work, like curriculum, up to my delivery. I can keep my health insurance and maternity leave that way."

Kari retrieved the ball that had rolled across the floor. "I'm sorry if this is a sensitive question, but what are you going to do about income and childcare after you have the baby?"

Jade put her paddle on the table and smiled. "This is probably a good time to tell you that Neill and I are getting married."

"What? When?" Kari asked elated.

"We don't know yet, but it'll be small. To be honest, Neill's the one really pushing for it. He wants the baby and me set up if anything were to happen to him on the job. He really, really wants to do everything he can since he'll be absent for a while." What had been a happy and uplifting conversation took a quick turn. Jade took off her glasses and wiped her eyes. "I'm sorry. I don't know if it's hormones or the fact that it's really sad he won't be there. He cried, too." She drew the last word out in a series of several heart-wrenching syllables.

Kari rounded the table and gave her a hug. "It can be both hormones and sad."

After a long moment, Jade gently pushed her away. "Good God, girl, your arms are strong. But I'll be okay. Both Neill and Diana are bending over backward for me. Did I tell you that Diana's narrowing her law school applications to a two-hundred-mile radius so she can help when she can?"

"That's really sweet of her."

"It is, but enough about me and my drama. What have you been up to?"

Kari served the ball. "Do you think it's weird that I don't date?"

"No. What would be weird is if you didn't want to date but did it anyway. So, I guess the question I have for you is, do you want to date?"

"I don't know. I don't know if dating will provide me with some sort of fun that I can't get from my friends. Or myself."

Jade grinned and lobbed the ball high over the net. "Honestly, I think it depends on the person you're dating. I've been on some real duds that I thought would be great. Conversely, I've gone on a few where I only went because there was a new restaurant I wanted to go to, then it turned out to be a great time. Have you talked about it with Ola?"

"She said dates are fine, relationships should probably wait." Or at least that was what Kari had interpreted from their last session.

"Well, then, date! You can do things on a date that you can't do by yourself."

Kari wasn't so sure about that; she had accumulated many accessories in her nightstand. Also under her bed. "Like what?"

"Can you kiss your neck?"

Kari sucked in her upper lip and released it with a pop. "You're right, I can't do that."

"There you go." Jade sent a fierce forehand her way, which missed the table. "I have to be nosey now. Who are you thinking about asking out?" She gasped. "Is it Belle?"

"She's currently in the US. Also, no."

"Well, who then?"

———

This was fine. This was typical. People all around the world asked others out. Why Kari was so nervous, she didn't know.

Among the soundtrack of muffled and clear music and conversations of the WU dorm hall, Kari wiped the perspiration on her hands off on her cargo pants. Then, she knocked. A young man with splotchy auburn facial and chest hair answered. He wore a towel around his waist and tube socks.

She would've criticized his manners except that she had also answered the door in only a towel once. "Is Sven here?"

"Kari?" Sven leaned into view and took out his ear buds. "What are you doing here? I didn't even know that you knew where my cabin was."

"It was pretty easy to figure out. Can I talk to you in the hall?"

Sven brushed past his roommate and closed the door so they were both in the passageway. "Why the surprise visit?" His silver-gray eyes grew wider. "Is something wrong?"

"No. Everything's fine. I had this idea that I'd show up unannounced and ask you out on a date."

"You are direct!" He smiled and bounced on his bare feet, which Kari noted had well-groomed toenails. "Date accepted. Did you have somewhere or something specific you'd like to do?"

Step one accomplished: He said yes. "I thought maybe we could take the tender in and check out a cafe. There's also a music museum that I think looks interesting. Does that sound like something you'd like?"

"I mean, I'll be with you, and I don't know if I'll ever be in Zanzibar ever again in my life . . . When would you like to go?"

Step two accomplished: He showed moderate enthusiasm for the date idea. "Would you be able to go on Sunday? Meet at the tender at noon?"

"That sounds great. I'll see you then."

———

Kari conducted a top-down assessment in the long mirror. Her pixie cut was both stylish and carefree, her fashionable turquoise sleeveless top presented an acceptable level of cleavage, her sand-colored skirt revealed recently shaved legs, but her sandals would definitely give her blisters.

She headed down to deck one in her canvas shoes and couldn't help but think people were staring. Was it really such an anomaly that she looked nice? At the tender queue, she saw Sven in khaki shorts, a polo shirt, and his Viking hair pinned up in a bun. Their eyes met and he jogged over to her. Poor guy, she could already see the darkened blue cloth under his arms. Even the gorgeous couldn't escape the unfortunate reality of armpit sweat.

"Hello." In a first, he greeted her by kissing her cheek. His lengthy stubble scratched her, which was also a first. Her ex-boyfriend hadn't been able to grow facial hair when they had dated and one of Finn's favorite pastimes was shaving.

"Are you ready for a fun day of heat and music appreciation?" she asked.

"I am. But, since this is a date, I should tell you that you look absolutely beautiful."

"Thanks. I did put in a little more effort than usual." She noticed the tender queue shortening as people boarded. "Shall we?"

On the ride over, they discussed Sven's upcoming final exams. He was nervous about a timed station practical but excited to go home for a few weeks after that. It was sweet to hear the loving tone in his voice as he spoke about his family. His father was his hero. Kari shared that's how she felt about her mothers, but unlike her only-child status, he had five siblings where they were always in some sort of competition for attention. And affection.

The museum was a fifteen-minute walk from the dock but only took an hour to go through. Kari had appreciated the handwritten lyrics and instruments while Sven was more impressed with stage clothes. From there, they had iced coffees near the beach and talked about music. While Kari gravitated toward rock and blues, his preference was pop and American rap. In summary, they enjoyed completely different things and were back on the *Hinewai* once the next tender showed. She couldn't help but think if she were with Belle, they'd still be in the museum. She would have really appreciated the lyrics.

Kari shifted on her feet and played with her hands in front of her door. "You have officially done your duty by making sure that I got home safely."

He clapped his hands together and shook them in front of himself in victory. "Does this mean I get a kiss?"

While their conversation had been mediocre at best, Sven was still attractive. Surely, she could get past the stubble for a kiss. "I think it does."

He bent down a slight distance and touched his lips to hers with soft, grazing passes before he increased the pressure and lowered his hands to her waist.

The kiss itself was fine, but the stubble had to go. She couldn't pretend to enjoy that. Kari broke the kiss.

"That was very nice," he said. "I'm sorry it ended so soon."

"Yeah. I'm having a tough time with your beard."

He rubbed his cheek with his hand. "You don't find it sexy?"

"No. I find it abrasive."

His eyes turned into those of a sad puppy. "I thought women thought it was sexy."

"It looks sexy, but it feels like sandpaper."

"There's not much I can do about it now."

Where he saw only problems, she also saw solutions. "You could shave here, then we could make out."

His jaw dropped. "You would really make me shave?"

Kari pressed her thumb to the scanner and typed in her code. "I mean . . . I wouldn't force you against your will, but if you want to make out then that is a requirement. If it helps, my shaving gel smells like lavender. It's very soothing. I'll put that and my razor on the sink for you."

His puppy eyes switched to those of an indignant human. "I'm not doing that! I'm growing out my beard for when I go home. It's below freezing there!"

She wasn't caving despite the urge to fool around. "I don't know what to say except that this won't work." Despite this, it was important that he understood she still liked and respected him. "It's no hard feelings though. We can still be friends."

Now his brow furrowed. In the span of thirty seconds, he had more emotions run across his face than an hour-long soap opera. "Okay," he said with uncertainty. "I'll see you after break then. Bye."

"Bye. Good luck on your finals!" She closed the door then checked the time. She could squeeze in the final few chapters of the latest Belle-Kari book club book before dinner service. She couldn't wait to learn what Belle thought of the character arc.

Chapter Eighteen

Dubai, United Arab Emirates

Kari knew Dubai would be their most epic stop. The list of VIPs coming aboard was the most extensive she had seen. Four staff cabins had been converted into two smaller luxury suites, and the tourism company on the ship had been subcontracted to help with the many tours of the glamorous city. A botanical garden with 150 million flowers, a mall the size of two hundred football fields, an artificial island in the shape of a palm tree, and a museum so futuristic that Kari was convinced it had to have been placed there by time traveling aliens. Every time Kari was impressed, Mom A's reminder that it had all been created with oil money and human exploitation came back to her.

That woman had a gift for buzzkill.

But before Kari went back to catering to the wealthiest of the wealthy, she had book and movie club with Belle.

"How's the jetlag treating you?" Kari asked as she opened the door.

Belle's bagged eyes opened wider and she shook her head.

"I'm sorry I made fun of you when you came back from Michigan. This is brutal."

"Were you able to sleep today? Or should I expect you to nod off during our movie?"

"Considering my nap lasted five hours—thanks to my roommate's absence—I think I'll be okay. Semester break will be a glorious, peaceful time." Belle walked to the sliding door and stopped. "Wow. Would you look at that?"

What captivated Belle was the view of the artificial World Islands of Dubai. It was a project that had cost billions upon billions of dollars and took several years to almost complete. And now, thanks to Mom A, she wondered how many enslaved people it took to build.

"Drinks outside?" Kari asked as she fetched the champagne and glasses.

"Oh, I have a surprise for you regarding that." Belle pulled a bottle of bourbon out of her bag. "I thought I'd bring some of home back here."

Kari pushed a glass across the counter to her. "Pass."

"Suit yourself." Belle poured the amber spirit until her iceless glass was a third full, then topped it off with a splash of cold water from the faucet. "Are you sure you don't want to try it?"

Kari took the glass, sniffed the woodsy-spiced vapor, and sipped. Her taste buds and tongue revolted from the Southern assault. "Hard pass."

Belle chuckled, then took a slow drink. "I'll try not to be offended."

"Seriously, why do you like that?" Kari scraped her tongue against her teeth as if that would help remove the vileness. "Did you bring anything else back that won't elicit some kind of gag reflex?" she asked as she popped the cork.

"Maybe. But you're not getting it today." Belle took her

drink out to the balcony and sat in her usual spot. When Kari joined her, they clinked their glasses.

"When do I get it, then?"

"You have to wait until your birthday."

A comfortable silence rolled over them as they watched the sun set over Dubai. From their spot off Port Rashid, they could see other beaches, the massive high-rises, the port for the other boats, and, of course, the lighthouse.

"How was your trip home?" Kari asked.

"I ate way too much food with too much butter. I took a trip to a ski resort. I had forgotten how fast you get to go!"

"Skiing is another hard pass." Belle was definitely the adrenaline junkie of the two. "Anything else happen? Were there birthday presents?"

"I got a nice watch for work. It's analog so Madeleine won't have to have a hissy fit."

"Or kiss your biscuits."

Belle coughed on her drink as she tried to rein in her laughter. "Exactly. So, what did you do while I was gone?"

Now was the perfect time to get Belle's take on her date with Sven, but she'd have to tread carefully since the conversation could get weird fast. Kari angled herself so she could see her expressions more clearly in the dim light. "Aside from the usual gaming with Jade and VIP shenanigans, I did do something new: I went on a date with Sven."

The muddled expression on Belle's face could only have been described as conflicted. "You did, huh?"

"Yeah. We went to a museum in Zanzibar and then a coffee shop." So much for comfortable silence. The air between them was thick now, like a wave of humidity had rolled in before a storm.

Belle looked in the direction of the waterpark where the light show had started. "And how was it?"

"It was okay." Kari sensed that every response she gave was like an extra grain of salt in the wound. Bringing up this topic was the worst idea she had since bargaining with Madeleine. Gods, she wished she knew what Belle was thinking. "We don—"

"How was the conversation?" The tumbler of bourbon stayed at her lips.

The idea of articulating her opinion made Kari's stomach roll. They were all friends and you weren't supposed to say unkind things about your friends. That was a rule! "Can I pass on that question?"

Belle's brow lifted. "That good, huh?"

"Yeah," Kari said with a sigh. "And, in a way, he made me feel like I used to in school."

"How do you mean?"

"Like I was weird because I wanted to learn."

"I've certainly been there. I remember those days of hearing whispers from my classmates after I asked too many questions in class. It was like you had two choices: be an annoyingly active learner or acceptably passive," Belle said into her glass.

"Yes!" She should have known Belle could relate in this way. "I hated that so much, but at least I only had to put up with it until I was eleven."

"Lucky you." Belle paused as though she was organizing her thoughts. "Are you going to go out with him again?"

Kari shrugged. "I don't know. Sometimes it's just nice to be wanted and have a different type of fun." Even to Kari's ears, her lack of enthusiasm was noticeable.

Belle's eyes softened. "I get that."

"Which part?"

"Both," Belle said. "But mostly the part about being wanted."

Over the course of six months, Belle's honest compassion

mixed with astute observations acted like a tuning fork inside Kari. After Belle's words had struck, the impact of the reverberation lingered. This time was no different. "Well, I want to have an intellectual yet silly book discussion with you and only you. Does that count?"

Belle rueful smile. "I'll take it."

"I'm glad. Do you want to go in now and start?" Kari pointed in the direction of the water park. "The light show doesn't come back on for another twenty minutes."

"Sure." Belle awkwardly stood from the lounge chair. "Hey, before we get to the books, what did you think of *Restraint and Seclusion?*"

"A hard movie to watch, but certainly puts the next two weeks of madness into perspective, especially with Amara and Aarti Gupta coming."

———

The last week in Dubai saw the most activity. Due to Belle's quick thinking, Doug was able to bring on two of WU's hospitality students to provide additional support.

Kari had never seen Nando so flustered.

"It's okay, Nando," Kari said in the calmest voice she could muster. "They get unreasonably angry sometimes when their batshit crazy last-minute requests aren't met. Like when Amara Gupta's daughter thought the temperature in her wine refrigerator was inaccurate. Just tell them William's working on it."

"Who's William?" Nando asked.

"He's an imaginary man to assign tasks or blame to." From poker, she knew Nando's scrunched nose meant that he was unhappy. "I do that because I don't have to throw anybody real under the bus, but at the same time it makes the VIPs happy 'someone' is actively working on their precious problem."

"Oh!" Nando beamed. "That makes a lot of sense. Thanks."

"You're welcome. Now, I have to see if both of the Guptas are ready."

Kari went to the matriarch's cabin first. She pressed the buzzer and patiently waited outside in the passageway. She plastered on her go-to smile once the door opened. "Good afternoon. I came to escort you to cocktail hour with Henry and Ray."

Aarti's ice pick heels gave her a significant height advantage over her mother but placed her at eye level with Kari. "Why is she here?" Aarti asked Amara in Bengali. "It's not like we can't find our way."

Thanks to the thorough lessons of her Nani Tanha, Kari knew the language well. "It's a security measure. It's my job to see that you get to your location safely." She repeated her answer in Bengali.

Amara's laugh lines deepened as she smiled. "You must be Henry's Karishma. Your name tag only has your nickname on it."

"Yes, that's me. Right this way, please."

As Kari led them to the lounge, she wondered what else Henry or the other In Virtute VIPs had mentioned about her. Did Jack Weatherby say resourceful? Did Ricardo Rojas say she was attentive? Had Jasi Monye said she could hold a conversation? Gabriella Fermi had to have praised her jiu-jitsu.

When they arrived at the outdoor lounge area, Henry was there, but the seat beside him was vacant. Henry stood and gave the same charming smile he gave to every In Virtute VIP. "Welcome to the *Hinewai,* Amara. I'm sorry I missed you when your helicopter landed. I had to attend to . . . Well, it doesn't matter now. What would you two ladies like to drink?"

"With weather like this," Amara said, "I'd love a gin and tonic. With cucumber."

"Same," said Aarti.

"Let's make it three." Henry unbuttoned his suit jacket before he sat again. "Karishma, after you tell the bartender our order, please go check on Raymond. Maybe he lost track of time." He regarded his guests. "I fear he may be jet-lagged from his travels."

Kari gave a quick nod and left. She provided the bartender with the simple drink order, plus the club soda for Ray, then continued down to the newer interior VIP suites, which lacked certain amenities like complete soundproofing. When she arrived outside his door, she heard a muffled sound. A scream.

Her thumb darted to the scanner. Kari typed the VIP code in record speed and rushed inside. She followed the cries of anguish until they led her to the bathroom.

Ahmed kneeled on the white tile while he shook Ray's naked shoulders. He was unresponsive to the violent jerks and his eyes remained half open.

Kari froze at the entryway. "Oh, my Gods."

Ahmed whipped his head around to her, tears streaming down his face. "Please help him. He won't wake up!" Ahmed moved back to give her space.

She got down on her knees to assess him. There was no visible evidence of his chest rising and falling, so she hovered her hand over his mouth and nose. Warm air struck her palm then disappeared. Good. Next, she placed her index and middle finger at his neck to check for a pulse. It was like a small drum beating in rapid succession. She lowered her head—to an outsider it may have looked like she was about to kiss him—and smelled his breath. It was sweet.

Kari sat back on her heels, retrieved her phone from her pants pocket, and dialed the emergency medical services for the ship. "I need an emergency team here in VIP cabin 806 immediately! Ray Wibawa is unconscious with weak respiration and tachycardia. I think his blood sugar bottomed out."

"Dispatching the team now," the ship's emergency operator said. "Do you see evidence of poison or drugs in the area?"

"Not in the area." She looked up at Ahmed, who paced and chewed his fingernails. "Do you know if he was using drugs? I know he has anxiety meds."

"I . . . I don't think . . ." he stammered.

"We don't know," Kari reported.

"Do you know what his blood sugar is?" the operator asked.

"Hold on." Kari pressed the button on the insulin pump clipped to the waistband of Ray's pajamas bottoms. It read 0.0 units. "I need Ray's phone, Ahmed."

He didn't respond.

"Now, Ahmed!"

He ran out of the bathroom and came back a few seconds later, phone in hand, which he handed over to Kari. "What are you going to do?"

Kari didn't have time to explain that she had watched him use his diabetes app dozens of times. She placed Ray's thumb on his phone to unlock it then went to the app. Her own heart started beating almost as fast as Ray's as she read the insulin dose history. An hour ago, he had a massive dose pumped into his system even though his blood sugar level was stable at 98. "Thirty. His blood glucose is thirty."

"What?" Ahmed yelled. "Seventy is low. How can it be thirty?"

The emergency worker was silent for several seconds. "Can one of you stand by the door to let EMS in?"

"Ahmed, go open the door and keep others out of the way." Kari touched the side of Ray's face and massaged his stubble-covered cheek. "Listen to my voice. There's a lot of art you haven't made yet. I've been thinking of commissioning you to do something to my car, which is still in a garage in New York." That was a complete lie, but countless studies had shown activity in the auditory portion of the brain when people spoke to individuals who had shown minimal neurological responses.

"They're back there," she heard Ahmed said, which was followed by the sounds of rushed footsteps and a squeaking wheel.

Kari pushed herself off the ground to give them room. The team of four, which included Dr. Zak, worked to set up the gurney for transport and took his vitals. One member of the team placed an oxygen mask on him, another pricked his finger for a blood sugar test, and Zak disconnected the insulin port.

"Oh, God," Zak muttered as she saw the number. "Set a 0.5 mg glucagon IV. Kari, call up to the helipad, confirm the pilot is ready."

Kari did as she was ordered.

While one of her crew dug into a cooler, Zak swabbed the crook of his elbow with an alcohol swab and then set the IV catheter on top of his vein. Blood flashed inside and her skilled hands worked fast to remove the needle. Another person hooked up the tubing. Another raised the IV pole.

"Let's get him out of here!" Zak said.

Kari watched in horror as they took Ray's barely alive body away. "Wait!" she chased after them. "Here's his phone. It shows that his app gave him a large dose of insulin when he didn't need it."

Zak nodded. "Thank you."

Kari and Ahmed helped clear a path for them as onlookers stepped into the passageways. When they reached the top deck, the Guptas and Henry sprinted from their lounge seats to the scene.

"What's going on?" Henry asked.

"We have to take Ray to the nearest hospital onshore," Zak said. "It's his blood sugar."

The scene that unfolded before Kari next was unreal. The EMS crew took the gurney up the stairs leading to the helicopter. Zak followed. Henry didn't rush over to see Ray; rather, he consulted with Josef and gave him a pat on the back. When their mini-conference was over, Amara went to Henry, took his hands, and gave him a kiss on the cheek. When they parted, the afternoon sunlight reflected off a coin. Henry placed it in his breast pocket and boarded the helicopter.

As the blades began to whirl, Kari stood frozen, except for her arm, which had found its way to stretch across Ahmed's back to comfort him. What had she just witnessed? Henry watched Ray roll by him on a gurney with life support and his immediate reaction was to give Josef an attaboy. Red flags whipped around faster than the helicopter's departing wind.

This couldn't have been an accident.

Anything electronic could be hacked. And Josef had plenty of experience in that department. There was too much at stake now for her not to gather as much information as possible. She turned to fix that problem.

"Kari, wait," Amara called out.

She gritted her teeth as she stopped and faced her. "Yes, Ms. Gupta?"

"Please, call me Amara. Do you know what just happened?"

She could have sworn she watched Amara's lip upturn in the faintest smile, but as quickly as it appeared, it was gone. "I'm sorry, but even if I knew, I wouldn't be at liberty to say." As much as it pained her to ask the next question, she had to play the part. "Since Henry had to leave, would you like me to arrange a change of schedule for you?"

"Yes. I'll see Henry again some other time. If you could

notify my pilot that we'll be leaving Dubai as soon as the helicopter returns to the ship, that would be helpful. We'll wait in our suites in the meantime."

It took everything Kari had not to scream. "Of course."

Kari would see to their travel needs as soon as her first priority was tended to. She didn't bother knocking on Madeleine's door, she barged in and slammed it behind her.

"I'll call you back," Madeleine said with an arched brow and ended the call. "You better have a— You're shaking. Why are you shaking?"

"EMS just had to airlift Ray to shore."

Madeleine opened her mouth several times like a fish out of water. "I'm sorry, what?"

"Ray is on a helicopter right now, barely clinging to life—probably in insulin shock—and I think Henry and Josef had something to do with it."

"That's a very dangerous accusation to make."

"I know it is." She took a controlled deep breath but released it as a shaky exhale. "I need you to get the remote."

"I have to say that this is a request I didn't see coming."

"We both know that Henry is up to something massive, and the only way we're going to find out everything is if you let me inside his head."

Madeleine pursed her lips. "That goes against his orders, which, at this point, is fine by me." She beckoned Kari back.

Kari followed her into the secret office and watched Madeleine go through the motions involving the little black box until she pointed the remote at her.

"Just remember that you asked for this." Madeleine clicked the button

"I understand, ma'am." Kari waited until she had returned to her typical office, went through the bathroom, and left the administrative center.

Can't do this. I don't speak Tagalog.
Never remakes the coffee.
Such a tight skirt.
Update taking forever.
WU has a full month off between semesters?

The experience of having her telepathy back on full throttle was a good reminder of why she had put herself through two separate brain surgeries with morally ambiguous doctors in the first place. Thoughts continued to bombard her as she made her way to Ahmed's cabin. Before she tended to the Guptas, she needed to check in on him.

She knocked on his cabin door, but there was no response. He wasn't in the VIP assistant office either. Her next stop was the kitchen.

"Hello!" Kari said into the belly of the VIP kitchen. "Is anyone here?"

Chef Jon walked out with a green splash on his white chef's jacket and a mournful smile. "Hey, Kari. What can I do for you?" *Wonder how she is.*

"Have you seen Ahmed?"

Poor kid. Jon nodded. "He told me what happened with Ray. That's just awful."

"Do you know where Ahmed went? He's not in his cabin."

Cheese. "He saw a cheese plate the Gupta's ordered for pickup and said he'd take it to them. I tried to stop him but he wouldn't listen."

Just great. Ahmed was off duty and delivering dairy to people who would exploit anything he'd tell them. "Thanks, Jon." She left the kitchen and headed to the Guptas' cabins.

She rapped lightly on the VIP cabin door. Aarti answered. "I'm sorry to intrude, but is Ahmed here."

Collect the crier. "He is." Aarti moved to the side—still in her impossible heels—and went to the bar.

Ahmed couldn't have looked more out of place in the lavish dining area with his elastic shorts, gaming T-shirt, and flip-flops. His head was buried in his hands as he sobbed. Amara Gupta had a hand on his shoulder and spoke to him in hushed tones.

"Ah, Kari," Amara said and stood.

Ahmed lifted his head, allowing her to see his mournful eyes.

"I'm guessing you're worried about your colleague here."

"Yes." Kari walked to the other side of the table, getting them both in range. Not only could she see Ahmed was okay, she could learn what Amara's play was. "I needed to see that he's okay."

Brother's gone. Ahmed sniffled.

Compassion. Need that. Balance JJ and Leonarda. "That's good of you." Amara sipped her gin and tonic. "I'm sure it would be better for him if he spoke to a friend, not some stranger or client."

Kari left fast. Ahmed's eyes were fixed on the decorative cheese plate.

She took a seat at the table beside Ahmed, where Amara joined her. "I'm sorry I ran off as quickly as I did. We had to activate the next emergency response crew and I needed to notify Madeleine. Ray's in the best hands."

Calm in crisis. Need that. Balance Ise and Aarti.

Makes sense. "I understand," Ahmed said. "Have you heard anything more about his phone?"

Phone? Amara kept her expression neutral. "I'm sure it'll be at least thirty more minutes before we get a call."

"No," Ahmed said and shook his head. "I mean, did they see what went wrong with the diabetes app?"

They know?

Even though Kari had personally handed over Ray's cell

phone to Dr. Zak, she wasn't going to place a target on her back by admitting she was handed it. "EMS might have grabbed it on the way out."

Don't understand. "How does something like that happen?" Ahmed asked.

Ray knew too much. Amara clasped her hands. "I'm sure Henry will do everything he can to see that it never happens again and that Ray comes out of this." *Sounded believable.*

Under the table, Kari balled her hands into fists. "Right. Henry will do everything in his power, I'm sure."

Then, Kari saw Amara's visualization.

Amara and Henry were in a dark chamber with several columns. Kari had seen the room once before as a rough sketch in the Brisbane notebook, but this time she saw a new element: a massive marble fireplace, and etched into the stone, above the mantle, was a carving of the head of an elephant facing forward. Its tusks were as long as the trunk. The elephant was a symbol of power and didn't come as a great shock to Kari that it could be a mascot for In Virtute.

What was startling was that it matched the description of Henry's vision.

Chapter Nineteen

Malé, Maldives

"I suppose that closes our last session of the year," Ola said. "Do you have New Year's party plans?"

Kari moved her extended legs off the chaise and planted her feet on the ground. The change of furniture on the far side of the room had made for a more relaxing session and kept Ola's thoughts away from her. "I have to work tonight. I'm sure I'll catch an eyeful of partying though."

"Any big-time VIPs?" she asked with a mischievous grin.

Kari had to chuckle. Ola was professional yet always tried to get celebrity gossip. She had insisted that because they had doctor-patient confidentiality she wouldn't let the news slip. While Kari trusted Ola, she still wasn't going to tell her about the Fermis, Gabriella and her younger sister, Leonarda. "Just some rich people."

"You are such a hard nut to crack." Ola's smile faded and was replaced by her concerned therapist face. "Just so you know, fireworks can be challenging for someone who has experienced your type of trauma."

Kari rubbed her hands on her thighs. "I already have my

positive associations cued. Fourth of July with funnel cake when I was eight."

"Very good. I'll see you out."

Kari left her office and moved to the next agenda item of her day: a communication to Adam in an isolated area. Which was more challenging at this port than she had originally thought. She had to get creative.

Once on shore, voices continued to attack her, but Kari kept her focus. She went into a crowded corner store, bought a burner phone in cash, and tucked it into a nondescript paper bag she had brought with her. As she walked to her next destination, she gradually added pieces to her look from inside the bag. At a stop sign she put on over-sized sunglasses, at a park bench she switched shoes, in front of a street performer she unfolded the wide-brimmed hat, and before she hung a left for the luxury hotel with private beach she put on a hideous yet extravagant beach coverall and stuffed the paper bag into the designer bag from the *Hinewai* VIP lost and found.

The affluent area she was headed to meant she had to blend.

Kari strode through the exclusive hotel lobby with her shaded eyes forward, her shoulders back and down, and her nice but knock-off sandals making slight clicks with every confident foot strike. For extra insurance that no one bothered her, she had a one-sided conversation in a German accent about a designer watch she desired.

If Daddy didn't buy it for her, it'd be the silent treatment for him.

Once at her outdoor destination, she found an isolated lounge chair facing the ocean and flipped the sign that said 'Do not disturb'. She stripped down to the bikini she wore under her original shorts and tank top and scanned the area to ensure no one was watching. They weren't.

"It's Sky Fisher," she said into the burner phone. "Ray W's coma is no accident. His parents are at odds regarding life support. There's no will or advanced healthcare directive. Henry wants to pull the plug because Ray knows something."

Kari hung up, discretely removed the SIM card, and then headed to the crystal clear turquoise water to let nature help destroy the evidence. The rest of the phone could go in the bins on her way back to the ship. Along with her fancy outfit.

———

Kari heard a jubilant twang from the inside of Madeleine's office. She knocked and was soon greeted by Belle's smile. But then it was replaced with a frown.

Still looks in pain. "How are you feeling?" Belle asked.

While Kari's telepathy allowed her to learn more about the shady and murderous tendencies of her boss and his friends, it had meant she had needed to revert back to a life of solitude to keep her sanity. Kari had avoided her friends—thankfully most of WU was still on break—with excuses of a migraine, guitar lessons, a planned call with her grandparents, and terrible menstrual cramps. Although, the cramps had been real.

As someone who had superpowers and was conceived mystically, the fact that she still had to deal with menstruation was bullshit.

"I'm feeling much better," Kari said as she took her seat. "Thanks for asking."

Madeleine leaned back behind her grand desk, ensuring even more distance than usual, and gestured to Belle. "I was just telling her about the big party tonight."

Belle's knees bounced. *Exciting.* "I had no idea it was such a big deal. You didn't tell me!"

"I didn't know," Kari said. "Last year I was home at this time."

"Well, it's a lot of fun. So, squeeze in a nap and come up to watch the fireworks," Madeleine said. "That's much more exciting than a ball drop."

Explosions. Loud. "Oh," Belle said with trepidation. "Um, that'll be fun." Belle stood, placed a hand on Kari's shoulder, and locked eyes with her. *Hope there.* "I'll see you later for the fireworks?"

Why was Belle so anxious? "I'll do my best to get out of the Fermi's grasp and find you."

Thank God. "Great."

When Belle left and shut the door behind her, Kari turned to Madeleine, who had a mischievous smile. "What?"

"Nothing. Just enjoying the show." Madeleine gave her desk a light smack. "Back to the important matters. Are you really doing poorly and haven't told me?"

Kari was momentarily stunned by the question. It sounded as though Madeleine actually cared about her. "I'm fine, but I've had to tell a few lies to avoid hanging out with friends. I don't want to hurt their feelings."

"Look at you lying for the sake of your own convenience."

"Trust me, convenient is the last thing it is."

"Touché. Let's move on to discussing your shift, then. Belle reported that the Fermi sisters are excited you're assigned tonight. I don't think you'll have to work too hard unless Henry has something up his sleeve, which . . . who knows?"

Kari blew a breath out from between tight lips. These days that was always a possibility. "What are they all doing now?"

"Currently enjoying the lounge before dinner. Except for Finn."

"Finn's here?" Kari shrieked.

Madeleine pushed back in her chair until she was nearly in

the bathroom. "Mind the volume. I assumed that either Belle or Finn would have given you a heads-up."

Still stunned, Kari shook her head.

"Well, now you know. You should also know that Finn's brought along their fiancé, Renata."

Instead of shaking her head, Kari gripped the arm rests. "Why didn't Finn tell me?"

"They secretly enjoy awkward surprises? I don't know." Madeleine opened her laptop and typed. "Ah, yes. It appears Henry added Finn to the VIP visitor log late yesterday evening when Ahmed was on shift. I'm sure Ahmed would have told you, but he's still struggling with . . . you know . . . things."

"Yeah, I know." Ahmed had been moving through life in a trance since Ray had been medically evacuated from the ship.

"That's all I have to say, except don't be petty because Renata is strikingly beautiful. You're better than that. Dismissed."

"I appreciate the words of encouragement," Kari said as she left and headed to the VIP lounge. Why hadn't Finn let her know? Instead of playing rich girl on shore that morning she and Finn could have used that time to have a drink and catch up. Or admired their beautiful red hair, porcelain skin, and toned legs.

Like what friends did.

"Karishma!" Henry hollered across the deck with a glass of white wine in his hand.

In the lounge area, Kari expected to see Finn sitting languidly in a chair with a bikini-clad, supermodel-esque fiancé on their lap while she twirled Finn's hair around her finger. Instead, Kari saw the Fermi sisters—no Finn, no fiancé —also raise their glasses to her arrival. Josef was nowhere to be seen.

Gabriella walked over and greeted her with a kiss on each

cheek. *Intelligence.* "It's nice to see you again, Kari. I like that you're growing your hair out." *Still too short.*

Kari instinctually reached up to touch the hair at her neck. "My goal is to have a stylish top half while keeping the bottom shorter."

Trendy.

Acceptable. Gabriella touched the shoulder of the brunette woman who was at least twenty years her junior. "This is my sister, Leonarda. Leonarda, this is Kari, the young woman Henry and I were telling you about."

They trust her? So young. Leonarda extended her hand to Kari in the style of a princess waiting for the back of it to be kissed. "Pleasure."

"Likewise," Kari said as she shook her limp hand in an odd grip. "I can see that each of you have a drink, but can I get any of you something else before dinner?"

After thoughts and dialogue about mangoes and nuts, Henry said from his lounge seat, "And get yourself a drink because we want you to be a part of this conversation, just like the visit with Jasi and Ise."

"Understood, sir."

Kari left to put in the request for the snacks and went to the bar. If she had to be quick, witty, and catch nefarious plans, she couldn't drink like them, especially with her two-drink tolerance. "Can you make me a ginger ale with club soda in a champagne flute?" she asked the bartender.

Weird. "If you want."

After her mocktail that resembled champagne was prepared, she headed back to the group where there was an empty seat beside Henry. Ray should have been occupying it, but she sat anyway and lifted her flute in the air. "So long last year." They all swarmed her with their wine for an actual toast.

More masculine hair does suit her.

Clink.

Bring crackers with bits of rosemary.

Clink.

If fidele change everything.

Clink.

Kari agreed with the assessment of her hair, hope for rosemary crackers, and that the conversation ahead would probably change her life.

"Before I forget," Gabriella said, "Finn wanted me to tell you that they needed a powernap but will come out later."

Kari's smile was genuine. "That's good to hear."

Don't know if Renata will like. "You should know that Finn brought his soon-to-be-bride."

The tinge of jealousy was still present. However, she sipped her cold drink instead of saying something catty, then rolled up her sleeves and released the top most button of her shirt. The Maldivian heat was no joke.

Renata wore out. "I didn't know someone could enjoy parties so much," Leonarda said. "Renata is rather energetic."

The sisters chuckled while the bartender brought over their snack board and small plates.

Down to business. "Karishma, I would ask if you remembered the conversation we had in my cabin in Cape Town, but I know that you never forget anything. Have you given any thought since then about acting as my fidele?"

"Yes, but I have some questions."

Of course. "Please, go ahead. We will answer what we can."

"So," Kari drawled, "what is this group you're are a part of?"

Don't know all. Henry gestured to his guests. "This would be best if it came from you, Gabriella."

Tricky. Not properly initiated. "We're a very important and influential group. You may be thinking that you already know this, but I assure you that you do not understand the full scope." *More power than any politician or monarchy.* "The goal is for the greater good of humanity. We aren't evil." She finished with a laugh.

Leonarda and Henry cackled along with her.

Kari concluded that they were definitely evil and delusional enough to believe their brand of morality was a-okay. "How long has Henry been in?"

I wish. "I'm not yet, but I can be soon. There are two hurdles and one last requirement I need." He motioned toward Kari.

"I'm a hurdle?" she asked Gabriella.

She's fabulous. Gabriella put down her wine glass. "The fidele is a requirement. It's important to have a loyal and trusted sounding board and assistant. Most, but not all, members have a family member."

Wish son out picture. "It's an overwhelming idea," Leonarda said. "But you should know that the role is not intended to be a replacement of the person." *Even if more qualified.* She sent a sweet smile to her older sister.

Kari sipped her diluted ginger ale while she studied this new dynamic. Leonarda played nice, but not only did she wish Ray was dead, she also resented that Gabriella was in charge. She'd pick at that thread later. "Not to sound selfish, but can we circle back to me? I mean, Henry has only known me for a little over a year. And you"—she pointed at Gabriella—"only know me from two encounters."

Love how she questions.

Know plenty. "Everyone here knows you are gifted in dozens of ways." Henry cocked his head. "Do you honestly not believe you were meant to change the world?"

Points to the megalomaniac in the tan suit. "The thought has crossed my mind."

"Everyone in the group who has met you sees greatness in you," Henry said, and Gabriella nodded. "They admire your intelligence, your wit, and your self-confidence. You are more than my pick to be my fidele, you are also theirs."

So true. "I couldn't have said it better," Gabriella said. *And can see to her safety.*

The flattery was nice to hear, as was the fact that Gabriella still wanted to see her safe. "Hypothetically speaking, say I agree to be this fidele person. What's my job on the ship? I can't travel on a whim with Henry if I'm supposed to be arranging jet ski fun for a VIP."

"If you accept this new role," Henry said, "you'll no longer have to be a VIP assistant. You can be anything you'd like, as long as you stay on the *Hinewai*, because that's where I am most of the time, and are available for my projects." *Bunker.*

This was it! This was precisely how she could get inside, learn their secrets, and blow up the system. And per the 'fidele' in his will, she could see that people and places in need received her share of the money once he died. "I accept."

Praise the Gods. "Excellent!" He raised his glass. "This is a grand way to start the new year!" *Now the two challenges.*

———

Kari had enough distance between the three other diners to enjoy a more peaceful meal of Maldivian lobster and champagne. The real stuff. But she still had challenges as she ate. She had to make her laughs sound genuine and her questions not sound suspicious or intrusive. Once the chocolate dome dessert came out, the conversation shifted into one where she could simply listen: the bunker.

All members of In Virtute were required to have a safe underworld haven to escape war, international tribunals, or even paparazzi. She had seen clues of Gabriella's bunker in the Maltese Islands last winter and had its presence confirmed shortly after. Now Kari learned that Henry's helicopter ride in Chile was when he had visited Ricardo Roja's bunker. Henry's task now was to narrow down the choices for his own bunker site.

"The Outback is perfect," he said.

Given that Kari was on her third glass of champagne—so much for the rule of two—she had no hesitation telling him why that was terrible. "It's so isolated that getting resources there to build it will be a nightmare. You'd need to build a camp for the construction workers." When the Fermis nodded, she continued, "Then, there's the heat. They'll probably have to work at night. That's when a lot of critters come out," she said in a warning tone. "Good luck to anyone who finds a snake in the portable toilet at that time."

The sisters' mouths gaped in identical ways.

"How about New Zealand?" Henry blurted with a smile. "It is my mother's home country."

"Are you sure about that?" Kari asked. "There are lots of fault lines there. You'd have to include earthquake-proofing."

He *tsked*. "And it has to be in my territory?"

The sisters nodded.

"Alright, I'll continue to brainstorm." Henry pointed to Kari's empty flute with his chocolate-smeared spoon. "Would you like another?"

"I don't want to be in pain tomorrow, so no."

"Wise choice," Gabriella said. "But leave room for one more glass at midnight, which reminds me"—she turned to her sister—"I'm going to relax a bit before the party starts."

"That's a good idea at your advanced age," Leonarda said. "I'm going to try to squeeze in a round of virtual golf at Augusta." As she placed her napkin on the table, she looked at Kari.

"Can you ensure that my masseuse for tomorrow doesn't use lotions containing methylchloro . . ." She snapped her fingers as if that would help her remember.

"Methylchloroisothiazolinone," Kari said in a single breath despite a lack of total sobriety.

"Yes. Please check that."

"Of course," Kari said, and began to rise from the table.

"Before you go and do that," Henry said, "I'd like to talk about the next steps now that you've agreed to the fidele position." He waited until the Fermi sisters were gone before he continued. "You can go about your duties on the ship as you normally would until your birthday. Around that time we'll both meet Botan Itoi, but his visit is just a formality at this point since I've passed the test with everyone else."

"What about those two hurdles mentioned earlier?"

"Ah, yes. When you excused yourself earlier, Gabriella informed me that there is a team working on it. They will not be hurdles much longer."

There was more to it than that. Kari moved closer, under the guise of reaching for the water pitcher near Henry. "What are the hurdles?"

Mystery. Ray more fight than expected. "It's better if you don't know."

There it was. A practical admission that he tried to murder his own son. Rather than shatter the glass pitcher over his head, she sucked in her cheek and returned to her seat to top off her water glass. She debated how to ask her next question, but there was no delicate way to ask. "When I become your fidele, will Madeleine still have control of my remote?"

"No." He raised his finger to make a literal point. "And I must stress that you cannot speak a word of this to her."

For this, Kari would obey because of possible Madeleine retaliation. Even if she had been nicer to her these days, there was a history Kari would never forget. "Are you going to be the one who tells Madeleine about my new job? Because it does conflict with my current contract."

"I will deliver all of the news to Madeleine in person. As for your contract? Poof." He mimicked dust in the air. "I should note that this new role will be unwritten. Absolutely no one, except for those in In Virtute, can know. But for the sake of practicality, like taxes and telling your family and friends what you do here on the ship, we can create a title for whatever it is you want to do with Wibawa Enterprises. Think it over. Think about how you'll want to start your twenties. In the meantime" —he stood from his seat—"I'm also going to power nap so I can welcome the new year with proper vigor. That'll also give you two time to talk without an audience."

She scrunched her face. "Huh?"

Kari spun in her seat and saw Finn walking toward her holding a dessert plate and a small sauce pourer. Their wavy red hair and white linen outfit billowed as they took casual steps toward the table. Were they still swoon-worthy? Yes. Was she pulled out of her chair by some invisible force to hug them? No.

"Hello, stranger." Finn placed the dish down beside her. *Didn't even stand.* "I thought maybe I'd get a hug."

"Sorry. It's been a weird day." Kari gave them a wan smile and stood to embrace them. "It's good to see you." The bergamot scent of Finn's hair products wafted off them.

Forgot feels. "I can't believe it's been almost a year since we've seen each other."

"Or about six months by my calculation."

Always too precise. They relaxed their arms and took a seat beside Kari. *Seems troubled.* Finn tapped their temple. "Is it on? Or is it off? I forget how it works."

Nobody could know she had defied Henry's orders when it

came to her device. However, Finn was an empath and knew her emotional state. She'd have to lie except when it came to how she felt. "I'm telepathy-free at the moment."

Relief. "Must be wonderful."

"I have to say that it is amazing."

Finn poured warm raspberry sauce over the white chocolate dome. "If you ever go back into lab work again, maybe you can research my brain?"

While Finn's abilities gave them the occasional headache, there was no way she would ever place that on the same level of annoyance as telepathy. "Has Gabriella inquired why you're exceptionally good at reading people yet?"

Strange she hasn't. "No." They dipped their spoon in the hole of the melted dome and into the torte. "I'm forbidden by Henry to say anything about your abilities or mine to her. Remember, I still technically work for Henry; I'm subcontracted out to Gabriella."

Of course, she remembered. "How about Renata? Does she know?"

Suspicious. "I don't think so. I downplay it quite a bit when we're together, which is often since we're colleagues, too."

"What does she do?"

Finn focused on another large spoonful of dessert. Then moaned. *Amazing.* "Clothes."

"Gabriella needs someone to put her clothes on her?" She didn't appear to have mobility issues.

Finn grinned, a small amount of chocolate at the corner of their lip. *Missed humor.* "Renata's a stylist. She picks out Gabriella's different outfits for the day but is also charged with buying new pieces, repair, and laundering. That kind of thing." *Jon outdid himself.*

It was just rude that Finn found the dessert more tantalizing than her. Especially with her shirt more unbuttoned than usual. Did they feel nothing for her anymore? "Does Declan like her?"

Adores. "He does. She loves to dress him up and then they put on little plays for me. Plus, there's the energy! She's the only one I've ever met who can keep up with him. Since he turned five, he's like on turbo speed."

Her jealousy hackles lowered. It sounded like Renata was excited to be a maternal figure in Declan's life, whereas Kari never saw that in herself. Except with dogs. "I'd like the chance to meet Renata. It's a shame she didn't want to join you for dessert?"

Finn enjoyed another bite. *Recovery needed.* "While she does have a lot of energy, she's exhausted from a boat party earlier and wanted to rest before the big festivities. She'd like to meet you, too, which I was surprised by because initially I had to be very clear with her about our friendship. She was a little weary of the texts you were sending, but she's good now."

So Renata had been a little jealous, too. Good. "You must have had a real intense connection to get engaged so quickly."

Such magic. Finn smiled with a faraway look. "We did. Were you surprised when you saw the ring picture?"

"I was, but I'm not judging. I think my moms had this instalove thing going on too when they first met."

Fair. "It's like what they say, sometimes you just know when you meet the right person." Finn put the spoon down. *My turn.* "Can I ask you some questions now?"

"What do you want to know?"

Mixed emotions. "How are you really? You're emanating a stress that I don't remember you having last year, and last year was pretty stressful."

"A lot's changed. A new job, new responsibilities, old responsibilities . . . I'm worried about Nani Tanha."

Strange. "Even with all that I'd have thought that therapy and your new friend group would have caused you to relax a bit."

"You and I both know I can't talk to them about everything I do."

"Surely, the other VIP assistants can listen. I know Ahmed is going through a lot now and Matthew tends to get distracted, but Belle seems great."

"Because she is great, but the VIP situation is different this year." She folded her arms across her chest. "I can't get into why."

Finn leaned back like they were assessing her. *Changed just then.* "Why not?"

"Things are really complicated right now."

"Then start simplifying. Oh, hold on." Finn reached into the pocket of their linen pants and took out their phone. A frown formed. "Renata's stomach is bothering her and wants some ginger ale."

"I guess I should see that that's taken care of."

Silly. "No, I'll get it. It'll be nice to catch up with the kitchen staff a bit more and give Jon my compliments on that dessert. Will I see you later tonight at the party?"

Belle wanted, possibly needed, Kari at the fireworks. That was a priority. "Maybe in passing, but hopefully we can talk some more before you leave."

Probably not. "I'll try." Finn took their dishes and headed back into the ship.

Before she abandoned the dining table too, she left a message at the spa about the lotion. Then, she filled a water bottle and walked most of the ship since it was too early to be seen at the party deck. That'd help her sober up and pass the time before what she hoped was a quiet night.

And peaceful entrance into the new year.

Chapter Twenty

The passageways were mostly vacant, especially those in the WU decks, since the new semester didn't start for another two weeks. Kari knocked on Belle's cabin door, but there was no answer. She must have gone to the party already. As midnight approached, Kari checked on the VIPs once more. The Fermis were both content and told her to enjoy the evening, so she headed to the party. As Kari took to the stairs again, she took a moment to appreciate the festive lights from the nearest resort.

On the party deck, there were hundreds of people drinking, dancing to bass-filled music, and talking. Talking in lounge chairs. Against the rails. In all the corners. She had never seen this many people congregated in one spot on the *Hinewai* before. The amount of people to sift through to find Belle would be annoying, but there was something special about fireworks with a friend that she couldn't pass up.

Even if the explosions were something she had needed to prepare herself for.

A guy from accounting with a neon green headband

jumped in front of her. *Name?* He lowered his eyes to her name tag and then her cleavage. *Fantastic tits.* "Hello, Kari. Do you have someone picked out for your midnight kiss?"

She didn't reprimand him for his staring, thoughts, or breast imagery because it only showed that he was observant. She knew her boobs were magnificent. Kari walked away without saying a word and headed away from the crowd. Along the way she saw couples cozied up to one another all eagerly waiting for the clock to strike midnight.

Kari still didn't see Belle.

Across the deck, Jade and Neill gave each other googly eyes as their four hands laid on her nonexistent baby bump. On the edge of the dance floor, Finn and Renata stayed in slow-dance formation even though the song was upbeat. Even Doug looked snuggly with the HR lady.

Then, Kari saw Belle away from the party, at the far end of the deck.

Dressed in an off-duty outfit of running shorts and a WU tank top, Belle rested her forearms on the railing and peered out in the direction of the resort. Under the soft glow of the ship's light, Kari could see a few blond hairs that had escaped her ponytail blowing freely into her face. When she lifted her hand to push the strands behind her ear, Belle caught Kari's eye and quickly spun to have her back to her. She brushed her hand across her face.

Kari headed her way but stopped once she reached telepathy range. "What's wrong?"

Belle turned to her with teary eyes and a quivering jaw. With a deep breath, she composed herself. "I made myself sad."

"Well, that was dumb." Kari's tactic of using an unantici-pated, callous remark was successful in both getting a smile and a genuine laugh out of Belle. "How did you make yourself sad?"

Belle bit her lower lip. She concluded her non-answer by picking her fingernail with her thumbnail.

It was obvious something was troubling her. Something so private or complicated Belle didn't know how to answer. Maybe it was the fireworks? Something bad had happened when she was younger with them? A cousin had severely injured themselves or something?

Kari opened her mouth and then closed it. She looked at the resort, then back to Belle. She fidgeted with her hands, only to stuff them in her pockets. Kari wanted to say or do something to help, but at the same time she hated it when all she needed was space and people wouldn't give it to her because they felt like it was their job to make her feel better. "Would you like me to leave?"

Belle's face contorted into a painful grimace.

"Or I can stay," Kari quickly added. "We can watch the fireworks together, support each other during the booms to create some sort of new positive memory. Maybe talk." The boisterous cheering from a group doing a water shotski carried over to their portion of the deck. "Or not talk."

"I'm sorry, I'm not trying to be dramatic." Belle sighed as she looked in the distance but then focused her attention back to Kari. "I try to be a good and strong person, but . . . sometimes things are too much, you know?" she asked with a voice crack.

Kari had no idea someone else's pain could be so brutal on her. "Yeah, I do. Especially around this time of year. Meeting goals, seeing or missing friends and fam—"

Tears erupted and streamed down Belle's face.

Kari rushed in for a gentle hug. "I'm here. I can help . . . maybe."

So alone. "You can't," she said into the crook of Kari's neck. "I wish you could help." *Can't do this.* Belle placed her hands on Kari's shoulders and gently pushed her way until Kari had no choice but to release the embrace.

The rejection stung more than Kari thought it would, but she shook it off. There were other ways to be supportive. While Belle may not have believed anyone could help, Kari could stay by her side to at least make sure she was safe and had a shoulder to cry on. That was if Belle changed her mind and wanted it. "I can still stay to keep you company. The quiet kind, if you want."

Want so bad. "I'd like that." Belle's voice was whisper quiet.

"Okay. I'm here until you push me away. Again." Kari gave her a soft smile as the crowd erupted into cheers on the deck. Kari turned to the bow and saw that the ten-second New Year's Eve countdown had been placed on the gigantic screen.

Be like to kiss her.

She turned and had to tilt her head up because Belle was so close. Kari subconsciously licked her lips but didn't close the distance. Instead, she reached up to brush away one of Belle's freshly fallen tears. "I don't know if my opinion has any weight, but I think you are a very good person and incredibly strong."

"Ten!" the crowd erupted.

Too good for me. Belle grinned. "At this point in my life, your opinion means the most," she said through countdown cheers.

"Six!"

How could Belle think she was too good for her when she knew that she was short-tempered, sarcastic, profanity-happy, and wished people dead?

"There's so much good in you, Kari." *So much beauty.*

Kari gazed into Belle's glassy dark blue eyes and her imagery set a fire in her belly. Belle pictured them kissing passionately against the wall directly behind them.

The crowd yelled, "Three!"

In different ways, loneliness had chipped away at both of their spirits. But that was the past. Why did they both have to be so lonely in the present? Kari cradled Belle's face in her hands.

Going to kiss me?

"Two!"

Kari inhaled the scent of sandalwood and licked her lips once more.

Oh my God, she is.

"One!"

Kari raised herself on her tiptoes and brought their lips together.

Really happening.

"Happy New Year!" the crowd yelled in unison as Kari followed through with what Belle had imagined.

The fantasy Kari had created was much different than reality. Belle followed her lead. Belle's skin was softer. Her hands gripped Kari's hips harder. Her mouth hungrier with the slightest hint of bourbon. Kari had never been kissed with this level of intensity before. It was like Belle craved her. And, in a first, hearing Belle's thoughts about their kiss didn't make the moment awkward or annoying. Knowing Belle's desire only enhanced her arousal as the fireworks lit the night sky and then pierced the air with their deafening booms.

Both safe. Not bombs. Can't do. One of Belle's hands moved to the center of Kari's chest and pushed her away. *Mistake.*

Kari stood, confused by the thought and the action. She hadn't guessed or taken a chance that Belle had wanted the kiss. She had seen and heard the yearning for it. Kari's mind whirled as the rest of her stilled. "I'm sorry. I assumed you wanted . . . that."

I'm terrible. "I do, it's just . . . " Belle shook her head. *Tired of lies. Undercover so hard.*

Kari's legs wavered as if the next firework had gone off beside her. She staggered back against the railing. "Undercover?" she muttered, barely audible.

Belle's eyes flashed open and her breathing came in short bursts. *How?*

The fuck. "Jesus Christ, Belle!" Doug said in a fierce whisper as he suddenly appeared before them. "What the hell are you doing with her? In front of people, no less."

"I didn't say anything, Doug, I swear to God." Belle's voice trembled as she spoke. *She UC too?* "I didn't."

The scorching tickle that had filled Kari's belly was replaced by a frozen fist in the gut. Belle was undercover? A spy? She couldn't be. Kari's breathing became shallow and irregular, but she recognized her hyperventilating and began four-seven-eight breaths.

Fuck. Bad. This is bad. Doug spun in a slow circle and placed his hands on either side of his temple. "This is . . ." He clenched his fists. *Fuck. Fuck. Fuck.* "Okay, this is what we're going to do, aside from keeping our voices down. I have to make a call. In the meantime, you"—he pointed to Belle—"go to your cabin. And you"—he pointed to Kari—"wait a few seconds and then run after her. Stay in Belle's cabin until I get you."

That fact that Doug was giving her orders took Kari out of her seven second breath hold. "Wait. What?"

Doug rubbed the back of his neck. *Remember Kari reads minds.*

Another gut strike, but this was more like a spinning back kick. "How do you know that about me?"

Belle's head whipped in Doug's direction. *What he know?*

Okay. This works. Doug looked at Kari. *Nod if you hear me.* Kari didn't comply.

Doug held his hands in a prayer-like formation in front of her. *Please trust that I'm on your side. Madeleine's office has a bug, so I know what all that thought spying on Henry talk was about now.*

Shit. Doug did know. Kari nodded.

Good. He alternated his attention between her and Belle. "We all have to play this very smart and make it look like something else for the cameras." *They're listening too, so get your work cell out. I'm going to knock it out of your hand. Be angry when I do.*

Kari's nose scrunched. "Huh?"

He began to pace and gesticulate wildly as he spouted random slurred sentences about sexual harassment, WU policies, ship policies, his ex-wife, and the fact that he just kissed the HR lady.

Now Kari understood. He was playing drunk and stupid so she would be embarrassed and angry. Although, that wasn't really acting on her part. "You're drunk off your ass! You know what"—she took out her work phone—"I'm calling—"

He spun back to her and knocked the phone from her hand. It hit the deck floor and bounced through the slats in the railing.

Kari stared at him, mouth agape, and then to the location where the phone may have fallen. Even though she had been warned, she didn't actually think he'd follow through with it.

"Shit. Belle, you should go to your cabin until I provide an update." *Kari, wait a few seconds, then go after her.* Doug walked away.

"Hold on!" Kari chased him. "I still don't understand why I have to go to her cabin?"

Your cabin might be bugged again. This whole fucking ship is bugged and they aren't all ours. Belle's cabin is clear. She's also completely in the dark about your mindreading skill. He placed his hands on his hips and folded in his lips. *This is fucking Montauk Project part two.*

Kari watched him head down the stairs. Then she dared a look at Belle, who gave her a sad nod and walked away.

After she gave Belle a five-second head start, Kari ran after her, ensuring it played out well for the cameras. She slowed her run to a jog, then to a brisk walk, once they reached her dorm level. Kari pounded on her cabin door. "We need to talk!"

Belle opened the door, but then went to her bed. She sat with her knees to her chest, still looking terrified and lost. Earlier, it was passion that had made Kari's blood run hot, now it was fury. She had questions and she would get answers. Kari moved closer until her knees touched Belle's mattress.

So angry. I did this. Never forgive me. When UC slip?

It took a moment for Kari's brain to process the new acronym, but given the circumstances she deduced that UC stood for undercover. "No one slipped. I have a very unique skill."

Belle pointed at Kari as though she were the devil looming over her who had come to drag her into hell. *My thoughts?* "How did you know what I was thinking?"

If Doug knew, then Belle would know soon enough. "I'm a telepath." While Belle's brows lifted, Kari moved to the next question. "Have you been using me?"

That's not real. "Wait. What do you mean you're a telepath? That's not real."

"You believe in aliens and that Jesus was a virgin birth! I think you can expand your mind a bit to accept the fact that my brain has an extra feature."

A sound of disgust left Belle which was quickly followed by a tilt of her head. *Good point. But need test.*

Kari crossed her arms. She hated this game but understood it needed to be played. "Think of an atypical color."

"What?" *Like chartreuse?*

"Chartreuse."

Belle paled—not turning a sickly yellow-green—like she had seen a gruesome ghost. "How?"

Kari unfolded her arms for the sole purpose of wagging her finger. "No, no, no. I get to ask the questions now since I'm the one who's been lied to. Have you been using me?"

Furious. "I haven't been using you, I promise. Please, believe me."

"Sure. No problem. I'll believe everything 'my friend' has told me for the past six months." She put her hands on her hips and paced. The more she thought about Belle's deception the more her anger transitioned to disgust. And disappointment. Her muscles tightened like she was about to go into a jiu-jitsu match, and she fought back tears. "I can't believe I actually thought you were my friend! Brav-fucking-o for that acting performance."

Not an act. "I am your friend." Belle picked at her thumbnail. "And I'm not here for you. You can't be why I'm here! You're a US citizen."

Kari knew of countless investigations conducted by the United States government on its own citizens. It was like their favorite pastime. "Americans are investigated all the time."

Intel. "I'm not investigating anything."

As soon as Kari put those two facts together, she remembered one specific agency that had no law enforcement function and only gathered information on non-US citizens. In theory. "Are you CIA?"

Damn. Belle dropped her head back against the wall with a thud.

"Holy shit! You're with the CIA."

"I can neither confirm nor deny that." Belle reached past the mostly full bottle of bourbon on the nightstand for the tissue box and blew her nose. Holding the tissue in her hand, she banged the back of her head against the wall. Each thud was accompanied by a *Damn*. "This is not how any of this was supposed to go. I was so careful but . . . But then I drank alone and got sad. Started thinking too much. Thinking about my life. Thinking about you." More head bangs and *Damns*. "While I've always liked you as a person . . . As I've gotten to know you, I've grown so . . . I mean . . . I can't deny that I like you in a non-platonic way."

"Oh, is that what your tongue in my mouth meant? I didn't realize."

Let her lash out. Deserve it. Belle took a deep breath to settle herself. "I'm sorry, I truly am, and I understand that you're hurt—"

Kari's anger surged once more. "I don't think you fully appreciate the scope of how hurt I am. I haven't had a friend I could truly confide in since I was twelve. Twelve! And on top of that, I developed non-platonic feelings, too. Has that sunk in yet?"

Yes. Belle nodded.

"Now, on top of that, I learn that you're a fraud!" Kari picked up the Halloween picture. "Is 'Tess' even real? Or did you pick her picture out of stock photos and thought, 'she'd make a good, sad story' for your cover'?"

"Tess is real. Was real." *Patrol IED. Explosion.* "I'm sorry, but I can't . . ."

So the killed in action reason Belle had told in poker was true. And this provided a clear reason for the firework fear.

"Her face is covered, so I'm allowed to have the picture." *Couldn't move to save her.*

A piece of the Belle puzzle fell into place. In a millisecond, other pieces rushed around it, snapping into place: her ability to identify a helicopter from a mile away, her perfect posture, her fitness, her ability to follow orders without question or comment, and her shoulder. Before Belle was CIA, she was military. "You were in that explosion, too. I knew that scar on your shoulder was too janky to be surgery."

Belle flinched. *Stop.* "I know you're mad, but I'd appreciate it if you showed some sensitivity to that portion of my life."

"I'm just learning which portions are real!"

Wrong. "My reactions and personality are genuine. You can't fake that." Belle inhaled deeply. *Tell poker.* "I'll admit getting you involved with poker was a selfish move on my part, but I only did it because I wanted to add some maturity to the table and I thought you'd like it. Getting together at your place was an organic progression to our genuine friendship. I didn't fake that." She reached for her water glass behind the bourbon and took a swig. *The kiss.* "And I'll also admit that up on the deck I was thinking about what it would be like if you kissed me. And"—her eyes shot open further and brightened—"I just realized that's exactly what happened. You read my mind."

Kari gritted her teeth and nodded.

Belle hung her head. *Damn.* "Still, I should have stopped you, but I just . . . I wanted it so badly." *Moment weakness.* "I needed that connection."

Kari's rage waned the slightest fraction and was replaced by empathy. "Even with your thoughts, I shouldn't have kissed you. We had a conversation about boundaries and working together which—oh my Gods—you thinking about 'staying focused on the job' when we first met and 'reports for Doug' have whole different meanings now." Kari walked away and leaned against the far wall. She had to process her own feelings without interference.

They gawked at each other as they each came to terms with the bombshell the other had dropped. They didn't speak again for what seemed like hours, even though only a few seconds had passed.

Belle cleared her throat. "Can I ask how you can be a telepath?"

Kari went to the edge of her roommate's bed for a seat and summarized everything from the development of her ability to what had happened at inCog. To Belle's credit, she appeared fascinated. "There's a remote to turn my telepathy off, but I don't have possession of it. A murderous bitch who loves Earl Grey does."

Oh no. "Madeleine has it. Why?"

"Why do you think?"

Blackmail, secrets. "So you can act as her spy."

"And Henry's." Kari crossed her arms. "Normally it's turned on, so I don't have telepathy for my non-working hours. That's why I can hear your thoughts now but couldn't during our hangouts. I probably would have figured out your whole 'UC' gig sooner."

Probably. So open. "I'm surprised you've been so forthcoming with telling me all of this."

Kari shrugged. There was still plenty she hadn't told Belle. "I figure you'll find out since Doug knows and my attitude makes a lot more sense when you know this fun fact about me. And I guess I still want you to know me." She shook her head. "I feel like such an idiot. Someone like me will never get a normal life with a true friend."

Awful to think. "You're not an idiot, and I think in another circumstance we could have been the best of friends. If it helps, I want you to know the real me, too, but I can't. I'm already thinking I'll have to catch the next flight out since I've been compromised."

"Well, technically, you don't have to say anything. If you catch my drift."

Sneaky. "True, but I'd feel more comfortable and our friendship would be more honest if it was information I volunteered."

"Fair point." Kari sat back against the wall, ensuring enough space. "I'm out of range now."

Her blond brow furrowed. "Like when you're far away you can't read minds?"

"That's exactly what it means. So, can I ask you a few basic questions? Nothing too invasive, I promise."

"Okay," Belle said unsure. "I'll answer if I can."

Kari nodded. "We'll start off easy. You're not twenty-two, are you?"

"No. But I am in my twenties."

"And is your birthday around Thanksgiving?"

"No."

"How about the accent and 'kiss my biscuits'?"

Belle chuckled. "Both genuine."

The accent led Kari to think about where she was from. "What you told me about your family and chosen family is true though, isn't it?"

Belle appeared to swallow a large lump in her throat. "I think you know that answer."

Kari did. And even with her feelings of betrayal lingering, she didn't want to hurt Belle. She changed her line of questioning. "I caught Doug's thoughts about bugs in my cabin and around the ship. Do you know anything about that?"

Thumbnail pick.

"I feel like I should tell you that when you have a tough decision to make or don't know what to say, you pick your nail with your thumb."

Belle looked down at her hand, then lifted her head. "That's more of a question for Doug. But this room and our poker room are safe. I check regularly."

"Okay." Kari took in the movie posters that covered Belle's side of the room and rewound the last few hours.

Drinks and fidele talk with the Fermis. Taking a new role on the ship. Seeing Finn. Kissing Belle. Learning Belle and Doug's secrets. Her sharing that she's a telepath. "This whole night has been unreal, but learning about you and Doug . . . I would have been less surprised if I had been hit by a truck on the ship."

Belle sipped her water. "Is it that surprising though? Do you honestly think that you and Adam Cho are the only ones in the world suspicious of Henry Wibawa? The only ones who see him as a threat?"

Suddenly, Kari's big brain deflated. "That might be a good point."

"*Mm-hmm*. And, I hate to say this, but the minute you accompanied Henry to that charity event in Stockholm last year, you put a target on your back. People are looking at you as a way of getting to him. Some probably even think you're in on his schemes."

Kari's eyes grew wider. The international community thought she was in on it? But then again, why wouldn't they think that? She had made her way into Henry's inner circle in less than two years. That was unprecedented. She placed her elbows on her bunched knees as she contemplated her next move. But she couldn't. The stress and emotional ups and downs of the past several hours had caught up to her to the point where she was exhausted. Kari shut her eyes and rubbed her temples from the headache building. She kept her eyes closed because it felt so good.

After a moment of quiet, Belle broke the silence. "Kari, I know I hurt and disappointed you. I can only hope that you understand why I did what I did and that someday you can forgive me for the pain I caused you."

Kari thought about her friend, the spy. The sweet woman. The cinephile. The adventurer. The Christian. The competitor. Her name wasn't Belle, but Kari knew exactly who she was. Even more than before.

The crush Kari had on Belle squeezed her chest until the air was forced from her lungs. "I understand why you did what you did and, while this will hurt for a long time, I don't want to stay mad at you. So, I guess I do forgive you."

"You do?"

"Yes. Even though I'm not allowed, I want to know everything about you, and the only way that can happen is if we can move forward together." She opened her eyes and saw Belle's hopeful face. "But, are we even allowed to be friends?"

"Kari"—Belle said her name like she was a child about to receive bad news—"this might be the last conversation we have."

"Seriously?"

Belle nodded with that same forlorn look. "I might have an hour heads-up when I'm given instructions on my extraction. I won't be allowed to tell you when or contact you until I'm given permission. It's awful and I don't want this to be the case, but it is for both of our safety."

The precaution was logical, but it didn't make the news easier to accept. Kari didn't have time to wallow as a loud thud made her jump in her seat.

Belle climbed off the bed to answer the door. Her shorts rose higher on her thigh, showcasing more jagged scarring.

Doug peered in. "Kari, come with me now. Belle, come to my office in thirty minutes."

Not knowing when she would ever see Belle again, Kari gave her a sad smile as she got off the bed. "It's been a pleasure being your friend and partner."

"Likewise. Oh! One second." *Present.* Belle held up her index finger, then scrambled underneath her bed and pulled out a brown paper grocery bag, rolled at the top. She handed it to Kari. *Early birthday.* "I went with a hand-me-down approach for your birthday present."

"You didn't . . . Thank you."

Un-fucking-believable. Doug spun in a small circle. "Let's go, Kari."

Before she followed him, Kari unrolled the top of the lightweight but full bag and looked inside. A toffee-colored dog stuffed animal that had seen better days peered up at her with black felt eyes. But the name tag was new. The bright white paper tucked inside had the name Rio written in fresh black marker. Kari immediately understood its deep meaning, but the thank you was lodged in Kari's throat.

Play guitar to dogs. "I hope you like it."

Kari fought every urge to launch herself at Belle for one final hug. "I love it. Thank you." She kept her eyes on Belle as she walked backward down the passageway.

Belle didn't say goodbye; she merely gave her one last smile and closed the door.

About time. Play the part, follow me. "I'm sorry about earlier. I can be a real asshole sometimes, or so my ex-wife says. I have some peanut butter cups in my office if that'd help make it up to you."

That sounded like a totally normal thing to do when a coworker wanted to apologize for erratic behavior at one o'clock in the morning. "Sure."

———

With the banners and world flags decorating the WU space, it had leagues more personality than the *Hinewai*'s administration area. Doug's office, on the other hand, seemed more fitting for a car garage. License plates from all fifty US states, and probably most countries, lined his walls and his ceiling. Chicken wire held them in place.

"This is a bit much," Kari said.

"I'm a collector, that's for sure!" *Faraday cage.*

"Oh." Kari was impressed. Faraday cages were metal enclosures meant to block electromagnetic signals. It wasn't a full proof method for blocking outside surveillance—after all, it wasn't a Faraday shield—but it had to help. She had no doubt more metal was hidden in plain sight. Maybe under the carpet.

Doug took a seat behind his desk. "When *Hinewai* maintenance questioned me about the chicken wire, I just said, 'The kids like seeing their homes represented, so do you want a couple dozen holes in the walls or a couple hundred?' And that was the end of that conversation. Have a seat." He pointed at the chair across from him. *Make this official and nod if you can hear me.*

She nodded.

Very handy. "Again, I'm so sorry for earlier." He opened a drawer and pulled out a gigantic plastic bag with a familiar orange and black logo, which he then plopped on the desk. The peanut butter cups made their meeting seem more American. "Help yourself!"

"Okay. But, before you say anything—"

Doug held up a finger. *Careful with your wording, just in case someone comes in.* "What's that?"

"Is there anything I can say or do that would prevent Belle from losing her . . . internship?"

"Let's not talk about her just yet. I want to chat about class instructors. CIs for short." He grabbed a chocolate and peeled away the orange wrapper. He put the entire peanut butter cup in his mouth and chewed while he stared at her. *You were going to be approached by someone to be a confidential informant, or CI, the week before WU graduation.*

That was more than enough to distract her from the mound of treats. "Why?"

You have access to Henry and we know you know he's dirty and are trying to stop him. We also know you're working with Adam Cho. So dumb. He led us to you. "We want you to be a CI, even if you've been careless and stupid on occasion."

Instead of saying 'fuck you', she responded with, "I've been extremely careful."

So-so. Other people, like Adam's assistant, aren't. He shook his head. "Careful would mean I didn't know." *You're very lucky that we don't think another agency has caught on to you working together despite the surveillance we've found.*

She supposed he had a point.

"What do you think about being a CI for us?" *What happened this evening has expedited my authorization to ask if you are willing to be a confidential informant.*

Again, careful. "I don't know." How in the world did she say this next part in coded language? "I'm worried how this could affect my family?"

The hell? His face morphed into confused wrinkles, but then it went back to normal. "I get it." *If at any point we think you or your family is in danger, we would step in and arrange protective measures. If you have doubts, let me tell you that this arrangement is leagues safer than what you're doing now.* "It's sweet that you care so much about your family." *Also, we do our best to corroborate everything you tell us, so if a different agency starts an investigation, an officer can testify that they witnessed the activity, not you.*

Kari unwrapped a peanut butter cup and ate a small bite. If she accepted the role Doug offered, the information handed over would be more secure, the risks were smaller, and it would be cheaper. Burner phones were expensive. On the other hand, Doug was with the United States government. They had a history of deceit and exploitation, especially against people with her background. "How can I trust what you're saying?"

He shrugged. *Fair question.* "All new jobs carry a risk. Will the boss suck? Will my job description suddenly change? I think the better question is, does the reward outweigh the risk?" *With your help we can bury Henry Wibawa and anybody he's conspired with.*

There was the dangling carrot she needed. That was justice for Mitchell, Santos, Ray, and probably dozens more. "Yes, I can be your CI."

He gave her a smile featuring chocolate wedged between his front two teeth. *Very nice.* "You just made my life a hell of a lot easier." *So, in acting as a CI for the Central Intelligence Agency of the United States of America, you are not to disclose any part of this investigation to anyone, and you will only share information with me.* "Do not at any time consult Belle about this role, even though she's also in the program. You are to remain completely independent of one another. If I want Belle to know something, I'll tell her. Understood?"

Wait. That meant . . . Kari's heart lifted. She looked down in her paper bag at Rio's puppy eyes. "Belle doesn't have to leave?"

He scowled and reached for another peanut butter cup. *Only because you agreed to be a CI.* "If it were up to me, she'd be gone, but the people above me in the food chain have other opinions." *Lastly, all laws, foreign and domestic, still apply to you.* "Do you agree?"

Kari relaxed in the cheap office chair. This hadn't ruined Belle's career and they could still see each other, even if it was only for a few more months. She set her jaw, feeling more confident with her decision. "Yes, I wholeheartedly agree."

"You should know that some CIs volunteer their services, but others are paid. Which would you like?"

The United States government would give her money and not strip away her people's land or illegally detain her? What a turn of events! "I'll take the money. How should I give you my account info?"

"Give me some time to do initial paperwork." *No accounts. We pay cash.* "Now, for the rules with Belle." He removed the wrapper on his next chocolate and popped the entire peanut butter cup in his mouth. Apparently, he was a stress eater. "The two of you need to limit your time together and absolutely no time alone."

"I promise I won't kiss her again and the first kiss was totally my fault."

"Oh, I know. I saw the whole show." *Pretty hot.* "A few dozen others saw you on your way to rounding first, too."

"They did?"

You're a telepath, not invisible. "Fortunately, everyone also saw the aftermath, so they know you two aren't going to be movie buds anymore." He reached for another peanut butter cup. "You can still go to poker games, if you want, and, obviously, you'll see her at work in passing. That's it. Understood?"

"Got it." She didn't know whether she should celebrate or mourn, so she ate the rest of her chocolate.

Good. "Good." He took a deep breath and rested his hands on his peanut butter chocolate-filled belly. "Everything will work out." *And put a bunch of these peanut butter cups in your brown bag so the security cameras in the passageway see.*

She swallowed the sticky mass. "Before I go, I need to know if you've told anyone else about my . . . special skills."

Negative. "Even if I wanted to, I haven't had time." *Right before the party I was reviewing recordings from Madeleine's office, that's when I heard it but it didn't make sense.*

But he hadn't heard it before? "You just found out today?"

"Correct. The dots finally connected."

He must not know about the secret office then. That was information she'd give at a later date. "To be clear, you're not questioning that I can do these things?"

"I won't lie, I think it's weird and I don't understand it, but I don't have anything to prove that your brain isn't phenomenal. This batshit crazy conversation we're having is proof enough for me." *CIA once believed telepathy was a thing and they know a lot of shit.* "I'm sure you're familiar with some of the science work my organization and others have done."

"Very familiar."

Doug had already thought about the Montauk Project, which was rumored to have done psychological and parapsychological experiments, like thought control and psychic behavior, in an underground military base. During the MK-Ultra Project, the CIA conducted illegal human experiments for similar reasons. The US Army used LSD against its own soldiers to test the mind's limits in the experiments at Edgewood. Who knew what else was out there.

"Whether people still do 'science' like that is way above my pay grade," Doug said. "But I can promise I won't tell others." *But only under the condition that you stop giving Adam Cho information and play by the rules I've laid out.* "If you don't play by the rules—say you want to thank Belle for your new doggie and it turns into another round of tonsil hockey—I will tell anyone with a white coat about you." *Who knows what they will do, and it will definitely lead to you being listed as an enemy of the state.*

"Seriously?"

Delusional. He laughed. "As a heart attack." *You can go into a room with the world's most powerful people and know what they're thinking. Any head of government would perceive you as a threat.* "For today, you can leave my office with the assurance that only I am burdened with this knowledge."

Kari cringed.

Fuck. "Did you tell Belle?"

"Maybe, yes," Kari said sheepishly.

The fuck. "Why the fuck did you do that?"

"I thought you were going to tell her! Plus, she was really freaked out and this provided an explanation."

"Jesus Christ," he muttered and then glanced at the ticking clock on the wall between the Switzerland and Germany license plates. "We're done now. I'll give you more specific details about your new role in Jakarta."

"But we go to Singapore next."

I can't show my face there. Incident. "Now, fill your doggie bag with apology chocolate and be on your way."

Kari put half a dozen peanut butter cups in her paper bag and headed to her cabin. She desperately needed a moment to herself before she returned to VIP work. Her bed looked so tempting when she walked in. Instead, she put her bag on the table and scanned her cabin. Someone had planted a bug in her personal space—most likely in her guitar based on that pick situation—to eavesdrop on her conversations with her moms, Belle, or even Jade. Not to mention the sounds of basic life functions when she was alone. Which, while natural, was embarrassing.

She had to know if there was another bug, but if it was visual surveillance, they couldn't see that she was searching for it. She had to make it appear natural, like if she were cleaning. That was it! She had one more day with the Fermis, Finn, and fiancé, then she could give her cabin a deep clean and maybe rearrange the furniture a bit for a fresh look.

Kari imagined new layouts when there was a knock. It was probably Doug with more rules. She opened the door. "Madeleine?"

Peanut butter. "You have peanut butter breath." Her sharp

eyes looked past her to her dining table where the paper bag tipped over. *American chocolate awful.* "I hate American chocolate, but a candy lecture is not why I'm here. You're not answering your phone or present on the VIP level. That's unlike you."

"There was a misunderstanding with Doug on deck ten where my phone took the brunt of his immaturity. Everything's fine now, but to make up for his actions he gave me a bunch of chocolate. I thought I'd detour here to drop them off before I went back to work."

Need details Doug later. "I'll need details about that when I get back from Melbourne." Madeleine walked down the passageway.

"You have to leave again?" Kari asked from her cabin's entrance.

"Family issues persist," Madeleine called out over her shoulder. "See you in Indonesia."

Chapter Twenty-One

Jakarta, Indonesia

"Henry has consistently stayed away from me since the Maldives," Kari said in Madeleine's main office. "Can we please go back there and do the clicky thing so I keep my sanity?"

"Not yet. Now that I'm back from my trip, I wanted to ask you about something Dmitri saw on the security monitors during the New Year's Eve celebration."

Kari's pulse quickened, but she kept her much improved poker face. "What's that?"

"You told me that Doug had acted immaturely"—Madeleine's smile was as if she had been told she was back in Henry's will—"but you didn't say it was because he caught you and Belle kissing. I thought I sensed chemistry between you two. It's a shame she pushed you away."

There was that blow to the ego again. "It is, but you gotta shoot your shot, you know?"

"I hate that expression, but yes. Also, I wouldn't have used the word 'immature' to describe Doug. He destroyed a company phone and tried to make it up to you with terrible chocolate."

This wasn't the place to debate her position of chocolate-peanut butter perfection. "You're right. Immature wasn't the best word, but it's only because I didn't want to make things more complicated. Belle's only a few months away from graduation. I didn't want to ruin her internship by making things awkward with Doug." Kari suspected this was also a reason why Belle could stay on the ship. To pull her off a major assignment with only a few months remaining would have possibly raised suspicion. "I can also promise that this incident won't affect my working relationship with Belle. We will have a no lips policy for the remainder of her time on the *Hinewai*."

"Pity." Madeleine stood from the desk. "Follow me for your brain thing."

———

"Thanks, Jon." Kari took the packed food and headed down to the poker room. When she walked in, the usual gang turned her way. "I hope you're all hungry for some local staples."

"I am," Sven said with a twinkle in his eyes. And no facial hair.

Belle was forbidden. Finn was taken. There was no surveillance in her cabin based on her cleaning and furniture moving. And she was horny. Kari pointed at him. "Can I talk to you outside?"

The gang, including Belle, chortled with murmurs of, "He's in trouble."

Once they had some semblance of privacy in the passageway, Kari prepared to lay out her mindset. "I like you, and I'm very attracted to you, but I don't see us in a long-term relationship if we go out."

"You're assuming I'd want to go out with you again."

Shit. That wasn't part of her plan. "You wouldn't?"

He chuckled. "No, I would, but I needed you to recognize that fact."

"Touché. Okay, so, if we do go on another date, it really is just for fun. I'm not getting emotionally involved."

"Can this fun include sex?"

"Possibly. But"—she counted reasons on her fingers—"not until you've shown me a clean STI panel and not without condoms. Also, I have an orgasm rule: If you do, so do I."

He pursed his lips. "Okay, all of this sounds reasonable."

"Fantastic." Kari reached for the doorknob to go back inside but stopped. "Hey, how did that poker tournament back home go over break?"

He smiled so wide she saw pink chewing gum between his back molars. "In my family, I went the farthest in the tournament! They were all very proud of me."

"Great job!" She gave him a high five then placed her hand back on the knob, but before she went back inside, she thought of something else to add. "Keep chewing gum. That might help you later with endurance."

———

"I'm out of breath." Jade put the paddle down and leaned on the table. "I don't like what this baby is doing to me."

"The rise of progesterone causes shortness of breath."

"Thank you, Dr. Science. Do you have any other pieces of helpful information for me, the experienced mother?"

The annoyed edge to Jade's voice caused Kari to frown. "Sorry. I assumed you were being critical of your cardiovascular fitness."

Jade released an agitated sigh. "No, I'm sorry." She meandered over to the lone chair in the corner they had brought in the week before to kill a spider on the ceiling. The lingering brown spot provided evidence of the arachnicide. "I'm still sour over the news Neill got this week."

"What happened? I didn't see him this week since I was on the night shift."

"They aren't shortening his contract with the ship."

"What?" Kari shrieked. "That's bullshit!"

"I know. He even offered to give them back the bonus he received this year. The real kicker is that they said if he absconds, they'll notify the South African military."

Kari tossed her paddle on the table with a loud *clack*. "Who told him this? Madeleine or Henry?"

"Madeleine. But from what I gather the decision was straight from the top. Why?"

So much for thinking that she could barter with Madeleine. And there was no point trying to persuade Henry, since he would rather kill family than bring them together. "It'd be so much easier if I could appeal to Henry's paternal instincts, but he has none."

Jade scowled. "That seems harsh, especially considering Ray's situation."

"You mean his son that he has lawyers fighting to pull the plug on?"

"Henry's just trying to end Ray's suffering."

Kari kept her scoff to herself. The insulin pump's 'malfunction' had been ruled a technological glitch. And, despite the fact that Henry was responsible for the foul play, that hadn't stopped him from suing the company that manufactured Ray's device. "Okay, let's talk about happy things. There has to be some happy here."

"Oh, there is!" Jade's face brightened once more. "Neill and I are getting married in a small ceremony in Papua New Guinea."

"That's soon! Will Diana be able to come?" Kari was pretty sure a last-minute trip that took a week of travel during classes was frowned upon.

"She can't." Jade twisted back and forth and held her clasped hands to her chest as she smiled mischievously. "Would you be my maid of honor?"

"Oh, my Gods! Are you serious?" When Jade nodded, Kari ran to the other side of the table and hugged her with little hops. "I would love to!"

They hugged and screamed like all of those girlie movies Kari had seen until Jade's shortness of breath caught up with her once more.

"I really hope this goes away soon," Jade said.

"It should, but then it'll be replaced by brand new pregnancy side effects, which you clearly know," Kari quickly added. "Who else is in the wedding party?"

"We're keeping it small, so best man, maid of honor, maybe another groomsman and bridesmaid, and the officiant, who doesn't have to be religious."

The gears started turning in Kari's mind and their teeth interlocked on a brilliant idea. "Neill should ask Henry to preside!"

"Are you crazy?"

"No! This makes perfect sense. Neill can present it in such a way that shows how much respect he has for Henry and how both of you would be so honored if he participated in that way. You know, really lay on the bullshit. After that, I'm sure Henry'd be more open to an early dismissal of his contract."

"I don't know," Jade drawled. "That seems real shallow."

"Trust me. For Henry, his ego is the way to his heart. He's not like the rest of us when it comes to romance."

———

"Why do you have a stuffed puppy on your bed?" Mom L asked on the video call.

Based on Kari's new furniture arrangement, the head of the bed was now in view. "Rio was an early birthday present from Belle."

The gift, and the day it came on, weren't the only surprises. Once she had taken the stuffed animal out of the bag, she noticed faded marker on the bottom of one of its back paws. She couldn't make out the word, but not because of its faded ink or the child-like handwriting. The word had been written in Cyrillic script. Before Rio had made its way into Kari's hands, somewhere in its history it had been with a child from a Slavic country.

The list of mysteries about Belle kept growing.

"Aw, she got you a little stuffed doggie." Mom A scratched Sage behind the ears. "Why did she give you your birthday present so early?"

Honesty worked here. "We may have been caught kissing—"

"Good job, chickpea!" Mom L said, but her joy retracted when Mom A sent her a disapproving stare normally directed at Kari when she misbehaved as a child. "What I meant to say was that as colleagues you need to exercise caution about that kind of thing."

"Yeah, we learned our lesson. Her supervisor caught us, yelled at us, and Belle felt terrible I was dragged into it, so she gave me my new puppy friend. Don't worry, it won't happen again. Instead, I'm going to see Sven. He's also a nice, pretty blonde who has agreed to my terms and conditions."

They both turned to each other with perplexed looks.

"That sounds . . . Are you sure you want to date him?" Mom A asked.

Mom L nodded. "Yeah, you're not leasing a car. He's a person."

"I know that, but I'm ready for the kind of companionship that Belle can't provide. So, I've concluded that Sven's worth a test drive. To use your metaphor."

"And now I regret that choice," Mom L said. "Hey, let's talk about your mom A's fun news!"

Mom A cocked her head. "What news do I— Oh! I had a virtual meeting with some of the ENN programming staff because they're brainstorming new documentary series ideas, and you'll never guess who came on at the end of the meeting: Adam Cho."

"You don't say."

"Yes! He said he's coming on the ship soon."

"Correct. He'll be a VIP guest. We're giving him exclusive access to the *Hinewai* to dispel some rumors." She watched Mom L avert her eyes. If the inside of her mug helped Mom L keep the secret that the *Hinewai* was bad news, then she was all for it.

"That's really exciting," Mom A said as Kari's reminder alarm went off. "Do you have a cake in the oven or something?"

"I wish. I have to catch the tender. Love you both."

"We love you too, chickpea!"

Kari disconnected, closed her laptop, and left her phone on the nightstand. She didn't want any devices eavesdropping during her next conversation.

The instructions Doug had given her when he'd stopped by the VIP assistant office were simple. She'd show up fifteen minutes early at the aquarium and nature center for the binturong, or bearcat, show. By pure coincidence, Doug would happen to be there and then she'd know her next steps in the role of a CI.

If Henry or Madeleine found out, they would kill her. Kari knew it. In the small empty auditorium, the walls started closing in. She couldn't get enough air. Kari recognized the signs of hyperventilation and initiated her four-seven-eight breathing. Gradually, Kari's breathing calmed, her lightheadedness waned, but her heart still beat like a hummingbird's wings.

At the sound of someone coming down the stairs, Kari peered over her shoulder.

Doug had a cartoon map designed for tourists and took the stadium steps down to her. "Thank God I found someone I know and who's smart. Maybe you can help me?"

She reminded herself that she needed to be real. "What's the problem?" She waited for his answer, but he said nothing. "What's the problem?"

He narrowed his eyes. "You can't do the thing?"

She shook her head. "I'm not at work. I told you I can't when I'm not there."

"Fuck. Alright"—Doug lowered his voice—"just listen and look at the map." He pointed at a fast food chicken restaurant at the edge. "You'll hand off intel via a coded report. When I leave here, I'm going to hand you a folded brochure with seven codes inside."

Kari stifled a laugh. That seemed super cheesy. "Seriously?"

"It's a classic for a reason. Write the info on a cheap napkin or tissue—no paper towels, they're bad for plumbing—and write with a pen that has water-soluble ink. Use the code for the day of the week we're supposed to meet. You'll hand it to me when

I ask for a napkin or tissue because I'm sniffling or have food on my face. Something like that."

"But when will I see you?"

Doug grinned. "I'm starting guitar lessons. I've always wanted to learn and you have more free time now that you can't have playtime with Belle. Questions?"

"Not a question, but it is about Belle. I think there might be a way she can stay on after she graduates."

"What do you mean?"

It was time for Kari to reveal her plan, but because of the reach of In Virtute, she couldn't spill all of the secrets. Surely Weatherby had a multitude of elected and unelected United States officials in his pockets. "Henry wants to promote me and has given me a few months to decide what kind of new job I want. I'm thinking about asking for Madeleine's job as the VIP Coordinator because I know she hates it. If that happened, Belle could take my current job when she graduates in May."

"Interesting." He dragged his finger across the map from the chicken place to the park. "If you could make that happen, it would have advantages. There's already a set weekly meeting to discuss the internship program, so you could deliver a weekly report to me that way. But I still do want guitar lessons, just to be clear." He folded the map and put it back in the travel bag he wore across his chest.

"But what about Belle? Could she try for my current job?"

"I'll run it by the boss." He took a pamphlet out of the bag. "Any other questions?"

"Out of curiosity, does this operation have a name?"

"Yes, but I'm not telling you, Sky Fisher." He handed the glossy pamphlet of Fatahillah Museum to her as he chuckled. "This museum was great. You should check it out after the animal show."

Once he left, Kari snuck a peek inside the pamphlet. The

paper had eight columns. The main column was the alphabet plus zero through nine, then seven more columns for each day of the week. Every day was different. There were 252 cells total. It was a cipher simple enough that she could commit to memory because keeping the physical code was too dangerous.

Of course, everything now felt too dangerous.

Chapter Twenty-Two

Darwin, Australia

"Kari!" Neill yelled in the passageway outside the security office.

She stopped and turned to her friend, who lumbered toward her. "Before you ask whatever it is you're going to ask, have you seen Henry? I need to talk to him."

"This works out well then," Neill said. *Mystery meeting.* "Henry wants you to come to a meeting."

"But I have a VIP."

Seems urgent. "I don't know what to tell you except you're supposed to come with me."

"Fine," Kari said, exasperated. She'd learn what Henry wanted, pose the future job opportunity question, then circle back to Mr. Northern Territory Sandwich King.

Oh, the thanks. Neill led the way down the passageway. "By the way, I can't thank you enough for what you did."

"What did I do?"

Wedding. "You suggested to Jade that Henry officiate the wedding."

"He's going to do it?" Kari asked, impressed by her own brilliance.

"No, but Madeleine is, and while she wasn't able to release me from my entire contract, I was able to shave a year off."

Kari put her hands in T formation. "Time-out. Madeleine advocated for you?"

Shocked. "Yes! It was a compromise between her and Henry. All I had to do was switch security positions and cabins with Josef." Neill pushed open the doors to the outside of the deck. *He'll be in charge.*

"Ah, Karishma! Thank you for collecting her so quickly, Neill."

He gave a quick nod, then put his hand on Kari's shoulder. *Thanks again.* "Have fun." Neill left, leaving her and Henry alone.

"Come with me," Henry said. "I want to get your opinion on some things and ask some questions about my projects."

That was a lot of information packed into one sentence. "While I have loads of opinions, love projects, and did want to talk to you, I have a shift right now. I can't leave."

"Yes, you can. Matthew is on his way up and will fill in for you until you return. So, follow me." He gave her a gentle push on the back toward the perimeter. *Be amazing. Can't wait meet Lydia.*

Henry wasn't acting like he knew she could hear his thoughts. "What are we going to talk about?" she asked as she caught up to him.

Bunker. "You're going to meet my favorite architect, Lydia, for the big dig."

"For your bunker?"

"Yes! This is why I need your input. I'm thinking that I want you to be the project manager. You'll miss lunch during Lydia's presentation, so I asked Jon to whip you up something."

Kari was struck by a major detail he had said and it wasn't about lunch. "You want me to lead the build of your bunker?"

"While you may not have construction experience, you designed that entire brain surgery study yourself and learn fast."

Kari supposed that was true. "But a bunker and a science experiment are vastly different things, requiring extremely different types of resources."

So silly. "That I know, but the heads of land management, engineering, the psychologist, etcetera will all report to you. You can keep them on schedule, answer most questions, and keep me updated."

"Okay, I guess I can do that." She followed him through the passageway that led to the secret conference room. To her shock, there was an older woman with silver hair already at the table.

Her weathered face registered surprise as she stood and made her way over to them. She gave Kari a firm shake. *Thought Mad would see this through.* "I'm Lydia. Pleasure to meet you," she said without a smile and maybe a Dutch accent.

"Same. I'm Kari."

Brilliant. "For twenty years, Lydia has led my builds. She's responsible for the *Hinewai*, including the secret passages."

She knows? Must be sleeping with him. Lydia turned around and gestured to the wall screen. "Shall we look at the model?"

"Yes!" Henry pointed to the charcuterie board on the table. "That is your seat."

Kari sat, and while she hadn't been hungry before, she was now. The assortment before her was robust and balanced. A glass of iced tea with a small boat of maple syrup joined it. Jon was a master of details.

More exciting than Star Conflict *on the big screen.* "Karishma, this is the project of the future. I want you—no—I need you to ask questions. Hard questions. Your role is not to be my yes person."

"Understood." However, Kari was more focused on which cheese would pair best with the different crackers or apple slices. "I guess the first question I have is how many bunkers has Lydia designed?"

"Five," she answered. "The one I'm going to show you is the most recent; however, I have scaled certain factors up with the information Henry has provided me."

Input from others. "It has to meet certain specifications."

"Such as?" Kari asked.

So, so many. "The nuclear winter scenario is the most serious. But also if we needed to escape a pandemic or I have to fake my death."

Kari chewed thoughtfully. Those were some varied reasons. "What's the intended size of this bunker?"

"Ah!" Lydia clicked the remote to start the presentation. "Ten levels underground, plus a level of soil above that. All in all it's about thirty meters down. The area is roughly two American football fields."

Thanks to her Ata Niq and Uncle River she had watched plenty of games. Two fields placed side by side would be 120 yards long and about a hundred yards wide. Kari calculated the math, including the unit conversion, while she crunched on an apple slice. "That's three hundred thousand cubic meters!"

Tough mental maths. Lydia hitched a thumb toward Kari but looked at Henry. "She is a bright one."

The compliment went over Kari's head because she was still dumbfounded by the size of this. "How long will this take to build? How expensive is this? How many people is this going to hold?"

Henry chuckled. *Fun as I hoped.* "The time it takes and the number of people are variable. The price tag is . . . negotiable, but I don't think we should go over a billion."

"Dollars?" she yelled, appalled. When they each nodded, she sat back in her chair and sipped the tea. This project was the definition of insanity.

"I understand that is a lot of money," Henry said. "As for the people, that's one of the items you and the psychologist will be responsible for." He went on to describe the other tasks, such as scenario building, population roles, and site monitoring.

"You're still going with New Zealand as your site?" Kari asked.

Why so paranoid? "Yes. I'm told the rock type is very good in the southern region and is away from the fault. If you still have concerns, you can discuss it with the geology team when you meet them. Go ahead and get started, Lydia."

Finally. "Okay, so I'm going to put us on walk-through mode," Lydia said. "Please note that this is not a detailed blueprint. This is just to familiarize you with the build."

The walk-through started like a dystopian reality show about someone's underground dream house. The tour started with a decontamination room and then split into four identical quadrants for redundancy reasons. Large areas were dedicated to maintenance and agriculture. There was a septic system that treated sewage with UV light then dehydrated it to form cubes. People could literally shit bricks down there. Amazing. Other dedicated spaces included a gym, medical bay, library, and kitchen. The living area was like the palace for the mole people, but the sleeping quarters and bathrooms were community-style.

Lydia switched off the wall screen. "And that's the tour. Questions?"

Just brilliant. "None from me. I appreciate your efforts and time to introduce the topic to the two of us." Henry looked at

Kari, his hands folded neatly on his lap. *Can tell intrigued.* "What do you think, Karishma? Do you have questions or any comments?"

Kari liked the thought experiment of a bunker. Though she found the actual practice of building it and determining who could stay there—who deserved to live, basically—abhorrent. However, that was why it was a job best in the hands of someone like her, a pansexual, Indigenous, second-generation Indian woman. "Sign me up!"

Excellent. Henry clapped. "That is just excellent! When do you think you can start?"

"Let's talk about that in private. I can let Lydia know what we conclude time wise."

Entire meeting could have been email. "That works for me." Lydia extended her hand to Henry first and then to Kari. "I'll see myself out to the helicopter pad." *Such waste time.*

Henry grinned at Kari as Lydia exited. *What she thinking? Only chewing. Cheese sliced too thick?*

She swallowed the not-at-all-too-thick cheese and took a sip of iced tea to wash it down. "Like you asked me to, I've been thinking of new jobs I could have on the ship."

So obedient. "What have you decided?"

"I'd like to take over VIP coordinating. I know Madeleine doesn't like it and I already have ideas that would improve what we have. It wouldn't be a lot of work, which would allow my focus and time to go to the bunker."

Interesting. "Out of curiosity, what kind of VIP ideas do you have?"

"For one, Belle has told me she wished she could stay on after graduation." Or rather Doug had told Kari his boss wanted Belle to stay on. Doug hated the idea. "If I'm no longer an assistant, then she could take my place. Another idea is using two interns from WU. That would increase meetings with Doug, but I don't mind him as much as Madeleine does."

Perfect timing. "The timing is perfect. Belle graduates a few weeks after your birthday."

"Correct. But how do you think Madeleine will take the news that I want her job in addition to all the other changes?"

"You let me worry about her."

Chapter Twenty-Three

Port Moresby, Papua New Guinea

In a two birds-one stone approach to evacuating the *Hinewai* for its dry-docking annual maintenance, the safety officers had organized an emergency drill. It was smart but inconvenient, as it had been planned during her scheduled guitar lesson with Doug.

But there was always a plan B.

Kari headed to the buses lined up for the many destinations the WU tourism department helped organize. Just like how meals were scheduled, everyone had to sign up for where they wanted to go since they couldn't be on the ship. Options were the airport, the hotels of Hohola North, the Inlet Resort, and Ela Beach. Most of the WU students signed up for the hotel near the shops. Kari signed up for the beach, because that's what Doug had told her to do.

Kari spied him in floral print board shorts, a long-sleeve beach shirt, and a boonie hat. He looked like a forgettable tourist, which was probably his goal. She followed him and boarded the same bus. The seats were filled, but he tipped his hat when he saw her.

Once Kari stepped onto the white sand, she slid off her sandals and laid out her towel. The last time she was on a PNG beach, she had been with Finn on their first and only date. Their kisses in the waves had been interrupted so she could do amateur spy work in Brisbane. Now she was working with professional spies, one of whom she wanted to kiss again but had to resist the temptation. Was that considered professional and personal growth? She wasn't sure.

"Hey, Kari." Doug waved at her with his wrapped peanut butter cup in hand. "How are ya?"

"Pretty good." If she could get information out uncoded, that would save time for everyone. "I'm really excited about a possible promotion I learned about the other day."

"Really?" He tore off the paper of the chocolate. "Something related to what you're doing now?"

"Some of it is. Henry's going to tell Madeleine first before it becomes official."

He nodded as he shoved the entire peanut butter cup in his mouth. "That sounds like it could be a great opportunity for you." He held up his hand, which had a small amount of chocolate melted on his finger. "Would you happen to have a napkin on you? I'm making a mess of myself."

"I do, actually." Kari went into her bag and took out the napkin with the coded message about Henry's bunker plans, her suspicions about Ray's attempted murder, Mitchell and Santos's murders, the MacDonald and Pawar murders, the hidden areas on the ship, and the roles of Madeleine and Josef. "Here you go."

"Thanks." He stuffed the napkin in his pocket without cleaning his hand. "Well, I don't want to monopolize your beach time. You enjoy the rest of your day."

"You too." With the most important task taken care of, Kari

settled on her towel and watched the waves. It was meditative. Her mind almost went blank as she followed a crest into shore and watched it move back out again. Seconds became minutes.

"Kari!"

She took her gaze off the water and turned in the direction of the person who'd called her name. Down the beach, in the area of the pick-up soccer game, Sven ran toward her in his black shorts. His legs weren't as impressive as Belle's, but she didn't hate that he had a toned torso that showed off slight pectoral muscles and a faint six-pack above his Adonis belt. Damp hair and grains of sand clung to his still clean-shaven face. "Hey, Sven."

He took a seat on the sand beside her. "What are you looking at?"

"The waves. It's pretty relaxing."

"I can see that you're taking it very seriously." He nudged her with his shoulder and smiled. "I came over because I wanted to ask if you'd like to have dinner with me Saturday."

Kari winced. "I would, but that's when Jade and Neill are getting married and I'm in the wedding."

"Oh, that's right. We're helping make food for that. How about lunch today?"

She did need to eat, and some time with Sven might be what she needed to get some fun back into her life. There had been a lot of doom and gloom lately. Especially doom. "Come and get me when you get hungry."

"Absolutely!" He kissed her on the cheek and ran back to the soccer group, kicking a wayward ball back to them in the process.

He might not have been the best for conversation, but he was nice, pretty, and wasn't off-limits.

Kari's back was pushed against her cabin door, and her hands moved under Sven's now dry shirt. It was only fair since he was doing the same to her.

Sven took a break from kissing her neck to whisper in her ear, "Let's go inside."

"If I let you in, I know we'll have sex and we can't."

He chuckled in a way that made the vibration from his laugh travel down her spine. "Because I haven't been cleared of STIs yet?"

She had actually forgotten about that self-set rule in her hormonal brainwash. "Sure, but also because we're both a little sandy, which will make everything uncomfortable."

"We could shower together. That would be extra exciting."

"My shower's too small." She gently pushed him away so she could no longer feel his extra excitement poking her hip. "But let's do this again soon. Meals are optional. Get that test."

He looked completely dazed but nodded. "I'll go to the medical bay tomorrow."

"Attaboy." She gave him a goodbye kiss, then watched him walk down the passageway that had Jade walking up it. Kari closed her eyes and didn't open them until she heard Jade's footfalls stop in front of her. "How much of that did you see?"

"Enough to know that in five more minutes you could have ended up like me." Jade patted her slightly swollen belly. "I take it you had a good day."

"I'd like to think that I made the most of it. How about you? Did you and Neill get to check out the resort together?"

She smiled. "We did. It's going to be so beautiful, and I ran through all the catering logistics with the other WU teachers. I hope you're not planning on seeing Sven in the next few days. He's got work to do."

"You have nothing to worry about there. He was happy he

could help with the wedding reception." The actual wedding ceremony reminded her of a key fact. "Are we having a rehearsal?"

"I'd like to, but it's too tough with everyone's schedule. Your job is simple: walk down the aisle with Josef."

"Ugh."

"I know, but you're a big girl. After that, stand beside me and hold flowers. The only person I'm worried about is Madeleine. I have no idea what that woman is going to say."

———

"I've never been married," Madeleine said with her hands on either side of the white podium, "but I've been to several weddings and have picked up a few dos and don'ts in the process." She exuded confidence as the wedding officiant in her lilac suit under a floral wedding arch. How was she not melting?

Had to be the glacial water in her veins.

Kari was warm in the silver-gray sheath dress she had received two days before. Poor Neill was in a full three-piece suit that matched her dress. Jade wore the lightest gray with a slight train of silver beads. Kari hoped her dress was a breathable form of satin. Jade kept her pink glasses.

"As someone who has sat in your metaphorical chairs," Madeleine continued to bellow her speech, "I appreciate brevity, a secular perspective, and even more brevity." She beamed as the crowd laughed at her joke. "Having said all of that, we are all here to witness and celebrate the official, legal union of Neill van der Merwe and Jade Boudreaux. They met on the *Hinewai*, so, of course, Henry wants to take some credit for this union and say something."

The bouquet of fire orange New Guinea impatiens at Kari's waist bounced as she attempted to muffle her laugh.

"Henry wanted me to read one of Shakespeare's quotes about love on his behalf. So, let's all learn what he discovered on the internet together."

"Oh," the crowd groaned and laughed.

Her snickering stopped, and Kari's eyes darted over to Josef. He wasn't nearly as entertained by the insult directed at Henry as the crowd was.

Madeleine flipped a page on the podium as the amusement quelled and then cleared her throat. "My bounty is as boundless as the sea, My love as deep. The more I give to thee, The more I have, for both are infinite." She pushed the paper away and regarded the crowd once more. "It figures he would choose from *Romeo and Juliet*, a play about teenagers committing suicide over a five-day crush. Maybe this is why he's divorced."

The crowd, Neill, and Jade howled at what had become the Madeleine Coultier Comedy Special. Kari fought back smiling. It couldn't get back to Henry that she liked the roasting, especially since Josef had taken out his phone.

"I personally don't have much experience with love," Madeleine said, "except if it's a dry martini at the end of an irritating day. This is why I'm going to get to the part where Neill and Jade can share the vows they've written themselves. I've been told they made a deal with each other to keep it short because the crowd gets restless when it comes to a delayed cocktail hour. And by 'the crowd' I mean me."

On cue, Jade handed Kari her bouquet, then held Neill's hands. He gazed at her with the same reverence, admiration, and wonder Kari had seen him direct at priceless works of art. But he also did something Kari had never seen him do. He giggled.

"Sorry, nerves," Neill said, earning a few awws from the

crowd. Once he composed himself, he directed an anxious smile at Jade. "I haven't had a peaceful life, and it lacked kindness on both the receiving and giving ends for quite some time. But something amazing happened to me last year: I met you. Without trying, you brought peace to my mind and kindness to my heart. You've made me want to be a better man, one who you can be proud of bringing into their family, while we expand it, too.

"I promise before all of these people and God that I will always be kind to you. I will always support you. I will always protect you. And, above all, I will always love you." He smiled. "Was that okay?" he asked his soon-to-be bride.

Jade cupped his cheek and, despite the tradition, kissed him. "You did really well, baby. I guess it's my turn now."

"Yes, that's how it works." Madeleine checked the time on her watch.

Jade turned to Kari as if to say, 'Really?'

Kari nodded as if to answer, 'Yes, she's a bitch. Funny. But still a bitch.'

Jade brought her attention back to Neill. "I never saw myself getting married again. Once Diana went off to school, I found a new life on the ship where I was happy, but there was this piece missing that I couldn't define, like when I try a new recipe but it's missing an ingredient. When I met you, I knew you were the missing and magical ingredient to my new recipe of life. As we've gotten to know each other, I've learned that not only do I love your flavor, but I love your texture and even the way you sound. Such a tough-looking, crunchy exterior, but on the inside, you're soft and sweet with just a little bit of rich saltiness."

Did Jade see Neill as a toasted everything bagel with cream cheese? Kari pondered that question.

"I love everything about you. Your strength of heart and

character. The fact that your InstaPic account is nothing but weight lifters, tattoos, and baby animals. The way you always greet me now with a hug before a kiss, so our baby can feel it, too."

That one pulled at Kari's heart strings.

"I'm so blessed to have found you. I'm even more blessed that in a few minutes I can call you my husband. I love you."

"So sweet," Neill said.

"Very," Madeleine said. "The rings, then."

Kari took a simple white gold band out from her dress pocket and handed it to Jade. Josef tucked his phone away to do the same for Neill.

They exchanged rings and Jade took a moment to admire the sparkle of the diamond inlay in her band. According to Jade it was impractical to have both an engagement and wedding ring, so she had asked for one that could function as both.

"Now," Madeleine said, "I pronounce you husband and wife. You can kiss each other again. Wedding over."

Neill and Jade sealed the deal in front of all to see. There was no music, but even if there was it would have been difficult to hear with the applause in the outdoor venue. The newly-weds made their way down the flower-sprinkled aisle with handshakes, hugs, and pats on the back.

Josef said a few words to Madeleine. She responded by rolling her eyes and heading to the bar. A freshly made martini waited for her.

Kari refused to loop her arm in Josef's as they walked down the aisle, but she smiled for the few people who snapped photos; one of whom was Doug. He tipped his head toward the direction of the server who balanced a tray of champagne. She could get used to working with Doug if he watched out for her like that. Once she was free from the aisle, she went to the dining area, placed her flowers down at her seat, and fetched her drink.

"Those were quite the jabs Madeleine threw at Henry," Doug said from behind her. "Trouble in paradise?"

Kari took a sip of the cool, bubbly nectar that was magic on her parched throat. "More like a riot in paradise."

"Interesting." Doug gestured to the area of the podium. "This was a nice ceremony. Short and sweet."

"You're welcome." Madeleine butted in with her martini. "It's nice to see you two getting along. That would make things awkward if you didn't."

Doug furrowed his brow. "I don't follow."

"It's not official yet, but in the next few months Kari will be taking the VIP Coordinator role from me because apparently there is a God. This will allow me to focus on my more interesting responsibilities."

It took a moment for Kari to decide how to play her response. "I hope you don't mind. It came up naturally in conversation when Henry asked me."

Madeleine shrugged. "Not at all. It's a logical progression, as is making Belle your replacement. Now, if you'll excuse me, they've brought out the appetizers, and I'm absolutely famished despite the fact that some people don't think I eat."

Kari's line of sight followed Madeleine. Along with her backside, she saw the group of WU culinary students, including Sven, come out of the hotel in matching khaki pants and vermillion polo shirts. She waited until Madeleine was out of earshot to say to Doug, "I really wasn't expecting that change of employment to go so well."

"Take your gifts where you can get 'em. The same goes for food. I'll see you later." Doug headed to the closest tray.

His presence was quickly replaced by Jade, who gave her a swaying hug. "Thank you so much for doing this!"

"It really was an honor. I still can't believe you picked me . . . even though I was your third choice."

Jade's first pick was a WU instructor who had a scheduled expedition. Pick number two, a WU admissions specialist, had debilitating anxiety in front of groups, but she did offer to record the event live for Diana.

Jade released Kari from the hug but kept a hand on each arm and looked at her with a sentimental grin. It was very mom-like. "I'm going to miss you so much when I leave."

"I'm going to miss you too, but I'm just a text, call, or email away." With a heavy heart, Kari asked, "You're still leaving Friday?"

"It just makes sense. The new instructor arrives Monday, so that gives him time to get situated on the ship and have a few transition days with the class. But let's do dinner and squeeze in a game before I go."

"I'd like that."

"Sorry to interrupt," Neill said. "Jade, there's a question about food that I don't know the answer to."

Jade sighed. "I better handle this." She gave Kari's arm a friendly squeeze. "Enjoy the party. Be good, though."

Kari watched them walk off hand in hand and finished her flute of champagne. A tap on the shoulder caused her to turn.

Sven directed a salacious look at her and held a tray of prosciutto-wrapped melon bites. His hair wasn't up in a bun, rather it fell to his shoulders. He gave her a sly smile. "Would you care for—"

"Yes. Yes, to all the things."

———

Kari took her seat across from Jade at the cafeteria table, both of their trays filled to the brim with egg drop soup, rice, grilled fish, and banana cake. She held up her iced tea in a toast. "To Jade, a woman who started off as my single neighbor and is leaving as my pregnant, married friend and metaphorical big sister."

Jade chuckled as their glasses clinked. "And to Kari, who started off as my people and relationship-phobic neighbor and is now a poker-playing people person who occasionally has mediocre dates and sex with them."

"As long as we avoid conversation, it's fine."

Jade folded her lips and shook her head. "I'm not an expert, but you may wish to change that if you want a relationship."

"I don't want one. He and I are having fun."

"I don't know if you're on the same page. I heard some rumors flying that he is falling fast for you."

That didn't make sense. "He knows where I stand with the situation. I have too much going on to consider a relationship right now."

"So I heard, Ms. VIP Coordinator of the *Hinewai*. Between you doing that and Josef taking over the head of security, there're going to be a lot of changes to the upper deck. Neill told me that Josef wants to instate a polygraph policy for any employee who has personal dealings with Henry."

The fish dropped from her fork. "Really?"

"Yeah, I don't know who put the idea in Henry's ear, but he thinks there are spies on the ship."

"*Hmm*," was Kari's non-committal response. She shoved a spoonful of rice in her mouth.

"Do you think there are spies?"

Kari chewed and willed a neutral face, but eventually she had to swallow and spin the question back. "Well, look at what the ship does. We go all around the world so Henry can meet with politicians and the super wealthy. It kind of makes sense that other people would want to know what they're talking about, don't you think?"

"That's what I thought, too! Who knows who is watching and listening. It's scary." Jade portioned off a piece of cake. "Promise me you'll be careful."

"I promise, I'll be as careful as I can be."

Chapter Twenty-Four

Henry's Island, Papua New Guinea

"Thank you both for being prompt," Madeleine said to Kari and Belle at their six am meeting. "Especially to Belle, since you have the late shift during Mr. Cho's stay."

"This time works better since it doesn't disrupt my sleep as much," Belle said. "Trying to grab some shuteye for an hour here or there has never really worked for me. I envy those who can nap."

"Always with a story." Madeleine sipped her Earl Grey. "I don't have to tell you both that this visit needs to go off without a hitch. He'll have questions, so answer them. If he wants to see something, show him. If he has a request for an orgy with adults representing very unique demographics, fulfill that request. But absolutely do not under any circumstances do or say something that makes me or Henry—even if he deserves it—look bad. To maintain full transparency, we've told Mr. Cho he can report anything he sees or hears as part of his piece for ENN. Do you understand?"

Kari nodded.

"Absolutely, ma'am," Belle said. "But, to be clear, I don't feel comfortable about the orgy. I'd rather delegate that responsibility."

Madeleine paused her teacup at her lips. "I'll miss working with you. You're dismissed, Belle. Kari, stay."

"Thank you, ma'am." Belle stood and grinned at Kari before she left.

The door closed, Madeleine stood and headed toward her other office. Once the remote was in her hand, the hard edges to her face appeared to soften. "If you could, see if you can learn if Adam's snooping around my family."

"You need to be careful making requests like that. People will start to think you care about someone other than yourself."

Madeleine gave her an almost sad smile and clicked the button. "Let's keep that between us."

———

At ten am, the helicopter containing Adam and his camera operator landed. The whirling air from the blades caused Kari's longer pixyish hair to fly about wildly. She had almost forgotten what it was like to have long hair in the wind. It was inconvenient.

Neill didn't have that problem.

Can't believe I get to meet Adam Cho. Exposé fraud in the art market.

"Don't throw your panties at him, buddy," Kari said. "I don't think Jade would like that."

Panties. He laughed and gave her a slight bump that caught her off balance. "By the way, she's settled in now and says hello."

"How'd the first appointment with her obstetrician go?"

Not happy with her. "Aside from some scolding that she didn't see one sooner, both she and the baby are doing well."

"I'm glad to hear everything is going to plan."

When the helicopter blades stopped, Adam stepped out in his typical on-camera fashion of a monochromatic suit. This time in maroon. He stood on the platform while he buttoned his jacket and seemed as though he took in every sight, sound, and smell around him. From his vantage point, he would have been able to see the vibrant shades of teal waters surrounding the private island, the palm trees, and natural flora providing brilliant pops of color against the beach. His chiseled traits were featured with each turn.

A petite Black woman in cargo pants, T-shirt, and field vest stepped out behind him. That must have been the camera operator.

"Hello, Mr. Cho," Kari said once his eyes landed on her. "Welcome to the *Hinewai!*"

He gave her a smile rumored to be insured for five million dollars and headed down the metal grated steps. "This is an absolutely gorgeous location. I can see why Henry chose to make this his maintenance spot." He stopped in front of her and extended his hand. *Play dumb.* "Kari, was it? I remember you from Stockholm."

She shook his hand, relieved he remembered to keep up the ruse. "Yes. I'll be one of the VIP assistants during your visit here. The man to my right is Neill, our head of security."

Could have guessed. "Am I being kicked off the ship already?" Adam joked and held out his hand for Neill to shake.

So handsome. "Not at all," Neill said and shook his hand. "I thought you may like extra assistance because of the equipment."

"Lucky guess," grunted the camera woman, whose forearms

rippled from the strain of heaving a case half her size. "Hi. I'm Dale."

Kari gave her the same welcome and introduced herself again. "We have a flexible agenda for your stay here," she said to both of her new guests. "Would you care to go over that once I show you to your cabins and stow your belongings?"

"That sounds like a perfect plan," Adam said as he visibly observed the deck. *Can't believe here. In lion's den.*

While Kari and Neill gathered their imposing luggage set for a three-day visit, Kari couldn't help but smile at Dale's excited thoughts for getting her own VIP suite on the ship. *The crew must not get the celebrity treatment at ENN.*

Neill carried Dale's camera gear and backpack to her suite while Kari took Adam's rolling luggage and slung his attaché over her shoulder. When they arrived at the door, she scanned herself first and typed in the sequence for guest coding. "Please place your thumb on the scanner. This will function as your lock during your stay."

Biometrics. Interesting. "Is this data wiped after each stay?"

"Yes, sir. If you'd like to know the specific process, Neill can explain it to you."

Maybe. He placed his thumb on the scanner, then Kari walked him through assigning his numeric code. "How many people have access to the VIP suites?"

"Only assigned VIP staff and security." She followed him inside. "Would you like me to leave your things here or take them to the master bedroom upstairs?"

"Here is fine," he said as he walked into the space and did a slow 360-degree turn. "This is very impressive. Have the cabins always been this nice?"

Kari knew she had to tread carefully. Doug had been very clear she couldn't act as a source of insider information anymore.

However, she could at least flag publicly available information that he may be unaware of. "Aarti Gupta, Amara's daughter, might disagree with you. They were here during our Dubai stop."

"I had heard whispers of that. What was it like working with them?"

"I really can't say more. We're held to non-disclosure agreements when it comes to our guests." Change of subject. Fast. "Would you like me to show you how to operate the virtual golf? It's very popular among our guests."

Odd. Cagey. "Not at the moment." He tucked his hands into his pockets and headed toward the massive window wall that featured another view of the island. "To be clear, I'm allowed to photograph and film everything I'm shown?"

"Of course. Anything in plain sight is fair game."

"So, no trying to find secret doors or something like that?"

Rather than answer, she laughed. It was so hard not giving him extra information. "Are you ready to start the tour? The way it's structured allows for lunch at the cafeteria once we arrive there."

"Yes. Let's check on Dale and make sure she has everything she needs."

When they arrived at her cabin, Neill opened the door. The swoosh of a club cut through the air. "She was very interested in trying out the golf," he said.

"Dale," Adam said with a terse smile, "let's start the tour. No interviews today, only shots of the ship and scenery."

She leaned the club against the couch and headed to one of the smaller silver cases. She pulled out a digital camcorder the size of a lunch box and several batteries, memory cards, and different gizmos that she tucked into her pockets like they were weapons and ammunition in a tactical vest. "I grabbed a light meter, just in case."

"Very good," Adam said, then motioned to Kari. "Lead the way."

Kari started the tour in the ship's administration area. "Welcome to the cube farm. As you can see, it's like most work environments. The perimeter are offices for the executives, including Madeleine Coultier."

Surprised not here. "Can we say hello to her? I thought that she or Henry would have greeted us when we touch—"

"Mr. Cho!" Madeleine beamed as she came out of her office. She also dressed in a monochromatic suit, but hers was in daffodil. "It's so lovely to have you on the *Hinewai*. I presume that Kari has started your tour."

So fake. "Yes. I have to say that this area looks pretty ordinary compared to the VIP suite."

"I think you'll find as you move about the ship that we really are a simple operation. Not many frills except the VIP accommodations."

See the dirty work. "Would I be able to see your no-frills office? I think it's interesting how executives set up their space."

Kari's facial muscles tensed as she fought the urge to smile.

Madeleine laughed, but the fake, nervous version. "It's a bit of a mess, but of course. Please come in." Once they were inside, Madeleine stood behind her desk and dragged her index finger over a bookshelf. She held up a mostly clean fingertip. "See? Absolutely dreadful. I'd make a terrible housewife."

Murder her spouse for sure. "Zoom in on everything," he whispered to Dale with his back to Madeleine. "What's that door behind you?"

"Personal bathroom. It's a perk. Do you need to use the facility before you leave?"

"No, I'm fine, thank you." Adam scrutinized every picture, book, chair, and even picked up the cheesy motivational pillows. His eyes lingered on the picture of her family. "How often do you go home to visit family?"

"Only a few times a year."

Bullshit. Was in Melbourne seven times last year.

Kari's attention had begun to drift, but that snapped her back. Madeleine had gone back home that many times? Was the family situation more serious than she had led on?

"Your office is smaller than I assumed it would be," Adam said. *Can't be right.*

The muscles around Kari's mouth were too taxed to fight. She looked down and picked a non-existent piece of lint off her pants to hide her smirk.

"Between digital files and hating in-person meetings here," Madeleine said, "I don't need much space."

Review this tape later. Adam signaled for Dale to exit. "I appreciate the access you've given us."

"You're very welcome. Henry is hoping the transparency will put some of your concerns to rest. You can ask him all about that at dinner this evening. Kari, please make sure you show Mr. Cho all the highlights."

"Yes, ma'am."

The tour she took Adam and Dale on was very similar to the one she had received when she first stepped on the ship. Per Adam's wishes they walked the length of the ship and peeked into every available facility. His thoughts about the ship remained suspicious.

I bet inconsistencies in duct work. "Can I use the gym tomorrow morning?" He craned his neck up at the rock climbing wall.

"Of course. If you'd like to take care of the legal waiver now, you can do that." Kari gestured to Dale "You're also welcome to use the facility."

"No thanks," Dale said. "I have a seven am tee time."

As Adam tended to his paperwork about general fitness and not suing Wibawa Enterprises if he tweaked a hamstring or had a heart attack, she texted the cafeteria to check on lunch. While Jon was the go-to person for VIPs, Adam wanted to see everything, and the operation that created three meals a day on a timed schedule was a large component of that.

Hope low carb. "Do we get the full dining experience now?"

"Right this way."

After fetching their utensils, condiments, and drinks, Kari led them to a large booth in the far corner. Several diners waved, said hello, or snapped pictures of Adam on their way to the table. She sat at the far end.

"Do we smell bad or something?" Adam asked.

"Not at all," Kari said. "Your cologne is quite elegant." He laughed, the first real one she had heard. "I was trying to give you space in case you had to get out your notes or something."

"I appreciate the gesture." He dipped his fork in his plain baked sweet potato, then looked at Kari. "May I ask you a question that may be a bit personal?"

"No, I do not have a sexual relationship with Henry Wibawa."

Dale coughed on her soda.

He smiled. "People think that often, don't they?"

"They do. And it never stops being annoying or offensive."

"What I wanted to ask is, why did you stay on the ship after the boat accident with your colleagues from inCog? I mean, you could have found work in another lab. You probably could work for either of your mothers. However, instead of doing any of that, you coordinate vacations for rich people. I find that odd."

"Me too," Dale added, then bit into her black bean burger.

Kari sipped her water. "This job does provide me with an

education I can't get anywhere else. It's fascinating listening to the VIPs' conversations with Henry, as I'm sure you can imagine."

Adam uttered a hmph.

Dale looked back and forth between them, apparently riveted by the conversation. Then, she put her burger down and pulled her phone from her pocket. She nudged Adam's arm with her elbow. When he didn't react, she did it again.

"What?" he said, annoyed. "I felt my phone buzz, too. I'll check it later."

"I think you'll want to see this." Dale handed him her phone.

Adam sighed, pulled out his reading glasses from the inside of his suit, and put them on. His shoulders jerked back, and a somber expression washed over him. He peered at Kari from over the frames. "Ray Wibawa is dead."

———

From behind Dale on the VIP deck, Kari could see that she had both Adam and Henry in the video camera's frame. They sat across from each other—the shore's palm trees between them— for the impromptu interview.

Adam looked into the camera with perfect natural light shining on him. "We're broadcasting live on the *Hinewai* with Henry Wibawa, who only a few hours ago learned his son died after being on life support for months." He spun in his seat to face Henry. "We can't imagine all that you are going through right now."

"That's why I appreciate you doing our interview now," Henry said in a neutral tone. "I have a feeling once reality and the grief sets in, I will not be able to articulate my thoughts and feelings as well."

The entire interview was maddening and in poor taste. News of Ray's death hadn't even passed the hour mark when Henry had texted her asking—no, requesting—that he wanted the interview with Adam as soon as possible. Henry didn't want privacy. He didn't want to grieve with Ahmed, who was a wreck, or any other person close to him. Henry wanted the world to see him that instant.

Kari had taken the news of Ray's death harder than Henry did. But, then again, she hadn't murdered him.

"I guess I'll start with one of the questions that's on everyone's mind," Adam said. "How did you learn of your son's passing?"

"I received a message from my ex-wife who was at his bedside. She told me he looked peaceful." Henry glanced down at his perfectly shined Italian leather shoes. "As morbid as it may seem to you, I prepared myself for this when Raymond's glucose monitor failed him while on the *Hinewai*."

Kari ground her molars so hard they should have cracked.

Adam placed a finger on his ear, presumably so the studio feed in his ear became clearer. He glanced at Kari. For a moment, he appeared startled, but as quickly as she saw it, he resumed his professional demeanor. "I've just been told by the studio that Amara Gupta and Botan Itoi have released statements issuing their condolences."

"I am fortunate to have many friends on this side of the world."

"I'm sure that's true, but they issued statements before the news outlets learned about it."

For the briefest moment, Kari saw Henry's hand clench his armrest, but then he relaxed his fingers. "In some regards, I am like most people. When tragedy strikes, I tell my closest family and friends first, not reporters."

"So, you consider them close friends?"

The faux-grief that covered Henry's face vanished in a flash and was replaced momentarily by fury. He rubbed his eyes to the point where they became bloodshot. He sniffled loud enough for Kari to hear. The faux-emotional act was grotesque in every way. "Yes. In fact, Botan is scheduled for a visit, but that may need to change because of the period of mourning."

"Of course," Adam said. "Since you stated that you had believed this day may come, is there a planned memorial?"

"His mother will plan that. I'll go when I'm required to."

"Required?" Adam leaned forward the slightest amount. "How would you respond to those who may think that sounds callous?"

"Because at times I need to be. You don't get where 1 am dwelling on death and failure, which Raymond now represents."

Dale kept the camera trained on the pair but turned to Kari. Her her eyes drifted down.

Kari followed her line of sight and saw that her fists were clenched worse than Henry's had been. White knuckles and all. Kari inhaled deeply. She had to maintain control.

"Do you have any more questions, Mr. Cho?" Henry asked.

"I have plenty, but given the situation, they can wait. Thank you for your time, Mr. Wibawa." He faced the camera. "This is Adam Cho for ENN reporting from the *Hinewai*." He mimed for Dale to cut the filming, which she did.

Henry wore his usual smile and unclipped the microphone pack at the small of his back. "I feel that went well. I have a conference call that will take several hours, but I promise that I'll be on time to our dinner. Karishma, please finish giving them the rest of the tour." Henry left the deck with Josef as his shadow.

Adam walked toward them with a slight grimace. *So weird. Does he care?* "That was . . . not what I expected."

Kari nodded. "I'd like to say, off the record, that Ray was a kind person. An artist. I liked him," she said with the tiniest crack in her voice. How was she supposed to finish the tour now? "Shall we pick up where we left off?" she blurted before she started to cry.

Really torn up. "Maybe tomorrow." *Get more secret intel.* Adam handed Dale the two microphone packs. "I think we have enough footage. It's been quite a day and I'd like to rest before dinner. Absorb what just happened."

———

Kari spent the remainder of her shift in the VIP assistant office. Adam wasn't going on excursions. There were no immediate VIPs to review. There were really only two things to dwell on: Ray was dead and Henry showed no remorse.

She had been staring into space when Belle stepped into the office. Worry lines creased her forehead as she approached. *Something happened?* "Kari?"

"Ray's dead."

Belle's hand went to the cross laying high on her chest. "When?"

"I found out at lunch. Henry requested a live interview with Adam minutes later. Despite all of these events, their scheduled dinner has not changed."

"That's despicable. How's Ahmed?"

"I don't know. I've tried texting him, but I haven't heard back. I was going to go to his cabin before I headed to mine."

"If you see him, please give him my condolences and tell him I'll be praying for him."

"I will." Kari got up from her spot at the desk and switched positions with Belle.

Wish could stay. Know hurting.

"I wish you could stay with me, too." Kari left the VIP office and headed to Madeleine's. She heard Ahmed through the closed door, so she knocked quietly.

"Come in."

Kari entered and saw a box of tissues in front of Ahmed. Madeleine was as stoic as ever. "Hi," Kari said softly and took a seat beside Ahmed. "I'm so, so sorry. Belle too. She's praying for you."

Typical. That brought a ghost of a smile to his quivering lips. "She would, wouldn't she?"

"Do you need an escort back to your cabin?" Madeleine asked him with more compassion than Kari had ever heard her use.

"No, I can find it, and I promise I won't do anything stupid. Again." *Stings.* Ahmed stood and left while rubbing his arm, closing the office door behind him.

"Something stupid?" Kari asked her.

"The interview Henry gave upset him. So much so that Ahmed went to Henry's cabin to confront him. I haven't seen the video, but Josef found his behavior aggressive enough to justify tasing him."

"He tased him?" Kari asked, outraged.

She nodded then stood to head back to office number two. Kari followed. "So, tell me about your time with Adam and I'll tell you something. A little quid pro quo, for a change."

Kari's curiosity was piqued. "Honestly, having Adam here was the best thing Henry could have done. The air of mystery is gone. I think he's going to move on to a new rich person to obsess over."

"Did he say or think anything about me?"

Partial honestly since leaving it out would be suspicious. "Your office size raised some questions as did your number of trips to Melbourne. I didn't catch anything about your family."

"Duly noted. After he finishes his interviews tomorrow, your next VIP will be Botan Itoi."

Kari opened her mouth to speak, but no words came out.

Madeleine waved her hand in front of her like she was gesturing to Kari's aura. "Are you having a stroke?"

"No. I thought that he wasn't visiting until Shanghai."

"I suppose current events have expedited his visit." Madeleine proceeded with the black box protocol. "I think you'd be interested to know that Henry went into the VIP logs and changed Itoi's visit a few minutes after Ray was pronounced deceased."

"Of course, he did." Kari folded her arms, disgusted. "Thanks for the quid pro quo."

Madeleine gave her a devious grin. "Oh, that wasn't the information I was referring to."

Her arms dropped to her sides. "What was then?"

"I learned why Henry wanted—or, perhaps, needed—Ray out of the picture."

For once, Kari wished Madeleine had a visitor chair she could settle into. "Why?"

"Ah. Well, let me ask you this . . . In all of that research you conducted about Henry, did you know that he had a much older half-brother? From his father's first marriage."

Kari stared ahead at Madeleine's eager face as her mind replayed all of the details she knew about Henry. Never once had she stumbled on that. In fact, the records of Henry were mostly vacant until he was fourteen. "No. Where's the half-brother now?"

"I believe you Americans use the phrase 'six feet under.'"

"He's dead?" Kari asked on impulse, even though she knew that was exactly what Madeleine had meant.

"Indeed. More specifically, his remains were found near an alcohol-filled cabin in a New Zealand forest. Evidence of a wild boar attack. The police report states that the two were on a hunting trip when his half-brother became drunk and belligerent. The thirteen-year-old young brother, Harold, left without a scratch on him."

The word 'remains' sent a chill up her spine, and 'wild boar attack' made her entire body spasm in fear, but her brain kept working. "Let me guess, his father wished to leave part of his massive estate to his half-brother, but due to the not at all plotted woodland excursion, Henry and his mom inherited all the estate instead."

Madeleine slowly nodded.

So Henry had started murdering people as a child. He was more than a power-hungry narcissist with a God complex. He was a legit psychopath. "How much of this did Ray know?"

"Only the deceased half-brother part. Ray mentioned it in an email to Henry when he was working on a family history tree. Some art project. The rest of the information came from good, old fashioned detective work." Madeleine took out the remote. "I think that's enough for today."

"Hold on!" Kari held up her hand. "Is Ahmed safe from Henry?"

"I believe so. However, it would be best if Ahmed stayed out of Henry's world as much as possible. Dismissed."

Chapter Twenty-Five

Manila, Philippines

Kari finally sat down and read the email Madeleine had forwarded to her. Earlier in her shift, she had received the verbal instruction, "Do something about this pest of a man!"

Greetings, Madeleine,

I wanted to personally thank you again for allowing my camera operator and me to come on board the *Hinewai*. Due to the unfortunate events, I wasn't able to get all the information I had hoped. Is there any way I could do a follow-up interview with you or one of the VIP assistants? Kari would be great!

Regards,

Adam Cho

The email itself didn't raise flags, but written between the lines was, "I didn't get nearly the scoop I thought I'd get. Cough up the information, Sky Fisher!" Back when she had proposed this visit, that was her intent, but now with Doug telling her she needed to back off or he'd send the No Ethics Science Squad after her, she couldn't. And she couldn't even suggest the most qualified person for him to interview because that would put Ahmed in danger. She had to choose someone totally removed. And oblivious.

Hello, Adam,

I think Matthew would be a fantastic person for this interview! Not only does he have more experience on the ship, but I don't believe you had the chance to spend much time with him while you were on board. I've cc'd him here, so you can work with him directly.

Thank you,

Kari

Belle barged into the VIP assistant office and slammed the door behind her.

"Is that your way of telling me that you'd like the chair to write your shift report?" Kari asked.

Kiss biscuits. "This puts the Weatherby visit to shame. I've never seen or heard Henry act so arrogant before. He must be putting on airs to impress Botan and Yuki." Belle put her hands on her hips and shook her head. "I still haven't figured out what kind of relationship they have. Aside from Yuki being Botan's EAT."

In her and Belle's research, the only facts they could find about Yuki was that his position for the technological whiz and billionaire was that he was the Executive Assistant of Travel, or EAT, for Botan. That was it. No place or date of birth. No education. No family. No surname. It was like he didn't exist before he'd started working for Botan. But, unlike Belle, Kari knew that Yuki was a fidele.

Kari tapped her device nub. "Lucky me, I get to learn all their relationship details."

They did their shimmy around the desk to switch places. *So hard.*

"If you want," Kari said, "we can rearrange the furniture in here so it's easier to move."

Belle stopped in front of her. "No, not that." *It's challenging enough wrestling with one's own thoughts and emotions on a daily basis. I can't imagine the stress of what you have.* "You handle it with an amazing level of patience."

Why couldn't Sven say insightful things like that? "Thank you. I think I needed to hear that."

"You're welcome. I hope your shift goes better than mine did."

Once Belle left, Kari took a moment to gather her wits. When she arrived in the VIP lounge, the raucous laughter was the first thing she noted. Next, she heard the greeting she dreaded.

"Karishma!" Henry waved her over. A bottle of whisky and three tumblers sat on the table between them. One glass was empty. "Come meet Botan and Yuki!"

As she crossed the deck, she noted the lack of servers and security. "It's a pleasure to meet you both." She extended her hand to Botan, who reminded her of a mad scientist with his unkempt white hair. His grip was cool, probably from his drink.

Very young. So curious. "I've heard much about you. This is my fidele, Yuki."

Yuki reached for her hand. "Hello."

Kari grasped his dry and fairly room temperature hand and, for the first time ever, she didn't catch a thought. Kari gawked at Yuki—which was easy given his model good looks—and waited to catch one, but none came. Weird. She cleared her throat. "Can I get anyone anything?"

"We don't need anything except for you to join us," Henry said. "Would you like ice?"

"Um." It took her a moment to realize he meant for a drink. "Sure."

Yuki used the tongs to remove a large cube from the bucket on the table and dropped it into the glass. He poured two fingers of Japanese whisky over the single cube, then handed it to her.

Best in collection. "I brought my favorite to celebrate," Botan said.

"Celebrate?" Kari took a seat and noticed a coin on the table near Henry.

Like with Gabriella. Henry smiled. "You can consider this more of an off duty—"

"I get it. I'm not here to act as a VIP assistant."

So smart. Henry motioned to her but looked at his two guests. "See what I mean; she's cheeky."

"It's good to have a fidele with that trait." Botan held his glass up. "Cheers!"

"Wait," Kari said. "Yuki doesn't have a drink."

"I don't drink," Yuki said. "I don't eat either."

She must have looked as puzzled as she felt because both Botan and Henry guffawed.

But Yuki kept an expression close to serenity. "I'm an android pro—"

"Shut up!" Kari shouted, causing both Henry and Botan to burst into laughter, but Yuki did, in fact, stop speaking. "Sorry, I didn't mean that as a command, more of an expression. How is that possible?"

"I am the latest in generational artificial intelligence," Yuki said. "Every day my program receives the latest information, which includes what I am exposed to while I'm with Botan. Therefore, I become more like Botan each day."

So wild. Brilliant and wild. Henry beamed.

Yuki 293. "The creation of Yuki has not been an easy process, but they are the achievement I am most proud of." Botan held his glass high. "To the future!"

Kari held her glass aloft and expected nothing but pure fire to touch her tongue on her first sip. Instead, it was gradual heat with a trace of vanilla. Verdict: It was better than bourbon, but not nearly as good as sparkling wine. She studied Botan and Yuki. They had their legs crossed in the same way and had identical expressions. "I thought that this level of technology and realism was decades in the future."

Father and robot rotated toward each other and smiled. It was almost sentimental.

"My company has made leaps and bounds in robotics," Botan said.

"But the last robotics demonstration I saw consisted of a weird dance by a silver machine that had a pure white pseudo-face. I also saw a weird game of soccer. Sorry, football."

Public. "Public companies share their advancements. As a private company, I only share what I want people to know." *Same with In Virtute.* "I think the sharing of knowledge is as good a segue as you're going to get, Henry."

So right. "Of course!" Henry smiled at Kari. "I gave Botan and Yuki a summary of what kinds of roles you'll have soon. Like the bunker."

Timeline issues. "I wish I could say that my build had gone to plan," Botan said. "I'd be more than happy to put you in contact with my team so you can avoid those inconveniences."

"Any lessons learned from the team that I can apply would be great. Why reinvent the wheel?" Kari grinned like everything was fine. Like she enjoyed the diesel fuel she was sipping and there wasn't a humanoid robot sitting across from her with perfect hair and muscles made of . . . silicon. Maybe?

Receptive. Botan gave her a sage nod. "I like that word, 'team.' I've heard us internally referred to as an organization, a consortium—a club, even—but rarely do I hear team, even though we all need to work together for our common goals." *Protect and perfect humanity.*

Kari sipped the whisky again only in the hope of hiding her face. In Virtute saw themselves both as protectors of global catastrophe and as the leaders of eugenics. Quite the dichotomy.

She put her drink down on the coaster nearest to the coin in the hopes of getting a better view of it. The green patina led her to believe that it was copper or bronze.

"It won't bite," Botan said. *Silly tradition.* "You can pick up the coin."

So she did. It was the size of a quarter and weighed about the same. She studied the design on the one side. Room with columns. She flipped it over and there was the elephant with its menacing tusks. It was the same image Amara Gupta had pictured in her mind. "What do these sides mean?"

Much power. "The elephant is the symbol of In Virtute and the other side represents our initiation space."

Kari placed the coin back on the table with a quiet tap. Her napkin to Doug would be filled to the edges next time. "Where's the space?"

Null. Botan poured a finger more whisky into his glass. "That's something Henry doesn't even know yet, but once his last hurdle is eliminated, you will both know."

Now that Ray was dead—not to mention anyone else who had threatened his wealth over the years—it must have been her. "My birthday will be here before you know it."

No. Botan shook his head. "You're not the hurdle." *Investigation slow.*

Was everybody involved with Henry in some sort of investigation? A vibration in her pocket caused her to jump in her seat and splash whisky on her pants. "Sorry. I need to check this." She read the text from Jon.

Can you come and get the appetizers? No one, per Henry, is allowed out there.

She tucked the phone away. "I'll be right back with our first course."

"Excellent," Botan said. "When you come back, I'd like to focus more on you. Get to know you better."

"Sure. I'm an open book." Yep, that was her. No secrets at all.

Chapter Twenty-Six

Busan, South Korea

Kari had thought she'd learn more about the investigation before Botan and Yuki left the ship, but she hadn't. Then, she thought she'd learn in Taipei. But the only things she had learned in that time was that Adam had not been impressed with Matthew's interview. Adam insisted on speaking with her. At this point she didn't know if he would ever get the hint and leave her alone. What she did know was that Adam had added more stress to her life and she needed to unwind in the worst way.

A party was what she needed.

"Jon really came through." Belle placed container after container of Korean foods on the side tables brought in for the combination birthday-graduation party. "How are we going to eat this much?"

When Kari lifted a lid and the succulent aroma of beef bulgogi wafted toward her, she almost salivated like a cartoon dog. "We'll manage, I'm sure of it." Once everything was out, Kari fixed herself a plate of bulgogi, a fried chicken thigh, and kimchi. But she did leave room for cake. After that, she would probably need to roll back to her cabin. Which was why she'd opted to have sex with Sven before the party.

"Where's Sven with the cakes?" Craig asked.

Nando hitched his thumb toward the door. "I saw him about a half hour ago."

"He wanted to grab a shower before the party started," Kari said. The crunch from the chicken reverberated through Kari's jawbone and up to her ears to make sweet, poultry music. But she caught Belle's pensive expression. "What? Should I have waited to eat until he got here?"

"No. Well, yes, you should have. But, I was thinking that I'd rather we focus on you and Craig since I'll be staying on the ship. Not much is changing for me."

"Did you or did you not complete a full undergraduate education?" Kari asked her.

"I did, but—"

"Then we share the party!" Craig raised his beer. At the sound of the door creaking on its hinges, he spun in his chair. "Nice! The delivery boy is here."

"Oh," Nando drawled in amazement as Sven pushed the cake cart into the room. "You did these?"

"You're surprised I have skills?" Sven asked.

"A little," Craig said, causing Nando to smack him in the back of the head.

Everyone left the table to admire the possible baking masterpieces. The graduation cake was in the shape of a mortarboard, complete with dangling tassel, in WU's vermillion, white, and black colors. *Congratulations, Belle and Craig!* was written in white icing script. There were no flowers or hearts, but there was a golden, puffy, most likely buttermilk classic, cut in the shape of a boat, at the corner.

Belle cackled. "Did you make a biscuit for me?"

"I did!" Sven nodded vigorously and smiled.

"That was really nice," Kari said. "As was making my cake. Thank you." Her birthday cake was a cube made to look like a wrapped present, complete with twenty small bows. "What flavor is it?"

"Chocolate and peanut butter. I noticed you had a lot of wrappers in your bin one time. The graduation cake is almond and toffee."

They returned to the table to enjoy their meal after they heard about Sven's small adventure of getting the cakes from the WU refrigerator and onto the cart without assistance.

"Any updates on where you're going after graduation?" Nando asked Craig.

"Quebec. I'd love to stick around so I could get some surfing pictures when you're in Hawaii, but I'm also excited to not be surrounded by the ocean. Kinda sick of it. What are your plans since you're not going to Uruguay?"

"I'm going to enjoy the perks of a roommate-less cabin while I start my internship," Nando said, then looked at Kari. "Are you my boss? I still don't understand how that works."

"Doug is, but I'll be giving him weekly notes on your progress either in the office or in the passageway when we run into each other. Like neighbors do." In a move that sounded like it had everything to do with CIA computer hacking, Doug had moved into Jade's old cabin.

"I might be able to boss you around though," Belle said to Nando. "I think you'll like that."

Kari nodded. In another life, she would have loved to have been bossed around by Belle. "You get to tell the other intern what to do, too."

"A second intern?" Belle asked.

"Yep. I got pre-approval of some changes I want to implement." One of the most important was Ahmed. She wouldn't fire him, but she could make efforts to keep him away from Henry as much as possible.

Craig chuckled. "You sound like a boss already. Are you going to wear a suit?"

Kari did like the idea of wearing a suit to go along with the new haircut she planned on getting. Her hair had finally grown long enough for some serious styling. "I think I might."

As they finished their meal and played one last game of poker, they spoke more about what the immediate future held for all of them. Who they would see. Vacations they might go on. Other events they looked forward to. Belle remained quiet, but when pressed, she said that she was content to live on the boat like a grown-up.

Kari couldn't imagine how annoying it must have been to pretend to be in college yet have to go through all the same shit.

When it was time to part ways, they packed the leftovers first. Thanks to Jon's foresight, Kari had half a dozen boxes to take back, which included a piece of cake for Neill. But she apparently had one more box to add to the mountain.

Sven approached her with a small, elongated wrapped box and handed it to her. "I forgot to bring this earlier to your cabin. Happy birthday."

"You didn't have to do that," Kari said with an uneasy smile because he really didn't have to do that. Between the request to cuddle and now the charm bracelet she held between her thumb and forefinger, Kari had a feeling this had stopped being casual for him.

He beamed and pointed at a guitar. "You can add all of your interests or change them from time to time. My mother said that's fun to do. There's a great charm shop back home that we can go visit together."

"Um." Kari turned to Belle, who shared her look of surprise.

But she was pretty sure Belle didn't feel smothered. Sven wanted her to visit his home? Where his family lived? To breathe again, she put the lid back on the box. "That'd be . . . new."

"Yes! And maybe we can see each other again before finals?" He kissed her cheek, then left with the cart. "Let me know."

Nando continued to focus on the table he had been wiping down. "He's got it so bad for you."

"Let's change who's receiving attention, shall we." Kari went to her backpack where she had presents stashed. She lifted the two gift bags and handed them to each graduate. "Happy graduation!"

Belle grinned. "I was not expecting this."

"Why not?" Kari asked. "As we discussed, you earned a diploma from WU, right?"

"Right!" Craig reached into the smaller bag and pulled out the fisheye camera lens he had been going on and on about. "I can't believe it! Thank you!" He came at her for an aggressive hug, which Kari happily obliged.

"You're welcome. It's not top of the line, but it's enough to get you started." Once she was free, she pointed at Belle's present. "It's more than a bag, you know."

Belle reached in between the pieces of white tissue paper and pulled out a driftwood picture frame with Kari's handwritten lyrics to *Mountain Home* showcased behind the glass. The occasional sketch of an object from the song decorated the paper further. Belle smiled sweetly at the gift as her forefinger traced the shape of a rocking chair.

Kari tucked her hands into her pockets. "I saw the frame at a market in Taipei and thought you might want to put your diploma in there. The lyrics are just a place holder." That was a lie. She hoped Belle kept the lyrics so that whenever she felt alone or homesick, she could be reminded of her chosen family who loved her back home.

Belle bit her lower lip. "This was . . . so considerate of you." She placed the frame on the table then embraced Kari. "Thank you."

Professional ethics be damned. Kari hugged her back and allowed Belle's warmth to fill her to the point where it gripped her insides. Literally. Her chest tightened, but in a way that brought comfort. It was a puzzling but wonderful sensation, until she realized what it meant: She loved Belle.

Which was not how she was supposed to feel toward her.

"You're welcome." Kari loosened her arms and stepped away. "I better get these leftovers in the refrigerator."

"That's right. You don't want food poisoning," Belle said. "I haven't taken your job just yet."

Kari smiled, said her goodbyes, and left with full, heavy bags. But the epiphany about Belle that she now carried weighed the most. By the time she reached her cabin and organized her leftovers in the refrigerator, she could distract herself from that by responding to the birthday wishes that had come in from Jade, Neill, Finn, and all three grandparents. She'd wrap up the festivities with a planned video call with the moms.

"Happy birthday, chickpea!" both of her mothers squealed in unison. Mom L blew into a party streamer, which woke Sage from his doggie bed nap.

"I can't believe my baby girl is twenty!" Mom A said. "Do you feel any older?"

"Actually, this year I do. I'm starting a job where I'm going to wear a suit and I can honestly say that I have decades—plural —of life experience."

"Just imagine how wise you'll feel when you hit your

fifties." Mom L pointed to the abundance of gray at her temples. "All of this is wisdom."

Mom A gave her arm a light slap. "What did you do for your special day?"

"I just came from a joint birthday-graduation party with a ton of food and played poker. Sven made the cakes."

"Was that his gift to you?" Mom A asked.

"He also gave me a bracelet." She didn't want to get into the awkwardness about Sven, especially considering the revelation she had about Belle. "The graduation festivities were very nice, too. Craig and Belle liked their presents. Although, it is a little weird for her since she's staying on the ship."

"Oh!" Mom A said loud enough to startle Sage enough to bark. "We'll get to meet her!"

Kari scrunched her forehead. "I'm not so sure about that."

"But what if," Mom L said, like she was a game show host, "we were *Hinewai* VIPs?"

Kari laughed. She knew her mothers were comfortable with their finances but not that well off. "You're hilarious.'"

"She's telling the truth," Mom A said. "We were invited to be VIPs by Mr. Wibawa."

"What?" Kari yelled loud enough for Doug to probably hear her through their shared wall. Her worlds couldn't collide. It wasn't safe. "Please, don't."

"We promise that we won't embarrass you," Mom L said.

"It's not that." How could she tell them not to come? But as soon as she asked herself the question, she knew the answer. There was no way they wouldn't come because she told them not to, they had to change their mind on their own terms. But she drew a blank on what to say, except when it came to questions. "When did you receive the invitation?"

"Yesterday, actually," Mom A said. "Leela got the call at work."

"Somehow Madeleine got my private number at city hall. Imagine that," Mom L said with a knowing edge to her voice.

Kari rubbed her face in her hands. "Yeah, she finds everything."

"I'm very curious to meet these people you work with," Mom L said.

Given what she had told Mom L during the trip to Michigan, she might ask too many questions. That curiosity could turn out to be deadly. "This makes me so uncomfortable."

"Don't worry," Mom A said. "The invitation said that we can enjoy the amenities and I can even learn more about the environmental aspects of the ship for ENN, which is really convenient since Adam said he hasn't been able to ask you follow-up questions about it."

Her outrage was stuck in her throat. Because she had ignored Adam's requests, he asked her mom to do the dirty work for him! "I'm going to say this again. You coming on the ship makes me—"

BAM! BAM! BAM! Someone pounded on the door.

"If that's how Sven announces his arrival," Mom A said, "you better have given him permission to do that."

"Probably Doug complaining about my screaming. Give me a second." Kari muted her laptop and switched off her video before she went to the door. "Josef?"

"Henry needs to see you in his cabin."

Apparently, he could speak in complete sentences. Or sentence. "Can it wait a few minutes? I'm on a call with my moms."

He stared at her.

"Fine. Let me say goodbye." She went back, unmuted, and unblocked her video. "I'm sorry, but I have to go. Henry needs me and it's urgent."

"Just call us back when it's convenient for you," Mom A said. "I love you."

"Love you too, chickpea. Happy birthday."

"I love you both, too. Bye." She disconnected, closed her laptop, and went back to her visitor, who stood in the passageway with his arms crossed. Telepathy would have been convenient at the moment. "Can you at least tell me what this is about?"

He answered by turning away from her and walking down the passageway.

"Cockwaffle," she muttered and followed. With each passing step, she grew more annoyed. And perplexed.

Josef stopped outside of Henry's cabin. "Go to the dining room," he said as he disengaged the locks. Once he stepped over the threshold, he veered off to the side.

The hair on the back of her neck stood on end. This was weird, but given that she knew the fidele role would take effect once she turned twenty, she should have expected something from Henry. It just would have been nice if it had been planned.

"Happy birthday to you," Henry sang as he rose from the table.

Kari waited until he finished singing the off-key song to give him a quiet round of applause before she sat. "Thank you very much for that special rendition."

"I hope you don't mind the late hour of the surprise, Karishma, but I can assure you this will be a positive conversation. Even more so than the one I'm sure you had with your mothers just now."

"Yeah, that was an interesting one." Just as Kari thought they were planting bugs, she remembered she had added that call to her shared calendar so no one would disturb her. It had been a good idea, in theory. "They told me they're going to be VIPs."

"Were you surprised?" Henry asked with a broad smile.

"That's putting it mildly." Even though she dreaded the moment they stepped on board, she needed to show gratitude. "Thank you for that wonderful gift."

He gave her a less crazed grin and bowed his head. "I know how much you care for both of them, so I thought it would be a nice present for you to bring them aboard. Also, the visit with Adam Cho went so well, it couldn't hurt to have ENN's own Aurora Okpik-Bakshi think of a specific environmental piece for the ship."

"Mom A didn't get into those details. Of course, our call was cut short." Her eyes drifted over to where Josef had meandered to the wet bar. He placed a wrapped present on the counter.

"This conversation won't be long, so you can call them back," Henry said. "Although, while this will be a short conversation it is a very important one. We need to talk about something serious before you start your duties as fidele: loyalty." His happy expression shifted to one of intensity.

Kari needed to stay poised, look innocent, and play along. "Of course."

He stood from the table, went to the gift, and handed it to her. "For you, on this very special day."

"Thank you." Kari studied the box that was the size and weight of a large snow globe. The white wrapping paper with a silver ribbon and bow added to the wintery theme. She tore the paper off until a plain white paper box was left. She popped its lid and opened it. The inner contents left her mute, except the gulp that came from her impossibly dry throat.

"I hoped you'd like it," Henry said at the other end of the table.

Kari couldn't believe what she held in her hands. As she touched it, she realized it wasn't a hallucination. She accepted reality and pulled out Madeleine's black box. Its locking mechanism had been taped to prevent its closure and the remote was nestled inside. "How did you get this from her?"

Like a switch had been thrown, Henry directed a look at her that was so cold it made the wrapping paper appear warm. "Before I answer that, I want to circle back to what it means to be loyal. Or rather, what it doesn't mean. Loyalty is not requesting that the ship analysts hack my lawyers' files, email, and the history of my father's estate. Loyalty is not making jokes at my expense during public events. Loyalty is not leaving the ship to meet with Australian authorities to work out a plea because of tax evasion."

Kari's heart skipped a beat. Madeleine had been working with the Australian government?

"And loyalty," Henry continued, "is most certainly not contacting Adam Cho's people and giving them a name like Sky Fisher to provide insider information. In summary, Madeleine was not loyal!"

There was no more skipping, Kari's heart simply stopped, and she knew her heart resembled Madeleine's in that way.

Henry shook his head while he walked over to the painting of Jesus. "All the great men and Gods have had people who've betrayed them. Who deceived them. I'm no different." He circled back to the table with his nostrils flared. "We were friends for decades, and if it hadn't been for the investigation of our new colleagues, I never would have known. She lied to me!" His shout resonated in the vast expanse of the cabin. "And because of that she needed to receive the fiercest punishment."

Kari's emotions manifested itself into a shudder so intense her teeth chattered. "How did she die?"

"Drowned in her bathtub," Josef said without emotion. "Very sad."

"I understand that this is shocking to hear," Henry said, "but it was import—no, it was imperative—that you understand what loyalty means to me." He gestured to her present. "But I also acknowledge that loyalty is a two-way street. Please accept this gift and the knowledge that your mothers are safe, as a sign of my loyalty to you, my fidele."

Her hand trembled as she picked up the remote. "Thank you, Henry," she said with words as shaky as her hand. She had the control of her own mind back, but she didn't want it this way. Even if the cost was the death of a woman she despised. "Where is she now?"

"Coroner on shore," Josef said.

"The story is that Madeleine called for Josef," Henry said, "but when she didn't answer he used his master passcode to enter. Evidence of alcohol and pills were nearby."

Like she had been the one who had ingested the toxic mix, Kari's birthday meal lurched out of her stomach, but she pushed it down. The taste of spicy gochujang mixed with bile lingered.

"I understand that you'll need some time to process this, and please know that her passing will not add more responsibilities to your plate. Josef will assume those roles—in addition to his security position—and take her offices." Henry approached her and offered her a hand to stand, but she didn't take it. "I understand that this is a lot to process, and I think you should see a friend."

Kari didn't want to hear his monstrous thoughts, but she needed to know. She clicked the button on the remote. "You actually want me to talk about this with someone?"

Shocked. Devastated. Henry nodded. "I trust you to keep certain details a secret." He reached out and gently touched her shoulder. *It's okay if you can hear me. I trust you implicitly, as you are my path to greatness. I have seen it in my visions.* He walked her to the door with a gentle hand on her lower back. "There are no VIPs tomorrow, so there is no need to report to work as the VIP Coordinator. Give yourself a day. Maybe even walk around the city to clear your head. Have a good night and, again, happy birthday, Karishma."

"Good night," she said but so softly she barely heard it. She left the cabin and zipped the remote in her cargo pants' pocket. That simple act of coordination challenged her enough not to trust her legs with stairs, so she walked in the direction of the elevator.

The horrors of what had occurred would stay with her for the rest of her life. If he had any clue that she was working with the CIA, the punishment would be worse than death. He would torture her. The moms. Maybe make her watch. She bit her tongue to try to keep her composure, but the pain added to her nausea. She sprinted to the elevator at the end of the passageway, knocked the lid of the trashcan off, and threw up her birthday meal until she dry heaved. Logically she knew that vomiting stimulated the lacrimal gland, but there was another culprit for the tears coming down her cheeks.

She had never been so afraid in her life.

Kari went inside the elevator and pressed the deck number for the friend who understood her situation the most. She took steady steps down the passageway as she focused on her breathing. One step, one breath. Once she reached the cabin, she knocked.

Belle stood in the doorway with her hair down and wearing pajamas of shorts and a T-shirt. *Looks terrible. Scared, even.* "Are you okay? Did something happen?"

"I'm . . . I'm so sorry to be here. I . . . I . . ." Vy looked at her, her brow crinkled, too. "I can't be here . . . I'm sorry. I'll go."

Terrified. "No. Come with me." Belle grabbed her hand and took Kari down the busy pre-final-stressed-out thoughts passageway until she pulled her into the party-poker room from earlier and shut the door. The smell of Korean food lingered. "This is a clear room. What happened?" *Like in shock.*

"I . . . I . . . " Clearly I statements weren't working. Kari unzipped her pocket and pulled out the remote so Belle could see.

Brain remote? "Is that what I think it is?"

"Yes." Kari's voice strained and eyes burned.

Oh my God. "Wait." *You can hear me?*

Kari nodded.

Belle held both of Kari's hands. *What happened?*

"Dead," Kari said above a whisper.

Who? "Who?"

"Ma-Ma-de-leine," Kari stuttered before everything inside her broke. She collapsed on the floor, blocking the door, as she imagined what Madeleine's dead-eyed stare must have looked like. Then she pictured her own, Belle's, and Doug's if Henry ever caught them.

Oh, my God. Belle joined her on the ground and continued to gently hold her hands. *Traumatized.* "Did you see it?"

"Henry told me. The report will say that she drowned in her bathtub." Kari gulped and shook her head. "You have to leave."

No. "You know I can't."

"You have to!" Kari shouted into Belle's beautiful and worried face. "If I fire you, you'll be safe."

Too on edge. "Kari"—Bell scooted closer and held Kari's hands to her chest—"listen to me." *This is what I signed up for. Your safety comes first. If this is too much for you, tell Doug. There is an exit strategy.*

"There is?"

"Yes." *Protection cued. You can go.*

But, at this stage, if she left it would draw questions and complications. Henry would search for her, and the first place he'd look would be her moms and grandparents homes. Even though Henry had said her family was safe that was most definitely under the stipulation she worked for him. She had two choices: Stay a committed CI, fidele, and VIP Coordinator, or put this life behind her and convince her family to go into hiding for the rest of their lives with her. Both choices were awful, but one only affected her. "I have to stay, but as long as we're smart, we'll be safe here, right?"

Still petrified. "Yes. You'll be safe."

Kari caught the change of plural to singular noun. "But you need to be safe, too."

"I will be, but you"—Belle cupped Kari's chin—"are my priority." *I will protect you at all costs.*

Up until that point in Kari's life, only her mothers had shielded her from the dangers of the world. "I get it. You have a job to do."

"It's not because of that." *Love.* Belle bit her lower lip and dropped her hand.

Kari's teary eyes widened. "What?"

"I'm sorry, I didn't mean to think that." *Can't love her.* "It's just . . ."

"You love me?"

Such conflict. "I'm sorry. I know that makes our situation so much more difficult." She lowered her head. *So sorry.*

Kari would have accepted any reason for Belle to want to protect her, but knowing Belle loved her strengthened her resolve to move forward. Belle needed to know that. "I feel the same way."

Belle lifted her head. *Really?*

Kari nodded. "But I won't apologize for it, so you shouldn't either."

Could be last chance. Belle cradled Kari's face with both hands and kissed her.

The chaste kiss created a euphoric wave that momentarily disrupted the turmoil in Kari's mind. Once the few seconds of peacefulness waned, she pulled away and leaned her forehead against Belle's. Kari fought the desire to kiss her again and so did Belle, but their thoughts mutually agreed that they shouldn't. They'd get caught, eventually. Then Belle would be punished, definitely.

Belle reached for Kari's hands and squeezed them. *Have faith.* "We will get through this."

"I believe you."

Chapter Twenty-Seven

Sapporo, Japan

"Thank you for rescheduling this so last minute," Kari said as she made her way into Ola's office. "There's been a lot going on that I need to talk about."

Thought mad about last-minute cancellation fee. "That's not a problem. May I ask what happened that was so urgent?"

Kari toed off her shoes and took her usual cross-legged position. "I'm guessing you heard the news that Madeleine Coultier died."

News everywhere. "Yes! What a shock. How are you processing that?"

"The short answer is that I don't know. I didn't like her, but at the same time"—she shouldn't have been murdered and had it made to look like an overdose—"no one should have to die like that. What makes me feel worse is that I like her sisters more."

What? "You met her sisters? Where?"

Kari took a deep breath. "At her funeral."

Ola uncrossed her legs and leaned forward. *She went?* "You felt compelled to pay your respects, I take it."

349

"Not really. Um, Henry—who I'm working with very closely now—insisted that I accompany him to Melbourne to represent the VIP staff. It was weird."

So weird. "Surely you were given the opportunity to decline."

"Do you think Henry takes no for an answer?"

Good point. Horror stories about that man. "Tell me about Madeleine's sisters, then."

For that thought alone, Kari was glad she had deactivated her device for therapy. That and she couldn't resist knowing Ola's true opinion about her. "Her sisters truly loved and admired her, even though they hadn't always liked her. Like their candy, they're sweet people and thanked me for coming." Kari had also learned that neither of them trusted Henry or his tears.

Honest. "I'm glad you had a positive experience." Ola resumed her usual position of her legs crossed in the chair. *There's more.* "I have the sense that isn't the only drama happening in your life."

"Your senses are pretty good." Kari waved a hand in front of her black uniform. "As you can see, I just got off work. Since Madeleine died, I've been working two jobs, but fortunately Belle graduates tomorrow, so I'll be down to one job, VIP Coordinator." *And the secret fidele role.*

Nerves. "I would think you'd be happy about that change."

"The job isn't the problem; it's that Henry has insisted that I move into Madeleine's old cabin for his convenience."

Narcissism knows no bounds. "I would imagine that is awkward. Hopefully, you can make it your own space."

"I hope so. I haven't unpacked anything yet, but I did request a new bathtub." Even though Kari wasn't one hundred percent sure Madeleine had been murdered in her bathtub, it felt too weird to be in there.

Ghastly. "I would have done the same." *Why Henry need her?* "You know that this is a safe space and what you say stays here, right?"

"Yes." But only because she occasionally checked it for bugs and Ola's thoughts conveyed a dislike of Henry.

"Good." *Inappropriate.* "Has Henry crossed the line with you in terms of professional and personal boundaries?"

If Ola only knew the amount of boundaries he had crossed. "He's never tried anything sleazy."

Dodged a bit. "Boundaries can be more than sexual."

Kari needed to spin the conversation away and fast. "Speaking of that, I started having sex with friend A to distract myself from the fact that I had a massive crush on friend B. I've recently realized that I actually love friend B, and it's mutual, but haven't broken things off with friend A yet. And, before you suggest it, polyamory isn't an option because of B's sexual orientation and religion." Although, her threesome fantasy would stay on standby. "Thoughts?"

Avoided the boundaries question. Verbal diarrhea. "Um. Yes, I think you know what you need to do. At least with friend A. Would you care to expand on friend B?"

"No. Do you have suggestions for how to break up with someone?" Kari shrugged. "I've never done it."

———

Kari listened to the World University president's closing remarks about leading a meaningful life to the graduating class. She had been watching from the back along with her VIP until said VIP realized that the ceremony was as boring as all the others and left to take a nap.

"There you are," Sven said from behind. "I have been trying to reach you the last few days."

Kari turned to face him. "Sorry. I can't keep my personal cell on me during work and I've been working two jobs since Busan." A crinkle appeared between his eyes. "I've been busy."

He gave a small nod that didn't convey complete understanding. "I stopped by your cabin last night, too, but your message board is gone. Belle is there instead. What's happened?"

"Per Henry, I had to move. For Belle, you'll have to ask her how she scored a balcony as a first-year employee." Kari was sure the answer to that was more CIA hacking, since she and Doug were neighbors now.

Sven continued to pout. "You could have at least texted me back when you finished work."

An urge to snap sprouted, but she reminded herself that he simply saw them as a couple and she saw the opposite. "Like I said, I've been really busy, but I am glad you found me because we do need to talk."

He took a step closer. "Have I done something wrong?"

If what she had done before had wounded his heart, then what she had to say next was twisting the knife. Even if it was for the best. "You haven't done anything wrong, it's just that we need to end our uncomplicated arrangement, because things are getting complicated."

"But . . ." He stuffed his hands in his pockets. "Should I do more?"

Ola had not prepared her for that response. "It's not that. I think you're a good guy and you deserve someone who can give you the kind of relationship you want. I'm not that person."

He downcast his eyes, but then he nodded in a way that did demonstrate understanding. "I thought I could change your mind if I did enough things for you."

As if she didn't feel like a big enough cockwaffle already. "That's not the way it works. At least not for me."

He shifted his stance and contorted his pretty face into one of discomfort. "Is it okay if I ask for the bracelet back? It was expensive."

"Sure. If you're not in your cabin when I come down, I'll put it in the mail delivery system you WU folk use."

He gave a nod. "Can I have a hug goodbye?"

"Sure."

After they embraced and he kissed her cheek, she watched him walk away. When he disappeared around the corner, she brought her attention back to the graduation.

"You didn't bring your cap and gown," Neill said as he sidled next to her.

"Neither did you."

He looked down at his jeans and T-shirt. "Not really my style for my days off. But I suppose it's more than just a day off when you use all of your vacation at once."

"As a new daddy, I really don't think you're going to have a lot of time to relax on this 'vacation' of yours."

His eyes brightened. "That reminds me, I wanted to show you this before I left." He took out his phone and showed her the selfie Jade had taken with their sleeping one-week-old baby in a black onesie with *Security* written across the back in white letters.

"Like father, like son." Kari chortled and handed the phone back. "Is Jade doing well? The last text I got from her said, 'Everyone's a liar, the second baby isn't easier.'"

Now it was Neill's turn to laugh. "She's improved and is settled at our temporary home. Our home. I still can't believe that."

They stood in silence until Kari noticed his nervous shuffle. "You're going to be a great dad. Now, go on. If you miss the tender, Jade's going to blame me for keeping you."

"You're right. I'll see you in Hawaii."

"Yep. Safe travels, buddy." As he walked away, she yelled, "Give my best to the family!"

He waved over his head and kept walking toward the stairwell.

Her gaze went back to the graduates and soon the vermillion caps went skyward and they scattered from their seats. Craig waved at her with a large smile. Next, Kari searched for a tall blonde in the crowd. She finally spied Belle celebrating and trading caps with a small group. She seemed as happy as the rest of them.

Belle caught Kari's eye and strode toward her. "Did you come to congratulate us?"

"I did and congratulations. Are you and the other graduates hightailing it out of here for some land-based festivities?"

"Some are, I'm not. I have to move into my new cabin."

"I heard that you're moving into my former space." Kari smirked. "Funny how that happened."

Belle's mouth formed an O. "How did you find out so fast? I just learned it myself last night."

"Sven told me a few minutes ago during the conversation where I told him I can't see him anymore. He was disappointed, but we hugged, so I guess that's ending things on a healthy note."

"Probably for the best, and I'm not just saying that because . . . You know. He's a sweet guy." Belle looked away and played with the cap in her hands. "Have you moved into your new super cabin yet?"

Kari exhaled a relieved breath from the change of conversation course. "Everything's there—in box and bag form—but I haven't had time to unpack and organize. It's so weird that I have to live in Madeleine's cabin. I just know her ghost is going to haunt me."

"Do you believe in ghosts?"

"One hundred percent." Given her own origin and abilities, the spirits of the dead saying, 'hi' to the living didn't seem that outlandish. "I think I'll be proactive and make a cup of Earl Grey every day to appease her."

"Don't forget the lemon." Belle turned to the group she had been celebrating with and then back to Kari. "A few of us are going to have some drinks on the ship once they open the bar. You're welcome to join us."

"I appreciate the invitation, but I shouldn't. I don't really trust the combination of you, me, and alcohol."

Belle breathed in deeply through her nostrils. "Fair point," she said as a long exhale.

After a silence that lingered too long, Kari motioned to the crowd. "You should have some fun and celebrate. I, on the other hand, still have to finalize my presentation for tomorrow's staff meeting."

Belle's eyes softened. "You've been working too hard."

Kari told herself that her pulse raced from the abnormally high level of caffeine coursing through her veins and not the depth of how much Belle cared for her. "Maybe, but thanks to you, I'll have one less job after today."

"Despite all that, try to relax tonight."

Kari gave her a sad grin, but then remembered something legitimately exciting. "My new bathtub was installed this morning. Maybe I'll hop into that. Turn on the jets."

"That does sound relaxing. I'll see you tomorrow."

"You better." Kari watched Belle join the group, then left the deck to finish the last few hours of her last shift. Tomorrow was the start of a new beginning.

———

Kari hadn't slept well, but she knew the reasons why: She had five cups of coffee the day before, the ticks from the ostentatious grandfather clock carried through the vents, and the sun had started to creep into her obscenely large bedroom window. She made a note to buy better blackout curtains. The only familiar elements to her new room were her mattress and bedding.

She refused to bathe in a murdered woman's tub or sleep in her bed.

Sick of hearing the clock, Kari tossed the covers off to start her day, even though it was almost noon. She went down the open staircase where more sunlight attacked her, causing the crystal chandelier near the clock to sparkle like lasers into her retinas. As did the glassware from her wet bar. And the granite countertop in the kitchen.

She was embarrassed by the lavishness of her new living conditions. She hadn't earned it; not that she felt anyone ever did. She was only a few generations away from poverty on both sides of her family. How could she justify the fact that she had a two-story suite to herself and an outrageous salary to those who came before her? The answer was that she couldn't. The only thing she could do to balance the scales was donate a substantial amount to the community.

And add to the newly implemented VIP staff reward fund for VIP meal vouchers.

Kari reached for the mechanism behind the clock and flipped the red switch to silent. Finally, the ticking menace had been vanquished. Before she headed back up the stairs, she set her electric kettle for tea. More coffee would set her heart rate to that of an Etruscan shrew with tachycardia.

After a blistering shower with precise temperature control and time to shave, Kari fixed her hair. Her completely badass hair. The new style had gelled wisps on top with a fade on her sides and neck. The quasi-punk hair was a nice juxtaposition to her professional attire. Henry had insisted she buy a collection of suits at his favorite shop and charge his account, so she had picked a few standard colors and styles with capri-length pants and skirts but chose several colorful options as well. Today felt like a tangerine and capri pant day. The addition of her firestarter necklace tucked underneath her camisole blended new Kari with old.

There was no need to go to the cafeteria because she knew her brunch would be waiting in a cloche on her desk. Once food was in her belly and all essential emails had been responded to, she went to the legitimate conference room and set the AV so that her presentation's non-catchy title, *Changes to VIP Operations*, projected onto the smart board.

Ahmed came into the room first wearing his black uniform but with his shirt untucked and unbuttoned. "Looks pretty official."

Kari sent him a grin. "Thanks. Did you have a good shift?"

"Not too bad. Matthew says he promises he'll read the slides you sent him."

"I have no doubt."

After another few minutes of small talk about the VIPs, Belle, Doug, and the new WU interns, Nando and Jia, came into the room and took their seats as well.

"Thank you all for being prompt and coming when you're not on shift. For your troubles, you get a VIP meal voucher." Kari forwarded the slideshow to *Introductions*. "I'll start. I'm Kari from the US. Next month, I'll be starting my third year on the ship, and the last good movie I saw was *Everest's Prison*."

As far as icebreakers went, that seemed to be a fairly painless template for the others to follow. It went quickly, and Kari learned some of Jia's story. She was from a town in the Hunan province of China, was starting her fifth year due to switching majors, and didn't remember the title of the movie, but it was body horror-comedy. Jia's first assignment was to get the title and report back.

That was going on Kari's To Be Watched list.

Kari went to the *Changes to Hierarchy and Schedule* slide. "Aside from myself acting as coordinator, there is another significant change. Starting today, Ahmed has been promoted to Senior of VIP Relations. He's in charge when I'm not here."

Belle gave him a pat on the back. "Congrats, Ahmed."

Nando, Jia, and Doug smiled politely.

Next, Kari showed a grid where each day was divided into three blocks, one was blacked out, and every employee or intern was color coded. "I did some data analysis and, long story short, we're moving to ten-hour shifts and shift consistency. There's no more frequent switching between am and pm shifts. That's not healthy."

Ahmed and Belle nodded.

Kari went to the next slide, *Changes to Internships*. "The intern shift has been reduced so they can take classes. Also, I'll be meeting with Doug once a week, in his office, since the program is driven by WU." The chances of Henry barging into Doug's office were slim to none. Plus, he had the whole Faraday cage set up for safer drops of information.

Kari advanced to the next slide, *Future VIPs*. "Our next significant stop is Hawaii, which has an extensive VIP list." She brought up the bulleted list.

"Wait." Nando sat up straighter. "Are your mothers coming aboard?"

Kari tried not to grimace. "They sure are, and believe me when I say I had absolutely nothing to—"

The door flew open with Henry on the other side of it. "Karishma, I need to speak with you now." As quickly as he'd entered the room, he was gone.

Kari ignored both Nando and Jia's starstruck faces at seeing Henry Wibawa for the first time. She didn't know what his pop-in—or barge in—was about, except that it was annoying and potentially murderous. Kari left, shutting the door behind her. "What is it?"

Henry smiled. "It's time."

"Time for what?"

"Our initiation," he said while bouncing at the knees.

Something even more troubling than Henry's official induction into In Virtute alarmed her. "Our? As in we're both getting initiated?"

"That surprised me, too." He placed a hand on each shoulder. "Does that concern you?"

Concern was an understatement. The idea that she would be initiated into a secret organization while working as a confidential informant filled her with so much apprehension that she had to empty her bladder immediately. However, every piece of intel she gathered moved her closer to seeing Henry punished for his crimes. "I'm very ready."

Kari's story continues in . . .
Project Underworld
The Kari Chronicles Book 3

Acknowledgments

For this novel to get into your hands, a team of people helped it along the way. Here are the individuals I need to thank who helped get this story to you.

To my wife: Yes, of course you get top billing! Thank you for all of the support you have given me (to include how I ended Project ORCA), pep talks when the imposter syndrome is high, and random questions I ask ("Does best ball ever have a hyphen?"). You are my biggest fan and I am yours. I love you!

To my wife and Aunt C: I tried my hardest to write Belle as a young woman who is strong in her faith but is not a stereotype. Thanks to you two I had inspiration to pull from. I love you both!

To "John McClane" aka Carl's husband: I really appreciate the time you took to discuss undercover and confidential informant work with me. I know I had to take certain creative liberties (I love Belle so much, she can't leave!) but I hope I talked around it well enough. Also, as I type this (October 2025) the Federal government consistently skirts laws and policies that are inconvenient for them, so I'm doing the same. To quote the famous 1987's anti-drug commercial, "I learned it by watching you!"

To my mom: Thank you for being an 'Angel Investor' so my work can see the light of day or night of lamps. I love you!

To my dad: I'm sure you didn't think the song writing assignment I gave you would end up here. I think the cues I gave you were: father figure, bittersweet, and Appalachia. I love you! (*Mountain Home* lyrics are after the Acknowledgements)

To Nan Campbell: You're a great friend and partner in the Sapphic Lit Pop-Up Bookstore, but for this I truly appreciate the time and suggestions you made to the draft. Double thanks for having your wife check medical and Aussie slang for me. To everyone reading this, Nan is a great author too, go buy her books!

To Lisa Caro: I appreciate you swooping in and giving me a hand with the blurb (aka: nemesis of authors). I hope you enjoyed the story! To everyone reading this, Lisa is a great author too, go buy her books!

To Brenda Murphy: Thank you for reading the initial draft of the Ray emergency scene and making suggestions. To everyone reading this, Brenda is a great author too, go buy her books!

To Lune: Thank you as always for the incredibly thoughtful feedback for developmental edits. You make my stories so much stronger and more well-rounded. I hope that you like the changes I made to Sven. I'm also deeply thankful that you provide an Indigenous perspective to Aurora's side of the family.

To my editing team, Eanna and Janice: I certainly keep you two on your toes! Thank you both for your patience with me and offering suggestions to make my story clearer and grammatically correct. Yes, I know I left you both hanging for book 3. You'll get it soon enough.

May Dawney: Your covers never get enough credit, especially considering the sketches and Powerpoint you receive at the beginning of the process with my ideas. Anyway, thank you for working with me to get Kari's uniform and hair perfect. My apologies in advance for the specifics needed for book 3.

To the Golden Crown Literary Society and Rainbow Space

Magic: Thank you for giving me platforms to promote my stories and providing such a lovely community.

To my fellow board members, authors, and partners of the Sapphic Literary Collective (aka Sapphic Lit Pop-Up Bookstore): Thank you for the support and being my friend. It's so hard to make friends as an adult! Keep writing and selling those stories!

To my readers: Thank you for hanging in there! I know that leaving stories off like I do is not the norm these days and fills you with antici . . . pation, but I rarely do things the way it's "supposed" to be done.

Mountain Home
Lyrics by Jim Hughes

Daddy said stay out of the woods
And don't hang around Uncle Jon
But come morning I'd always be there
Rocking on his porch in the early dawn
Born dirt born in the little town of Claysburg
If he had a quarter you know he'd always share
Always kind to strangers
Although his loads were hard to bear
Uncle Jon was an Army veteran
He lived and worked until the very end
But I smile and remember when Uncle Jon was my only friend
I remember the laurel blossoms and lilies white as snow
On that day I lost Uncle Jon, I cried and hated to see him go

About the Author

Serena J. Bishop is an accidental author. After writing technical, science-based pieces, in 2015 she decided to start turning her daydreams into stories. She writes novels in the speculative fiction, thriller, and romance genres with sapphic main characters. She always sprinkles in some humor along the way.

When Serena's not writing, narrating, or working at some job to pay the bills, she enjoys being a nerd, time with friends and family, and drinking coffee. Black, no sugar. Deck time or dock time with her wife is another favorite.

Serena lives in Maryland, USA with her magnificent wife and precious Chihuahua. She's also a member of the Sapphic Literary Collective, LLC. You can follow her by signing up for her newsletter at www.serenajbishop.com or following her on Facebook, Instagram, Threads, and Bluesky @serenajbishop.

www.ingramcontent.com/pod-product-compliance
Lightning Source LLC
Chambersburg PA
CBHW070208310726
48976CB00001B/254